LIVING
UPSIDE
DOWN

Inspired by a True Story

JOHN **HICKMAN**

ABOUT THE AUTHOR

John Hickman was born in the UK at the end of WWII. He grew up in the shadow of his war hero father, Bill.

Attending numerous schools due to the family moving for Bill's work, John learned quickly to enjoy the most of the moment, and to not take life too seriously.

His books are a glimpse into his world and the imagination that has grown from those life experiences; working in a bank, as an hotelier, and in the Pest Control industry before migrating with his family to Australia as 'ten pound Poms'.

After specialising in global pest control, fumigation, and timber preservation, John and his family diversified into farming Javan Rusa deer, in the South Burnett.

After retirement in 2003 and unable to play golf, he discovered a latent passion for writing.

Living Upside Down is John's debut novel to feature the adventures of Sue and Roger, after writing three true stories.

This novel was inspired, in part by the author's thirty-five years of experience in the global pest control industry, life in the Archipelago, and migrating as ten pound poms.

Chapter 1

ALWAYS AN ENGLAND

Sue dreams about making ends meet and a better life for her family. She is now fully awake and attending to her second child, baby boy James.

Roger is fast asleep searching for, of all things, Seal Flipper Pie.

His ridiculous dream has clipped along at a furious pace until a change in direction, as dreams often do. He encounters a brief loving chat with his mother whose ashes were scattered five years previous, then into a spectacular nosedive. His Father's second wife Zelda, a woman devoid of any warm fuzzy feelings for Roger, scolds him over the failure of their family hotel business, as she blames him! She is over groomed and prissy as a pampered poodle while caterwauling at him in German.

At this point, in danger of shitting a gasket sideways thanks to Zelda and still bereft of his Seal Flipper Pie, Roger is waking up.

Feeling fuzzy and exhausted from his dreams, Roger cautiously opens one eye.

After a moment he realises it is a no-work-day, Saturday. All he has to do today is nothing if he can get that right.

Dazed, he is rubbing sleep from his other eye when Fred starts his panic whining. Thinking he must get to Fred quickly, Roger attempts to become Action Man. Hampered by bedsheets and blankets, he kicks himself free; his bleary eyes trying to keep up with the rest of him.

Before Sue can put the kettle down and attend to the dog, an animated striped pyjama of flailing arms and legs rushes through the doorway towards the back door.

Canine Fred is now in a state of panic and performing repeated u-turns.

Making contact with the newspapers laid down the night before as a precaution, Roger's socked feet fail to gain traction. He slides, skips, and is sent airborne with a Nureyev double turn leap. Without a controlled

1

touchdown, he lands spread-eagled on a sharp toy. Ouch! That has got to have hurt an important part.

Sue's badly stifled shrieks of laughter prevent her from assisting the prone Nureyev.

"Oh, fuck!"

Sue glares, "Standards, Roger!"

"Bloody standards? I've nearly impaled my jewels," hands clasping his gonads, "on…on, something."

"Breathe," Sue's holding her hand across her mouth to stifle her laughter, "BREATHE!"

As if breathing will ease my pain," Roger whines.

Not breathing certainly would ease Roger's pain but now he feels like a complete Knucklehead.

Lying out prone, their back door rearing above him like the southern face of Everest, an excited Fred farts in Roger's face.

Still clutching himself Roger exclaims, "Wow! That's got some hang time!"

Sue screws up her nose, glaring at Roger. She is making strange noises. A little like those his Gran makes whenever she sees a live mouse.

Sue knows well that in the first thirty minutes of any day her husband's cognitive abilities are quite similar to those of a toddler — not a very bright toddler at that, and not a silent one.

Sighing, Roger begins picking up the newspapers. "What an awful end for the *News Of The World.*"

Sue grins, "Maybe Fred's fussy what newspaper he puts to the sword?"

"That's a good, boy." Roger praises him for not making a mess, then watches helplessly as Fred wees himself with excitement where the paper would have been.

Roger shakes his head in exasperation. "Damn! God's being unfair, again!"

"Takes a lot of the fun out of it, doesn't it?" Sue replies with a fixed grin, "Kettle's boiled."

Sue cracks open the back door, gently pushes Fred outside before shivering and quickly closing it again; exactly as she had intended before Roger's fiasco.

Clutching at his sore jewels, Roger wraps himself in his heavy dressing gown over his winceyette pyjamas, shuffles back into his well-worn fur lined slippers.

"It's snowed, Sue. Damn! Now we'll need to buy more heating coal for sure."

Sue turns her attention and considerable patience to preparing the first feed of the day for James.

Roger wears his proud father grin and tickles James under his chin.

James is unimpressed, maybe because he's hungry. Roger remembers that when James was born, his stomach was the size of a walnut. Now it is a cavernous pit.

Under determined clear blue eyes, with her chubby cheeks pinched by the cold, James's three-year old sibling, Jayne, is climbing a chair.

"Clever, Girl. Did you know it snowed while the sun was still in bed?" Roger says excitedly.

Jayne is three, going on seven, noticing everything and missing almost nothing of significance. Her curly hair shines the colour of sun-dappled straw.

James begins to jabber and point. An awkward, gummy smile playing about perfect lips he could not yet control.

"He's big for his age," Sue remarks, "with the prospect of him becoming a tall boy, just look at his long feet."

Jayne is staring at James as if he has just hatched from an egg.

"Better let Fred in, Roger."

Roger opens the back door but there is no sign of Fred. To avoid losing heat he steps outside where a gust of freezing wind whips up a cloud of dirty snow that sends an involuntary shiver up Roger's already frigid backside. The bite of the cold wind snatches at his ears and turns them in to rocket fins.

Fred is now bouncing around as if on a pogo stick.

"Weak bastard Hound. Conjure up one last tinkle, or do a crap, and you can come inside!"

Fred casts that well-known hang-dog look while Roger wedges his bare hands under his armpits for warmth.

"Won't save you. Just because you're a dog, doesn't mean you always get a bone."

Back inside Fred wisely keeps a paw's distance from what Jayne might have in mind for him, yet now wants to play with the big people.

Sue, wearing multiple layers of clothes and thick wool socks enveloping her feet inside her slippers is stating the case of the bleeding obvious.

Roger has not yet noticed that Sue is wearing more layers than an onion.

At twenty-five years of age, Roger's idea of culture is a half pint of lager and a *Z Cars* marathon or *Callan*, but it's too early for any of that. Instead, he stokes the fire in their lounge room before settling beside it and turning on their colour television set. While the set takes a few minutes to warm up, he reaches for a cigarette and lights up his first of the day.

Inhaling deeply he realises, too late, that not only will Sue be annoyed with his smoke but she will likely have another reason to avoid any polarising kisses.

The television emits its robotic noises, bleeping and zooming with piercing jingles, as the crash and tumble of advertisements commence.

Calling out to Sue in the west wing that is their kitchen, Roger carps, "That bloody Australian Government's on the TV again. The amount they're spending on this crap is not only excessive, it amounts to the equivalent of granting the entire population of the Democratic Republic of the Congo each fully paid Oxford university scholarships."

Arriving with two welcoming cups of steaming hot tea Sue makes a face at his disgusting cigarette smoke.

Might two strikes out of two be not bad for his first try?

"Love your little bit of cigarette at the same time as my tea! If you must smoke, why don't you do it outside?"

"Outside! Be fair, have you looked? We've had snow."

With an involuntary little shiver, Sue kicks off her slippers and shuffles her covered feet closer to the fire.

"Bit over the top this Australian advertising," Roger announces, while sipping his hot tea.

"What do you mean?" Sue asks whilst talking to her cup of tea.

He jounces at the television. "The amount they're spending on this crap would bankrupt most nations. You know governments waste

4

money. You're always saying it's because they've no vested interest in their expenditure."

"True!"

"Might few in government have moral compasses? Day after day we're being stuffed like geese with sun drenched beaches and bikini clad women."

Nodding, Sue holds her cup in both hands, her nose just above the rising warmth.

"The catch," Roger continues, "is you have to migrate. Go live Down Under in a penal colony."

Sue glances sideways from the rim of her cup. Twenty-seven years old with curves in all the right places, she wears her auburn hair up; as when down, it is long enough to sit on.

As an ex-hair stylist, professional hair is like a religion to Sue. Top and bottom of the spectrum, hair and shoes.

Giving her husband an impatient look, her alert green eyes pack a wallop.

"They're trying to attract liberal minded people like us, from the heart of the British Empire."

"It's not so long ago the Crown sent them for free."

Sue becomes a tad terse. "Well, now they want £10 each."

She is looking down for a moment so that Roger will not see the resentment reflected in her features. Sue is in an age when male chauvinism is expected and a certain amount of it is popular at this time. She likes him to lead but not totally dominate. It's a fine line that sometimes Roger has difficulty with.

With his voice now approaching an audible level only to canines, "A whole ten quid! Ten to fifteen years more likely with a chain around their ankle. That's more appropriate."

Looking back up Sue forces a smile, replying in a comical way. "You think?"

Purebred canine Fred is impressed but unsure why. Jayne and James do not care.

"Today politicians spout on about getting tough on crime but as everybody knows that's bullshit, as they genuflect to the left for votes. Not like in the good old days."

Roger's oration is interrupted by a colourful bevy of bikini-clad girls appearing on their TV, kidding about on a near perfect sandy white beach. A wash of colour makes the line between the sky and sea indistinct.

"Admittedly, it's easy to watch," he concedes.

Sue purrs as bronzed iron men from the surf join the girls. "They say it's easy enough to apply."

"Yes, I know. Moreover, if you qualify they'll sponsor you, which means employment is guaranteed. They haven't shut up about it. All anyone has to do is pack up their shit and move to the arse end of nowhere!"

Sue's emerald eyes bore in to Roger. "They say Australia is a huge continent that's only sparsely populated."

Roger's gut tightens and the feeling of cement shoes forms around his feet.

"I'm unimpressed. And anyway, much as some of the scenery appeals, don't I have a good enough job here?"

"Yes, you do."

Jayne! Don't let Fred lick your face, Sweetheart, you don't know where a dog's tongue's been."

"£1,200 per annum, Sue, plus commission on sales; can't sneeze at that."

Sue counters, "When they don't renege."

"They have been known to move the goalposts mid game but don't forget there's a company car."

"Luxuries are beyond our reach, admittedly a gap made wider since the failure of your father's hotel businesses."

Sue did not marry Roger for his money. Sometimes he wonders why indeed she married him at all.

Their agreement was to have children and at twenty-one years of age that was alright with him. A view currently shared by her, but she is finding him increasingly difficult to please.

"There's not too many around here on that sort of moolah in their mid twenties. We can't live on the square root of nothing. I've got two children under four to support, no degree or trade qualifications."

Now the cement is inching up his calves.

Sue frowns. "But you don't really like working in pest control, do you?"

"I wanted a profession. All those years of studying Latin and the General Principles of English Law, turns out now I just need money."

"You're not Robinson Crusoe, Roger. Most people are short of money."

"Who'd have thought I'd end up killing vermin for a living. It's not that I don't like it. I'm physically repulsed, Sue. Frankly, some pests frighten the shit out of me. I have the odd nightmare of being trapped in a cellar, I can hear them but unable to find them. Then again as a consultant I don't have a great deal of contact with them."

Ironically, the cement is now reaching his throat.

Sue juggles James and her cup of tea. "I can honestly say I enjoyed hairdressing — every moment — I truly loved it."

James grizzles.

"Not surprising as you were rubbing shoulders with stars of the silver screen," Roger patronises, "but I've never done anything I truly liked since college, and I wasn't rapt in that. To me a job is just that, a job. At the hotels I cooked, cleaned, served at table, bar, and now I'm chasing money, which is about as easy as levitating right now."

"To most people going to Australia would be their adventure of a lifetime." Sue fingers her nightie nervously. "Who knows? You might even stumble over a job you like?"

Roger shrugs. "Adventure? I don't think so. For thrills I'm thinking milk a death adder, castrate a raging bull, or..." he pauses caught for another suitable example. "Or, go sing the *Scarlet Flag* outside Buckingham Palace."

"Why?" she studies him closely.

He feels himself shrink from the scrutiny. "There's a time to be boring, Sue, or being a man. Think of the adrenalin rush before being arrested."

Sue takes a deep breath. "Imagine a life with sunshine, then."

"I'm so fair-skinned, I get burned by the fridge light."

"Then wear protection. It could be the best £50 you'd ever spend."

"Fifty quid!" Roger shrieks. "How come?"

"Well," Sue replies testily, "unless you've not noticed lately there are five of us in this family."

Roger grunts, "Can Fred go for £10?"

"I don't know," for an instant Sue's smile falters, it no longer reaches her eyes, "he is part of our family, isn't he? We can hardly leave him behind."

"That reminds me he's due to be neutered at the vet."

Roger lights another cigarette.

"Ignoring the vet taking a higher percentage of our earnings than the mortgage this month, I see my future prospects as reasonably bright. My region's supposed to be expanding." He chances a bright smile. "I have you, our two children, and the dog. I'm not complaining."

Sue strokes his arm, "But we're still without curtains."

He now feels like a fully kilned concrete statue, ready for primer and paint.

"You could always pretend it's deliberate because we've nothing to hide," he tries weakly.

Sue frowns. "Heavy curtains would help keep the house warm."

Not long and they're back to another advertisement.

"Their beaches do look good," Roger acknowledges, "I'll give them that, but our local beach at Great Yarmouth is sandy enough, don't you think?"

"Maybe our sand isn't quite as white as theirs," Sue smiles, "nor our sea or sky as blue. Although you have to admit beach life here does lose most of its appeal."

"Why?"

"Well, being adjacent to the North Sea, for starters, it's too damned cold."

"Being unable to stand upright in a force eight gale, you mean."

Sue looks at Roger triumphantly. She barks back. "Unless you're congenial to being rugged-up to the eyebrows, it doesn't make for a great day at the beach, does it?"

Roger pries himself reluctantly from the warm cushion of his armchair and reaches for the coal scuttle to replenish the fire. Tense as his wife is, he realises that she would likely go off as easily as nitroglycerine dancing on hot coals. He decides to tread carefully.

Certainly, their small two-bedroom brick veneer house, Casa Del Coxwell, is not remarkable by any means, looking out as it does over a street of identical small homes with small front gardens, ranging from immaculately tidy to jungles of death.

Tiny kitchen, living room and dining area combined. Their bathroom would suit Tom Thumb. The only people for whom the house is in any way special are Sue and Roger, as it happens to be the one they live in.

Coxwell is an uninspiring village by any name. Frankly, quaint though it may be, if it were on a main road it's the sort of place you would drive through on your way to somewhere else. Rural with a shop, a pub, and an out-of-work windmill.

"When the children get older they'll need their own bedrooms."

Roger sighs his deepest sigh.

After the failure of his hotel businesses, his Dad had the perfect excuse not to pay Roger for all those years of hard work and to make matters worse, Zelda blamed Roger in part for the failures.

Roger was left in charge of a business that had already failed and, pending his Dad's bankruptcy, the company chequebook had been surrendered.

"I should never have trusted Dad, Sue."

Sue is gentle. "You both ended up directors of a failed business."

"Yes. Dad went bankrupt, which sort of ruled out his culpability, but I'm still liable."

"Liable for what? Surely as a director you're in the clear?"

"Yes, except for personal guarantees. Banks insist on them in addition."

Sue stares fixedly at Roger like a rabbit trying not to be run over by a car.

"Oh, Roger what will happen?"

"Well, they can't get blood out of a stone, that's for sure and so far we've heard nothing."

"How long?" Sue is clearly worried.

"About twelve months now."

"At least the bank wouldn't want our furniture, and they can't take curtains we don't have."

"Banks take everything, why not the furniture?"

Sue raises a shapely eyebrow. "Everything we own are hand-me-downs spread across the 1940s and 1950s."

"You mean the furniture is worth fuck-all."

"Yes." Sue wraps James in a shawl and checks Jayne's fingers to see how cold she is. "She can't eat her breakfast wearing gloves, Roger," her voice becomes tense when talking about the well being of her babies. "I hate the cold, hate it, hate it, hate it!"

"As if I didn't know *that* by now, for Christ's sake Sue, give it a rest. I know we're on our uppers."

When she leaves the house, Sue's bones ache from the piercing easterly wind that is so lazy it seems to pass right through. She doesn't like the English weather, not even in summer, and definitely not in winter. She never has, not even as a child born there.

"The Bible refers to forty days and forty nights as a disaster, but here that's just an apt description of winter," Sue reinforces adamantly.

"On the bright side maybe salt spray from the North Sea will blow further inland and melt the black ice on our roads this year," Roger joins hopefully.

"We're supposed to be coming into spring," Sue comments over her shoulder, "it doesn't feel like it."

In a demonstration of brute strength, Roger limbers up. "I'll stoke up the fire."

He pulls a face like a smacked arse, which gets a good deep chuckle out of Jayne who by now is tired of climbing chairs.

"So you reckon compared to our Antipodean friends in their tight swimmers, we're no match in our Arctic clothing."

Sue draws a deep breath, "With our feet planted firmly in double socks. And don't forget the Wellington boots and fleece lined overcoat to the beach."

"Last time I went beach fishing at Great Yarmouth I was nearly toppled by a wind so strong I had to lean hard on the car door to get out. It felt like an Arctic wind; come to think of it even the seagulls sat quiet with their beaks huddled deep into their ruffled chests."

"And that's Autumn, not Winter," Sue's mouth is pinched into a thin line as she prepares to redress James.

Jayne is adamant, she points at James. "Can't want him. Take him back."

Sue grins at their enraged toddler. "Her new baby brother is too small to play with her. Without doubt, if he were bigger, she'd punch his lights out."

After a brief game of *Eeny-meeny-miney-mo* Roger continues his tale.

"There I was all rigged up, struggling to the edge of the water in near hurricane conditions. A supreme effort and a great cast."

Noticing he has the floor with three pairs of eyes on him, he goes for it.

"The wind was so strong it lifted my sinker mid cast and blew it right back up behind me on the beach."

Jayne giggles. Roger sits her on his knee to continue with his story.

"Undeterred Daddykins puts on a heavier sinker," he raises his eyes, "but it was so heavy now that the tip of the rod's sagging from the weight. Have you any idea the thrill of satisfaction Daddykins felt catching a fish for our dinner under difficult circumstances like those?"

Jayne shakes her head and says, "No!"

Roger makes another face. "No! You're right and neither did Daddykins. Not even a herring! All was lost. So thoroughly fed up I came home."

His audience laughs.

Seeing himself as an enlightened dictator in his own home, a left-over attitude from earlier in the century, pompously Roger feels the need to reinforce not wanting to go to Australia.

"For twenty-five years I've practiced the fine art of being an Englishman that has been my defining quality in life."

"Good for you." Sue is unimpressed.

Roger pushes, "Why would I suddenly decide to send myself into voluntary exile 16,500 miles away for Christ's sake? That's a bloody long way to go for a sandy beach and a job in a factory I don't need or want."

"We live from hand to mouth, literally. I do my best. I buy proper meat once a week, maybe sausages on another. I'm tired of the Israeli Army Diet."

"What's that?" Roger asks.

"It means existing on two days of cow cabbage, two days of cheap dairy products, two days of tinned sardines, and one day of fasting."

Roger looks impressed.

Sue continues, "We'd discharged ourselves from the Israeli Army

Diet by Week One but I've kept balancing two sardines on a lettuce leaf, topped with a few carrot shavings for colour and a sprig of parsley, as dinner. It's cheap."

"Mussels and offal are cheap, although I'd rather stick my dick in a blender than eat tripe."

"That can be arranged." Sue becomes serious. "There's nothing left over from your salary for small luxuries." She wrings her hands. "God knows how we'll manage when the children get older."

Sue draws her deepest 'all is lost' sigh.

"I'll need to get a part time job."

"*What!* No! Absolutely not!" Roger shouts. "Sue, when we married it was agreed you would be a stay at home wife and mother. I'll not go back on that. No!"

"You'd miss me if I went out to work, wouldn't you?"

"No more than I would my eyes," Roger replies tersely.

Sue had agreed to be a stay home wife and mother, which was not unusual among their other family members. Roger never changed a nappy, nor got up in the middle of the night to attend to Jayne or James, because Sue saw that as her role. Roger is the breadwinner. He works. She feels it only right that he has uninterrupted sleep.

She breaks away to serve cereals, boiled eggs, and buttered toast for their breakfast.

"I suppose we could always sell a child." Roger jokes in a whisper, to lighten the mood.

Sue is not amused.

"You wouldn't mind though, would you?" Sue asks, as Roger clears table.

"Mind what?"

"I'd like to know more about Australia. You wouldn't be too upset if I sent away for their brochures, would you?"

"Me? Upset? Course not. Why should I get upset? I've got balls the size of Planets."

Sue pats him on the knee, much as she would pat Fred on the head. "In your dreams, Darling."

The continual dull monotony of attempting to keep body and soul together in such a grey and cheerless place as England is getting Sue down. The bags of tiredness and stress under her eyes seem to swell whenever she speaks.

That night his dream searching for Seal Flipper Pie continues. He is walking through The Lanes in Brighton, every shop is selling Haddock testicles, and no-one knows anything about his pie. His dream ends with him chasing a bikini clad Sue along a sun drenched beach of white sand.

Monday Roger sets off to greet the start of his working week with lime enthusiasm.

After he has gone, Sue sits glumly at their dining room table, her temples throbbing from lack of coffee. Sipping some instant, the strength of such she can almost feel her pulse rise with each swallow, she recovers shaking her head at their predicament.

Looking out the window at the front of the house the view offers little entertainment. Living on one of the quietest streets in the Village of Coxwell, like her life, it was leading nowhere.

Hugging the cup, she wonders if she should send off for those Australian brochures.

It is as if her life is unravelling. She can feel it, sense it, like a big ball of string someone has tossed down a long flight of stairs and yet, that post box is just outside the Coxwell shop, and they do sell postage stamps.

She worries about Roger's guarantees to the bank for his father's loans, but as he said, no news is good news.

Chapter 2

THE TOILET SEAT DEFENSIVE

Another working week is done and dusted.

When Roger arrives home to hilarity HQ Sue is grinning like a prospector who has just struck the mother lode

"Look!" she cries clutching armfuls of brochures. "The postman had to make *two* trips."

What arrived from Australia House three weeks after Roger's twenty-fifth birthday, six weeks after James's birth, sixteen weeks before Jayne's third birthday, seven months before Sue's twenty-eighth birthday, and twenty-seven days shy of their fourth wedding anniversary, was far too bulky to pass through any letter box. Sue is almost unable to contain her excitement.

"I'll bet the postie was overawed making two trips," he replies sullenly.

"He was," Sue beams, "and he asked if we're going to Australia?"

"And what did you say?"

"I didn't say anything."

Roger plays with Jayne and cuddles James.

Ignoring the pile on the dining table, he says gently, "He cheers my day with his cooing and grunting."

"Let me take him. That's a changing grunt."

It is not long before brochures and pamphlets hinder Roger's every move. Patiently he moves them from every chair, he turns around, and they are back again. They go from chairs to footstools, then back onto chairs, the kitchen table, the kitchen bench, even their bed.

Roger's mutterings of, 'Musical bloody brochures,' can be heard around the house.

Roger finds one on his car windscreen. That makes him more determined than ever as he pries the damp brochure from the glass.

"That'll teach you," he mumbles to himself, "ruining their glossy brochure of their white sandy beaches!"

The next one he finds on his driver's seat with a backdrop of mist and flashes of moonlight that escapes through the clouds.

"They're your brochures, not mine," Roger repeats for the umpteenth time. "How's about you have them close to you? They're multiplying and I don't want to look at them! Dodging them is about as easy as swimming the English Channel — and I can't swim."

A stony silence follows. All is not well at Camp Sue.

At their zoo feeding Sue asks, "Most months here are cold but don't you think this year seems colder and longer?"

He sits his lame arse down before saying rather tamely.

"Yes. I've just ordered another load of coal for the central heating system. Damn, the budget's blown, again!"

"If we sit any closer to the heaters they'll become pregnant," Sue jokes.

Feeling now that all her ducks may be lined up in a row, Sue is no longer subtle nor as welcoming as an eggy fart at a first date dinner table.

That afternoon she gives Jayne a quick couple of laps around the bath while adding hot water being careful not to scald her. Her contented sounds and associated crescendos of bath bubbles from under her bottom confirming she is happy with the water temperature. Getting her out and dried off with big fluffy towels before she shivers becomes a military operation, even with the aid of a twin-bar electric fire to warm the room.

Next morning Roger retreats to the toilet for his morning fart for merry England.

"I'm going to the library, Sue."

His Dad used to take his cup of tea in with him, which always disgusted Sue, but it is far too cold for that.

Looking at Roger with a practiced glare that would shatter glass Sue hands him the fresh air spray.

Roger is preparing to curl one out with pride when a glossy brochure slithers under the door and bounces off his foot.

His turtle head quickly retreats.

Sighing and rolling his eyes at the lost chance to celebrate something

15

he was dedicated to birthing he comments to the closed door, "That's below the belt, Sue. Is nothing, nowhere, sacred?"

With nothing to read and nature proving fickle he reluctantly picks up the brochure.

What he sees is an overview of climate in Australia produced like a textbook on the run. In the north, it is described as tropical.

Roger ponders his Rodin's Thinker pose. *Tropical?*

His mind ticks over; maybe a bit too hot and sticky for his pale Saxon flesh.

I could go a bit of that tropical warmth right now, he thinks, as ice is forming on the insides of his nostrils.

In the south being the opposite of north, he observes it is cold.

It is now so cold in the library that Shackleton would not have left a Husky dog outside for long. He is now so cold the poor bastard cannot feel his own testicles. Maybe his turtle is frozen? Perhaps a new archaeological find in the making?

Looking at the brochure, his attention catches their coastline about half way up the Australian continent on the left hand side. Their summertime is the same as British wintertime because of the reversal of the hemispheres, he understands that, but, from what he is reading, it is warm to hot by British standards.

With his usual optimism and unclear lateral thinking, Roger suddenly becomes somewhat hooked on the idea of not spending about one third of their disposable income on coal heating.

Could it be that simple?

Finishing up with a smile, he even waves farewell to the turtle as the water swirls it away to its watery grave.

"Amazing how once in a while having a shit can be such a wonderfully revealing experience," he murmurs as he almost collides with Sue, busy with additional odour neutralisers, her face a picture of concentration.

"You know, Sue…, according to these statistics a family could live in say, Perth, wherever that is, and never need to buy coal for heating."

"Wow! You're sounding wonderfully positive today." Sue brightens.

Sue looks as if she is about to crawl out of her skin from excitement.

"You're right," Roger beams, "optimism is beginning to infiltrate every cell of my body."

In a devil-may-care moment, brim full of new found knowledge about fuck-all but temperatures Down Under, they race out and buy thermometers.

Placing these at strategic distances, in and around their cooker, they plan to get the edge over the highbrow meaning of the statistics.

"You mean we'll feel for ourselves what sub tropical temperatures Down Under really feel like?" Sue asks.

"Exactly."

After a while Roger announces shrilly, "It is very hot."

"Your hand is almost inside the oven," Sue says defensively.

"Trouble is Australia's in Celsius and our thermometers are in Fahrenheit," Roger groans staring at their appliances with an air of hopelessness.

After attempting to do their school day conversions in their heads, and with limited success, they decide rather than go completely bonkers — to take a short cut.

"How's about anything above our thirty-two Fahrenheit is a bonus?" Sue gushes.

Roger toys with this thought for a while before dismissing it. "Here we're used to a life threatening ten above at peak of day, so a move is looking good, but what about the children?"

Sue's smile brightens. "I think it best we take them with us, don't you?"

"Yes. I meant how'd you think they'll cope?"

"Why? They're children; they'll adapt well, probably better than we cope. Your legs are white and skinny. You'll look like a flamingo."

"Presupposing we are to leave this land of our birth. Admittedly a land of benighted fools and spoon fed unremarkable people who've been born into unearned privilege," Roger pauses to collect his breath, and further supposing that I'm even employable in Australia."

Sue is hanging on his every word. In her mind's eye, she is already visualising a life Down Under as a panacea for most of their ills.

Anything to get out of this mind numbing, grey, lifeless, British climate and the extra distance between them and Roger's bank guarantees might not be a bad thing.

"And further surmising other costs measure up similar to here,"

17

Roger continues counting again on his fingers, "whatever is left to spend after taxation could mean we'd be one third better off financially than we are now."

"Simply by moving to the other side of the world and living upside down," Sue prompts gently.

"Yes."

"Their 'ten pound assisted passage' is a big pull, but still no mention of Fred." Roger ignores Fred. "It's a no-brainer, Sue. Money-wise I'll never be accepted here as anything above lower middle class, because I wear the wrong School tie. Can Down Under be worse?"

Sue perks up. "It's worth a try, isn't it? Do you think we'll be forbidden to walk on the grass in their parks, like we are here? Will we have to keep Fred on a lead?"

"I have no idea what to expect. Do they even have green grass in Australia? Or even parks, or dogs?"

"Maybe now is the time to try and find out?"

The following afternoon they visit their local librarian. He explains, "The name Australia is derived from the Latin *Australis* meaning *of the South*. Matthew Flinders was the first person to circumnavigate the continent when the only inhabitants were Aborigines, and he referred to them in his book."

"Aborigines? What about the Aborigines?" Sue asks.

"Well, from what's in the library, they invented the boomerang, which in aboriginal probably means, *'Don't stand there'*, but they don't appear to have come up with much else in the past 40,000 years, or so. According to newspaper articles, they only recently got the right to vote, which means they've certainly been disadvantaged. Maybe you should take an interest in the Aboriginal culture?" the librarian suggests.

"What like join in their rain dance on a Friday evening?" Roger asks tongue in cheek.

"Why not?" Sue smiles, but it does not reach her eyes. "Great idea — weather permitting."

"If Aborigines spend much of their time outside, sitting under trees, you do realise something very important?"

"What?" Sue and the librarian ask in unison.

"Everyone needs a hobby?" prompts the librarian with a smirk.

"No. I mean it can't be that cold, can it? Not where they are, because if it's freezing their nuts off they wouldn't be sitting around outside. Would they?"

Sue has another of her involuntary little shudders, "No-one lazes about outdoors here. Not even in Arctic clothing and around a big bonfire."

Each afternoon for a week after work, Sue and Roger run around in ever decreasing circles in all their local libraries looking for books about Australia.

"Australia's so far away it might as well be on Mars," Sue says dejectedly.

"What we want," Roger explains to any librarian who will lend an ear, "are books, preferably big books, with lots of glossy coloured pictures all to do with Australia."

At one particular library, after some soul searching and rummaging about, three books are found.

Eagerly Sue picks up each one to check them out.

"No!" She places the books back on the counter. "It's not the nesting habits of the Pelican that we want to know about."

She does an eye roll to Roger that is so massive it almost gives her a headache.

"Frankly, if we wanted to settle on the Moon there'd be more up to date information available," Roger says gravely.

"You're probably right," the librarian's soft voice replies, "experts have recently been there and documented it." He scratches his head. "Come to think about it there's more interest about the Moon — than Australia."

"All available information comes back to what the Australian Government is putting out by the dray load, but that's all heavily slanted in favour of their sponsored areas," Sue explains.

"How can we find out something worthwhile about Australia without actually going there?" Roger asks another brainy looking librarian.

"Why, Australia?" Brainy asks.

"Because we're thinking of becoming 'ten pound Poms' and going there to live." Sue explains patiently.

Brainy shows interest. "You've seen their television advertising?"

"The son of Fu Manchu couldn't avoid it. It's never off the television. If you buy a newspaper it's got full page advertisements."

"They're supposed to be a weird lot," Brainy says softly, "you'll need to take care." He begins rummaging through his card indexes for books. After a while, he pulls one out. "Will you want to build a boomerang?"

Roger looks at Sue. Sue looks at Roger.

"No. Probably not," Roger replies. "Well, not straight away, anyway."

Brainy puts it back, rummages further, and draws out another. "What about a Didgeridoo?"

Roger looks blankly at him. Sue raises a shapely but sceptical eyebrow.

Brainy shrugs. "Another confusing thing about Australia is their animals."

"Why?" Sue asks. The smile has melted off her face.

"They're divided into three categories; venomous, odd, and sheep."

"You amaze me," Roger grimaces.

Brainy beams. "Thank you. It's true."

"I don't doubt it," says Sue in a resigned tone as she attends to James in his push chair.

Jayne tightens her small grip on Roger's hand.

"Of the ten most venomous arachnids on the planet, Australia has nine," Brainy announces proudly.

Roger is thoughtful. "Wouldn't it be more accurate to say then, that of the nine most venomous arachnids, Australia has all of them?"

Anything else?" Sue asks; she is becoming bored.

"There are snakes."

"You mean the spiders haven't killed them all?" asks Roger.

"Most snakes live near the sea, even the spiders won't go near the sea, but be careful to check inside your boots and shoes."

"When?"

Brainy is thoughtful. "Best before putting them on. Oh, and under toilet seats before sitting down."

"What, for snakes, or spiders?"

"Both I'd say, oh, and always carry a large stick."

"What else have you got in your bag of tricks?"

"Watch out for Drop Bears." Brainy continues. "I've heard there are these Bears that stay in trees, they wait for you to walk under them, then they fall on top of you and attack."

Sue and Roger are mortified. Jayne perks up at the mention of bears falling out of trees.

"Surely not!" Roger gasps.

Brainy smiles appreciatively and winks at Roger as he flicks through more index cards. "Did you know over half of the entire flora and fauna that exist in Australia are found no-where else? And yet, to top it off, that it is the most inhospitable place to support life outside of Antarctica."

"Good to know," says Roger snidely, "actually it sounds a great place to live and bring up a family."

"Another confusing thing about Australia is the inhabitants," Brainy continues.

"Surprise me," Roger retaliates.

"Well, about 50,000 years ago Indigenous Australians arrived from the north possibly in boats."

"But if they arrived by boat or on foot, how come they're Indigenous?" Roger asks. "I thought the definition of being Indigenous was that they were always there?"

"Because it was 50,000 years ago, apparently they qualify."

Roger shrugs.

Brainy peers at Roger over the top of his bifocal glasses, "They're called Aborigines, you do know that."

"Yes, that's easy to find out."

"I've got a number of books about them. The tree hasn't grown too far from the apple if you get my meaning?"

Roger looks puzzled. "Isn't it the apple doesn't fall far from the tree?"

"Yes, but remember we're referring to Down Under? Anyway, they ate all the available food and a lot of them died of starvation. Those who survived learned respect for the balance of nature, man's proper place in the overall scheme of things, and the spiders. They learned about spiders and snakes."

"What happened then?"

"They ate the spiders and snakes."

"Then what?"

"Well, they settled in and spent a lot of the intervening time telling strange stories they call the *Dreamtime*."

Roger sighs. "It's more about life now for people like us that I want to read about. Not how to throw a spear or make a boomerang."

Brainy grins like a schoolboy, "Well, it all boils down to some bloke landing on a beach in a silly hat about 200 years ago."

"Silly hat? You mean their three cornered hat?"

"Yes, but it was known as a 'cocked hat' during its time and later known as the Tricorne, until in the 1800s when it fell out of fashion."

"Well, yes. I suppose it's unlikely they'd have been wearing Akubras back then." Roger smiles. "That would be the European convicts sent by the Crown in chains to a penal settlement in the south?"

"Well, yes, you're probably correct. Crime and punishment would have been like a bushman's holiday for many, only with a few deranged officials in charge. Anyway, after they'd killed more aborigines than malaria, they tried to plant their crops in autumn. They failed to realise that the seasons were reversed you see. They ate all their available food and a lot of them died of starvation."

"It has a familiar ring to it."

"What them killing the aborigines?"

"No, the British have always killed everyone in their way. Look at any atlas to witness the extent of vast, pink Imperialism. That's one of the reasons we're so damned unpopular."

"Oh, ok." Brainy beams. "Well, there's no substitution for a winning personality, but it was about then that the sheep arrived and have been a treasured resource ever since."

"So really the only information I'm likely to find is that I should eat more lamb and always carry a stick." Roger sums up.

"What else?" Sue sighs. "We're drifting off topic."

Brainiac looks a little beaten.

"Well I'm afraid that's all I have on the matter."

Back home Sue attends to Jayne and James while Roger sits at the dining table twiddling a pen as though it is a well-earned cigarette.

"Time for a bottle of Chateau cardboard and another rethink."

"It's earth shattering stuff," Sue calls out from the east wing, its entirety affording their bedroom, "Now it's going to cost us a whole £10 each and we're being extra choosey."

Sue joins Roger at their table.

Both now into the plonk, Roger is thinking it could be a great time for him to try the horizontal limbo, as Australia is an awfully long way to go for a shag.

He raises his glass to his wife, and smiles, "Here's to us then, Sweet Pea."

Sue toasts back, "Good luck to you then, Knucklehead."

Roger frowns. "Maybe I should act royally."

"Alright, how's about Lord Pist-a-lot then."

"According to Brainy, it's the driest, flattest, and at times hottest, place imaginable. The most merciless place north of Antarctica. Remind me again, Sue, why are we going there?"

"For a better life."

"No guarantees. No idea about housing, or costs," Roger sighs, "and if we go to Australia we'll be saying goodbye to everything we've ever known here."

"Such as?"

"Oh, I don't know. Country of our birth. Maybe Ena Sharples, Len Fairclough, and Stan Ogden of *Coronation Street*. Ronnie Barker, Dave Allen?"

Sue takes a sip of wine. "What else, seriously?"

"We may never see any more re-runs of *Steptoe & Son*. I'll miss the rasping and manipulative voice of Wilfred Bramble and the comic antics of Harry H. Corbett."

"We'll also be leaving a country of strange names. Prisons like Wormwood Scrubs, Strangeways, and Parkhurst. In the county of Sussex there's Devil's Dyke," Sue adds with a smile. "Does any of that matter? It's like complaining about potholes when they're among the few things left that are still being made here."

"And in London I never did find out why Tooting Bec was so called, and will we or the children miss being able to ride the tube trains or the double decker buses?" Roger adds, "Or the donkeys on the beach?"

"Well you don't ride them now, and anyway why should you miss a bus?" Sue pauses. "Are we going Down Under or not?" she asks firmly.

Roger sighs. "Yes. I suppose so, okay."

"You mean it?" Sue brightens.

"Yes, a bit of roast kookaburra, or some nicely fried platypus will be a change from sausages and sardines."

"What's a platt-ie-pus?"

"I don't know, not even sure how to spell it."

"What about roasted kangaroo?" Sue asks.

"Might taste alright."

"Are you sure we'd go? Even without a job and no money?"

"We're broke here. I'm supposing we've got little or nothing to lose."

Everything that has happened to them to date, the untimely death of Sue's dad at only 58, the premature death of Roger's mum aged only 38, and their financial hardships working at the behest of family, has finally led them to this juncture.

"Okay." Sue replies, drawing out the word. "Yes, then we'll go," and with that she takes Roger's face in her hands and gives him a kiss that nearly sets his clothes on fire. Roger finds his baser instincts creeping firmly into place.

"If we do go Down Under," Roger muses, "will the missionary position be upside down?"

"Trust you to bring sex into it."

"Now might be a good time to sing God Save the Queen."

Instead, in low tones so as not to wake their babies, they butcher *Waltzing Matilda*.

"Are you happy about all this, Roger?" Sue asks between humming and softly singing.

"I will be, if it works."

Chapter 3

THE TREE OF KNOWLEDGE

As part of the application process, Sue and Roger are assigned to see separate doctors to avoid any risk of collusion.

"Heaven only knows why? What on earth concerns them? Collusion about what?"

"Don't worry, Sue. Remember we're dealing with a government department, and to boot one with an unlimited budget."

"We should be thankful, that Fred is not booked in to see the vet."

"Agreed. Then we'd probably see some real paperwork!"

As Jayne and James are not considered health risks by the Australian government, they tag along with Mum.

Roger's doctor studies the forms in silence.

"I've had no prior experience with these Australian forms but I'll complete them stage by stage as instructed. I see they require crosses and not ticks, most unusual. Go behind that curtain to fully undress, please."

The doctor follows him and draws the curtains tight, so tight not even a microscopic particle of light penetrates through. Well and truly encased in a cocoon of gloomy solitude, he undresses quickly and then regrets it as the bone wrenching cold permeates every pore of his exposed skin. "This is why I'm doing this," he mutters miserably to himself, "to avoid this bastard cold."

He piles his clothes together and as he is about to leave his cold haven turned torture chamber, he realises he is still wearing his socks. *Fully undress, please…* resonates in his brain. Hopping from one foot to the other he removes the burdensome items and with a theatrical sigh attempts to exit but has difficulty finding where the curtains meet. For a few stalled seconds, which seem an eternity he looks as if he is trying to battle his way through an impenetrable wall of nylon.

After the doctor rescues him and guides him back into the room, Roger quips, "If that was the intelligence test, Doctor, I fear I failed."

The GP allows a thin smile, "Please stand with your feet shoulder width apart, looking straight ahead."

His hand cupped under Roger's shrunken testicles, he instructs him to cough. "Does that hurt?"

"Only if I try to squeeze toothpaste at the same time," Roger jokes.

Unfazed by Roger's humour, he frowns darkly and asks, "Do you exercise?"

"Only when I have to," Roger replies, and then with a leer, "although, I do try to get about twenty push-ups in at least three times a week."

"Any exercise that doesn't involve a coronary is good." He writes, 'Active'. More study and careful thought slows the process as he further studies the forms.

"How much alcohol do you drink?"

"Too much."

The doctor frowns. He writes, 'two beers a week'.

"I don't like the way these government forms are framed but the road to hell is paved with good intentions, or so they say." He pauses. "I suppose if you insist on going to Australia I can't see anything medical to prevent you."

He takes Roger's blood pressure and checks his pulse with his wristwatch, then motions to Roger's clothes indicating he can now return to the English modesty that is world renowned.

"That's great, Doctor," Roger crows struggling to get back into his clothes. His body it seems is used to the chill now and slow moving. He feels as if he is wallowing in Treacle.

Finally back in familiar territory Roger stands in front of the GP, about to leave, when his judge continues with a quote from the Bible, "You'll probably get your three score plus ten the same there as here."

"One thing though, do you need those?" The doctor is pointing to Roger's packet of Chesterfield cigarettes in his top shirt pocket. Thinking he is short on words and asking for a smoke, Roger offers him one.

"No, no, I don't want one!" He insists, waving his arms in the air in horror. "What I meant was can you? Would you? Stop smoking them?"

The doctor pauses, as if searching for the correct comment.

"If anything I can say to you here today," he begins, "that might extend your life, it's giving up smoking those damned, awful cigarettes."

"Are you serious, Doctor?"

The GP nods enthusiastically. "Every cigarette you don't smoke is definitely doing you good."

"I've heard smoking may not be the best of pastimes health wise, but nothing has ever been stated officially other than it being a nicotine habit. My Gramps refers to them as coffin nails but in a joking way."

The doctor enforces with a philosophical nod, "You really would be better off without them."

Whilst smoking maybe harmful to his health, Roger is unsure if he wants to stop sucking down those magic bullets. On impulse he takes the opened packet out of his pocket and hands them to him, "Best throw them in your waste bin then, please."

"Are you sure?"

Roger thinks that strange. "Yes, I'm sure."

"Might you prefer to give up smoking after you've finished this packet?" The doctor asks.

Roger's mouth erupts into a smile before he can reel it in. "You've never been involved in sales, have you, Doctor?"

The GP shakes his head. "No, I went straight to medicine."

"Well," Roger grins, "you'd closed the sale. No need to reopen it."

At home, they compare visits. Sue's was walk in walk out. Her Quack took one look at her and the two children, and signed the forms.

Sue is chuckling and pointing at Roger's incorrectly buttoned shirt. "You have Tuesday's button in Wednesday's hole."

"Sue," Roger pauses, "On the Quacks advice I've given up smoking." His Cheshire cat smile is as wide as though he has been conferred a junior spelling bee award.

That news almost receives a standing ovation by Sue. Within minutes every ashtray in the house is washed, dried, and disappeared as if by sleight of hand.

Roger turns his attention to Jayne. "What day is it?"

"Today," Jayne replies, "Daddy not smoking anymore."

"Bright girl." Roger turns to Sue, "Our three year old daughter with the seven year old brain scores again." He reaches out and grasps a wriggling, giggling Jayne for a big cuddle. "Turns out to be Daddy's favourite day, Sweetheart, because it's also your third birthday."

Sue grins, "Time to celebrate with a cocktail cherry on a stick."

Jayne has cordial and cake while Sue and Roger share a bottle of cheap calamity. Jayne wants their wine. Sue dips her finger in her own glass and puts it to Jayne's mouth.

Sue whispers to her, "Drinking wine is like angels peeing on your tongue."

"She appears to like angel's pee," Roger smiles warmly, "welcome to the family, Sweetheart."

Sue becomes heuristic, "Remember wine is made from grapes, and grapes are fruit, and fruit is good for us," then with a frown, "do you think we have a problem with alcohol?"

"Absolutely," Roger replies, "as self-appointed sommelier I can confirm we don't have enough of it. I'm also craving a cigarette as much as Fred devours his treats. Maybe it's more of a habit than I realised?"

Sue is supportive. "I'm sure the cravings will grow less frequent for you."

"I've got a plan to beat it, Sue"

"Oh, Roger that's wonderful, what plan?"

"I haven't got a plan really, but at work they love it when I say I've got a plan."

Roger's only difficult time is at work, when other people are smoking and offer him one, otherwise, Sue is proven correct. Roger finds if he inhales stale smoke from butts in an ashtray, any ashtray, it kills the moment.

"Admittedly carrying a full ashtray around with me would be an excellent plan, Sue."

"It will make you look a complete Knucklehead, that or close to wearing a wrap-around, tie-at-the-back, white jacket."

Soon he is turned off by the mere thought of sniffing an ashtray.

In the meantime, more forms, and choices to make, arrive from Australia House.

"All this would have confused Einstein," Roger ploughs on as he grumbles.

"Melbourne appears to do what she does best," Roger is thumbing through their statistics.

"What's that?"

"I quote: 'Often provides wet and cold days'. They admit to 'changeable as in four seasons in any one day.'"

Sue has an involuntary little shudder. "What about Adelaide?"

"It's a pretty city, well laid out, but cold enough in July for snow."

Sue looks at Roger with a raised eyebrow. "Right, not Melbourne or Adelaide, got it."

"They're not interested in Fred, but it's up to us if we want to pay for him."

"Oh, Roger. Can we take him?"

"Don't see why not, but it looks extremely expensive, Sue. Can we afford it?"

"No we can't, can we?"

"No. Sorry. It's too expensive."

Pushing unpalatable thoughts about Fred to the back of their minds, they press on regardless with due consideration about fuck-all but climate. They draw a beeline northwards on their only map and lo and behold find the very place that initially appealed to Roger.

"Perth!" They say in unison.

"Okay. Let's avoid anywhere further south."

"Agreed. It's too cold. Can anyone wearing thermal underwear be happy at all times?"

"That's one decision down, Sue. Now they only want us to choose mode of travel. Ship or plane?"

"Maybe we should get ourselves some brave or stupid pills?"

To try to relax, Roger switches on some soothing music; — Chopin is one of his favourites. They continue to contemplate. He prepares to make inroads on a bottle of Chateau cut-price red wine, which starts going down rough. Very rough! Like a rough diamond that has lost its sparkle they are about to slide into it like a ferret down a drainpipe.

"I know that tomorrow morning my head will hate me," he is offering another glass to Sue with a grimace.

Sue sips her wine slowly. "If it comes down to twenty-four hours of misery in the air or throwing up on a ship for six weeks, at least on the boat we'd get fresh air."

Roger sets his wine glass down in front of him, and gazes into it as if glimpsing an uncertain future.

That night in his dreams, he is still searching for his elusive Seal Flipper Pie, interrupted by female seals skipping across vast empty grey oceans in a chorus line carrying freshly made whale pies.

After scraping three glaciers from his car windscreen, he is unable to stand upright. Then in semi-foetal positions, they take turns at clutching the cold ceramic curves of the only toilet bowl shared with many on an 1850's sailing ship. Retching and arching like sick cats amid the wild and brutal seas, while being offered and declining freshly baked pies, he receives further ridicule by his father, 'What bloody fool chooses to go live upside down in a place inhabited only by convicts?'

Roger awakes in a clammy sweat. Silence. Fred must be asleep. No frantic whining. Good. His heart still races at the fading thoughts of throwing up. Quickly he realises that he has run out of dreams but now dozes afraid to repeat his nightmares.

Roger's oblivion is clinched by Sue's brilliant observation at breakfast.

"You do realise that we won't have any money to spend on the journey, either way we go. Perhaps the *SS Wanna Be* isn't the best choice of transport. We'd be tempted to go ashore. Spend money."

"We've never had a holiday."

"I know. Neither so much as a sun lounger in the rain, nor a dog eared book to read over a period of days."

"Join a book club that only reads wine labels, and get guzzling, Sue. Maybe we'll need a holiday after we arrive just to recover from all this?"

"Alright, now we're aware that *Poseidon* is possibly not on our side; we don't need any more soothing music."

Roger's mental awareness is ranging from that of a butter knife to an over-ripe plum, but they are on it like a fat kid on a cupcake.

With their forms, certified copies of birth and marriage certificates, employment records, proof of financial standing, or as in their case severe lack of, a request to fly and last but not least payment of a whole £10 each they drive to the local post office and send the hefty envelope to the Government half eagerly and half with a slight feeling of trepidation.

Quite quickly for a government department they receive a letter back.

"Might they have tired of sitting on their fat arses all day bending paper clips?" Roger announces, "Hey, look at this," Roger is dumfounded, "it insists a personal appearance is mandatory, no excuses, or our application will be cancelled forthwith. All four of us have to attend."

As usual, Roger is up early, although Sue is unimpressed with his horizontal jog before their important meeting.

"Not the best of timings, you selfish bastard," she mutters.

Roger feels nuttier than a Snickers bar. Moreover, he realises to boot that outside it is a miserable day trying to rain but cannot. It is cold, windy, and bleak as an embittered ex-wife. The tightening of his scrotum only added to Sue's idea of an uneventful day!

"We need a bigger car." Roger groans. "I'm carrying enough gear to collapse a donkey and it's only just a London meeting."

"Be grateful they don't want to see Fred," Sue replies, buzzing around like a frantic worker bee.

Roger grins, "Fred, you lucky hound, you're staying home. See? Today the dog does get the bone."

Pooch Fred is excited, hoping Roger will leave the cathode ray tube on. It is his only source of warmth when they are out.

At Australia House, they are warmly greeted by a charming man whose stiff wattage of smile almost blinds them. He is taller than Roger, sporting the style of parting that only a fretsaw down the middle of his crown could achieve.

Fretsaw shows them through the reception area with pride. Plush as any bank's HQ it has more locks than the Bank of Scotland.

"So you're applying to go to Australia," Fretsaw's big wattage smile lights their way.

"Yes," Roger replies, thinking *it's bloody astounding he realises that's why we're here.*

They see many security guards.

"Why all this security?" Sue whispers to Roger.

He whispers back, "Dunno! With only a few Victorian oil paintings on the walls of buttoned down girls, what's to steal?"

"Thanks to their overzealous cleaners the place is as clean as a nun's drawers," Sue giggles, "but why are our ears being assaulted with boring piped music by Muzak?"

"Agreed. Why don't they play *Waltzing Matilda?*"

Briefly meeting Fretsaw's boss, Sue smiles like an actress auditioning for a coveted role. He is trim and fine boned, immaculately dressed in a suit the colour of claret wine; handsome with a square jaw, dark hair, and broad shoulders.

When he speaks, he sounds pompous. "Oh, you're the pest man."

The way Pompous said that sounded synonymous with lunatic vermin. "I'm regional manager for a specialist pest control company," Roger corrects cheerfully.

"Quite so."

Pompous does not sound Australian; he has the kind of voice shaped by Sandhurst, the Guards, and a lifetime of drinking Pink Gin. His dulcet, educated tones could make it worth listening to a shopping list recital. When he smiles, he exudes an air of designer barbed wire that makes Roger feel about as conspicuous as a Great Dane at a cat show.

In demand are painters, bricklayers, labourers, steel workers — not fancy arse pest controllers.

Sue is tapping her fingernail against her front teeth. Nice nail. Nice teeth. She is melting next to Pompous as surely as a butterscotch chip into a warm, sweet cookie.

Female staff busily tap away at typewriters. The younger ones wear blouses unbuttoned to show some cleavage. Roger appreciates their effort while getting a stern look from Sue. Others run around with important looking folders.

"Maybe they contain their advertising budgets," Roger comments to no-one in particular.

The staff have their special smiley faces on but offer little output. It becomes obvious they understand everything really, really well until they are asked a question. Any question. This directs Roger and Sue back to Fretsaw who slips into auto waffle, or suddenly becomes deaf.

Eagerly Roger pursues each of their carefully thought out questions about Perth in the fervent hope that their six Pools numbers might magically come up, but Fretsaw is unwilling to part with more than smiles that do not reach his eyes.

"I don't think they know one end of a dog's bowl from another," Roger lowers his voice to Sue, "and in addition may they be culturally unaware?"

"They're about as bright as post codes," Sue opines quietly. She is annoyed. "If they can't answer even our simple questions, and everything they want to know about us has already been detailed on their forms in triplicate. Then why are we here?"

Roger, putting on his hopeful smiley face, speaks to Fretsaw, "Here we are, brimful of questions for the experts, and no-one seems to know much about anything." He pleads. "What about property values?" He pauses. "A guide would be helpful. Are we likely to be able to replace what we have here, with a similar mortgage? Can we get an indication of median property prices?"

"Our house's value represents about quadruple Roger's annual salary." Sue cuts in, "Any comparisons *would* be helpful."

Fretsaw thoughtfully projects, "Australia is a very confusing place. Most staff here are not Australian and the few that are, come from Canberra."

"Is that why you know nothing about Perth?" Roger asks tentatively.

"Australia is such a huge landmass it takes up the major part of the southern hemisphere."

Fretsaw has a smile, the beam of which resembles that of a Jehovah's Witness who has just added a brand new member to his congregation.

"In the outback many children have never seen the sea. They've grown up without television in towns little more than T-junctions or a wide spot in the road. Vast stretches of major highways are little more than dirt tracks. If you break down you could be stuck for days. Jobs could be few and far between. Red dirt country. I'm sure you'd be more suited to city life in our nominated areas."

Roger is thinking, *Better than Bum-Fuck-Idaho or the never-never.*

He nods in agreement, "Attractive though country life could appeal to our inner pioneer spirit, I'm sure you're right. City it is but that's why we nominated Perth. The brochure states it's the Capital City of Western Australia."

Sue is thinking, *Can it get any less rural than that?*

"Put another way," Sue adds with a smile, "we prefer our milk delivered from a bottle rather than a teat."

Fretsaw begins nodding enthusiastically, "Quite so. Western Australia, indeed Perth is its capital. It's too far from anywhere to be really relevant." He pauses. "I'm not even sure if they have television yet in Perth."

Roger turns facing Sue, "That answers our question about television programs. No more Ena Sharples or Len Fairclough of *Coronation Street*."

"I think they have 240 volt electricity in Perth." Fretsaw is shaking his head, "but I'm not certain, you understand." He is speaking softly, almost as if life is one big conspiracy.

Fretsaw then blows a cloud of nicotine that even the French would be proud of but Roger is about as shitted off as any Frenchman could be about now.

"We might as well be talking in Korean for all the assistance we're getting," Roger groans to Sue.

"He's about as much use as an ashtray on a motorbike."

They both chuckle.

"They're totally fucked when we ask them any questions related to Perth. In fact anywhere outside of their nominated areas might as well come from Planet Sock." Roger whispers.

Roger shakes his head, if only to release steam building up in his ears, "They may know how to fill a BOAC 707 but maybe they're a long way off knowing what to do with the people after they arrive?"

Sue keeps nodding. If she is not careful, her head might fall off with the repetition.

"I bet you it's because of their White Australia Policy. I'm convinced they only ever wanted us here for a visual."

"You're right you know. I bet a pound to a penny if we'd had so much as a tinge of anything other than pure unadulterated snow in us, that would have been the end of it. Not even allowed to step over the threshold here. I wonder who would have greeted us instead of Fretsaw?"

"The Ku Klux Klan, perhaps," Sue opines.

"Have they said, yes?"

"I don't know, have they?"

Roger asks Fretsaw another question. "Where's your boss?"

He casually scans the area. "No-one ever knows the answer to that question," he smiles.

"Maybe we should get going, Sue?"

"But we've only just arrived."

Fretsaw thinks of something. His voice, barely above a whisper, is irrepressibly cheerful, "If you're accepted under the migration scheme your journey will be seamless. Remember to take nothing and carry as little as possible on your flight, as BOAC supplies everything. That includes baby food and nappies on the plane."

Sue gives Fretsaw her generous smile. "That's wonderful. I was worried. It's such a long way and how much to carry?" her voice tails off.

Fretsaw beams. "Absolutely. Once assigned everything will be taken care of including accommodation. Guaranteed."

"Anything else?" Roger prompts eagerly.

"According to our government rules everything has to be sold and finalised before you leave. You can understand the merit of that. No unfinished business to be left behind. You'd be surprised how many people flee Down Under to avoid commitments here."

"Absolutely," Roger enthuses, "no loose ends." Roger's insides are a little less confident than he is showing.

"Yes and if you have any specialised kitchen equipment, like say a technologically advanced kitchen cooker. Please ship it out. That sort of paraphernalia is in short supply Down Under."

Conversations continue but have long, pregnant pauses that make Roger and Sue feel uncomfortable.

With their visit completed, their new friends at Australia House appear content in the knowledge that they are not *black fellas* in disguise.

Fretsaw has one final piece of paperwork to be signed and witnessed.

"Both of you press hard, please," he instructs, "as the bottom copy's yours."

Sue manages to sign her name without falling over in a dead faint.

Roger mumbles to Sue as they head out. "Maybe his eyes are brown because he's so full of bull shit? Getting worthwhile information here is like trying to get Cork out of Ireland."

"That man can say absolutely nothing and make it sound as strong and noble as the Ten Commandments.

Did you pick up his comment about people migrating Down Under to run away from their commitments?" Sue asks, her conspiratorial tone sounds concerned.

"Yes, but it hardly applies to us, as father's bankers have never contacted me."

Sue mouths the words to Roger, *"Good, then let's leave quickly before they do."*

Outside another downpour is well into its stride. Rain pelts down in heavy sheets. For a while, it bounces off the pavement like one long drum roll.

"I wonder if it rains much in Australia." Sue yells above the din. Roger merely shrugs.

"For tail end of summer the wind is bitterly cold."

Roger cannot see the children thanks to their bundles of clothes. They resemble Michelin Men as they hurry to their car to make their way home.

After their visit to Australia House, they receive a registered letter.

"Might it be a change of heart about Fred?" Sue opines.

Roger frowns. "Not likely, let's open it and see."

He scans the letter, with Sue leaning heavily across his arm.

"What's it say?" Sue asks anxiously.

"It states they don't like our preferred destination of Perth."

Their disappointment is palpable.

Sue's face is as if she has secured a ticket to a Rolling Stones concert only to be told at the last minute that it has been cancelled.

Her face drains of colour. "So, what's our next move?"

Trying to appear cool, calm, and composed when he feels none of those things Roger ponders their tabletop at length.

"Why that damned harpoon to my brain and on a day when it's already suffering impaired activity." He whines on. "Why us?"

Sue grabs his wrist with surprising strength; her voice is phlegmy, "All is not lost."

"Maybe Fretsaw and the way he avoided questions about Perth was a clue?" Roger ponders.

"Or, if he saw the content of this letter, after all it is from another department, might he be as surprised as we are?"

"Don't call him to try and find out," Sue cautions.

Roger nods in agreement. "If there's one thing Dad instilled in me, it was trust no-one."

"I'm guessing that made for some interesting Sunday lunches?"

The letter expressed in polite terms how someone with Roger's qualifications, *or lack of them*, would be better placed in one of their Eastern States. They gave the following choices:

1. Sydney   2. Adelaide   3. Melbourne

"Now what do we do?" Sue asks.

Out comes their only map, again.

"Its use is proving as reliable as my bowels," Roger jokes.

In a state of shock and disappointment, they stare stonily at the dot on the extreme left that represents Perth. They then traverse the latitude from Perth in the West across towards the Eastern States. They double-check their letter.

"Seeking is the goal and searching will be the answer," Roger sounds totally without conviction.

"Yes," Sue confirms, "it's written — Eastern States."

After attempting to drown their sorrows about Perth being a no go, Roger has a shot at drawing a straight horizontal line across the map from Perth in the west.

"*Look*," Sue is cheering up a little, "the line you've drawn sits just below a place in the east called B-R-I-S-B-A-N-E that's Brisbane, capital city of Queensland."

Looking at each other Roger snorts, "Climate wise it's a no brainer, being further north, and nearer to the equator, it has to be the right side of warmer than Perth."

Sue is thoughtful. "I'm not sure what to do? We don't want to upset our chances."

"They say Eastern States. Brisbane, my Love, is Eastern. Actually, you can't get any further east than that, or you'll be in...the drink.

Look, we shouldn't get frustrated by these Australian rules one, two, or three. They say east but don't mention Brisbane. How's about we hedge our bets."

"How?"

"I'll attach a hand written entry; 'Sirs, we respectfully request we be considered for Brisbane—please, blah, blah, blah!'"

They send their missive away. Days slowly trudged into weeks.

Now they wait for the powers-that-be to sprinkle their pixie dust.

In the meantime buoyed by a non-response, which they find strangely encouraging they try to find out something, anything about Brisbane at the Norwich library. It is the largest in their area and Brainy greets them as old friends.

"Based on what we need to know today, I'd say these are good for lining budgie cages," Roger retorts smoothing the newspaper with the palm of his hand.

"Admittedly, they're old newspapers," Brainy agrees with a wry smile, "but Brisbane is rarely mentioned. I deduce therefore that Brisbane must be a very plain and uninteresting place. There's quite a bit about Canberra and Melbourne, though. Sydney gets a few mentions."

After a while Brainy finds them a book that shows a small part of the Gold Coast in South East Queensland. On the map, it looks slightly more than an afternoon's drive from Perth but on closer inspection Brainy suggests they might require taking a picnic lunch.

Sue who finally has her hands on the book is excited. "Look there's a recent photograph. Oh, this is so much better than those black and white drawings of Captain Cook."

Whoever had written the segment about the Gold Coast included a single colour photograph.

"A novel change from etchings of convicts in chains," Brainy agrees amiably. Nodding like a Pekinese doll on the dashboard, he loans them the book.

At home, they do more than peruse. They study that photograph of a man hosing down the drive-way to a house.

Without question that photograph was never intended to provide the hours of in-depth investigation that Sue and Roger devote to it. The expression *'a picture is worth a thousand words'* comes to mind. Roger briefly scans the image looking for something of interest, like a woman's cleavage or a dog doing something despicable in the background.

Sue dissects the picture with a considering look as if conducting an autopsy. "Other than being referred to as banana benders it clearly states: *A fastidious Queenslander*. That's a bit unfair; it's as if Queen-Z-landers are not overly popular with others in Australia. Why call him fastidious just because he likes hosing down his driveway?"

"A good point, if it is his driveway. Unless of course you don't like Queen-Z-landers anyway."

"The hosing down looks more like some sort of relaxation ritual. There are no obvious signs necessitating a clean down."

"There's a big timber house," Roger chimes in. "Means it can't be that cold, otherwise it would be brick. Wouldn't it?"

"Not necessarily; colder places do have timber homes. At least he has reticulated water and apparently plenty of it." Sue observes with excitement. "Look, he's using a hose draped from what looks like a car wheel mounted on the side of his house."

"Maybe he can't afford a proper one, but it's not a novelty him having the means to splash water around. There can't be any shortage of water. Just makes you wonder sometimes how close an anthropologist's deductions are…"

"He's dressed in shorts, so we can assume he's not freezing his nuts off."

"Nor is the water icing up on contact with the ground and look, he's barefooted."

"He's not starving either. His stomach's sticking out over his belt. He looks overweight."

"He doesn't look wealthy by British standards but he can at least afford to eat well."

"With a gut that size it's unlikely he could out work me physically," Roger adds optimistically.

"Unless he's an Einstein in disguise hosing non-existent crap off his driveway?" Sue offers sceptically.

"As long as if he's asked what he does on his day off, he doesn't answer 'celebrate Christmas,' you might be right."

Sue continues, "The sky's a deep clear blue, look, see up there, a couple of brilliant white wisps of cloud, you can even see shadows on the driveway, from what look like trees."

Sue is turning her head sideways to change the rotation of the image. "The grass is green, the other shrubs and flowers all look healthy. Huh, I just realised, he's hosing a concrete driveway, oh, and look right down the bottom here, you can see the road, it's black bitumen, not dirt."

Sue's eyes are alive and dancing as she devours every minute detail of the photo. The whole scenario captured in a nanosecond by some passing photographer of the time.

They remain enthusiastic but worry creases their faces without word from Australia House.

Sue is convinced, pressing her white-knuckled fists to her mouth. "You've blown it. Oh, why did you have to go against their wishes?"

Roger is pacing back and forth like a caged animal. He turns. Her eyes are glazed, as if she is elsewhere. He knows that look well. He has seen it in the mirror often enough after the failure of the family business. Four years of his life working twenty-four seven for food and keep without wages only to be kicked out by the receiver's liquidators with nowhere else to go, except more of the same.

"I hate many things, Sue, but most of all I hate waiting for something to happen. This is like all retch and no vomit."

"You've been giving this a lot of thought, haven't you?"

"Yes, but only once a day," he smiles, "just all day long."

The postman knocks on their front door with another package too large for the letter slot.

"Hello," he says cheerily to Sue, "I see you're going to Australia then."

The age old ritual of the Postie knowing everything about everybody is how Sue and Roger first learned going Down Under.

The package contains, amongst the obligatory government paraphernalia and crapola, four air tickets to Brisbane, departing 13 March, 1971 on a BOAC charter flight from Heathrow.

Sue starts doing crazy little dance steps. She looks as excited as a small child waiting for Santa Claus.

"Say something."

"Wow!"

"Say something else."

"I'm gobsmacked. You know what this means."

"No. What does it mean?"

"This means the staff at Australia House decided to wait until after James's first birthday."

"Why the hell would they do that?"

"Because he'll have a seat to himself on the plane." Excitement crackles off Sue like static electricity, "Don't you see? That qualifies us for an additional luggage allowance."

Roger is amazed. "I don't believe they did it on purpose, but, I'll go with it. We're now well and truly government sponsored migrants, then."

That night Roger snores like a contented hippo about to give birth. Snoring and grunting in brute slumber, instead of dreaming about Seal Flipper Pie, Roger is dreaming of when nothing goes right, try going left.

Thanks to the postman spreading their unbridled news, Sue is approached by local women wanting to buy items they might not be able to take with them.

For the next week, Coxwell swarms with villagers, who are agog. Nothing this exciting has happened since 1942 when Annie Bancroft, a chambermaid at the Maid's Head Hotel in Norwich, was bludgeoned to death.

"Look at all this stuff," Sue's surveying their contents strewn over the lounge room, "looks like the inside of King Tut's tomb."

"Pity it's not as valuable."

Their neighbour Doreen is first to put dibs on their late model *Silver Cross* pram.

Roger is on his hands and knees busily cleaning the wheel rims level with Sue's thighs.

"I hope you know what you're doing down there, Roger," Doreen says coyly.

"That's just what Sue always says," Roger offers with an awkward side look at Sue.

Cecilia is hot on Doreen's heels wanting children's toys. Her friend put dibs on pots, pans, and glassware. Someone suggests Roger buy a mower so he can sell it to them, cheap.

They are making new friends from everywhere.

The downside to their move is the Australian Government does not consider Fred a suitable candidate for Down Under. The high costs involved in Fred becoming an Aussie canine include six months in quarantine.

Roger shakes his head, "That and his live freight passage make the costs of taking him highly prohibitive."

Their decision has nothing to do with Fred chewing shoes or digging up the vegetable garden next door.

"Maybe we should get professional advice?" Sue suggests.

Dr Doolittle, their local veterinarian, is about as pet friendly as *Hyde Park*. The decor hints at old fashioned values and efficiency. The view from the surgery window is not great: a variety of angles, gables, ridges and tiles of the old high street are splattered in bird poo.

The vet and Fred are in raptures over each other every visit.

Dr Doolittle frowns. "I'm of the opinion that Fred should be put down!"

Sue is horrified.

"I have trouble accepting that," Roger replies evenly.

"Well Roger, the cost of taking Fred with you would bankrupt most people. Do you have time to sell him or give him away? No. Well, I've stated the obvious really."

Dr Doolittle cups Fred's face in his hands and speaks in that chirpiest of voices that people use when talking to animals or babies.

Back home their mood is glum.

Sue is mournful, "If we had a goldfish, then that has to be killed, too."

"It's one thing to take Fred down to the vet surgery to lose his manhood," Roger explains gloomily, "but now this! I can't understand why a family doesn't want to take him for free."

"We'll ask around again, and see if we can find another family for Fred."

Chapter 4

MOVING ON...

At work Roger needs to broach the subject of leaving with his boss. He wants to give plenty of extra notice but he is working himself up into a nervous knot about the whole thing. He reasons getting a good reference will be important Down Under. He decides to bounce the idea off his colleague in London.

"Give them too much notice and they'll sack you," his London colleague advises. "Try and avoid being sacrificed on the altar of his ambition. He's a prick."

"I feel like a damned tomcat waking up to the reality of his neutering," Roger replies, "Either way shit will happen."

"You've been reading too many bumper stickers, my friend," came the amiable response.

"They're entitled to four weeks, Roger. One month's notice. That's it." London's words echo in his head.

His dreams now have dramatic sound tracks while still searching for Seal Flipper Pie with Boss Man looming over his shoulder as the Anti-Christ.

His horoscope this week advises minimal communication with those who pay lip service to the truth. For Roger, it has never been more than a job at best but it delivers a good, regular income. They desperately need this income. He decides to tread carefully around Boss Man; the added knowledge that he has confided in London is playing on his growing gut knot!

On the morning of his scheduled visit to Boss Man he is awake early. It is still pitch-black outside.

He drives slowly, as if hoping in some juvenile way that he might never arrive at his destination. The radio is on but he hears only white noise preferring the sound of silence. With the heater on full blast, he can feel his eyebrows starting to smoulder. As he approaches his destination, he grips the steering wheel so hard his fingers hurt.

Where the hell is Dr Who and his sonic screwdriver when you need him?

After an agonising ten minutes of turning himself into a mental pretzel, and urinating enough to water a dusty country, he mans up.

Entering Boss Man's office, he hopes his face will reveal none of his anxiety. Or the fact he desperately now needs to dump a log the size of a small animal.

Roger is not a *Yes Man* and holds a poor opinion of those who are. He has never played that game of kissing ring fingers, bowing and scraping in order to please. With his debonair attitude, often he would have more chance of selling a drowning man a glass of water than blowing smoke up Boss Man's arse.

The office bears few of the usual Christmas decorations as Boss Man is humourless. He has lost his lip toupee and gained a few facial lines around his eyes since last they met. His bloodshot eyeballs are swivelling. If he turns his head quickly, they might pop out of their sockets. A long streak of misery, Boss Man is not wearing his normal suit and tie. Roger is quite sure he sleeps in them. Must be his dress down Friday on a Monday, Roger concludes.

He is obviously not intending to call on clients today. *Good, at least that means he will be staying away from mine.*

Roger has finally decided to damn it all to hell and give plenty of notice, now is the time to formalise his intention.

"I'm tendering two months notice to finish up mid February 1971 as we're due to leave for Australia in the March," Roger blurts, "hopefully, that will give you plenty of time to find my replacement?"

Before Roger can draw breath he realises he has just blabbed the whole scenario. Not exactly the best example of tact and diplomacy, he thinks.

Boss Man looks at Roger through fish-cold eyes swimming behind chunky glasses, as if Roger has just announced he is selling burial insurance.

"Two months should suffice, Roger. Any chance of extending if I have trouble replacing you?"

"No, sorry."

Roger has an unmistakeable urge to reach across the desk and slap Boss Man silly. He almost said, instead mouthed to himself, "Two months notice and you want more, this isn't Oliver Twist."

Smiling Roger continues. "Sorry, but our March departure is confirmed."

Boss Man is grimacing slightly, as if he has just swallowed his cuff link.

After a month of knock backs their decision about Fred seems painfully inevitable. Unfortunately, Dr Doolittle is proven right.

Fingers trailing up her cheek, Sue summarises. "The problem is Fred still being so young, a puppy really."

"He's still in the process of being house trained and Bassett Hounds are notorious. No-one wants a free dog, even with a good pedigree, that digs up everything outside, chews the whole kit and caboodle, and still shits and wees inside."

Sue tucks her hair back from her eyes. "The vet's advice is Fred will fret in a new home without Jayne and James. He calls it separation anxiety. Maybe we have no choice but to consider his professional advice."

On the appointed day, Roger takes Fred on his last visit to the veterinary surgery.

Dr Doolittle looks mournfully at Fred and shakes his head, "Such a shame to have to put him down, Roger. I won't do it right now, it'll be too hard on you having to watch. I'll keep him over night out the back in comfort, well fed and I'll take care of it, later."

Roger is relieved, the drive down had been heart wrenching enough.

As he pays the bill for euthanizing Fred, the dog looks at him pitifully.

Roger strokes the dog's nose one last time and departs a little blurry eyed.

On the weekend, they decide to pay Roger's Grandparents a personal visit; a first since the breakup of the family business. This is not something Roger feels they can do justice by writing a letter. As Gran and Gramps have no phone their visit will indeed be the biggest surprise since Eve ate the apple.

Roger knocks loudly. Nothing. He knocks again and hears almost incoherent voices.

Gran and Gramps are delighted to see them and their great grandchildren on their doorstep despite Gramps being sick with a bad chest.

"Too many smokes and neglect over the years has finally caught up with me," he announces with a rattle.

In the flat Gran's crocheted doilies, china figurines, and knickknacks are everywhere.

Sue comments nervously, "Jayne would have a field day if she stayed here."

Gran is as fat and jolly as ever. She has a habit of sucking on her dentures.

Both Gran and Gramps appear to have aged about ten years in three. They have transitioned from mature-aged to the much less optimistic label of 'elderly'. Their flat is dated; their furniture has lost its lustre.

None of this matters to Roger because he is blind to their faults. To him they have become historic treasures.

Sue sips some tea from a chipped rose-pattern cup and toys with a biscuit on her plate, while Jayne explores the china figurines and James grunts.

They laugh and joke, and their planned departure to Australia is applauded with so much enthusiasm that Sue and Roger become embarrassed.

Gramps rattles, "If the weather and economy stays like this through summer, half the country will become suicidal, and the other half seriously contemplate it."

Gran and Gramps hold James and Jayne while reminiscing about Roger.

Gran recalls. "The way your face radiated joy as a baby, you were such a happy child. Unlike your father who was the opposite. You'd lay in your cot all gummy grins and twinkling eyes, podgy arms and legs."

Gramps closes his friendly eyes and his lips tremble, "I enjoyed holding your tiny hand to the shops and giving you horsey rides around the scullery." He sighs and looks sad when he tickles James and adds, "Sorry, James, I'm too old. I'm out of horsey rides now."

"If he gets down on the floor now, we'll never get him back up again," Gran reinforces with a pixie grin.

"And when you used to run along the landing but miss the two steps down at the end," Gran laughs, "your legs just kept going. Like in a cartoon."

"Priceless," Gramps adds with a wheezy laugh.

Memories flood back, the old man and his stories of Coco the clown. Roger riding on his back like a jockey around the small kitchen at their flat in Barlby Road.

Unbeknown to all except closest family Gramps is illiterate and he told stories because of this. He remained a guard on the railways because promotion to train driver would be like walking through a minefield with him having to prove his literacy. Even filling out their Pools coupons had been a big step for Gramps struggling to put the crosses in the correct squares.

"Goodness so many memories. I even helped bring you into the world." Gran pauses and wipes her tired old eyes on a corner of her apron, "I bought him his first typewriter, didn't I, Roger?"

"Yes, a *Remington* portable from *Whiteleys* department store at Bayswater, Gran. It was an expensive gift, thank you."

Gran continues, "Took him to playgrounds in the Kensington parks when he was only young, and you remember how we cooked all those wonderful fresh mussels, whelks and brown crabs back in our little scullery kitchen?"

"Just so many good things to remember and it all seems now such a long time ago in another lifetime even," Gramps wheezes.

In this instance "good" is not enough, Roger thinks.

Roger wants to remember them the way they had always been, not old and sickly as they are now. The emotion is filling him from the toes up.

Gramps hugs Roger. Tears are beginning to gather. Gramps' eyes, are changing from the faded blue of old china to bloodshot but his voice is steady and strong now. "It's been a privilege to be your Gramps every day of every year since you were born, Son."

Tears well up in Roger's eyes with the sorrow of leaving them. He is struggling to recover his emotions that might rob him of speech in his shrinking world.

"Remember, Sue," Gramps advises, "don't let fear hold you back, fear is like an invisible dragon. And sometimes you just need to say move aside dragon, you're blocking my path."

After a few more tears from Gran and Sue, they leave feeling sad and buoyed up at the same time.

Their ride home is a silent one, each lost in their own grave thoughts. James is sleeping and Jayne is looking out the window, obviously on one of her own adventures.

"My tummy's doing flip flops, Sue."

"You're probably upset after our parting with your grandparents. Do you want to stop somewhere?"

At home, Roger and Sue break open a bottle of money-be-damned Red wine.

On the advice of their newly found friends at Australia House, they decide to leave most electrical appliances behind, the choice made for them by neighbours wanting to buy them at bargain prices. They are adamant, however, about taking their almost brand new state-of-the-art, electric kitchen stove. They are assured this should go, as for some reason cookers or electric ranges are in short supply, in the land of upside down. The lucky appliance is set aside for a sea voyage.

Appropriate forms completed in quadruplicate, personal possessions finalised, they are ready to pack and go.

Roger makes his final visit to Boss Man who throws a faltering smile.

"I'd be pleased if you'd change your mind and stay. Particularly as I'm having trouble finding a suitable replacement for you. There are plenty of applicants but none who want to move to this area."

The accusatory tone of Boss Man implies that by leaving Roger is a dog turd.

With a half-hearted handshake they part.

At home, sitting as close as possible to their heater, Sue and Roger take stock of their situation.

"The only things left to do is pack and get to Heathrow in time to board our flight," Roger announces smiling.

The next day their home telephone rattles. It is a call from Mrs Doolittle the veterinary surgeon's wife. "Do you have papers for Fred?" she asks Sue.

Sue shifts her weight, looks belligerent, and goes into Rhino mode before handing the telephone to Roger. She whispers, "They want Fred's papers. Can you believe it? A week after he's, he's, …. and they call wanting the papers!"

Frowning Roger takes the call. "We have papers somewhere but I'll have to dig them out."

Allegedly, Dr Doolittle wants Fred's papers so he can complete his befuddling paperwork for putting him down.

"I know I'm no sharper than a butter knife, Sue, but I find that very hard to believe."

Sue sets her teeth. It is as if wisps of steam are curling from her ears.

"With what he charges, I'd expect him to walk on water and have a direct line to pet heaven."

"Never mind, if there's the slimmest chance for Fred, that he might go to a loving home instead of getting a sharp green needle…"

"But to have been told the truth and spared the costs of euthanasia, would have been nice."

"Agreed, I'll take the papers down tomorrow."

Roger turns up to the surgery where Mrs Doolittle advises her husband the vet is out on a house call. She takes the papers from Roger, gushing as she does so with admiration of their transatlantic move to the colonies.

Roger leaves feeling confused. He is hoping that pure bred canine Fred has found a more or less legit home with the Doolittle family.

Chapter 5

THE LAST FAREWELL

Friday, 12th March, 1971.

"The house sale has fallen through at the last moment, whatever will we do, Roger?"

Roger is beside himself. Fretsaw's words echo in his mind. Government rules state everything has to be sold and finalised before they leave. That is a cardinal rule, no loose ends, no unfinished business.

"I refuse to let this stop us, Sue; and there's another thing."

"What?"

"Well, if migrants have been known to disappear to Australia leaving debts behind, why wait until the damned house is sold? Maybe we should get a move on!"

Unwilling to put the kibosh on their plans at the eleventh hour, they leave the house and unsold contents in the hands of the local estate agent.

"What if we get caught out?" A worried Sue asks Roger.

"Pounds to Pesos I don't see how they can. Not unless we tell them."

"Okay," Sue takes a deep breath but her look is one of relief.

"History shows we shouldn't take governments too seriously. After all the best way of creating a famine, surely, would be putting any government department in charge of agriculture."

They arrive in London the day before their departure with limited time to do last minute shopping, sightseeing, and people watching prior to their big event. They find the city too noisy, too crowded. Amid horns blaring, they took in multiple deep breaths of diesel fumes.

"Even Lord Nelson looks pensive in Trafalgar Square, stood on his giant granite shaft."

"Worried because of all those damned pigeons crapping all over him," Sue replies. "He's wearing a wig of bird poo that's visible from down here."

At the Telecom Tower, boredom settles around them like a thick coat. There Roger plays with Jayne by pretending to be a lift operator.

The lift is a rocket, even too fast to bother with music.

"Going up," he announces, "25th floor Ladies lingerie, Men's apparel and Children's shoes." Jayne giggles. Sue smiles. James grunts.

The distraction with their children helps to take Roger's mind off his fear of heights. He looks to Sue for sympathy.

"It's hereditary," he explains, "it always amazed me how my Dad could climb up into a Lancaster bomber, let alone fly one."

As they hurtle skyward he tries behaving as normal while the pulses in his neck threaten to burst out over the lift walls. His legs and feet begin to tingle and lose feeling; all he wants to do is sit in the foetal position on the floor in a dark corner and rock himself to his happy place.

Jayne and James show no fear, even when they reach the top floor. Poor Sue is bravely stifling her sobs.

The lift doors open revealing Sue and Roger leaning heavily on each other, each clutching onto a child for support. If it had not been for their false pride, Roger would have been out and back in that door, like a honeymoon dick. Blind paranoia has Sue by the throat like an enraged boa constrictor.

"Using children as an excuse for covering our fear of heights is pathetic," Roger mumbles.

"Agreed, but doing it crouched on the floor of the lift is not a pretty sight either," Sue admonishes.

"This entire outing is becoming even more of a cluster fuck than I envisaged!"

"It was your silly idea to visit this damned tower."

"Experts say with heights you need three points of contact."

"You should be alright then, because counting your knees and forehead — I count seven."

Sue makes a dash for a security rail, and then pauses before venturing towards the entrance to the skywalk.

Roger meanwhile resembles a giant crab unwilling to leave the security of the lift wall. It is only after he has circumnavigated the lift more than once he chances to exit. If only the message he is sending to his feet would not be ignored.

Less than one minute in to their visit Sue turns to Roger.

"I have to get down now," she is dragging Jayne and James back in to the lift. Roger is hot on her heels. A couple of people pass them without making eye contact.

"The nightmare trip down seems interminably long."

"Where the hell is the ground?" Sue sobs.

He is so nervous by the end of their trip down that had there been a water feature out front he would have been tempted to use it as a lavatory. Dimes to doughnuts he feels as jittery as an old maid balanced on a picket fence.

Madame Tussauds completes their outing of outings.

"It delighted me as a younger man," Roger explains optimistically.

"The Chamber of Horrors looks awfully macabre, Roger."

"That's because it is, Sweetheart. It's not widely known but they used to run competitions with prizes for anyone who could stay in here alone all night!

Few were successful unless they downed enough whisky to put Falstaff to shame."

"It is very dark, Roger."

"You're right, maybe a bit too realistic with all that imitation blood and gore and creepy noises."

"And their spooky music! Really? Men hanging from obscene hooks isn't a place for an impressionable young child, Roger. Actually, it's no place for any child. Not for me either! I refuse to venture in, with or without, the children."

Even Roger feels disturbed; they peruse the less controversial exhibits. Even those are daunting to younger minds, and that done, decide to call it a day.

On the way back to the hotel, they sport themselves a taxi to avoid the hassle of buses and tube trains.

The driver speaks what sounds like the English language but being dragged through a pit filled with sludge. Roger has difficulty understanding what he is saying.

"I take you — only £5."

"Can you improve on that?" Roger asks hopefully.

"How's about £10?"

Their fare-inflated route further boosts the meter with the taxi inching forward at the pace of an asthmatic snail.

"His gearbox has a whole lot of gears slower than the postal service," Roger whinges aloud.

"Not helped by his clumsy left foot," Sue replies.

While forward progress is accompanied by the odour of burning oil, the driver tries to become, albeit temporarily, part of their family.

Roger is intrigued. He notices the driver has a strange name, and wonders if his swarthy complexion precludes western European origins? An Asian appearance, or Arabic maybe? He is certainly not dark enough to be Nigerian.

The taxi stops with greater ease than it moves.

Genuinely curious about the driver's background, paying him Roger asks, "What nationality are you?"

Surprised, his injurious response is, "I'm Engrish!"

"Good to know," Roger, covers his faux pas with a handsome tip they can ill afford, at which point the cabbie's frown softens into a leering gap-toothed grin.

Roger barely manages to close the taxi door before he speeds away leaving devils in his wake.

As they enter their hotel bedroom, Roger feels moved to postulate.

"You know, if ever we needed a more fitting epitaph of our final night in the old country," he spouts on, "I doubt we'd find anything better than being told by a toothless, migrant cabbie, 'I'm Engrish!'"

"Oh well, sums it up, but on the bright side at least we found out why Tooting Bec is so called."

"Agreed. Who would have thought it's named after Bec Abbey in Normandy as part of the land carve up after the Norman conquest. Such evidence of bottom line shenanigans is everywhere in the Old Dart, even back then."

Exhausted after their day's misadventures and apprehensive, they try to sleep.

Finally their big day arrives.

Roger stares into the bathroom mirror absent-mindedly. His thoughts instead of about money, sex, and food, are about Australia. A strange land down under to where they are about to transport their small family.

"My shoulders feel tighter than balls of wool held together with knitting needles," Sue confides.

Nervously they take deep breaths and enter Heathrow Airport.

"It appears functional," Roger comments, "not an attractive place."

"I'm sure most airports are ugly, Roger. 'As pretty as an airport,' isn't an appropriate saying anywhere!"

"I'm amazed at its bluster, people everywhere, and all in a hurry."

Roger is a little solemn, "As our suitcases are headed to Australia, I suppose we are too."

"Take heart," Sue offers, "if half what we hear is true many might have just discovered their luggage has not landed with them."

"Oh, the full horrors of tourism. No change of undies for some!"

"James being one year and seven days old qualifies him for his own seat on the plane, today," Sue beams.

Roger smiles at his son. "You get a birthday each year, James."

"I want one too," Jayne declares.

"It'll be expensive but we'll stretch to one each year for both of you, provided you behave," Sue smiles warmly.

Their formal goodbyes are confined to a few family members gathering around to hug and kiss them and their babies.

Roger's grandparents are absent but excused, as they would have had difficulty with the return journey by expensive convoluted public transport.

Through all the pain and mental anguish, Roger is trying to remember his Dad fondly. Named William Edward, everyone calls him Edward, rather than Bill.

Once his best friend, Edward had always talked with his son, even confided about his career as a Lancaster bomber pilot in WWII, telling Roger the gory truth about war. Often at dinner parties when others told jokes, Roger would tell one of the wartime stories his Dad had told him. This suited him well as he is incapable of telling any joke successfully, usually forgetting the 'punch-line'.

Any father and son relationship involves communication and right now that is finished. They are both stranded on an island as if attempting to decipher smoke signals. Problems include the wind blowing them to bits, smashed to smithereens by Edward's greed in the family businesses and by his second wife, Zelda. A woman proven to have a flexible relationship with the truth.

"It is a shame, Roger, because, from what you have told me, your supportive mother, Alice, kept him in line wanting him to keep a proper job."

"Even as the crooked, manipulative bastard of a father he became after Mum died. He always saw me more often while I was growing up than every third Saturday, and then only on an outing to somewhere like a zoo.

He changed dramatically after he met Zelda and she drew out his dark side. They might as well have been married by an old, blind holy man on a donkey for all June cared, it happened so fast.

Never mind. Drum roll! Now we're gallivanting off to Oz without a proper job to go to. Mum would have been displeased. Crestfallen even."

To Roger's mind, any doubts about how badly they were treated at the first hotel business were reinforced tenfold at the second.

Sue's mother Minnie, now a sad and lonely blue rinse widow, has made a State visit to Heathrow. Her entourage in tow, she exudes charm greeting with, "There's a cup of tea and a biscuit waiting for me at home, dears."

"Would you like Roger to get you a cup of tea?" Sue offers.

"Oh, don't go to any trouble, dears," Minnie is thoughtful, "I'll just have half a cup."

Silly woman, thinks Roger. *Same difference!*

"How are you, Mummy?" Sue asks as she nervously picks at the cuticle on her right thumb.

"When lately have you seen me happy, dear?" Minnie lets out a long sigh. Lately she has been letting out many long sighs. She turns her painted smile to Roger, which he finds insipid. Holding that smile is one of the hardest things Minnie's done in a while.

"And dare I ask how you two are getting along after that dreadful hotel business of your father's?"

Roger braces for any pre-emptive nuclear strike. "In a regular job, Minnie; we don't actually see as much of each other during the working day as we did at the hotels. But we have a much better home life."

Minnie becomes frustrated and begins rummaging in her handbag; she pulls out her cigarettes.

"That must have been quite suffocating, dears."

She glares at Roger. "A gentleman always lights a lady's cigarette, Roger. Or have you forgotten?"

"Sorry, Minnie. I don't carry a lighter anymore because I've given up smoking. Here, allow me to use yours." As he takes Minnie's lighter to her cigarette, his hand shakes slightly with nerves.

For what seems an eternity Minnie inspects the lighted end.

As does Roger. He is sorely tempted. If this keeps up he might need a distraction; a cigarette.

Sue's younger brother Philip has combed his hair to commemorate the solemnity of the occasion. Devoid of his transistor radio, usually adjacent to his ear monitoring the unintelligible gabble that is air traffic control, he appears lost.

"The fun just never stops," he mumbles to no-one.

Auntie Audrey, God bless the old crone, is dressed all in black, which seems appropriate to her under the circumstances.

Sue's dear cousin April with husband Kevin are part of the entourage.

As April possesses a disproportionately large natural bosom, she has always been a favourite of Roger's.

Despite an age difference of some ten years between Sue and April, they behave as though they sisters, lovingly joined at the hip.

Husband Kevin, an ex-merchant naval man, shakes hands solemnly but with a gentleness that is faultless. Well muscled and of middle age he wears a white buttoned shirt, subdued tie and charcoal slacks. An easy twinkle in his eye for the ladies, Kevin is renowned for saying all the right things.

"Would you like a drink, Kevin?" Roger asks, "something a little stronger perhaps than tea?"

"Sure. I'm a drinker of opportunity," Kevin grins, "I get my hands on it, I drink it."

They all adjourn to a café come bar but Sue and Roger are too highly strung to partake of food or drink. Kevin is busy looking about at people. He spies a Jamaican with dreads and a crocheted wool cap. "What d'you reckon of him, Roger?"

Roger is thoughtful. "What, the Jamaican who's wearing a tea cosy on his head?"

Kevin smiles smugly at Roger. "I've been Down Under a few times back in the day on the ships. They've a great sense of humour the Aussies. I'm sure you'll do well there. You do know what they'll call you?"

"I have no idea," Roger smiles invitingly.

Kevin looks mischievous, "If they like you, you'll be a ten pound pommy bastard."

Roger grins. "And if I'm unpopular?"

"Be like pissing on your own fire, Mate. Ten pound *bastard* pommy, but with an unfriendly emphasis on the word *bastard*."

April behaves as if Sue is a comet about to leave its star for a lonely trip through the cosmos. "No sign of Roger's family today, Sue?"

"No. True to his word he's given his Dad and Zelda the Ernest Hemingway treatment as in stoic silence."

As far as Roger is concerned they are unaware of their departure, but irrespectively, Zelda's presence would only have proven antagonistic.

Better they be at each other's throats than lunging at mine, Roger thinks.

"Probably for the best," April sighs brightly. "I wouldn't accept a reverse charges call from that man if he was haemorrhaging to death on the pavement in front of me."

Audrey at 72 does not look a day over 90. She wears a pale blue coat, her hair tinted to match. "And that awful German woman he married. What's her name?" she asks, biting out the words.

"Zelda," Sue replies.

"Yes, she'd even complain Nuns pray too much in a nunnery."

"She and staff go together like frogs and lawnmowers," Roger offers not to be outdone, "I can vouch for that."

"Why did he marry her? I didn't think he liked Germans. He must have killed thousands of them during the war." Audrey states in an icy, condescending tone.

"If you ask me," intones Minnie, "the only good German is a dead German. I've never forgiven them for what they put us through. And what about all those poor Jewish people. It was a disgrace. She should be ashamed to be German."

"I do believe Dad's intentions were good," offers Roger, "as he wanted a Mum for June."

After he speaks, he realises with some surprise that he has actually defended his Dad when really he wanted to reproach the lying bastard for his back wages.

"It could always be worse," Roger offers with a sigh.

"Worse! How?" Minnie asks.

"Well, he could have married a Japanese," Roger suggests with a brief smirk.

Mostly Audrey ignores Roger. "How'd it go with Roger's family?" she asks Sue. "I see that none of them are here."

"Oh, you know. Tears, the usual hysteria."

To Roger at that time his wife's voice is as welcome as a fine summer breeze.

Audrey glares.

"Oh, not me," Sue replies with a forced smile, "that's Roger."

"I'd have liked to have seen June," Roger adds, "but she's only fourteen years old I couldn't see her, without Dad and Zelda."

Audrey turns her attention to Roger. "Just because I look at you when you're talking, Roger, don't think I'm interested in what you have to say."

"Oh, this just keeps getting better and better," mutters Philip under his breath.

A long moment passes.

Sue looks on in embarrassed amazement.

"If Zelda was here might she speak German?" Philip asks Roger with an impish smile.

"Probably, but only complicated German stuff," Roger smiles back. "Like mein linker blinker ist kaputt."

Philip's face is alight with interest. "What's that mean?"

"My left blinker's not working," Roger replies dead pan.

Auntie Audrey is looking at Roger as if he is wearing a live fish on his head.

Well meaning though their intentions doubtless are, our emigrants could have done without any of them. Having to make polite conversation, while trying to overcome their apprehension and concerns about what lay ahead.

Roger draws close to Sue, "I suppose emigrating is a bit like getting married," he whispers to her, "part of us would prefer to slip quietly away."

All around them similar scenes to theirs are playing out. It is as though everyone leaving Heathrow that day is emigrating.

"Had you been departing Ireland rather than England," Minnie's face is full of despair, "a wake may have been more appropriate."

"Thanks for that," Roger replies sensing more hostility. "Maybe this is reminiscent of the siege of Rorke's Drift, Minnie. Just the overwhelming Zulu army didn't have our resolve."

"You're talking in riddles again, Roger," huffs Minnie.

"Where's Rorke's Drift?" asks Philip, "somewhere in Australia?"

"Good question," Kevin answers, "No! It's somewhere in South Africa."

"Nothing at all to do with Australia, then," confirms Minnie.

"Nothing at all," Roger responds sadly.

"So," Minnie swings her attention back to Roger. "I suppose this silly idea of going to Australia was your brainwave?" Minnie's unblinking stare continues accusing him sternly as though he is a certifiable fool.

Roger panics but sees an out. "No! Actually, Min. It was your daughter's idea."

Minnie is thoughtful. "And when did you decide to go along with it, then?"

"Honestly?"

"Yes, of course."

Roger considers the situation carefully and then decides to go for it. Like a hot knife through butter. Take some of the starch out of the old biddy.

"While I was sitting on the toilet taking my morning dump."

Minnie's smile falters and drops in wattage. Recovering well she continues coldly. "What job will you do when you get to *Australia*, Roger?"

Minnie states the word Australia as if it is a malignancy. Such is her attitude, it is nearly enough, to make Roger's ears bleed.

"I haven't got a clue. About my only preference is to steer clear of catering and pubs if I can. If it all works out, we'll be better off than here. Otherwise Sue might end up living in a cave, eating tofu and sucking on tree bark? Interesting thought."

Minnie ignores Roger's response.

Kevin is quick to assist. "Will you get a job in pest control, Roger?" he asks, "they have plenty of bigger pests Down Under."

Visions of Roger being chased by spiders so big he could hear their footsteps, and snakes of obscene proportions, terrifies Sue, "Oh, my God, Roger will we be inundated with flies at every turn, and carried away by the ants?"

"Pests here are surely smaller and less dangerous," Minnie states with some satisfaction.

There is a prolonged uncomfortable silence.

Roger feels about as comfortable as sitting on death row waiting to do the last dance with Mister Hangman.

"Are you looking forward to the flight?" April asks sweetly.

"I'd rather be going by train," Sue replies nostalgically, "that clickety-clack sound can be quite soothing."

"Never mind, dear. I expect you'll be eating the best of foods and off fancy china forever," April continues. "It's such a long way."

Too late it occurs to Sue that as the children will be seated for such a long time they should have organised some strenuous exercise before the flight to tire them.

Realising it is too late to break away from the embarkation committee for a Herculean triathlon. That or instal Minnie with an 'off' button they prepare to depart.

They sit and gather their wits for a few more moments. So far the morning had been one to forget as far as Roger was concerned. Sue is looking drawn.

After they have exchanged a few awkward last hugs, they slink away like bilge rats abandoning a sinking ship. Waving their final goodbyes, they prepare to board their plane.

In accompaniment Roger hums Roger Whittaker's recently released *Last Farewell* but adds his own words; "Our plane lay rigged and ready for departure…far away to a land of endless sunshine…far away from our land full of rainy skies and gales…"

Outside, the air is cold, the fat clouds holding the promise of snow or sleet. Behind them a sea of faces blur as they are herded towards their BOAC Charter flight.

Roger shuffles his feet the last few yards.

Sue giggles "Why are you walking like that?"

"In sympathy with those who've gone before us. I'm wearing ghost shackles."

Chapter 6

EDWARD AND ZELDA

In the seaside municipality of Brighton, famous for among other things its cobble stone beach, Edward is sitting quietly in his drawing room. After being discharged from the RAF in 1946 without a job to go to, an unfair dismissal from a senior management position in the early 1960s seemed to herald his downward path. He is convinced the last few years have been significantly cruel to him and yet he is able to convince himself, without any difficulty whatsoever, how impeccable his planning has been. His misfortunes are obviously at the behest and instigation of others.

Zelda, his second wife, who has only recently returned home from full time office work is sitting exhausted in one of her favourite antique leather armchairs.

"Edvard, vhat vill you do? Ve are short of money," Zelda barks. "I vork but cannot perform miracles."

Zelda is leggy, tall, and elegant with dyed brassy, blonde hair. Edward is thinking her hair today resembles more the colour of dirty egg yolk. Slightly stooped at the shoulders, she is slim almost to the point of being consumptive. Her slightly turned-up, if not judgmental, nose gives her a supercilious air.

Her physical downsides are the lines of a heavy smoker etched around her bright red lipstick thin mouth that makes her look as if she is sucking on a sour lemon.

Dressed impeccably as always, Zelda is wearing a long pleated black skirt and white blouse. Her touched up hair and makeup expertly accomplished.

She is indeed a handsome woman, Edward thinks. After the death of Alice, Zelda was eye candy personified to Edward. A tidy dresser with a 1940s look, accentuated by the way she wears her hair. Her daughter, Charlotte, is one year younger than his own daughter, June.

"True, we are short of money," Edward replies slowly, and then with an edge of sarcasm, "but as we are ensconced in this luxury flat. A flat we can ill afford, what would you have me do, Zelda?"

Zelda glares at Edward. Her eyes catch and hold him, intimidating as hell.

"You done bad, Edvard."

Edward sighs deeply. He realises the failure of his recent hotel ventures hardly herald a success story.

He senses that Zelda is becoming a hovering black eagle observing him as the uneasy mouse.

"You are a valking bill-board of zhe personal problems," Zelda looks hard at Edward.

Here we go, again, thinks Edward.

"You came into mein life at a difficult time for me, Edvard."

"Yes, Sweetheart," Edward sighs deeply, "I know. You've told me many times how hard you tried before your divorce, even allowing your now ex-husband to bring his motorbike into your house."

Edward's sarcasm kicks in as part of his defence mechanism.

"I'm sure your ex's fan base meets with him every afternoon in a telephone booth down the road," Edward continues.

"And den you come along, Edvard, vhen ve met through zhe agency."

"I thought, we agreed, Zelda, not to mention the introduction agency. It sounds so much better if we get used to telling everyone how our doctor introduced us. Especially as we both had the same GP."

"Ja ja, fiddle faddle."

Edward primes his pipe and as he does so, he feels the anger of betrayal rise in him more than usual. "You chose divorce, Zelda. I did not choose my wife to pass away. Alice died in 1965 she was only 38. A sudden, terrible, cancer that took her in a matter of weeks. My situation was entirely different to yours."

"Mein Gott, Edvard. I know Alice vas a good vife und mudder. She was very lucky to have you survive de var as a Lancaster bomber pilot."

Zelda is right. Physically whole, Edward displays none of the horrific war trauma carried as shocking trophies by so many surviving RAF crews, but he still feels down.

The relaxed ambience of their surroundings is doing nothing to make

Edward feel better about his situation right now. The small but elegant crystal chandeliers, floating overhead like candlelit funeral shrouds, are supposed to cast a calming light, but he and Zelda are far from enjoying calm.

Too late, about three years too late, Edward realises he is having doubts about his marriage to Zelda; she is a proven fine actress, he gives her that much, but a very dangerous woman to cross.

According to her ex-husband, whom he has met with on occasions when releasing the girls for visits, she is a beautiful liar who her ex is pleased to be rid of.

In her younger years, might she have been the scourge of many a middle-aged man?

"Uh huh." Edward agrees. "All I want is a little peace and quiet, Zelda." He cast his eyes around their expansive drawing room, taking in the discreet wall lights illuminating the embossed, velour wallpapers in their rich burgundy colours. The expensive fabrics evoke a high style of sophistication while the deep pile carpets swallow their footfalls adding to the exclusive ambience. If he has to be miserable, he would rather be miserable in style.

"Vhat rubbish you talk!"

Edward loses his calm. "For Christ's sake, Zelda, what part of fucking peace and quiet don't you understand?"

Zelda sulks.

Edward cast a further glance towards their rattling front windows. Fierce rain lashes the glass turning any view into a muted shade of grey.

Edward knows Alice loved him despite his attempts to get rich. Schemes that despite his dedication and hard work, never came good. Alice wanted him to work in a steady day job that paid regular money. In hindsight, she was right; Alice was always right. Edward eases away into his memories.

The first thing Zelda noticed about Edward was his blue eyes, which she decided were pleasingly impish. A surviving bomber pilot and recent hotel owner, he was about as full of himself as any man could be.

Edward is aware that to his wife from a council shit tip, she feels that she married up. As his German Boudicea, she would surely enjoy putting a chain around his neck — if only she could. Edward smiles at his thoughts; *Then force feed me Italian spaghetti meat balls to maintain my strength.*

Zelda softens. "Vould you like a cup of tea, Edvard?"

Edward nods. "Yes, thank you, Zelda, Sweetheart."

Zelda moves through their flat to locate Charlotte and stepdaughter June; as she goes she sets her Teutonic antennae onto dust or disturbance alarm.

Good, she thinks.

Now her Obsessive-compulsive disorder has kicked in and is operating at full pelt, all the rug fringes appear to be combed in to place, exactly how she likes each one to be. Fluff on the carpet unsettles her most.

Best I get the girls to re-vacuum the entire carpets, tomorrow! she thinks.

Paramount to Zelda is that Charlotte is alright and coping well with her homework. Not that she has any reason to suspect otherwise.

She finds both girls playing quietly together in their shared bedroom. Running a severe gaze over both, she sees little sign of homework being done, which puts her in a darker mood than usual.

"Vhat is dis? Vhy ist dere kein homevork done?"

The girls express some rebellion. "We'll do it later, before bed," Charlotte giggles.

"Be sure your homevork is done or de TV vill be verboten."

June stares back at the tall, bony woman her Dad chose to take the place of her Mum. If only she had the strength, she would strangle the life out of the cow. Instead, she beams her happiest smile and thinks her Dad is barking mad. Can he not see Zelda is part viper, part fairytale evil?

'A cobra in high heels and lipstick,' is how her brother Roger describes her. 'Not unlike the witch out of *Hansel and Gretel*,' Roger said. June has learned the hard way. Not every secret shared with Charlotte, stays between them.

Zelda stares back at June, her dark eyes holding an indefinable measure of unfriendliness. She rummages for her soft pack of unfiltered Camel cigarettes and after finding her *Ronson* gas lighter, lights up. Her face a picture of displeasure as her exhaled smoke hovers in the air.

June is seriously hoping that Zelda will spontaneously combust.

"Your fadder vants a cup of his hot, sweet tea. You vill make it for him, June, and I vood love anudder coffee, just de vay I like it."

Turning on her high stiletto heels, Zelda struts back to join Edward.

June has been a problem for Zelda since marrying Edward. The little bitch kept calling her 'Thingy' instead of Mum, Mother, or Zelda. She soon put paid to that nonsense by disciplining the wayward child in a number of imaginative ways, ways that appeared harmless if not examined too closely. She could not help but smile at her own creativeness; excluding June from the clothes buying process by getting Charlotte to try everything on worked a treat, as had giving her stepdaughter more chores, such as making her father's tea now.

Oh, how pedestrian is she now? thinks June.

Zelda sinks back into her favourite luxury leather lounge chair. She breathes in the aroma of Edward's pipe tobacco hovering in the air like miniature cumuli and considers other battles she has won; such as establishing herself within the family as 'Nanny' and not being called 'Granny'. She gave an involuntary shudder at the thought, but at least that is behind her now.

"June vants to make your tea, Edvard," Zelda sighs her deepest sigh.

Overheard by June, *Oh, yes,* she thinks, *but no, not quite. How the cow twisted that one! Can Dad not see through all this crap?*

Whilst Edward remains paralysed in his memories, hoping his dreams might become realities, Charlotte joins June in the kitchen. Both girls cannot stop giggling.

"I'll make Dad's tea," June offers, "you make *her* coffee." Then, in a whisper, "What will you put in it that she doesn't like?"

"How's about Strychnine?" Charlotte replies with another giggle.

"No, silly I'm serious. Even if we had any that would show up on a post-mortem. How's about too much milk, or not enough milk?"

"What about lukewarm water instead of re-boiling the kettle? We haven't done that for a while."

"No! She'll catch on when she can't hear it whistling."

"Okay," Charlotte draws the word out, "I'll stir in a very small amount of sugar because we know she doesn't like any at all."

"But only add a small amount so it tastes a bit off but isn't that obvious. And I'll overfill the cup."

Charlotte is no more star struck on her own mum's behaviour than June is.

Together the girls make a good team as they enjoy being with Charlotte's Dad and baiting Zelda.

Zelda being German had not sat right with Edward. After all, he did bomb the crap out of her country and killed thousands of Germans.

In bed after their first night, Edward's husky voice wavered when he confessed, "I dropped my bombs, Zelda, and watched Dresden erupt in flames beneath me; flames a thousand feet high, temperatures of over a thousand degrees, even the air was on fire, the roads melting, rivers and canals boiling. I saw it burning to the ground."

"An entire city, Edvard."

"Not one combatant among them. Women, old men, and children numbered over 100,000 people dead that night."

"Der is no doubt in my mind dat if die Allies had lost the war, Dresden should have been declared a war crime, Edvard."

"You're right. To my mind that deed turned Bomber Command into a byword for slaughter. I felt ashamed, which was why under target in my log book I wrote only three words; *women and children*."

"That vas very clever of you, Edvard."

"Clever?"

"Vell, if de Allies had lost de var dan Germans could have exonerated you."

"I never thought of that. But I did check my RAF logbook before proposing marriage to you, just to ensure I wasn't over Hamburg the night your house was bombed."

Unfortunately for Edward, his parents, Roger's grandparents, were too ensconced, too brainwashed by the British establishment, to accept Zelda. His own mother had said, "Bloody shame you didn't bomb the house with the German cow still in it."

Family wise that was the beginning of their big family split. He could see that now, but even so, then as now, he felt helpless to do anything about it.

After his hotel business venture failed, with son in tow, he secured a lease on another hotel, and in Zelda's name. Creative accounting at a high cost helped him with that, but now he and Zelda, married by convenience, are as united as any two people could be. Together there is some financial future. Apart? Well, that is an entirely different story.

Edward likes long walks and good books, Zelda prefers to party. Where Edward is introspective and brooding by nature, Zelda tends to move at lightning speed and let the chess pieces fall where they may.

Zelda's daughter Charlotte is proving easier to get on with than his own flesh and blood.

Edward relights his pipe. Zelda's smoke joins his. Both seemingly hang from a single cloud of cigarette smoke. He continues puffing rhythmically.

"Your pipe reeks of burning leaves and vet dog, Edvard."

Don't sugar coat it, Zelda. Give it to him straight! thinks June.

Edward refuses to rise to the bait, instead he ponders as he puffs.

"Roger mustered well after the death of his Mum, I'll give him that much," Edward tells Zelda, "he did everything I required of him."

"Ja ja, fiddle faddle," Zelda exclaims. She blames Roger and his wife Sue for the failure of The Harewood Hotel. If they had been decent and appreciated all she had done for them, she and Edward would not be where they are now.

"Give him his dues, Zelda, it was remarkable he found a hotel I could buy without any money. That in itself was a master stroke."

"Vee all vorked, Edvard."

It is well known to the whole family that Zelda did nothing. She mostly upset staff with her Teutonic attitude and avoided front of house contact with customers by hiding in the office with Edward.

"Nevertheless, Zelda, I do feel that after I went bankrupt, Roger and my own parents should have been a lot more understanding of my plight."

"Roger vas a director mit you, Edvard; he should not have got off scot free. It vas you who vent bankrupt, Edvard. Roger hasn't suffered as you 'ave."

Edward nods slowly.

Zelda continues. "Den dere is Roger's wife, Sue, mit deir two offspring from that union — Jayne and James."

"I don't fancy much being a grandfather," Edward glares at Zelda, "not any more than you wanted to be a Granny."

"Edvard," Zelda's firm voice has all the warning signs.

"Sorry, Sweetheart, I meant Nanny," Edward smiles inwardly at his dig.

Zelda works normal shop hours at a local office while Edward manages a small chain of sex shops requiring his presence at odd hours. Edward detests his job and all the people associated with it.

Edward cannot help but think about the highlight of this week's news.

"Word is Roger, Sue and their two children are migrating to Australia as participants in a ten pound assisted passage scheme."

"I feel no anguish at their departure from the UK, Zelda. Those in charge here are only sponging toadies ready to receive any favour and give nothing in return."

"Ve are to be left behind mit a rising pile of debts," Zelda adds crushing out her cigarette and lighting another.

Zelda needs to relax. Talking about Roger and Sue has left a foul taste in her mouth.

She runs her bath and lays in it with one leg hooked over the other. She knows that they are good legs. The hot water takes the chill off her bones. With trembling hands, she reaches out to light a cigarette, and smokes it with her nerves all a-jangle.

The bathroom is dark; she likes it that way. Edward will stay away from her. She has a lot of thinking to do. Their finances are in poor shape. Edward is not a stayer in any job, probably never has been, even when Alice was alive. Zelda enjoyed her relatively high life at both hotels, but that was too short-lived. Now a new variable into the mix. This recent news of Roger, his wife Sue, and their two rug rats going down under to Australia. *Good riddance*, she thinks. Her face turns into what is loosely considered a smile as the bathwater finally works its magic.

Her thoughts are interrupted when Edward appears in the doorway dressed in a smart yachting jacket, white turtleneck and beige slacks. He steps over the threshold hesitantly, like a well-trained dog that knows better.

"Zelda, I'll have to leave for work soon, Sweetheart."

She ignores him.

"Zelda, Sweetheart."

When she speaks, her strident tone is not one of warmth and sweetness. "Vhat do you van't, Edvard?"

He smiles thinly, "Would you like to cook, or should I get some fish and chips, take-away?"

"Cook! Mein Gott. I've not long finished vork Edvard and you vant me to, to, to prepare a meal?" Zelda waves her hands in the air, exasperated, her point clear.

Edward swallows nervously. "I'll send out then." He is complicit. His head cast down as he leaves her quietly alone, content to wage an inner debate with himself.

He smiles sideways at June and Charlotte and June catches herself smiling back.

If only they could have their life back but without Zelda. June thinks that often.

How much she misses her Mum, and why, oh why did she have to leave her. She misses her more each day becoming an icy heaviness in her heart threatening to topple her over.

If June was subjected to a natural disaster, it could not have come in a worse form than Zelda. A death in the family that broke their biological bond was tragic. She now feels as if flung aside like a piece of seaweed.

Zelda clears her bath, takes a large fluffy wrap around towel, and dresses.

The rain has eased and night is upon them. Edward returns from work with dinner. Back in the drawing room, she can see both her reflection and Edward's in the window glass. He never takes his eyes off her but she doubts his interest is romantic. No. His interest, she knows, is the now fast failing light and not wanting to be alone.

Later that evening Edward struggles to fall asleep. Outside has returned to being wet and windy. *What use are expansive sea views if you can rarely see the sea?* he thinks.

His mind continually needs to unfold the day's events and his dreams often return to the 1940s when he struggles to survive his bombing missions. Often he relives his Lancaster holed by flak and he is without controls. His flaps and hydraulics shot away, oxygen tanks exploding, flames spreading throughout his plane. As the plane begins its rapid decent, he leaves what controls he has to his co-pilot, unhooks himself from his seat and squeezes through the hatch into the belly of the flaming beast. There he goes looking for his crew crawling on bended knees but he cannot find them. In his dream he watches through a gaping hole in the fuselage another Lancaster go down. He feels another shockwave from a direct hit; beneath him a larger hole appears from a ground to air canon. The air rushes past him then turns and sucks him from his platform. He falls from the plane into the abyss. Edward awakes in a cold sweat.

Fuck!

He lays afraid to sleep should his demons revisit him. He feels as if he has been connected to an improperly calibrated drip of adrenalin as seemingly every ounce of belly bile begins to incinerate his throat. He draws long, grateful breaths.

As 57,000 RAF aircrew perished, Edward's concerns were indeed very real. He knows how fortunate he was to survive that madness.

As he lays in the darkness next to Zelda, Edward struggles to collect his thoughts and return to being hopeful about his future. He speaks to Zelda essentially to see if she is awake.

Zelda's sleep was thin.

"I've just had another awful dream. My Lancaster crashed, again."

Zelda raises herself up on one elbow, moves closer, and takes Edward's hand in her own.

"Ve all get de bad dreams, Edvard. I lost family and friends in dose raids. Mein Gott, Edvard, your bad dreams, don't you tink I have zese nightmares. I vas a young girl in var torn Germany. De constant bombing, de hunger it vas no picnic. At least you ver a young man, I vas a young girl. Dere is a big difference. A girl must do many tings to survive und eat in vartime."

Zelda has not told Edward about her pregnancy to her tall, squinty-eyed Sergeant in the SS. She had become well practiced at pleasuring a man by her mid teens.

"I know," Edward squeezes Zelda's hand in friendship. "I too lost people in the war Zelda but I've never quite mastered being alone at twilight."

"I know Edvard. Shush now. I do know."

Zelda moves away and lays quiet in deep thought. If she does not want sex, she knows now is the best time to fein sleep. In that all men are the same, she knows that.

As Edward drifts off to sleep, he wonders if the English novelist Aldous Huxley was correct when he philosophised, 'Maybe this world is another planet's Hell?'

Chapter 7

THE JOURNEY

Saturday, 13th March, 1971.

Cleared for take-off marks the no-turning-back-now portion of the journey, like breaking a bottle of champagne on a ship's bow.

Sue, Roger, Jayne, and James are sitting across one row near a wing. Sue and James on one side of the plane, while Jayne very senior at nearly four years of age and Roger are across the aisle. Jayne and James both scored the window seats to amuse them.

Sue fusses with James to calm her frazzled nerves, while Roger's bony structure jams back hard against the seat, he is trying to fold himself up, but that presents its own problem as he is not bendable enough.

Jayne is outgoing, social, talkative, and eager to please in her own way, while James is the opposite, living in his own head, lost in his own world as most babies are.

The Captain announces flight time to Beirut as four hours and thirty minutes.

"Oh, Roger. I didn't leave the bath running at home did I?" Sue asks in panic.

"No, Dear. I checked and anyway, if in doubt, I turned off the water."

"Was the back door locked?"

Roger clenches his teeth and forces a smile. "Yes, Sweetheart," he leans across the aisle and holds Sue's hand "everything's taken care of, please try to relax my Love."

Sue smiles back, her normal wonderful warm smile, "thank you."

An air hostess walks down the aisle handing out cardboard menus.

"Their menu does look excellent," Sue gushes, her face flushing with excitement.

Roger opens his menu, and lets Jayne hold hers.

It reads in part:

London	—	Dinner	4h30
Beirut	—	Refreshments	4h55
	—	Breakfast	
Delhi	—	Refreshments	
	—	Lunch	5h15
Singapore-	—	Dinner	4h30
Darwin	—	Breakfast	4h05
Sydney	—		

Their first dinner is: Truffled pate Waldorf
                                 Escalopine of Veal Marsala
                                 Sugared garden peas with glazed new carrots,
                                 Buttered noodles
And for dessert: Fruit flan or Mousse
                                 Cheese   Cream crackers
                                 Coffee   Caffeine free coffee
Bar Service: Champagne 1/4 bottles

The latter catches Roger's eye and had he not given up smoking, the packets of 20s both English and American, plain or filter tip, are on offer…welcome aboard.

"Their posh nosh menu along with their blurb looks excellent," Roger chirps to Sue.

As they taxi out towards the end of the runway, the air hostesses take them through the safety lecture. At the part where in the unlikely event of a crash, it is important to assume the position with your head between your knees there is some good natured banter emanating from the row behind.

A man destined to become their flight wag chortles in a cockney accent, "Is that so I can kiss my bum goodbye, Love?"

"They sound like Fred and Wilma Flintstone on a second pipe of opium, Sue."

With engines roaring at full thrust and hands waving frantically at every porthole window for no-one else to see, their BOAC Charter flight bumps its way speedily through take off.

As the plane lifts off and continues to gain height, Roger reaches across the void between them and holds Sue's hand. She responds by gripping him so tight it hurts, but he is reluctant to pull back.

Grey roofs diminish in size before they climb through bouncy dark clouds.

Although in an aisle seat, as the plane tilts, Roger can see down. He briefly glimpses the River Thames through broken clouds. Its pewter surface glitters like polished lead. For a fleeting moment, Tower Bridge comes into view but he loses sight of them as the plane straightens up.

Roger's mind becomes a Ferris wheel of recall. They are leaving behind the only lives they have ever known and a welfare state that has promised to look after them from cradle to grave.

Suddenly, the enormity of what they have taken on and his responsibilities to his small family strike him like a sledgehammer. He begins feeling nauseas.

Sue notices his changing demeanour, "Are you alright?"

"Yes, fine," he huffs, and then attempting to make light of the moment, "but I already miss the English beer, oh, and not forgetting the weather. I miss it like a yeast infection."

Sue craves a cup of addicting coffee, savoury smelling and loving coffee. It seems to quiet her brain; her body is starting to go down on her after the stress of their morning and airport farewells.

A pretty, young air hostess, with legs up to her eyebrows and in a uniform that manages to enhance a body that does not need much enhancing, politely asks if she can get by. It is only then they realise that they are still holding hands across the aisle. As the air hostess moves up the aisle Roger cannot help but think she is someone most men would like to forge a relationship with, no matter how brief.

"Let's celebrate," Roger suggests, "a small bottle of champagne if nothing else, it might help take the edge off our nerves."

A commotion in the row behind them signals that flight wag is experiencing some difficulty opening his champagne.

"He's wanting pre-mature cork-u-lation," Roger sniggers to Sue.

Sue gives him a withering look.

"I'm wrestling with a conundrum."

"What?"

"Should I appear a connoisseur by taking small sips, or go straight to piss-pot and order another bottle. I'm undecided."

Sue wrinkles her nose. "If you want to but I don't want anymore."

Food is about to be served.

"It does comprise rather small portions on large trays, doesn't it?"

"Had it been on large plates there'd be a rather big gap around it, wouldn't there?" Roger replies.

When he ventures to the toilet, he sees a teenager troughing down his meal and his sister's as well, while using the armrest as a serviette. He tries not to show his displeasure at the younger man's poor manners. They would all be taking up Colonial appointments at some juncture. Who is he to judge others?

On his return Roger enquires of their hostess, who turns out not to be the pretty young one but a menacing crone of middle years, her complexion as wan as a cadaver. Her stern expression is made all the worse thanks to the severity of her hairstyle — scraped back and knotted in the tightest of buns on the back of her head.

"I was wondering if we could get some baby food for our son James?"

"There's no baby food on this flight, sir," the sour one states in a voice that would serve Boudicea well, while turning the full glare of her lip gloss onto Roger.

Sue and Roger sit stunned. Then they look at each other in utter disbelief.

Bloody hell!

"Are you sure?" Roger presses. He's perplexed. "We were told by the staff at Australia House to the contrary. 'Bring nothing and carry as little as possible as baby food and nappies are supplied on the flight,' they said."

Scary lady shakes her head with a stern expression of contempt. Roger feels as if he is something distasteful stuck to the bottom of her shoe.

"And before you ask," she takes on a calculating look at James, "if you are expecting nappies as well, good heavens no."

The committee inside Roger's head is about to call an emergency meeting.

He turns to Sue, his actions are expressing frowning with confusion.

"At this stage, we're not looking too flash. I'd try asking the prettier one but not while dragon lady has her guardian eye on us."

"Dragon lady continues to exude an appalling lack of charm," Sue whispers.

"Her attitude suggests she's in urgent need of a refresher course in customer relations," Roger whispers back to Sue, "that or maybe she's Swedish?"

"Why Swedish?"

"Some say Swedish women are bizarre."

"That's of little help to us. Oh, Roger, what do we do? This is horrific. Fretsaw was so sure. Why did we listen to him? I've come so totally unprepared."

Roger moves quickly into panic mode and starts making uncomfortable u turns in his seat.

In an effort to take charge of the deteriorating situation he tries to reason with dragon lady, "Surely, on the basis that BOAC had prior knowledge of the passengers they're carrying, James should be catered for."

The Crone leans in with that veiled look of disrespect usually practiced by those who prefer performing below par in their jobs. "Since the boy represents a full fare and is occupying his own seat, it's expected by BOAC he dine on what's being provided." Scary lady then flounces off.

Roger rests his forehead on the rear of the seat in front of him. Anger is winding him up like a watch spring tightening around his head. With no-where else to take their concerns he forces himself to calm.

"I suspect that with the no nappies and baby food we're the victims of nothing less than the fluid rules of commerce," he half growls. "Although admittedly it was a ten pound special."

Sue becomes understandably, very, very, distraught.

"A flight of this duration with no assistance for a twelve month old baby is horrific, Roger."

"It's a cock up of mammoth proportions, but we'll have to cope. What worries me is," Roger takes a deep breath and lowers his voice, "if Fretsaw's wrong about this, what else might we find wrong with our one way trip to disaster?"

The pretty young hostess has overheard the conversation, she approaches and kneels down between Roger and Sue. She suggests in hushed tones an alternative to the handbags at dawn scenario. Her body language is almost placatory. Her perfume scents the air.

"We'll be in transit at Beirut Airport and you might be able to purchase something there," she offers keeping her voice low. No more details are forthcoming for the untutored.

"Oh, Roger. Can we do that?"

"A lifeline for sure. Thank you for the suggestion," Roger sinks back in to his seat. "Rock on Beirut."

Flight wag, whose arms are emblazoned with more tattoos than a merchant seaman, is sounding off like a pneumatic drill, "This food is shockingly bad even for an aeroplane. This escalope of veal looks like a silicone implant."

As if by response, Roger sprays a mouthful of champagne out of his nose. Stinging his schnozzle into that brain freeze feeling. Jayne bursts into laughter at Roger.

Sue is not calming. Jayne appears to be impressed, whilst James could not care less. More balls than talent, he has been playing with an empty envelope for over half-an hour.

Mrs Wag mutters, "Eat it and shut up." Then, more kindly, "You know if you do, you'll never need to prove your *courage* in any other way."

Amid titters from Wag's group, Sue tries to mash little pieces of their pretentious wannabe veg up for James with plastic cutlery, which keeps giving in to the task. In the end, she gives up and partially chews some for him.

Roger is working up a storm in a teacup.

"We shouldn't annoy the flight attendants," Sue cautions. "I'm sure they can make or break our flying experience. This could end badly."

"Don't be such a pessimist, you mean we shouldn't ask for anything silly like food or water!"

Carry-on bags, big enough to conceal dismembered bodies, are being visited and revisited for rummages around them about every ten minutes, but James is the only one year old they can see on board.

Everyone is beginning to settle when the plane hits a particularly stubborn air pocket.

"The sooner our bus driver gets off the gravel and back on the tarmac, the better," Mr Wag announces.

"He has a true ability for stating the obvious," Roger confides to Sue.

Caught in a layer of turbulence they lurch from one rung of cloud to the next, rocking in between like a deranged drunken person.

As the turbulence worsens, children begin crying. When the plane drops, their stomachs go into orbit. Adults groan while children scream. Screams end in louder sobbing.

As she sucks in air, Sue assesses her abysmal options that she has no control. She closes her eyes and realises this beats the hell out of the worst nightmares she had as a child.

Their plane is jouncing around like a rag doll in the jaws of some savage celestial animal.

"It's as if Thor and Zeus are hurling great thunderbolts from the heavens," Roger tries alleviating their situation through clenched teeth.

"It's enough to strike fear into the hearts of the bravest men, Love," chortles Mr Wag, desperately hanging onto his seat, "brave sober men that is."

Roger is beginning to wish he had ordered another bottle of Dutch courage. By the Wag's comments, he is not alone.

Mrs Wag is most sympathetic. "No doubt the pilot's got his hands full."

"He's under the pump for sure, Love," agrees Mr Wag.

"All of the air hostesses have scattered like cockroaches when the lights come on," observes Mrs Wag.

Even the crone has disappeared, thinks Roger, *and their piped music is now the loudest since our departure.*

The *'Fasten seat belts'* and *'No Smoking'* signs are flashing in syncopated panic modes.

"Bloody no smoking," cries out Mr Wag. "Are you kidding me? How anyone could light a cigarette without burning their nose off's a damned mystery."

It is at moments like these that send people drifting off into their own little worlds. Sue and Roger are no exceptions. While Sue fears with intensity for the welfare of her babies Roger imagines Mr Wag trying to light a cigarette.

The comedy of it brings him momentary relief. He almost laughs out loud as he imagines the Wag twisting and squirming in his seat, as he tries to direct the flame from his gas lighter to the end of his cigarette. It is as though he is trying to perform the feat while drunk. He flinches and dodges like a boxer as the flame first misses his nose, catches his eyebrow, and then singes his cheek. He finally gives up, exasperated as the lighter becomes too hot for him to hold, and then he burns his thumb.

"Are you alright?" Sue grimaces.

That moment when arriving back, from your own private world of chuckling at your own idiotic imagery, can prove most embarrassing.

"I'm just considering our options, Sweetheart."

Sue looks earnest, "And?"

"Well, we don't have any." He shrugs, unnecessarily.

Sue continues to stare at Roger in a most disapproving fashion. "You look demented, sitting there, chuckling to yourself, while everyone else is frozen in a state of panic."

"I'm just hoping we're not on *Candid Camera*."

The fuselage has come alive with inanimate objects! Any food remaining on seat trays, together with hermetically sealed plastic anythings, are airborne, scattering around the cabin. Roger lifts his foot, so as not to impede the progress of a number of plastic cups heading towards the rear of the plane as it now gains altitude. Then wonders if he might encounter the same items on a revisit, as they plunge back the other way? It is like being on a massive big dipper but the cries around them are not of fun and excitement.

Wag announces very loudly, "I'd like four treble whiskies on my bill, please. I'll pay after we arrive."

Drinks are not forthcoming. More plastic cups and a child's toy roll across the aisle. Slowly like the drum of an overloaded washing machine.

"Now we're banking more to the left than Fidel Castro." Adds the wannabe drunk Wag.

From the look on Sue's face, she is sure they are all about to die. Eyes shut so tight Roger cannot see her eyelashes; her skin is almost transparent from lack of blood and her head and body are pushing so far back into her seat Roger cannot see where one ends and the other begins. Her hands are clutching the armrests so tightly he wonders if she might leave nail marks in the metal. Thoughts of James sound asleep are furthest from her mind.

"Jesus Christ!" exclaims Mr Wag, "in one second, life can change from super good to tits up, can't it?"

It is about then that the undeniable sound of people dry retching and heaving can be heard. Then comes the unmistakeable acrid aroma. Roger's nerves are close to running away from him. The butterflies swarming in his stomach are fighting the involuntary urge to join in.

He thinks of Groucho Marx, *"I intend to live forever, or die trying."*

As quickly as the turbulence started it stops, although it seems a lifetime in between.

"Thank Christ, we're off that gravel track and back on the tarmac," chirps Mr Wag. "Now what do I do with these full sick bags, Miss?"

The pretty, young hostess with the open-necked blouse and her neat, bottle blonde bob framing cheekbones sharp enough to cause an injury, assists with the bags, shooting Sue a look of sympathy.

"Are we there yet, Mummy," Jayne asks.

"No, not yet, Sweetheart. It's a long way to go yet."

"How are you, Sue? My bowels are in uproar, thighs so tight I could crack walnuts with them."

The veins on the side of Roger's head are threatening to erupt like Mount Etna.

Sue is grinding her teeth.

Roger is humbled by the reality of their mortality, while Sue is grateful to have survived.

"Oh, Roger. Is it over? Are we safe yet?"

Absentmindedly Roger begins reading the instructions on a vomit bag.

"I'd rather be reading the meditations of Marcus Aurelius," he mutters.

"Marcus Aurelius? Who was he?" Sue asks.

"A Roman emperor and a great philosopher."

"Oh, that's good then. What would he know about aeroplanes?"

A girl aged about five is returning to her seat. As the plane levels out, she is caught mid stride and falters beside them. Clearly in the process of commencing a great technicolour yawn, her head pitches slightly back, her hazel eyes distant. She wants her mum.

Roger's arse clenches like a boxer's fist just as Sue, with the speed and reaction of an Olympic gold-medalist sprinter, reaches out her free left arm and applies gentle pressure to the child's back simply preventing her from back pedalling, which also has the unintended effect of propelling her gently forward. This brilliantly contrived action takes the child and her puke two rows further forward.

"More strength to your arm," Roger jokes, swallowing hard against the acid that is creeping up the back of his throat.

"She needs her parents, not us," Sue opines with some guilt. "No child likes throwing up, they all panic."

Fresh vomitus matter adorns carpets and seats. Ugly haemorrhage slicks, which together with their noxious odour, will remain for some time. The thought causes sweat to suffuse Roger's skin in a sudden wave of additional nausea. He worries that he might join the chain reaction and add to the potpourri.

As far as the cabin crew are concerned, it is as though nothing untoward has happened, other than to slow down their food trolleys.

Sue takes Jayne to the toilet while Roger calms down to a mild panic.

"What goes on in that plane toilet," Sue says quietly, after she returns with Jayne, "is seriously disturbing. It's showcasing the sort of poor aim and behaviour that would never be excused at home."

"Miss," Mr Wag calls out to a hostess, "I say, Miss, there's smoke pouring out of a motor."

"Is there a problem?" Calls out a worried Mrs Wag.

Rubbernecks crane and bob to see, while the nearest hostess shows little interest. When she does eventually look and actually sees the smoke her muscles as taut as ropes she displays speedy progress to the flight deck.

Sue and Roger exchange 'what now' looks. If ever hope and fear can be displayed on two faces as one, it is there in spades.

Roger becomes mesmerised by the strange look of smoke outside of their flying machine. It appears in little wisps. Almost like dark cloud but the unmistakeable look of, well, smoke.

Sue becomes more anxious. Her jaw is tight enough to crack her teeth.

"Jesus! Tits on a turtle, would you look at that," calls out Mr Wag, "fire at 30,000 feet and me already with a serious bowel related problem and not sitting in an aisle seat."

"Will the wing fall awf?" asks Mrs Wag breathlessly.

The smoke appears to be increasing in quantity. An announcement blares over the loudspeaker by the Captain, "We are experiencing a minor mechanical fault."

"Yes!" shouts Mr Wag, "you've got that right old chap. But maybe if you were back here and could see what we're seeing, you'd not think it so bloody minor."

"Don't panic," yells Mrs Wag, "if you do, you'll lose all sense of reason."

"Yes, we know," Roger agrees loudly, "I'm doing it all the time."

After absolute silence, the sound of acquiescence pervades. All around the murmuring of discontent mingling with fear grows louder.

Someone else calls out, "Can they please define minor?"

The flat well cultured English voice of the Captain continues, "I am about to make an unscheduled landing, at Nicosia in Cyprus. Do not be alarmed."

Mr Wag perversely claims, "Thank Christ he didn't say an unintentional flight to the ground. That's BOAC speak for crash you know!"

The Captain advises, "To accelerate our descent I'm lowering my undercarriage." Then almost as an afterthought, "Do not be alarmed by the loud rumbling noise it will make."

They hear the hydraulic groan of the landing gear locking into place.

"Cabin Crew please take to your seats immediately. We may pass through some turbulence on the descent."

"Oh, Christ," cries Mrs Wag, "what's happening to us now? I didn't sign on for this! Am I hallucinating?"

They are dropping like a canary in a coal mine.

Anything unanchored hits the ceiling. The stench of stomach acids and decaying food tinging heavily with bile no longer matter. It all becomes a Jackson Pollock painting on the ceiling. Roger feels as though his heart is twisting in his chest.

Flames from the motor are now lighting up the cabin interior. It is a sort of eerie orange glow that accentuates their white as chalk faces.

During the decent Roger no longer cares what is happening around him; he finds himself gaping as if a fish gasping for water.

He cannot move a muscle to see how Sue is doing. He hopes to Christ James is still strapped in his chair, concluding as much as he is not yet visible on the ceiling. Roger has no clue whether James is awake and crying.

Everyone is shrieking, voices indistinguishable of adults and children. All hell has broken loose. A long, low howl escapes Roger's lips, terror intermingles in one hard, hot knot in his stomach.

Roger tries drawing his knees up under his chin, which is not easy. There is that awful feeling of his stomach trying to leave his body through his bottom, while his brain is trying to exit through his ears.

Sue sits frozen in fear, her feet firmly wedged under the chair in front of her. It takes every faculty of her control not to cry out. The pressure on her intestines feels like something is trying to extract the last bit of toothpaste from the tube.

Around them prayers are being mouthed to Deities. Fingers are wrapped around Rosary beads.

In between the serious stuff, barf bags are reached for. Jayne is laughing. She is watching her feet moving up and down without her doing it for them.

Roger envies that innocent bliss and is now grateful he never ordered the second bottle of wine.

Vomit slicks now have plenty of company. It is as if they have played the whale everywhere! Roger wishes he had never had anything. No champagne, not a scrap of food. He is desperately trying not to chunder.

Now their drop is shearer than Marilyn Monroe's stockings.

Adrenalin burns through Roger's bloodstream like flame on a short fuse, but there is nothing he can do. Fight or flight has nowhere to go!

There are gaps of quiet in-between screaming children and yelling parents. Jayne is now distressed with all the noise, something is wrong but she does not understand what exactly.

They hit the tarmac with all multiple reinforced wheels facing down, and after three hard bounces, the thrust reversers engaged. The most incredible feat of high speed landing imaginable. Top marks to the Captain. He has literally dropped his big bird out of the sky. All souls accounted for.

"Obviously their minor engine fault was a tad more than that," Mr Wag says crisp and distant as they taxied to a stop.

A welcoming committee of airport emergency vehicles greets them like a pack of over excited dogs.

The muted sounds of screeching police cars, the yelp of ambulances, and the bass bark of fire trucks blend into a howl sounding more of sorrow than help. The whole place is illuminated with flashing amber, yellow, and blue lights.

For all their flickering and noisy commotion, they sit there unneeded.

"Welcome to Nicosia! The tits are well and truly off the turtle! Thank you Lord we owe you one!" sighs Mr Wag.

Everyone claps and cheers.

If Roger could have managed the co-ordination he would have given the pilot a standing ovation.

To lighten the mood, Roger tries, "I'm as hard as nails you can tell just by looking at me."

"I'm struggling to reduce my heartbeat to safe levels," Sue replies. "Thank goodness the children are too young to understand. Would you believe Jayne wants to do it, again? Our child is insane!"

"Good, she's barking mad because it stopped her from joining the throw-up club."

An announcement: "As this is an unscheduled emergency landing no-one is permitted to leave the aircraft."

Groans, gasps, and complaints begin to filter through the cabin.

The entire plane is audible in their amazement at being confined in the tin can of vomit and stench. A few passengers have lost bowel control, and the toilets have done a reversal. Not good.

A large canvas style tent is put over the offending engine and part of the wing. Not so much as to prevent passengers from seeing what was happening but protecting the mechanics outside. It is now a driving blizzard of snow.

The Cabin Crew open the front and rear doors, and turn off all lighting and air-conditioning. They all sit quietly in the gloom. An Arctic breeze swirls down the tin corridor, thankfully alleviating some stench.

"How incredibly smooth and quiet it is," Mrs Wag marvels, "when we're at a reckless zero mile per hour and zero degrees."

"Why can't flying be like this?" Mr Wag says wistfully.

They are told repeatedly by their Cabin Crew that they are unable to leave the aircraft through any open door and not to use the toilets as the aircraft is in shut down mode.

"I 'ave to spend-a-penny," says Mrs Wag.

"Go for your life, don't fall in," adds Mr Wag.

Without enough blankets to go around they wish they had worn their thermals. James and Jayne are double wrapped while their parents go without. All they can do is encourage their children to sleep.

"Pity the poor people sitting near the open doors," says Sue looking sympathetic, "look snowflakes are blowing into the plane. It's like sitting in a chest freezer with wings."

"We're in Cyprus," declares Mrs Wag, "Let me out. I want to eat octopus and play *Scrabble*."

She receives worse looks from the Crone than were thrown at Roger.

Eventually, as a peace offering of some modest significance, an orange for each passenger is sagaciously distributed by the cabin staff throughout the streamlined metallic body.

"Only one each," announces the crone, "no cheating and no seconds. As this is your only sustenance for some hours on the ground with not even water being made available."

Passengers welcome their oranges like alley cats circling around fish bones.

"No water!" complains Mr Wag, "nothing for hours! If I'd have known it would be like this I would have gone by sea."

"You're not *Robinson Crusoe* thinking that," Roger replies, loudly. "We wanted to go by train."

A few bitter and tired passengers snort small laughs.

Sue touches his arm keeping him focused. She ventures a thought. "I doubt the benefit of giving citrus to children who have just recently parted with the entire contents of their stomachs but at least sucking on an orange helps pass the time."

Given the seriousness of their situation, Roger remains quiet; his daily hygiene ritual such as cleaning his teeth, has gone to pot, and now to top it off he is forcibly incarcerated in a foul smelling aeroplane.

In a whirlwind of skirts and buckets, a squad of cleaners, speaking little or no English come aboard. They huff and puff and help greatly improving the sanitation of conditions.

Roger finds himself avoiding their gaze, embarrassed as he is about the condition of their plane. He wants to assure them. "No, that vomit there, no! That's not ours. That belonged to that young fellow. The greedy little pig that ate not just his own fruit flan dessert but his Mum and Dad's as well."

"Probably the fruit flan was a better choice," echoed Mrs Wag, "that mousse was like a solid block of ice."

They sit interminably bored while trying to make the sort of polite conversation that everyone else listens to, but pretends they are not. It drags on for about five long stressful hours. Those who have to go to the toilet, go, but the toilets are disgusting.

Eventually their plane is repaired.

As the engines spool up, a great cheer goes up to the news that they are to take off again.

"At last," says Mr Wag, "fuckin' A." Most passengers laugh along in agreement.

Sue and Roger twist and turn in their confined spaces trying to achieve a modicum of comfort.

The flight from their unscheduled stop at Nicosia to Delhi in India is a longer haul than planned with only light refreshments served. Roger contemplates ordering up as much alcohol as possible to survive but Sue is against it.

"If you must," she warns.

The sunset of a lifetime shines through the windows. Gold above the clouds turns them to crimson in unbelievable patterns.

Unfortunately, due to the emergency landing at Nicosia they have been denied the opportunity to shop for baby food and nappies in Beirut.

The next stage of their flight passes without incident and mostly in comfortable silence, as all passengers are probably going over the horror of their previous ordeal in their own minds before moving on from it.

As the aircraft slowly shed altitude into Delhi, everyone tries to find where their seatbelt buckles are hiding.

On the ground, they stand up from their seats for the first time in too many hours.

"Might we be able to buy nappies and baby food here?" Sue asks hopefully.

"Don't see why not," Roger replies.

They are told by their Captain, "Delhi being a troubled place politically our scheduled landing is only for the purpose of refuelling. Passengers will not be disembarking. There's no guarantee if you get off the plane that you'll be allowed to re-board."

Roger looks at Sue. Sue looks at Roger.

As the Cabin Crew never open any doors, it is unlikely anyone would have been able to put that challenge to the test.

"Doubtless Bombay would have been as bad," chirps Mr Wag. "What a god forsaken fuckin' 'ole this is."

"Shush, watch your language," cautions Mrs Wag, "and think yourself lucky. Every restaurant here would serve curry, and you don't like spicy food."

Another passenger offers, "At least we got here, and in one piece."

Passengers crowd together at the windows looking out. They see unfriendly looking soldiers standing in a raggedy line around their plane. Rifles in one hand and lit cigarettes in the other. None of the passengers have a clue why armed soldiers are surrounding their plane.

The soldiers do not understand either.

Outside there are more young men with guns than Roger has ever seen outside a Bollywood film. With all guns there is a right end and a wrong end. Anyone at the wrong end is in danger of things going badly. Roger is all too aware that if a gun goes off it makes not only a loud noise but also a big hole.

None of the armed soldiers outside is returning the passengers' enthusiastic waves and smiles.

This could go badly, reasons Sue.

"Most of the soldiers look not much older than children," observes Mrs Wag, "but get a look will yer, they're all carrying guns nearly as big as themselves."

"Bloody hell. Watch where you're pointing that gun, mate," panics Mr Wag, "you could shoot yourself in the foot."

"Not the smartest thing to do while refuelling the plane," Mrs Wag panics now. "They keep this up I'll get the runs for sure. I can feel them coming on. Get a look will yer, at the ones looking forward to their fourteenth birthdays?"

Another passenger calls out in panic, "Please put out your cigarettes."

Worry and confusion playing all over their faces is rampant throughout their plane.

Roger feels queasy. They have survived to date only to die a miserable death incinerated in a plane in a foreign land, because some ignoramus who does not speak English, wants to light his cigarette.

"Roger, are you alright?"

"Yes."

Roger is far from alright. He is making whimpering sounds and can feel his dignity slipping away. He feels as if he has aged ten years during the re-fuelling. He has just added getting to their destination to his bucket list.

They take off again.

Heaven knows how old he may feel by the time they actually get to where they are supposed to be going.

Where is that? Oh, right, B-R-I-S-B-A-N-E.

They had been told they would be landing at Darwin via Singapore, which meant less than nothing, but now another change of plan. For whatever reason, they are now re-routed direct to Perth for the purpose of Immigration.

"Better facilities in Perth," they are told by the Crone.

From Delhi in India to Perth in Australia seems a very long way indeed.

"Where is Perth?" asks Mrs Wag.

"Somewhere in Oz," Mr Wag replies.

"Yes, okay, but where is Oz?"

"I think after you leave Singapore, you turn right, or something. I'll really have to talk to my travel agent, Love. This journey is getting worse all the time," says Mr Wag.

The original menu has been discarded since the plane is out of food and can only take on snacks, refreshments, and limited breakfasts.

"Service has flaked away like an old croissant," Roger moans.

"At least we're alive," Sue counters.

They try eating some food. Roger attempts to open a small

hermetically sealed packet that even King Kong would have had trouble with. He ends up spilling the contents all over himself.

"Better than vomit I suppose, but it probably doesn't matter anymore, there's so much crap everywhere, anyway," he bleats to Sue. "I don't know what's worse, the appearance of the ever present carrot ingredient, or the smell?"

Jayne chomps on a ham and cheese sandwich while James sits contentedly in the same nappy without any remedy.

"With delays, and time changes I estimate we've been with BOAC over thirty hours!" Roger says.

Another hour into the next leg and Jayne becomes distressed. "I feel sick, Mummy."

Sue and Roger look at each other. In the blink of an eye Sue hands Roger an open sick bag. He manages to get it in front of Jayne as the first of her gut wrenching heaves echo around the plane. She does not like throwing up anymore than they like listening to it. At one stage, Sue thinks Jayne's feet will pop out of her mouth, her heaves are that intense. With no water to offer her to wash her mouth out, Roger ventures into the pit of hell that is the toilet. His dry heaving while he helps does not seem to concern Jayne. She is shaking like a leaf in a gale and turns several whiter shades of pale. After the attempted clean up Jayne soon drops off in to childlike stressed sleep.

Sue rubs her forehead. "Oh, Lord, why me?"

Roger and Sue are wide awake, waiting in constant vigil for the next conundrum to unfold. James is dead to the world strapped into his seat, his nappy smelling anything but of roses. Jayne is still unwell from her food poisoning and dehydrated; her eyes red and puffy from throwing up. By the time they descend in to Perth, they feel like the journey has taken two lifetimes.

"By my count we've missed a couple of night's sleep," whimpers Roger, bleary eyed.

Sue is clearly in a state of emotional overload. She has the look of a person who has not slept in over a week; eggshell pale.

"My teeth feel more than furry, it's as if they've sheepskin coats on."

Roger peers at Sue. "You look terrible. Your eyes look like tomatoes."

"You're no oil painting yourself."

Roger looks at his slender wristwatch, "Supposedly it's two o'clock," he peers outside. "Seeing as it's as dark outside as it's going to get, it must be early morning."

After their descent stairs are attached to the exterior of the doorways to facilitate the passengers disembarkation. Preparing for their descent into paradise, travellers begin standing up and moving about locating luggage that moved during their plummet into hell.

Sue's legs will not play. They keep letting her down. Her head is spinning, her co-ordination is skewed, her limbs are convulsing. Roger fears she will begin shaking like a blancmange, with more mange than blanc.

Passengers depart in the orderly but eager fashion of those who have been cooped up in a metal tube for too long. Sue holds onto the back of Roger's trouser belt so tightly they look glued at the hip like un-coordinated Siamese twins.

Sue is unable to cope with their children. Roger cradles a reeking James, and holds onto Jayne who is almost a leach to his leg.

"This was our first time on a plane," Roger jokes to Sue, "I hope they aren't expecting a tip."

They inch ahead in the slow motion procession to the front exit. As befitting the head of his family, Roger is the first to emerge into the welcoming embrace of their new world. Australia at last!

"What the fuck," he gasps.

Slapped in their faces by a strong wind that ruffles their hair, it feels as hot as a pizza oven. They have never felt a hot wind pummelling them before and marvel at the novelty. Even if it is slightly scented with jet fuel and cannot make up its mind which way to blow.

"Every bit of me feels like one solid knot," Sue groans.

Roger becomes excited. "Look, Sue, kids…there are black swans at the Airport."

Too numerous to count they are reflecting in the powerful arc lights.

On the tarmac, a ground staff stewardess offers a wheelchair for Sue.

The magnitude of what they are attempting to do, the trauma of the journey with the combined stress and tension, the awful flight and the distress over her babies' welfares is just too much. Barely able to prevent her little mushrooms from being trampled into the dust Sue's response is less than enthusiastic, but the provision of the wheelchair becomes a little miracle of orderliness and goodwill in her despair.

Their conveyor belt of humanity moves toward the terminal.

They enter the terminal to pass through Customs and Immigration.

"Why is it that the first pieces of luggage on the carousel never seem to belong to anyone?" Roger asks.

After what seems an eternity, they recognise their tatty looking suitcases containing all that they need.

Gathering their gear is like trying to wrestle a king size mattress off a waterbed.

Sue musters to sort her little man out.

"He's developed nappy rash sores, his delicate little bottom'll incur discomfort for days as a result of this brutal treatment."

Roger hears himself say, "How easy it would have been for us to carry nappies and some baby food with us in our carryon luggage."

"As parents we should have been better prepared."

James is unperturbed. Sitting in his own soil bin for too many hours has not upset the little chap at all.

Sue takes charge right there at the luggage belt, kneeling and using the wheelchair as her work table she tends to James using a nappy and powder from their main luggage. Not one passenger gives her a second glance, most are in their own hell and want to wake up to find themselves back in the humdrum of England.

Now that James is changed and powdered he is the star of their group.

Roger looks like a dirty buffalo, feels like one on Valium, and smells like a submariner. He cannot even walk straight.

By the time their little group arrives at Immigration, somehow they have become equally spaced, like chocolates in a box.

For Roger the cumulative tiredness is the misery of phasing in and out of consciousness.

At Immigration he finds himself standing in front of a smiling middle-aged Australian in a uniform that had seen one too many washings. The broken in look suited the man. His upper lip is partially covered by a bushy moustache, his face is tanned, and the corners of his eyes are heavily stacked with wrinkles. Despite the hour, he is friendly enough, even looks pleased to see them, although heaven only knows why? The man's blue eyes drill into Roger.

Roger watches his mouth move but for the life of him, hears no sound. It is like a silent movie. Everything around Roger appears in slow motion and his head and his ears feel as if they are wrapped in cotton wool. He worries he might be closing down. Immigration man's face softens in a way that offers understanding.

There appears to be other matters, all much too numerous and too swiftly presented, for Roger to take in. While his senses reel with overload.

Immigration Man twinkles all smiles. He wants something. Some documents, that haven't been forthcoming. Roger does not know what he wants. As an automaton he has handed him what he has, what is to hand, but not enough.

Immigration Man wants something else.

Roger feels about as helpless as a rabbit destined for a hawk's dinner.

Roger looks at him. He looks at Roger. Roger's shoulders slump. He feels helpless, and then, Roger shrugs his shoulders as if to say, *I'm spent*. It is not that Roger is being awkward with the officer, nor intentionally rude. Roger hopes he will understand that he is not.

Immigration Man gives Roger the sort of wink that uses up most of his facial muscles.

A kind, benevolent, caring sort of smile that epitomises generosity, empathy and compassion, rarely known by Roger.

Immigration Man steps down from his pulpit, comes around the separation barrier and stands with Roger, who can hear him now, he is saying amiable things. He is calling Roger, "Mate."

Roger wants to hug him but has not the strength. Immigration Man expertly sifts through Roger's top pocket. A most welcome invasion of his privacy Roger does not mind at all. Compliance is sweeping over Roger like a spell.

Immigration Man finds whatever it is he is looking for and says, "Thanks, Mate, you'll be right."

He returns to his workstation and expertly completes his befuddling paraphernalia.

Still smiling, and still calling Roger *'mate'*, he comes back around the separation barrier.

This time he pins important little labels to the fronts of each of them. He seems moved by the experience and is particularly gentle with Sue and the two children.

Suitably addressed almost like overseas parcels, coded, and numbered, they are gently shunted and guided towards the next stage of the process. Their tatty suitcases are taken from them at another juncture and disappear to who knows where.

On autopilot they are back on another plane, bound for Sydney, or is it the same aircraft cleaned up? The crew has changed, the crone is nowhere to be seen. They depart Perth with a few lines of clear pink beginning to burn against the sky.

Roger leans down in an attempt to try to pick up the clean travel sick bag Jayne has dropped. At the same time, the lady in the seat ahead of him decides to throw her seat back into full recline, pinning him helplessly in the emergency crash position.

Jayne is too young to assist him and dozing, finally a break from her vomiting. As Roger can barely move or speak, his muffled sounds emanating only centimetres from the otherwise un-pristine carpet, he fears he may remain in this position until seats are in the upright position prior to landing.

Sue rescues him, while making uncomplimentary comments, "Really, Roger, at times it's like having a third child."

The backs of his eyeballs hurt and the pain radiates out to the rest of his skull but after another five hours of total misery with appalling food and service, they land in Sydney.

They transfer seamlessly, their final flight with *Ansett Airlines*, the short leg to Brisbane in Queensland.

"Well at least we're in the same country," Roger says groggily. He gathers his tribe and belongings, and, as a group of stunned Mullets, follows the crowds.

Another wheelchair, which Roger affectionately nicknames Boudicea's chariot, carries his wife with Jayne on one leg and James on the other. Roger applies one last gargantuan effort, and pushes.

"Make way, Tour Bus destined for Brisbane, coming through!" Roger jokes.

Their second wind helps counteract unpleasant states of mindlessness.

No sooner are they in the air, they begin feeling better about their situation. Everyone they now encounter reminds them of that wonderful Perth Immigration Man.

Almost sorry to only be with good ole' Reg Ansett for about an hour, all the familiar faces of their fellow passengers from BOAC are gone, except for Mr and Mrs Wag. Whether the rest have stayed in Sydney, or boarded other flights to Adelaide or Melbourne, they will never know. The flight is less than one third full and they are able to spread out. The Wags mainly doze. Although no baby food is expected on their final leg, what the Cabin Crew lacks in material comforts they make up for, by giving what they can in spades.

"We have no shop on the wing," a senior girl jokes with a relaxed smile, "but we can manage a crushed biscuit in warm milk prepared in the galley kitchen for James, if that's alright?"

"Alright?" Sue is ecstatic. "Thank you, so very, very, much."

Roger is impressed with her Australian accent.

Umpteen cups of airline coffee stiffen Roger and Sue's upper lips. Jayne is amused with colouring-in books, crayons, and plastic toys in between her dry retching. Her deathly pale almost translucent skin is beginning to get some of its English pale back.

A hostess perches next to Sue. They chat girl to girl. Roger appreciates how well his wife responds. It is like a medicine she needs.

Roger is amazed how friendly the Ansett crew are. How truly wonderful is the power of a friendly smile and a kind word in need.

Chapter 8

BRISBANE

To Roger the plane feels his jubilance; it hops, skips, and bumps its way down the runway coming to a jolting holt outside the only terminal at Brisbane Airport, the Nissan Hut.

Roger and Sue strain to get a better glimpse out of their portal, and from their limited view, it is not love at first sight, but close.

"The sun's shining," Sue is in a euphoric daze.

"Not a cloud in the sky," Roger adds, "it's as clear as a baby's conscience."

Their eyes water as they strain to take in everything from their tiny viewpoint.

Walking down the metal stairs of hope and stepping down on to the concrete, the sun is high and blazing. The heat on their faces is like a lover's first kiss.

"Wonderful warmth — heat!" Roger then launches into his soliloquy of quotes from various famous historical characters to Sue.

"When the Romans invaded Britain back in the day they burned their ships on the shore. A symbol, as well as a practical gesture, that they were there to stay in their new home."

"Well, BOAC nearly burned our plane before we got here. Maybe that counts for something?" Sue opines.

"That or build your bridge, get over it — then blow the fucker up!" laughs Mr Wag.

"Christ, this humidity is pressing the life out of us," Mrs Wag complains. "I can't breathe."

"Do you think the Aussies have forgotten we're coming?" Roger asks nervously.

"Why?" Sue queries.

"There's no bunting," he replies, "no flags, not even a balloon."

Mr Wag grins. "No welcome 'ome signs either. Shame! Not even the release of a single white dove."

Sue walks beside Roger holding his free hand. No wheelchair is required this time. James is cradled in her free arm and Jayne is being half carried by Roger.

"Just think, in England it's raining, and mostly cold." Sue cheers, "here we have thirty-five degree sunshine with wall to wall blue skies. Oh, it's so brilliant, isn't it? Oh, Roger, I actually feel warm."

"Good to know," says Mr Wag. "Christ the fuckin' flies here ain't alf friendly; aren't their bastard feet sticky, too."

"It ain't 'alf hot!" repeats Mrs Wag, fanning herself with her handkerchief.

Wide-eyed and excited, their little entourage gaze about the airport building.

"It's been given a bit of a tart-up," says Mrs Wag, "maybe that means they found some paint somewhere."

"Looks like it was done by the same mob who fixed up our old railway stations back in the 50s," Mr Wag adds, "a lick of new paint, but barely enough to cover up the old."

"From where we're standing it's sorely in need of something," complains Mrs Wag.

"Maybe a broom and then some more paint," adds Mr Wag.

They are met by a rotund, middle-aged man, neatly groomed, in shorts, long socks, and highly polished brown shoes.

Mrs Wag in a whisper to Mr Wag, "and a tie that's choking the life out of him."

Tight Tie Man explains with a beaming smile how their two families comprise his Brisbane contingent. Bubbling with enthusiasm and bonhomie, he shouts them their first taxi ride down under.

Sue's body language is all about relief. Curiously, Roger feels ready for anything.

"See you at Wacol 'ostel," Mr Wag calls out.

They are off on the last leg of their journey to where Wacol Hostel is expecting them.

Brisbane in 1971 is not going to win any beauty contests but for the boy from London, and his girl from East Grinstead, it is their favourite style of city.

"No conveyor belt of cars and traffic jams like London," Roger observes.

A sprawling overgrown country town, Brisbane is large enough for some good hospitals and a variety of employment, yet small enough to be friendly and liveable for its jubilant herd. Perching astride the watercourse of the same name, this is the primary reason for the city's establishment although the river no longer plays a prominent role in Brisbane's economic future. It is as though Brisbane is trying to be taken seriously in the overall scheme of things but the herd look happy. Not deliriously, stupidly happy, as in wearing funny hats type happy, but smiling and friendly.

"I'm not surprised Brisbane gets less publicity than other cities," Roger states sagely, "it seems to enjoy keeping a low profile."

Their friendly cab driver quickly acts as travel guide extraordinaire. "Welcome to the lucky country," he commences, "You've chosen the best State. Queensland is beautiful one day, perfect the next," he chortles on, "I love the sun, the heat, the beaches. This is literally my favourite place in the world. Friendly and unhurried, with just a whiff of excitement, that's Brissie."

With their cab windows down, a warm breeze flows through. In the cozy mid thirties, trilling birds are wheeling aloft in a huge tent of crystal blue sky, while the morning literally chimes.

"You can almost hear the red tin roofs cracking like empty chip bags in the high temperature," Roger comments excitedly.

He grins at Sue and lowers his voice. "Their lack of chimneys surely supports our notion of it not ever being a cold place here. Not even in winter."

"Never gets really cold 'ere in Brisbane," their cabbie chirps. "Although after you've been here a while and acclimatise, you'll feel cold in winter alright; especially at night. Doubt you'll ever see more than an occasional frost though. My kids have never seen snow."

"Bloody terrific," Roger exclaims. "We've seen enough of the white fluffy stuff to last us a lifetime."

Any self respecting gum tree is stilled to silence by the mind melting heat while the cabbie warms to his task of pointing out how green everything is.

"On account of the recent rains, we were flooded 'ere, only last week," he informs with genuine pride. "Otherwise you'd find the grass lay panting on top of the dirt.

I expect you'll want to buy land for a house when you've settled. Remember the cardinal rule though."

"What rule is that?" Roger asks.

"Don't ever live at the bottom of a hill or in a gulley. Water runs down hill you know."

Roger laughs. "I'm sure we'll remember. Thanks for the advice."

"Just remember to ask yourself, how long can a horse stay up. You'd be amazed how many make that simple mistake."

They all laugh.

A blur of shops and used car lots between colourful weatherboard homes cruises past. The place has a *lived in* feel, not in the slightest bit touristy. It's a dizzying kaleidoscope of movement and colour.

"I've travelled all over," continues the cabbie. "Melbourne's worldly with lousy weather, Sydney's too damned expensive; Adelaide's churchy and too damned cold in winter. Perth's nice but too isolated, Darwin's only liveable in winter. Brisbane's the pick if you ask me."

"Why?" Roger asks.

His lips almost twitch to a smile. "I grew up 'ere, out at Kangaroo Point. How many places have groovy cliffs in the middle of their city? Growing up my biggest problem was fitting all the good stuff in; West End on the weekends, and on the long weekends we either went fishing or Roo hunting. We had a ball. Good place to bring up a family.

But you'll need to get some colour into you. You look like poms. Work on some third degree sunburn. Not so you look like a biscuit, though. And look at losing some of the accent, you sound like Royalty."

"Do I?"

"Mate, you might as well hang the Union flag across your chest and hum God Save the Queen."

"Yes," says Roger. "Agreed. Get a job, a place to live, and master the art of living upside down!"

"That's it, Mate, you've got it in one. It doesn't look too difficult, does it?"

"No," laughs Roger, "but for now, all we want to do is sleep like drunken sailors."

They farewell their cabbie to greet Wacol, only just ahead of the Wags who are less than cheery.

"I thought my arse was on fire sitting on that black leather seat," Mrs Wag complains, "I'm pleased we're 'ere."

"Looks like the only things that thrive around 'ere are their fuckin' flies," mutters Mr Wag as he queues behind Roger.

"You don't dare open your mouth for fear of swallowing the bastards," Mrs Wag adds, pulling her mouth into a shape resembling a drunken comma.

Chapter 9

WACOL-HILTON

Previously an army camp Wacol Hostel comprises accommodation in timber bungalows raised off the ground on short stumps.

"It's nothing fancy," Roger observes. "We'll call it Wacol-Hilton."

The complex has the usual administration buildings, canteen facilities, segregated toilets and showers. They are assigned to half a bungalow. Solidly built, it has seen better days with plain cheap furnishings. Shaded light bulbs hang from aged flex revealing walls that originally were a shade of light green; now a sorry shade of darker green. Other drab cream fittings stand out against a constant background of Army camouflage greens.

A kindly, meringue of a woman is the matron whose eyes vanish amid her rosy cheeks when she smiles. Being competent, she promptly calls a doctor for Jayne.

"There you go Love," she smiles again, her hamster cheeks puffing out, carefully handing them a brass key on a plastic fob, two slivers of soap, and four hand towels, as though they are priceless relics. As they dump their suitcases inside the door, reality pops like a fuse.

"We're here!" Sue gasps.

"Finally!" Roger sighs.

Their room has three single beds each no wider than a windowsill, a cot, an old chest of drawers, and an enormous wardrobe.

"If push came to shove that looks substantial enough to sail in back to England," Roger jokes.

Unremarkable in design though the beds are, they draw the migrants immediate attention to them, as though cast from pure gold and etched with diamonds.

Thin sheets, greyed by a few hundred washes, grace their green framed beds.

"Paradise," Sue says, "and I mean it without even a hint of sarcasm."

Timber-framed windows open outwards without a breeze to disturb the chintz curtains. When closed, the windows have frosted glass for privacy.

The GP is quick to arrive. "I'll give Jayne an injection to stop her vomiting and help put her to sleep," he says. "If you still need me tomorrow please advise Matron, but I think she's over it."

"Thank you, Doctor. What do we owe you?" Roger asks.

"On the house," the doctor beams.

James is naked, clean and powdered, and out to the world.

"Neither James nor Jayne care if they're sleeping on nails or in a hollow log," Sue says flatly. "For them it's a welcome oblivion."

"As for Matron; that woman is surely a force of nature. She's a blessing with more drive and ambition than Napoleon." Roger shrugs, "It is very warm in here, it's as if they've turned the heating up."

"I don't see any sign of heaters," Sue screws her nose up, "but it doesn't smell very good either."

"I wasn't going to mention it. I thought it might be us."

Sue and Roger lay motionless on their beds. Without their winceyette nightclothes, they cover their nakedness with the thin, light sheets. A warm breeze embraces them. It floats through their open windows and caresses them as they prepare to join James and Jayne snoring in familial unity.

"I think I'm over tired for sleep," Sue says slowly. "Over tired, and over wired."

"I feel like someone's stuck a pin in me and let out the air."

The best they can do is snooze a little, but the noises are different. The dizzying cacophony of insects; cicadas sizzling in frypan high temperatures, the didgeridoo drone of a blowfly, together with occasional snatches of laughter or chatter nearby.

"I recognise the Wag's voices," says Sue. "I do believe they're next door to us."

"He's certainly a character."

Sue dozes for a while and then asks, "do you know what I used to fantasise about as a teenager?"

"No. I'm afraid to ask."

"No seriously."

"I am being serious."

"Coming to Australia."

"Why didn't you?"

"I didn't have the guts to go on my own."

"I'm pleased you didn't," Roger replies, and he means it.

Roger's brain is busier than a Friday afternoon rush hour at Piccadilly Circus, and then he finds himself cat napping through the distant melody of a pooch barking empty threats and the constant noise of crickets, like tinnitus.

Unfamiliar bird calls. One in particular sounds like someone laughing. They lay quietly, both of them feeling almost awkward now that they have arrived.

A strangely light but repetitive tap, tap, tapping noise almost like a mini-person approaching in dwarf style stiletto heels, keeps stirring them as they drift off. Sue opens one eye and glances in the direction of her unwanted distraction.

She does not scream exactly, but lets out a low moaning sound that becomes something like, "Ohhhh, nooooo Roger, looook, loooooook!"

Roger's heart gives a lurch.

"Fuck me!" Roger yells sitting upright in bed.

A very large cockroach is meandering across the floor.

The sounds are the noise from its untrimmed toenails on the ends of its six clod-hopper feet, like high heels click-clacking as it rattles across the smooth polished floor's surface.

"My God, Roger, it's big enough to be someone's pet."

"Should I get it a collar with a bell? We could name it. Maybe Hercules?"

Sue has never seen an insect quite as large.

When Roger moves to get a closer look, their uninvited guest reciprocates his interest.

He sends Sue what he hopes is an enigmatic smile. "In a fair fight of three rounds or more, I'd stand little chance anyway."

Summoning all of her maternal instincts at one time, Sue conserves on words. "Kill it!"

As she senses Roger's total inability to perform, she adds. "Get a shoe."

Roger is sitting on the edge of the bed looking bewildered.

"Any shoe," she says again with more desperation, more feeling.

"It isn't fair, after all we've been through. I'm not up to this challenge at all."

Roger looks about for a shoe.

The closest unattached footwear is a child's shoe. Roger is about to reach out for it when Sue reads his mind.

"Not that one! Get a big shoe, one of yours. You're going to kill it. Not play footsie with it."

By this time their unwelcome visitor, has decided to backtrack and check out their luggage, which is only partly unpacked.

As Jayne and James are sleeping soundly, Roger is trying not to make any noise.

Sue sits upright on the edge of her bed, her feet off the floor, looking as though she is doing some sort of Army training.

Sue shudders and tries to avoid seeing any performing cockroaches on the curtain rail.

Trying to maintain eye contact with the cockroach Roger looks at Sue in the impending gloom. Her face looks alive for the first time in what seems days.

"Don't let it get away. Oh, I'll never rest with that *thing* in our room. Oh, it's awful, Roger."

"Better watch your feet, there might be more wildlife in the carpet than the whole of Borneo," adds Roger unenthusiastically.

Their unwelcome visitor is an Australian cockroach *Blatta australis*. Similar to the American variety, it is easily identifiable by the yellow markings near its head. It only appears grotesque to some because of its size.

As Roger approaches the monster, he feels the hairs standing up on the back of his neck! Insecurity reaches deep into what dangles between his legs, his captain and two sailors.

'I'm convinced,' he thinks, 'I'm not enjoying any part of this.'

Instead he says, "This so far has all the elements of the cartoon 'the Road Runner' but without any of the funny bits."

Roger glances over his shoulder at Sue, now disappearing under her bed sheet, as Roger's upward swing descends. His first swipe is a disgrace. He misses by a country mile and the muffled groan from Sue speaks volumes.

"If you weren't encased like an Egyptian Mummy in your bed sheet, Sweetheart, I'm sure you'd do a lot better."

Roger says testily. "Here I am facing my first serious altercation on Australian soil and by my dead reckoning we've been in our adopted new home all of about two hours, fifteen minutes, and thirty-five seconds.

I'm building on a good pattern of grouping, Sue and given time, I'll eventually close in on the *bastard*. If only it'd remain still. Work with me here you *bastard!*"

Roger may have caught it a glancing blow.

The cockroach saunters away and toddles off under the wardrobe with the same complacency as Muhammad Ali versus Joe Frazier.

Roger lets out an exasperated groan. "Game, set, match…I've lost to the cockroach."

He peeks under the wardrobe but can't see anything. "I was caught with my pants down."

"That's not a pretty sight."

The wardrobe, now a tad larger and heavier than he would have liked, will have to wait until morning to avoid waking the children. He skulks back to bed like a scolded dog.

"Sorry," Roger's voice is contrite, knowing he has not cut it.

Roger senses more than sees Sue nearly grinding her teeth to dust with frustration in the dark. Now Sue has another reason not to fall asleep; the fear of cockroaches the size of dragons.

"Why are you hugging your slippers in bed?" Roger asks, as he settles down.

"Because, I'm so terrified of big cockroaches and I don't want them in my slippers come morning. Trouble is they smell like crap!"

"What the cockroaches?"

"No! My slippers!"

To top off their jet lag, they can now hear some familiar noises from some heavy action going on next door.

"Sounds like they're going at it hammer and tongs," Roger says.

"Lucky Wag. Don't you get any ideas, I'm too tired!"

After a while, the bumping of the headboard seems to increase in tempo.

"Maybe Mrs Wag likes it rough," Roger says, "reminds me somewhat of when I was a young man of nineteen."

"I'll buy it. Why nineteen?"

"Without a current girlfriend my sex life was like a Ferrari."

"Why a Ferrari?"

"I didn't have a Ferrari."

"She's not howling yet. If they could move it along a bit we might get some sleep."

"Let's hope the wall holds."

Eventually, Roger does not hear their alarm clock, nor the hiccupping frogs and possums that make use of their roof as a highway.

When he finally gains release from morpheus and joins the conscious world he looks at the bedside clock. The big hand is on twelve and the little hand is on eight. He has overslept due to listening to the Wags half the night.

Roger sees Sue standing near the door, and son James awake and bouncing up and down in his cot.

James is attempting to catch a large cockroach that is just beyond his reach up the wall oblivious to the heat and mosquitoes.

"Good, boy. When you've sorted him out you can climb under the wardrobe."

Sue is attempting to dissuade James by wiping his hands clean.

They attend the rhythm of breakfasts in the communal canteen. There the heightened odour of chlorine hammers their senses. Mysteriously that makes their gluggy porridge seem even more unpalatable. Jayne turns her nose up at the watered down cordial; the orange juice is not much better. Nothing on offer entices them to want to hang in.

"Maybe they want us weak and compliant," Roger jokes.

"Like sheep," Sue opined.

"Yes, but offering their throats willingly to the ritual knife."

Sue is dejected. "If breakfast was anything to go by, I'm not looking forward to lunch or dinner."

Back at their digs, they prepare to move the wardrobe.

"Deep breaths," Roger coaches. "Keep our minds buzzing like a top, and bend-a-zee knees!"

Roger cautiously opens the wardrobe door to peer inside and its smell of mildew immediately hits him.

Sue wrinkles her nose, "I'd prefer not to put our clothes in it."

Roger braces for action against the other side of the wardrobe.

After a joint Herculean effort, moving in tandem, they gape at nothingness. There is no sign of their unwelcome visitor behind or under the wardrobe.

Sue gasps, "that gap along the skirting board's so large, it could have left in a double-decker bus."

"Or on horseback. Anyway we're ill equipped."

"No guns, not even a knife."

"I have no intention of crawling under this building with a torch," Roger adds in case Sue has ambitions.

No words are strong enough to survive the acid eating through her throat at that moment. She is unhappy having no control over Australian fauna in their quarters.

Sue peeks out the window. "Oh, well. At least it's not snowing."

A few feathery clouds have stolen into an otherwise perfect blue sky.

Roger's world might almost have been back on kilter until Sue cuddles Jayne. "We can't leave here yet, Sweetheart, because Daddy still hasn't got a job."

"Great, get a job. Yes, of course. Piece of cake."

Roger is unsure whether to laugh, cry, or go jump in the Brisbane River.

Chapter 10

A JOB INTERVIEW

As Roger makes his way to the courtyard of Wacol-Hilton, standing with hands on hips is an impressive, fit looking fellow dressed in a once-white-now-stained tank top and brown shorts, with his feet spilling out over rubber flip flops. His name tag: Activities Director. Tank Top man is busy mustering his small group together in assorted clothing.

By his appearance, this gym rat works out, enjoys an alcohol free diet; grazing on bean curd and sprouts, but there is not much he can do about his weak chin and his little piggy eyes.

Why do vegans hate animals so much? wonders Roger. What did they ever do to them?

One hopeful is running enthusiastically on the spot. He is pounding the compacted earth like dough hitting the baker's board. Heaven only knows why unless he feels lonely or bored. Surely the humidity would knock a fly off its wing.

Another is doing a version of the hunchback's scuttle. Roger would almost certainly not fit right in. By the size of the group, Tank Top Man could have scrounged up more takers in a cemetery.

Roger does not enjoy exercise; unless it is the horizontal jog with Sue!

He steals a look at a bosomy jogger in a midnight blue silk tunic, tight pants, and gold sandals on adorable feet. Her mouth forms a provocative O of exertion as her cleavage leaps before her. He cannot help but notice her nipples are so hard she could dial a phone with them.

Tank Top Man, gym master of ceremonies, smiles at Roger.

Roger smiles at Tank Top Man.

Roger can see that Tank Top thinks he might be onto fresh meat.

"Just arrived?" Tank Top Man asks. His voice sounds hopeful, soft, Welsh, and pleasantly melodic.

"Yes. From London," Roger replies, feeling non committal. "We've come for the climate."

Tank Top Man sticks out his hand like a bayonet, "Humidity's high today."

Roger and Tank Top Man shake hands.

Tank Top Man asks, but sounds almost too hopeful. "Would you like to join us?"

Roger shakes his head. "Afraid not. I've already done my workout for today."

From his toothy grin, Roger feels he has misconstrued what Roger meant, not moved a mountain of a wardrobe to find Mohammad.

"Do you run?" Tank Top tries a serene smile.

"Only when I have to. I do jump, but mainly to conclusions. Occasionally I run in circles."

The thought crosses Roger's mind talking about exercise that getting a job might improve his sex life, which is at an all time low thanks to the local wildlife and the Wags.

Later that morning, Roger and Mr Wag are invited by Administration to be formally welcomed as immigrants. "We're to be given the *drum* about our new surroundings," Mr Wag gushes.

"Men only are represented from our families," Roger says. Frowning he adds, "Maybe it's seen by Admin more as a meeting to brainstorm ideas."

Sue dresses Roger for the occasion in a suit. She reasons, that as they are being sponsored by the government this is not a social gathering.

"You should treat it seriously," she advises, straightening his crooked tie, "as if attending a job interview. You need to keep an open mind."

"My mind is so open my brains could fall out.

Jayne's got one sock on and one sock off," Roger comments to Sue as he glances over her shoulder.

Sue beams. "She's not sure yet, if she's coming or going, cold or hot?"

As Roger enters the meeting room, he sees that he is in the minority. Everyone else assembled is wearing bathers, board shorts, stubby shorts, and thongs, which the Wag refers to as Japanese riding boots.

The meeting is held in a type of conference room with paint peeled fold out chairs dotted about. Windows thrown open to allow what breeze there is to flow through.

"Might this be where the visiting generals gave them the good news about going to Vietnam?" Roger suggests quietly to Mr Wag.

"Poor bastards."

They receive an absolute mine of information. Everything from the penalties for misuse of Wacol-Hilton facilities to the dangers of Magpies and protecting their young.

Their rules are stated over, and over, and over again in his reedy voice by their Deputy Director of Operations. *Probably to avoid legal ramifications,* Roger thinks.

A thick-chested, pot-bellied man of middle years, he is wearing a necktie but when he tries to swagger, he has too much tonnage on his hips. He reminds Roger of the man pictured in the Norwich Library book hosing down non-existent crap off his Gold Coast driveway.

"In particular one important thing to remember," Necktie speaks with a fake smile in a neutral tone, "is that everything here is entirely free of charge. No reimbursement is required for your accommodation, your meals, the utilities provided, not even laundry powder. Here everything is supplied free of charge."

"He really wants to 'ammer out the free of charge fuckin' aspect," whispers Wag to Roger.

"It's more than generous, but well overplayed," Roger agrees.

"In addition," Necktie continues, "any family can stay for as long as they please, even get jobs and send your children to the local school. And still..." he continues to emphasise, "remain here entirely free of charge. Many families have already stayed here for more than six months. Some are going for their annual anniversaries...!" he jokes. "But remember, once you move out, there's no coming back, no way at all of getting back in here. That door of entry," his arm waves towards the front entrance and they all follow it like automatons with their eyes, "can only swing one way in the once."

After the eye drooping monotone droning meeting finally tires itself out they mill about.

A representative from the CBA (Commonwealth Bank of Australia) helps Roger establish an account to receive future wages and hopefully an anticipated large deposit from the sale of their house.

An MBF (Medical Benefits Fund of Australia) representative busily signs up new members waiving waiting periods as an incentive.

Roger notices Mr Wag has a faraway look. "What's up?" he asks.

"Nothing much."

"How's your wife?"

"She's got a splitting head ache today."

Wonder why?

Roger practices his faraway look suppressing the urge to reinforce he may know why.

"You know a fair bit about history, don't you?" asks Mr Wag, changing the subject.

"That's a big subject."

"Did you know the Greeks claim to have invented sex," Mr Wag says with a brief smirk. as if a thought might have fluttered close to the surface, but then disappeared.

"So they may have," Roger replies tersely, "but we English introduced the better idea of using women."

"That's funny and true," Wag replies with a broad smile.

"That said," Roger continues, "the closest to a sexual experience I've been lately was finding lipstick on a wine glass."

"Me too."

You lying bastard, thinks Roger.

Roger is taken aside by another of their welcoming committee.

Another Necktie with sceptical eyes set in an unremarkable face that only a bulldog's mother could love. They are breeding, thinks Roger.

He offers Roger and his family superior alternative accommodation in the form of a fully furnished unit at Wooloowin. Apparently, their new benefactors own two blocks of such units; each available on a six months lease but only to approved migrants.

After Roger returns to their digs and tells Sue, she is ecstatic.

"Maybe it was your suit and tie that had helped us qualify?"

"It certainly wasn't our staggering under the weight of our pound notes."

"Whatever it was," Sue beams, "we've really been offered fully furnished accommodation out of here?"

"That's right, and at the princely sum of $56.00 per month rental, plus services. We'll be in Hunter Street, Wooloowin, wherever that is."

With Sue's voice ringing in his ears about getting a job Roger adds the odd four-letter pleasantry and quickly sources a copy of Saturday's *Courier-Mail* newspaper from a local shop.

"It's a pity," Roger says, "that the powers-that-be don't provide them on campus as everyone surely needs one."

As churches are the only places allowed to open on Sundays and even mowing a lawn is frowned upon by some, Roger reasons he will have all day to scan the situations vacant.

"Now, on whose arse should I attempt to plant my lips for a job interview?" Roger jokes.

"You might need to reassess being a *Yes Man* in this new environment," Sue opines.

Roger finds a few Situations Vacant and next day armed with a pocketful of change he performs a little known Native Australian dance that involves hopping from foot to foot, while wedged into a sweltering telephone booth.

Not long and he loosens his tie. Five minutes is all he can stand at a time in the sweatbox.

Newspaper balanced in one hand, Biro in the other, he is set. Poised and confident he is doing alright.

"Where are you living?" the friendly voice at the other end wants to know.

Roger has given his name without much difficulty but after he explains his address is *Wacol Hostel* the next sound he hears is:

Click.

The line disconnects before Roger has a chance to speak. Pushing his glasses further up the bridge of his sweaty nose, he grumbles in his head that could probably have gone slightly better.

This continues for the duration of his torture in the sweatbox with good progress right up to the point where he is to give his address and then click.

Emotionally beaten, sweat dripping off his nose, sweat splotches on his glasses, his shirt soaked through, Roger finally escapes the glass maiden to enjoy the stifling hot breeze. He stood fully upright and put both hands to the small of his sweat sodden back, letting out a groan.

This is getting more complicated than an algorithm, he thinks.

A sign of the times, perhaps? But the chances of him procuring an interview from this Wacol address looks about the same as the *Bolshoi Ballet* calling him out of the blue for a tryout.

Roger reports back to the other half of his support team about his unlucky day.

"You could use the unit," Sue suggests thoughtfully, "we may not be in yet, but it's worth a try."

Another turn in the glass torture chamber, he uses their semi fake address and is short listed for a job interview straight away.

Exhilarated he reports back. "That worked, worked a treat. One problem though."

Sue pokes her tongue out and blows a soggy raspberry. "Only one?"

"I can't carry a fan around with me. My necktie is strangling the life out of me, but I need to make more impression than a fly-in-a-frenzy makes against a closed window."

"I'm sure the suit is important, even if the sweat does sting your eyes. It did get us the flat."

"Unit, Sweetheart, they call flats units here."

Roger's first job interview is in Brisbane City. "I'll catch the train from the station nearby. Then hop off in the city and walk."

Wacol-Hilton has no fly screens on their bungalows and even if they had it is doubtful the pesky mosquitoes would stay out. That afternoon the winged critters leave their abodes and circle in holding patterns around Roger. In a night as still as a corpse they sound like kamikaze planes heading for any gap in his defences. Mosquitoes as big as crows.

"Bloody mosquitoes are making my ankles their own world dart championships!"

In the morning Roger notices an ankle is badly swollen.

He has difficulty getting a dress shoe on. He is feeling a little lightheaded, and then he realises that he has trouble even getting a sock on.

"Might I have to go barefoot?" he asks Sue.

"I'm sure most people are bitten by mozzies but you appear to have suffered more than most," Sue replies with tenderness. "Maybe your English blood is good for something after all," she giggles. It was the sort of giggle a man could live with.

With a struggle, and enduring much pain, he eventually finishes dressing. Rock on!

"I think things might be turning for the better, Sue. Now all I have to do is limp about two kilometres to the train station. But I'll still have to find my way around the city."

They are both quiet for a full minute while they consider his chances of success. It has taken him so long to get dressed with the agony of getting the shoe on, he is now behind time to catch the train. He must hurry!

"My foot feels like ten pounds of shit squeezed into a five pound bag."

The station seems like about ten kilometres. Roger hurries between spurts of pain.

He tries running.

Nimble as a Water Buffalo with a broken leg Roger is nauseous with the effort of hurrying. At least I'm not carrying a 50kg backpack in the jungles of Vietnam, weak bastard. Nor am I suffering from Guardia, farting and shitting for so long, I can't feel my arsehole anymore. That or amoebic dysentery on a 36 hour bus journey to Kathmandu. That or a six month bout of hepatitis in the Himalayas. He cheers up on account of how damned lucky he is compared to others.

After what seems ages, he suspects the train station is a mirage looming out of an unconquerable desert.

Far away, a few clouds dot the sky. Roger wonders whether they may team up and deliver a downpour.

He is deep in thought about missing his train and how best to get a job while appearing as a cripple, when he is stopped in his tracks by an older gentleman, dressed in shorts with long socks to the knees in enclosed shoes and an open neck shirt who has a question for him.

"Why are yer running, Mate?" the older gentleman asks.

Roger's smile from his sweaty face is somewhat forced.

"I have a train to catch for a job interview," he explains between taking breaths.

The older gentleman looks somewhat puzzled, scratches his balding head, and then ruminates, "Running? Running to catch a train you say?"

Roger nods, he is hardly intending to stretch the man's mental capacity.

"To catch a train you say?"

Roger does the nod thing, again. He is still out of breath.

"I've been working on the trains for years, and I still don't know it all. But train timetables are all works of fiction, Mate. But anyway, we Aussies don't do that, you must be a Pom. Are yer?"

Roger nods again, grateful for the one-way conversation. He supposes the suit and tie may have given him away.

"The only way an Aussie will run for a train is if he's in front of the bastard, and only then if it's moving towards him at the time, Mate." He scratches his head again. "Mind you walking's alright. Shouldn't bother you none," with a radiant toothy grin he finishes with, "Burke and Wills proved that Mt Isa is only walking distance from Melbourne."

Roger hates to admit he has not a clue what the man is talking about, but as he does not want to miss his train. He smiles and nods.

Shaking his head as if he has seen it all for one day, he smugly finishes with, "Good luck with your interview young Mate!"

It is a good job the older gentleman has delayed him because otherwise by the time he reaches the station he might not have been breathing at all.

Roger has high hopes for a selling job with a company car.

Roger who is still breathless buys his return ticket and sits on the only wooden bench seat in the shade. There he waits with nervous anticipation, constantly checking his watch, for his ride to arrive. The eardrum bursting, black smoke belching diesel train rumbles to a holt. Roger finally over his forced exercise takes a seat near the door. A quick getaway is in order.

The trip into the city passes painfully slowly, he gazes out the window not seeing what passes, because his mind is on the interview.

Once in the city he finds the address without much delay as he decides to play the immigrant card and ask directions each step of the way.

A kindly man of middle years interviews Roger, overlooking his painful limp after taking in the full flavour of his suit and tie. Interview

Man is dressed in comfortable shorts, long socks and an open-necked shirt.

"There's a basic goodness in most Australians," Interview Man smirks, "but someone of a more robust appearance," he eyes Roger up and down as though assessing his life's worst deeds, "might be better suited to the task of humping heavy, crates full of glass bottles."

The job is for a soft drink delivery company, with the emphasis on the delivery.

No company car, no office chair, no phone. No chance of a paper cut.

"Thank you for the opportunity, Sir," Roger smiles with a touch of regret in his voice.

Outside, after he has composed himself, he feels as dull as faded paint.

Back at Wacol-Hilton he reports to Sue, "I've got off to an incredibly bad start, but at least he let me down gently. Even if he did eye me off as he would a rabid dog."

Sue nods good-naturedly.

"I'll try not to make the same mistake more than three or four times, Sue. Maybe in future I'll be more selective about the sales positions I pursue?"

"On the bright side you at least found your way to the train station, around Brisbane city, and back again, without getting lost," she praises.

Roger perks up like a dog catching a scent. "Yes. I suppose you're right. Not bad for a first attempt. Brisbane city's not without a few surprises. Up until now, I haven't seen adult men in shorts and long socks other than scout masters, but here they're everywhere. It's the in thing, and a lot more comfortable than how I'm trussed up like a sacrificial chook."

Chapter 11

G'DAY WOOLOOWIN

Their plans to depart Wacol cannot happen fast enough.

Sue is constantly turning her nose up in the canteen while pushing food restlessly around her plate. "Once it's down, I hope it doesn't come up! It's the punishing, strong, smells of disinfectant that turns off any craving I have for this food."

"It's pervasive alright, worse than what I remember about school dinners," Roger adds.

Mr Wag stares down at his plate. "This is dryer than their Simpson Desert and about as 'ospitable."

"Surely a little gravy without lumps would cheer it up a bit," Mrs Wag suggests.

"Anything might help make it look edible," complained Mr Wag. "This food might be free, but it smells of sour milk and soap. It's worse than the shite on the plane."

Sue stares down at her plate. "My Mum said, 'You don't have to put anything in your mouth you don't want to.'"

"Just how true's that. You've followed her advice all these years to the letter," Roger replies playfully.

Sue leers, "Trust you."

Mr Wag looks confused, Mrs Wag roars with elfish laughter.

"What work did you do back in the old country?" Sue asks the Wags.

"I was a painter," Mr Wag replies.

"Big brush or little brush?" Roger prompts.

Mr Wag looks blank.

"Roger means are you an artist — small brush, or houses — large brush, Love."

"Oh, I see, I'm a house painter, inside and out. I do good work. What about you?"

"Well, I used to work in a hotel," Roger explains, "Jack of all trades; waiting on tables, barman, relief chef. But more recently I've been selling pest control."

"Ooo," gushes Mrs Wag, "plenty of pests 'ere, Love. You should be kept busy. Good on yer."

Later away from the Wags and back in their quarters, Roger suggests to Sue, "Maybe we should go to the canteen less often. After all Jesus fasted in the desert didn't he? Why not us?"

"HE had a choice," Sue replies. "We have to do something, Roger. I'm not happy feeding the children with this, could we pay to have something better?"

"Agreed. We're desperate. Means we need a desperation plan."

"A proper plan, Roger, not a pretend one!"

Sue looks relieved. "There's one small shaft of hope. Not far from the entrance, I saw a shop that sells bits of everything. Probably been there since this was an army camp."

Sue's expectations encourage Roger. "That's where they sell the newspapers."

Sue remains at the Hilton with the children, no sense in drawing attention to what could possibly unfold. She gives firm guidelines with a Mission Impossible smile, "Should you choose to accept your mission," she pauses, "which includes no cold cooked chicken nor ham sandwiches. Understood?"

"Yes." Roger understands that it is not to repeat the problem Jayne experienced on their BOAC flight.

Roger feels like Hansel and Gretel following the crumbs to said mirage of hope.

Primed like a Fifth Columnist he finds the shop's door locked. Adorned with a helpful handwritten sign: *'Back in 20'*.

He glances insignificantly at his watch.

Here's hoping the sign means minutes, not hours, or days.

With his stationary face pressed against the grimy, glass door, he peers in. He cheers up when he sees the harsh fluorescent lights are on.

He looks again at his watch. Assuming their sign is accurate he has twenty minutes to wait from the time the sign was displayed, but that poses the inevitable question. How long ago was that? Is he in for a wait of one minute or nineteen minutes? He settles in for the long haul, attached to his shadow, with his back to the door.

"I feel like Moses on the road to Damascus," he mutters to himself, "or was it Noah?"

The shop proprietor arrives after ten minutes. A large, middle-aged man, with a ruddy complexion and a prominent beer belly. Looking bored, he is wearing a dirty white apron and has three days' worth of white whiskered growth on his face.

When he sees Roger glance at his watch he reacts in a gruff manner.

"Sorry, Mate. I have to lock up to use the public toilet. I'd redo the sign but the army never liked too many words and the migrants don't understand unless I use mime or pixie cards."

"That's alright, if you hadn't returned when you did, I'd just keep reading the sign."

The store is a bare bones version of a larger style supermarket; daily necessities, food items, and take-away.

Roger wants nothing more complicated than a bubbling feast from a cauldron of hot oil. It is calling to him, he can sense it. Maybe fish and great greasy chips? Yes, he wants fry-o-lated arts and he wants them all, now.

He peruses the menu board. This is a time of celebration. Hamburgers…Maybe? Toasted Sandwiches…Maybe? Cooked chicken portions. Maybe not. Pie and chips. Would it matter what style of pie? Sausage rolls? He does like a good sausage roll.

He settles for fish and chips and hamburgers.

Gruff repeats his order, "Five portions of fish cooked in deep fat with crispy batter and six loads of Irish trifecta."

"Irish trifecta?"

"Yeah, chips hot and soggy! And two hamburgers coming up, Mate."

The battered Barramundi floats adrift in a sea of life giving oil. It boils and bubbles and the smell is truly amazing.

Roger manages a sage smile. "Do you miss your army customers?"

"Well, most of them went to Vietnam. Bad fucking war that. I doubt if most made it through." He brightens, "But Army life's like that. A bit like getting career advice from Ronnie Biggs."

"We're ten pound poms only just arrived. It might take a while for the army to realise I'm here."

Gruff looks Roger up and down. "It'd be like leading a cane toad into the sugar fields if you ask me. But you look too old, mate. They like the young uns with no brains."

Thankful for the chatter to pass the time, Roger eagerly accepts the parcels of hope and sustenance as though it were the scriptures themselves being delivered in the new land and hopefully the promised land in a few hours.

The smell of fish and chips trail after Roger as he makes his way back. Smuggled take-away wrapped in newspaper is more like the crowns of dead kings.

In the sanctuary of their room, Sue accepts Roger's gifts almost in awe, "Roger," she purrs in such a way it reminds him yet again of his lack of sex life.

After Sue has chomped into her fish and chips, she remarks, "Mmm, Oh, Roger. I'm so ashamed, this is delicious."

Sue glances to her daughter, no encouragement needed, Jayne has stuffed hamster cheeks, "Jayne, chew your food," muffles Sue between mouthfuls.

James has his Farex and Heinz baby foods.

For a rare moment no-one speaks, each captivated in their own thoughts and euphoria of food, real food.

After due silence in honour of their meals, Sue observes, "Maybe we aren't enjoying our new surroundings with quite the same enthusiasm as many of the other guests appear to be."

"Yes. But interestingly the hamburger contains beetroot, maybe it's a must have here?"

"Unusual. Though I never thought I could fall in love with an egg," opines Sue.

Their meal over they wash it down with ice cold milk and set about trying to remove the tell-tale odours of their contraband with more than a nodding use of deodorant.

Roger clandestinely sets off to find a suitable receptacle for their rubbish.

Desperate for the keys to their unit and fearing mail could soon be arriving from prospective employers Roger pleads with Admin on bended knee for the keys.

They must have taken a shine to him, or that he was really on bended knees begging, either way they left Wacol-Hilton with a cheery wave from the matron who wished them well, "You certainly don't let the grass grow under your feet, I'll give you that," she says with an unbelieving chuckle.

Mr and Mrs Wag line up to see them off as if they are old friends.

"We'll 'ave to keep in touch with you when we get settled, Loves," Mrs Wag called out.

Mr Wag looks as if he has just lost his best friend.

As the taxi whirls them away, "We hardly know them, Sue."

"They're just lonely in their big new world," Sue replies, "like us."

"That's all well and good, but I hope they don't keep dropping in."

"We can always be busy, or out." They share a sideways glance.

"Four days, Sue, we did well, sadly no more free government cab rides."

They both chuckle and talk aimlessly to the driver, not really listening or wanting to until the cab pulls up outside a block of unremarkable units, but to Sue and Roger it is the Taj Mahal.

The unit is a big step up from their Wacol digs. Two bedrooms, kitchen come dining, and lounge.

Sue is ecstatic, "Look, Roger, there's a bathroom with a shower over the bath."

Their first introduction to showers was at Wacol. How clean they felt when they showered, how preferable they found it to bathing and how badly they sing, although James and Jayne are of an age when they still enjoy splashing about in a bath.

March is still hot, very hot, and humid.

He is snapped from his thoughts by Sue, "We have fly screens on the windows."

"Thank Christ."

The unit is furnished with regular sized double bed, single bed, and a cot for James. A three piece suite, a dining set, with a few portable fans. Downstairs hosts a garage, which stands empty.

The train station is an easy stroll from the unit, across the road is a little shop that sells the basics of life and lollies for the kids, which becomes designated as Jayne's 'holly' shop.

Anxious for quick employment, Roger soon snags a job selling office equipment on commission only, in Brisbane City.

He befriends a fellow salesman called Arthur. His senior by one month in the company Arthur prefers being called Art. He is a Brisbane boy through and through, born in deepest Brookfield a rural suburb. Art's handshake is firm and proper in duration.

"Are you married, Roger?" Art asks.

"Yes, I'm sorry. I'm spoken for Art."

Art laughs.

"I've got one child by my first wife. No rug rats yet by my second wife. But that's probably because I haven't met my second wife yet," Art jokes.

Art is a natural salesman. His toothy grin lights up not only his own face but also any room.

Roger enjoys hearing about his life as a 'true blue Aussie' and in return, Art enjoys Roger's tales about the old country.

Art's physical appearance is hunk-surfer type. Muscular, he has the weighty presence of granite. Stout neck and his wide tanned face frames blue eyes, topped with a mane of blond hair.

Art appears salt-encrusted, windswept, and at one with the dolphins.

"Their star performer," Art explains, "is an overweight Kiwi who keeps big noting his Maori origins. He does his strange little dance most mornings."

Roger looks blank. He has no idea what Art's talking about. "Dance?"

Art sighs, his voice is uneven, "Maori warriors used to make faces and stomp their feet on the ground to intimidate their enemies."

"Did it work?"

"Sometimes, they claim it worked against the British."

"They pulled out in 1870, but only because they had something more important to go and do."

Art beams, "Then — it wasn't all Captain Cook's fault."

"No. Plenty of others to blame besides him."

"All a long time ago then." Art continues with a wink, "Mate, most Maoris wouldn't know if it was Christmas Eve or Cracker Night, unless you told 'em. Just remember Oz comprises Sheilas, blokes, and wankers.

A few too many of the latter come from the Land of the Long White Chip on the fucking Shoulder, Mate. If you know what I mean."

Roger has no idea what he means. "Where's that?"

"New Zealand, Mate. Somewhere called Why-Kick-A-Moo-Cow."

Roger looks even more confused.

"Look, don't worry about it, Mate. Just avoid him. He sports a twenty-four hour stubble on his neanderthal chin, his tie always hangs at his neck, and to top it off, he's a man who never looks happy to be at work. Not that I blame him for that. Anyway he never shuts up talking about a bunch of dead Maoris."

"Dead Maoris?"

Art rolls his eyes. "One of the Kiwi's finest fucking achievements, mate. Their other is to convince everyone how nice they all are."

"Well, aren't they?"

"They've conned the world, Mate. Conned them I say. Except for their rugby team they're a spent force. He's not indispensable, just thinks he is. Anyway he's a Kiwi from Dunedin, Mate."

"Is that special?"

"Special? It's that place with horizontal drizzle. Special enough for you? Word is he joined a support group to get laid. He's a selfish and egoistical prick. Look, I wouldn't have him on my toe for a corn. Forget him, mate. Alright?"

Roger is skeptical. He wants to belong. To be part of this new Aussie culture, but doesn't want to become too extreme. "What about the Aboriginals?" he asks.

"ABBOS!" Art's reaction is extreme. "*Bloody Abbos!* Cloistered in their alcoholic, glue, and druggy life, with an enormous bloody chip on their shoulders. Good for nothing most of them."

Roger is thoughtful as Art continues to bang on about them. *As likeable as Art is, he might have a few issues.*

Sales do not come easily even for their Kiwi star performer.

"I dun't do so good, ey," the big Maori says shaking his head, "better luck with thut, Bro."

Roger witnesses a revolving door of staff turnover that is consistent but with perseverance, it pays well on results.

Roger quickly settles into a routine. Salesmen generate their own leads by cold calling with a typewriter under their arm door to door. Aim is to sell on approval. Some days Roger fakes enthusiasm while he keeps an eye on the *Courier-Mail* for something better. He almost pisses himself with glee on Wednesdays and Saturdays, which are the big days for the new Situations Vacant pages.

Art's standard joke is, "I want to be the first to get Wednesday's paper but on a Monday morning. I know, I know, I'm more likely to witness a mating ritual between a Tasmanian Tiger and a Yowie on Lassiter's Reef."

Most days Sue meets Roger's train at Wooloowin station with Jayne and James in tow and they stop to buy ice blocks at the 'holly shop' on the way home. Roger's income, which is hard won, pays the rent, food, and utilities with some left over to save. He has learned when life gets you up against the ropes and those punches keep coming, the key is to keep going. Persistence, but somehow in sunshine, and with better food, he feels sure he can melt granite.

"We need to prioritise a list of things we need, Sue."

Sue is thoughtful. "Somehow might a stereo and television vie for exclusivity below a car?"

"With no news from the old country about the sale of our house we must tread cautiously," Roger warns, "but I agree we want wheels."

Saturday morning while strolling down Sandgate Road they spot a car yard at Albion. With next to nothing down and on hire purchase at $35 per month they are popular with the salesman.

The once dark green Volkswagen now lacks its sheen and has an eternally rattling tailpipe; the windscreen has a crack off centre that looks like a bolt of lightning.

"We'll need to name our car," Sue gushes. "What about *Kermit*, it's green and if I squint it reminds me of those green tree frogs we saw at Wacol."

"Now we have something large and metallic to put in the garage."

Sue beams. "How good is that?"

Kermit features skin-peeling, sun faded brown vinyl seats with more springs than upholstery and a scratchy AM radio. At top speed, they cannot outrun a dairy cow but trundle along on about a shot glass of fuel.

Toombul Shopping Centre is new and exciting. With their trolley full of ingredients for meals to come they wander and soon find a record player and sound system.

Being on a tight budget of zero dollars, they opt to hire a black and white television set. Delivered the same day it stands in pride of place in their lounge, with rabbit ears aerial.

The freedom Kermit offers helps cement a firm friendship with Art and his wife Kim.

Kim is in her mid twenties, cute with fair skin and long brown hair, which she often keeps in a pony tail. She likes wearing loose, flowing dresses in subdued greens and browns with light-weight scarves and metal bangles on her arms. Her voice is high and quick, and when she speaks, she emphasises with her hands.

They are easy people to like and have a new baby for Sue to cuddle. Their home is what once had been a lovely example of a Queenslander, now run down. Their house is perched up on timber stumps with a wide verandah that once went all the way around, but filled in over the years to create additional rooms and living space. Half of the exterior is in need of a coat of paint. The other half is covered by creeping jasmine so you cannot tell whether it needs painting or not. Bougainvillea holds up the front fence and at the side, a rusty, lopsided Hills hoist looks like a giant umbrella frame.

Inside the ceilings are covered in brown stains, the tell-tale signs of a leaking roof. To top it off, many of the old floorboards have sprung.

"We don't own it, Mate. Just rent it cheap from a bloke up the road. I've just put a deposit on a big corner block out at Ashmore, haven't I, Love?"

Kim smiles broadly. "It's a lovely block. Cost $4,000, didn't it Art?"

"Wow! $4,000 for your land," Roger whistles, "that's a bit rich for our tastes I'm afraid."

"With good commissions we'll soon hopscotch through the minefield," Art laughs, "I'll have it paid off in no time. $800 I put down on it."

"Will you have more children?" Kim asks Sue sweetly.

"I wanted to, I wanted lots of children but after the difficult time I had with these two, I've gone off the idea."

"Difficult?"

"Jayne was a forceps birth, James was induced with labour of more than twelve hours. And when he was about to come out they had to push him back in and get instruments because I wasn't wide enough."

"However big was he?"

"Ten pounds, but it felt like he came out sideways."

"Oh, you poor thing."

Roger has gone a paler shade of grey.

"Poor Sue, it's at moments like those, that my testicles retreat up under my ribcage."

"As for our run-down Queenslander home," Art continues trying to change the subject, "it's huge! With space enough to shelter a fertile catholic family without seeming crowded."

Roger involuntarily crosses his legs.

Embarrassed he says, "Sue was in labour longer than Harold Wilson."

"Who's Harold Wilson?" Kim asks.

"An unpopular labour party prime minister back in the old country, in the 1960s."

Sue smiles at Roger. She arches a heavenly eyebrow as she asks Kim, "Did you cutback on the wine during pregnancy?"

"Heavens no," Kim giggles. She presses Art's arm, "I didn't want to have to do him sober."

"Wasn't the only thing that entered her, the Holy spirit," Art grins sheepishly.

"I wonder at times what Kim sees in you, Art," Roger simpers.

"Being a bloke, it'd be weird if you did see it, Mate. But at times like this I'm convinced."

"Convinced of what?"

"She carries my balls in her handbag."

"Thanks," Kim responds, "At times I'd rather be in a phone box with an amorous octopus."

"The angle of the dangle equals the throb of the knob," quotes Art piously.

"He's as free from brains as a frog is from feathers," counters Kim.

Art's retort. "Sex is like air. It's not that important unless you aren't getting any."

Chapter 12

GREAT EXPECTATIONS

"Well, Brisbane doesn't have any sites of major historical interest. Mozart never visited," Art says with a chuckle, "there's nowhere you can stand and reminisce about wars and revolutions, decapitation of kings, torture of heretics, and stuff."

"Not a bad thing really then," Sue ponders. "We've left a country of strange names. Prisons like Wormwood Scrubs, Strangeways, and Parkhurst. In the county of Sussex there's Devil's Dyke."

"Ah, but we have even stranger names," counters Art. "Such as Yeerongpilly, Enoggera, Caloundra, Bli Bli, Goondiwindi, Wagga Wagga. How's about that?"

"Makes us feel quite homely," laughs Sue.

Roger is caught mid mouthful of beer and almost snorts it out his nose.

"Charming," admonishes Sue handing him a hanky.

The next afternoon after the week's figures are released Art is brimful of good news.

"We've both beaten our sales budgets for the week," he explains to Roger. "You know what this means?"

"We're employed for another week?"

"Yes, but more than that. Cash in your skyrocket."

"Cash in my what?"

"We've been paid, Mate. We've cash in our pockets. How's about celebratory drinks on the way home?"

On their way to the pub Roger points to a vehicle towing two trailers, "Look at the size of that lorry."

"Where?" Art asks, gazing hopelessly skywards.

"In front of yer, Art."

Art laughs. "I think that highlights a few differences in our vernaculars, Mate. When you said lorry I'm thinking that's short for lorikeet. A bird."

"It's amazing how we speak the same language but need translations."

"Like when someone comes up from Sydney, Mate. A tinny goes from a can of beer to a flamin' boat and a Gregory's becomes a Referdex."

As they stroll, they chat, and further agree on differences. "Your sweets are our lollies or ice blocks."

"*Durex* or French letters in England are condoms."

"We drive on the same side of the road here, the left, but remember that you always give way to the right."

"Go figure that," laughs Roger. "I'll bet the insurance companies enjoy fighting over that."

"You're not wrong, Mate. It's like watching two people fighting over a stapler."

Art slows and becomes more serious. "We're becoming somewhat yankified here. Suppose it could be worse. Better the yanks than the Japanese."

"In what way?"

"Every fuckin' way; street signs, stop signs. Everybody's a 'guy' even the girls are 'guys.' Their Amtrak is our Austrak, it's like being scalped by Yankee Apaches, enough to get a bloke down."

"I must admit I've never liked 'Hi' as a greeting, I do prefer the more English 'Hello.'"

"That's easy, Mate. In Oz we use 'G'day' remember your Down Under now!"

"G'day Down Under, it is. I like it."

"We'll get just pissed enough to handle that arduous walk up the hill to the station" Art announces, and then breaking into Roger's thoughts, he stops at the pub's entrance door, his hand on Roger's arm.

"I feel the need to brief you, Mate. Before going in."

"Brief me?"

"Yeah," Art looks embarrassed, "try not to sound too English, Mate."

"How come?" Roger asks, with a look of bemused astonishment. "What's that got to do with the price of fish?"

Art lowers his voice, it sounds tight and thin, "I'm serious, Mate. You're so Kensington Gardens and Aussie blokes are Wannabulu. A lot of Aussies are still upset about Gallipoli."

That takes a moment to register with Roger.

"Fuck me, Art. That was during the First World War in 1915." Roger starts counting on his fingers, "About fifty-five years ago."

"Still, I don't want any of the pub blokes going crook on yer."

"Why should they go crook on me? I didn't orchestrate Gallipoli! Shit! I wasn't even born back then. Christ, they should go crook on Churchill it was his mad brain idea."

"No, I know. But you're a Pom."

"A lot of British and Americans aren't too fucking rapt in the imbecility of Gallipoli. It's right up there with Lord Cardigan's charge of the Light Brigade."

"Poms have a reputation," Art continues, but he looks pained.

"What sort of reputations?"

"Being as dry as a Pommy's bath towel," Art grins and calls over his shoulder. "We say Poms smell that bad so that blind Aussies can hate them," as he almost runs through the pub door.

Inside Roger observes the bar staff and customers look friendly and smiley.

A good start, he thinks.

"Everyone's as happy as Larry," Art gushes. He's on them like a praying mantis. "**EVERYONE,** I want you to meet me mate, Roger."

Roger beams his Cheshire cat grin. "As a recent migrant to your shores I'm being made to feel most welcome, thank you."

Art gives Roger a reproachful stare. He leans in, "Just a simple fuckin' 'thanks, Art,' would have done, Mate. Fuck you do sound too English."

A tall, heavy set man called Shorty, who has deep sweat circles in the armpits of his collared shirt and his shoes glazed with a fine layer of dust from the boondocks, asks, "Do you miss home, Mate?"

"I am home," Roger replies with an easy smile.

"Good answer, Mate. Wanna beer?"

"No good story can be told without a full glass," Roger replies wiping the sweat from his brow. "Thanks, Shorty."

A well endowed smiling barmaid in a low cut frock helps the boys ask for another round and another, as they repeatedly approach the bar and wish that she would just lean over that little bit more.

Shorty laughs. He appears to be delighted. He winks at Art, "You've got a good one 'ere. Better show him the ropes."

"This 'ere's a 7oz glass, but we'll step it up a bit, Roger. Middies? Schooners? Do you like our Fourex?"

"It's excellent beer," Roger acknowledges quickly making his way to the bottom of his pitifully small glass of full flavoured, icy cold brew.

"We'll make an Aussie of you, yet," Art downs his first and quickly orders another round. "Good people are hard to find, and bad bastards aren't worth looking for."

Shorty laughs. "D'ya know what we say to bad bastards, Roger?"

Roger shakes his head, thinking his response might be a little too old country.

"I hope all your chooks grow into Emus and kick your fuckin' fowl house down!"

Everyone laughs, the barmaid the loudest.

Art is keen to promote Oz to Rog' in front of his mates.

"We're the best in the world at all the sports that count, Rog', like cricket, netball, rugby, AFL, swimming, roo-shooting, two-up and horse racing."

"Horse racing. The sport of Kings," quotes Roger, "or more accurately to some, quadrupeds circumnavigating a 360 degree strip of verdant vegetation."

Grinning Shorty continues, "We also have the biggest rock, the tastiest pies, the best looking Sheilas, and the worst dressed Olympians in the Universe."

"I'm loving it," Roger says in one quick rush of noise.

"We shoot, we root, we vote and we want to be pissed by lunchtime," Art continues.

By the eighth round of drinks, Roger is on the decline, but feels obliged to accept the next glass as it is his shout.

"How's our Aussie beer compare with that English beer now?" asks Art.

"I think," Roger burps, "that Aussie beer is pretty damned good. And stronger than English. It's also chilled, which is unusual in the old country."

"We drink cold beer because our summers are hot, mate," Shorty explains.

"How hot?" Roger asks.

"About as hot as a snake's arse in a wagon rut," Shorty says deadpan.

Roger meets his rheumy eyes with his own blank stare.

Art offers additional assistance. "Put another way Rog', it's when it's so hot the crows fly backwards to keep the dust out of their eyes."

After the raucous laughter subsides, Roger notices that his tie is the only one not loosened or undone.

"How yer goin' Mate?" someone else asks.

Roger appears somewhat surprised and pauses to focus.

Art answers for him, "He's goin' alright, he's just having a bit of a bludge between rounds."

"Fancy something to eat, Rog'?" someone else asks, "How's about a rat coffin?"

Art explains, again, "He means do you want a meat pie? Same as bush oysters are animal testicles."

"He was a bold man who first ate an oyster," Roger hiccups. "But we could go another beer. My shout."

"It's fact that in the 19th Century oysters were a staple food of the poor, now they're a prized delicacy," Roger offers, to anyone interested. None are.

"He needs another beer like he needs a hole in the head," Shorty declares. "But at least he's not another bloody I-tie."

"Pull yer head in," Art pleads, "he's a good bloke."

Another True Blue coughs, agrees, and offers his cigarettes around. Art takes one.

Roger declines. "No. Sorry. I don't smoke. Given it up."

"Smart man," Shorty says. "We're different this side of the rabbit proof fence. Some are brighter than others."

"What about the bush-tucker I've heard about?" Roger asks.

"Living off the land doesn't necessarily mean eating road kill, Mate, but if you must, you must. Just beware it isn't rotten. Crows picking at a carcass of a kangaroo that's just kissed the bumper of a truck the night before might be best left alone."

Art groans. "You can survive on bush-tucker if you're hungry enough. But it tastes like shit."

"Like eating a rag doll's arse through a wire mattress," Shorty offers.

"We're looking forward to having a BBQ," Roger says.

"Good idea. Just remember, Rog, Mate, sheilas don't do BBQs. Sheilas do the preparation, Mate. We blokes just bugger the food. If you get confused just remember like the cocky on the biscuit tin lid, you're not in it."

Roger feels the need to make a short speech. "As I'm surrounded by the knowers of so much good stuff maybe the *Beatles* were right after all."

"How come?" Shorty asks.

Roger smiles, *"Love is all you need."*

Shorty downs his last beer. "I'll be off now, mates. I'm as full as a State School. By the time I reach home and the little woman, I'll be ready to eat the crutch out of a low flying duck."

Art looks at Roger. "Last one."

On the way to the Ann Street railway station Roger notices a sign. "Look, Art."

"What, Mate? Not another bloody lorry?"

"No. Look in the window at that seafood shop."

"Yes. I got it, so what?"

"They have fresh sand crabs for sale!"

"Yes, and according to their sign they're on special, Mate. Nothing unusual about that."

"They look nothing like Cromer crabs, Art. I'm going to get one."

"Don't get too reckless. Don't eat your one whole crab all at once," Art jokes as he departs to catch his train west. "By the way, we buy them more than one at a time," he calls back pointing out Roger is a real twat.

Rapt in his new found food delight, Roger is oblivious to Sue waiting impatiently at Wooloowin station, and now he is somewhat later than intended having failed to phone home before leaving work.

Sue who is stood watching train after train come and go, decides either Roger is selling a room full of products, lying bleeding to death in a gutter, or having a drink with work mates. Any of which she is less than impressed that he has not picked up the phone to tell her. Finally with the children getting bored and unruly, she trundles home.

Roger arrives to the flat still in the euphoria of his after work libations

He furnishes his peace offering with great enthusiasm, which goes only a small way to lighten Sue's mood.

Standing at the kitchen sink, Roger dissects the crab slowly, methodically as though defusing a bomb.

"It looks alright," he says, after discarding the lungs, or dead man's flesh.

"The meat's firm and white, and smells fresh," Sue reasons in a conciliatory fashion.

With some trepidation, Roger tastes a small piece. He grins with pleasure. "Sue, it's sweet and delicious."

They share the one crab, and Sue gives Jayne a small taste.

"I have only one regret, Sue."

"What?"

"I realise I'm not the brightest bulb in the chandelier but even Art said I should have bought more crabs."

Sue nods and then indulges in a disciplined sip of wine. "Maybe tomorrow then, but a little earlier, please."

Chapter 13

EUREKA!

"You know I've never complained about your weekly visit to the pub after work with Art, Shorty and the boys," Sue is staring at the carpet as if searching for lost valuables.

"I know you haven't, you've even waited patiently at the station for me."

"Yes, and with the children."

His thoughts like confetti, Roger sighs his deepest sigh. His lungs deflating like two balloons. "I realise that's not fair on you and our children."

Sue continues a little unsure, "In England we always did everything together," she pauses as though about to walk on thin ice, "but you never were much of a pub person, were you?"

"No, I wasn't. Working in hotels beat that out of me. But it's different here and the boys seem to like the pub. From what little I've seen the majority of Aussie drinking holes are unlike the English pubs."

"Different? How?"

"Well, women are not always as welcome in bars," Roger replies, "it's just different."

Sue raises a shapely eyebrow.

"Why not suggest a change in thinking to Art and Shorty, then?"

"Such as what?"

"Like how's about we all drink at their places, or ours, where us girls can join in the fun. What's Shorty like?"

"Shorty's a big man. Art says he could hold a bull out to piss."

Sue chuckles, Roger nods, "I see your point, you're missing out on adult fun, I understand, leave it with me," Roger gives Sue a reassuring hug. Her head rests on his shoulder, the fragrance of her freshly shampooed hair fills his nostrils, and her heartbeat radiates through his chest. The emotion of the moment takes hold and they kiss hard, that in turn leads to something more.

Next day when Roger approaches Art, he agrees wholeheartedly.

"I'll let Shorty know, Mate. Good idea. Kim will jump at the chance; a pub's no place for a newborn."

Roger realises he does not know much about Shorty, and if they are inviting him into their home, he should find out something about him.

"Where does Shorty work?"

"Shorty's job is high wire work, Mate. He works long hours in construction selling concreting products. His wife, Judy does shift work at a supermarket."

"Any children?"

"No kids, not yet," Art replies. "I think they're trying though."

At their next gathering, Sue and Kim are deep in discussion.

"I've been dying to ask how you two met?" Sue asks.

"Actually, it was on a golf course," Kim replies. She looks sheepishly at Art, "Wasn't it, Art?"

"Yeah," Art grins. "She was following up and she sliced her ball really hard and it hit me."

Kim explains, "I was horrified. He doubled up in the foetal position. I thought, my God, what on earth have I done to him?"

"What did you do?" Roger asks.

"Well, being a nurse I knew a bit about pain relief and so I told him to straighten his legs, breath slowly and deeply and then I asked him if I could massage the area. He nodded through his pain and so I undid his trousers, slipped my hand down around his tummy and started massaging his groin and his balls. Very, gently of course.

After a while I asked him if he was feeling better?"

Roger looks at Art who is smiling broadly. "What did he say?"

"Well, nothing at first. Then he said he did feel better. But…"

Kim laughs and then looks at Art with an expression that could melt titanium, "Go on, tell them what you said. *You bastard.*"

Art's coy, "My thumb still hurts!"

"And that was that. We became a bloody item," Kim sighs, "he was on me like a moth to a flame flexing every muscle he had."

"Yes, all three muscles, actually," Art agrees enthusiastically. "Then we cried, and went back to holding hands, didn't we, Love?"

"That's better than our story," Sue says. "I met Roger at *The Wire Mill Club* in East Grinstead, and he asked me out on a date."

"What happened?" Kim asks.

"The *bastard* stood me up," Sue replies.

"Stood you up!" Kim shouts in an overly dramatic way.

"*Bloody stood me up.* No-one had ever done that before. I was so angry I tracked him down at the hotel where he worked with his Dad."

"What happened?"

"Well," Sue's thoughtful, "he shouted me dinner and we had a few wines, and we talked a lot. He explained why he'd stood me up."

"Why?"

"I forgot," Roger says, looking a bit sheepish.

"**Bloody forgot!**" shrieks Kim. "Did you believe him?"

"Not at first, but then after I'd stayed the night I sort of gave him the benefit of the doubt."

"What happened then?" Art asks.

"Well, I never really went home."

"Phew," Art says. "We make for an interesting group, don't we?"

"Be interesting if Shorty and Judy can top that."

After a few more drinks with Art and Kim, they leave.

Next day, Sue goes shopping with Roger in tow.

Shopping expeditions for Roger are born out of necessity, which he thoroughly detests. He used to tell his sister how he'd rather shove his head into a bucket of cold vomit than go shopping!

He knows that he had better shape up for Sue's sake.

The shoe industry needs her! Spend, spend, spend up! Sue is determined not to leave the shops empty handed, as that is a sure sign of madness in her book!

"I just can't get over their wide range of fresh foods," gushes an excited Sue. "Just stand out the front of any butcher's shop. Admire their pork, lamb, beef, and all their cuts of meat, and we can afford to eat it all, Roger."

"Maybe not all at once, Love."

Weight conversions give Sue pause as she is used to pounds and ounces.

"I either buy half of what I really want, or twice as much, but as we can afford double, anyway, it doesn't really matter. Does it?"

Roger is getting rapt in Sue's enthusiasm. "Seafood shops here sell prawns from only about 50c per kilogram and the man said that's most of the year round."

With dazzled eyes Sue ads excitedly, "And fresh sand crabs at 50c each."

Suddenly summer leaves and the sky becomes the colour of steel. Not a threat, rather a reminder that winter is approaching; or what passes for winter in Brissie.

At a visit to their local bayside suburb of Redcliffe, Jayne and James enjoy playing in the coarse orange sand, and splashing about in the safe shallow water.

"Can it get better than this, Sue?" Roger asks.

"It's winter, and we're on a beach with the children splashing about in the water, it's incredible isn't it?"

"Certainly is. A millionaire's view as far as Moreton Island in the distance and even the seagulls are friendly."

They are approached by a middle aged Australian, who is balding and without a hat.

Hatless asks, "Where you people from?"

Sue and Roger look blank.

"Well, you're either from Victoria or you're Poms! Bloody Poms!"

"Doesn't sound as if you like Poms," Roger answers cautiously.

"I'm not overly struck, no!"

"Well, you're right," Roger simpers, and then with a furtive glance at Sue, "we are Poms."

Hatless shrugs. "One thing's for sure, being as this is our winter, next year you'll think differently, I'll wager that, Mate. See ya, 'ave a good one."

On the way home Roger keeps telling himself he is not at all concerned about being a Pommy in Oz. Not at all.

Sue is not, she is ecstatic at being in Oz, and happy to tell anyone who will listen to her.

Back at Casa Del Wooloowin, a letter from Gran has arrived.

Roger reads it out to Sue while she is busy rattling around in the kitchen;

"Gran says, 'The Nazi party may be gone but their regime is alive and well and definitely kicking in Zelda.' I'm aghast," Roger exclaims, waving the letter about.

"What? You know Zelda was always sympathetic to the Nazis."

"No not that. I know she admired Adolf; probably wanted to have his babies."

"Well what then?"

"About Dad not repaying his parents the money he owed them."

Roger had hoped his Dad would have done the right thing by Gran and Gramps after the closure of the hotel businesses and repaid them their life savings. He promised Roger that he would do that.

Sue placed her hand tenderly on Roger's arm.

"No doubt about it. But it's time now to blow away the old thoughts like dead leaves in a storm."

"Dad can eat crow until he spits out the feathers and chokes on the beak."

Sue's fatigued frown softens. "He had few graces. But to move on, we must forgive."

"Alright, I'll try." Roger smiles weakly, reluctant to let go of his father's lies just yet.

Sue seeing this becoming a storm in a teacup changes subjects.

"The house in the old country remains unsold."

"Our home, such as it is, remains in tea chests and boxes that'll soon arrive, and I want us to buy a house."

"An old Queenslander?" Sue brightens at the idea of a home with verandahs all around.

"No. I want a new house. Doesn't matter if it's small, and in timber not brick — but new."

Memories of the house Art and Kim live in are swamping his thoughts.

Sue smiles, and raises her glass, "To Maison Nouvelle, as the French would say," and they clink glasses.

Next morning while Art quickly scans the situations vacant over morning coffee for better jobs, he has a question.

"Didn't you say that back home you worked with some mob in pest control?"

Roger is taken back that Art has remembered, let alone mentioned it. "That's right, I did."

"There's an ad you might have missed," Art smiles impishly, "just thought you might want to know. Pests Erased are wanting a typist in the girls section. Kim might fit, I'm sure you won't," he sounds enthusiastic.

"I've never liked pests," Roger confesses, "sort of hoped I'd fall into something better."

"Mate," Art emphasises, "you know pest control, don't you?"

"Sort of."

"Better to specialise then, Mate. Should pay better than this crap peddling typewriters door to door, and they might give you a company car."

"If I'm in sales or management, then I don't have a lot of day to day contact with pests. Frankly big spiders and rodents frighten the shit out of me."

"So what? The thought of dropping a fucking typewriter on my foot worries the hell out of me!"

"Alright. Should I write a formal letter of application?"

"They're not advertising for a bloke, Mate. No. Just ring 'em up. If they're interested they'll offer you a job for sure!"

Roger prepares to prime himself full of bullshit and make the call.

The switchboard operator puts him straight through to the man in charge; The big cheese, Mr Jack Woodley, their Director.

Roger politely summarises his introduction.

Listening carefully and asking a few leading questions, Mr Woodley has a stellar suggestion.

"Why not come and meet me for lunch tomorrow," Jack suggests, "we can have a quiet chat away from the office."

Jack Woodley is a long-standing director. Himself an ex-pommy, he proves personable and knowledgeable of the industry. He is medium height, trim, with a pale complexion, and appears to be in his fifties. A pair of reading glasses, which he keeps putting on and taking off, gives him a professional air. Not surprisingly, he is keen to talk about Roger's knowledge of pests.

By the time their steaks hit the table, Roger has sifted through his memory warehouse and searched out most of the information he needs to try to sound knowledgeable. He discusses his initial field training and subsequent employment in the UK. His knowledge about the control of public health pests, rodents, cockroaches, and feral birds sounds impressive, even to himself.

Jack seems impressed.

After a careful quizzing of Roger's background, Jack grows silent.

Roger is uneasy, he thinks he has blown it.

"How do you feel about making cold calls, Roger?" Jack asks.

Roger smiles his most relaxed smile. "Absolutely no problem at all."

Jack's frown deepens. "I've found the majority of Australians don't like making cold calls."

"Well, I'm certainly used to doing cold calls."

Jack is thoughtful.

"I'll make room for another Technical Sales Consultant in Brisbane. How does $5,000 per annum to start, plus commission on sales, and a company car sound?"

The suddenness of the offer takes Roger back.

"Thank you very much, Sir, I accept."

After they shake hands, Jack rubs his hands together. "Thank Christ," he beams at Roger, "Now I won't have to explain about how *Warfarin* works to a new recruit."

Warfarin is an anti-coagulant; stops blood from congealing, and as such it proves to be a popular ingredient in pest control rodent baits because it has an anti-dote namely vitamin K.

Chapter 14

CRICKETS

Roger takes a deep breath. He feels that if he lets his mind catch up, he will crumple in a heap as everything is moving so fast.

Reality pops like a fuse, this is his first day at his new job.

Standing at the reception desk is a lady slender and refined with carefully groomed short, brown hair and colourful round glasses fronting her face. Her name is Lucy. She smiles revealing two rows of bright, even teeth. Teeth so straight and white they could have been dentures.

"You're Roger!" Lucy declares it so forcefully, and with such conviction, that even if he were not Roger, he would have been compelled to agree.

Jack appears from nowhere to greet Roger with the firmest of handshakes.

"As Roger lives north side and is new to Brissie, I've decided, Lucy, he'll be our north side consultant."

The other consultant, who is about the same age as Roger, squints slightly through narrowed eyes. Not boss-eyed Roger notes but quickly forgotten as he is quick to shake Roger's hand enthusiastically.

"Hello, I'm Percival but everyone calls me Tweedy," he says in a well-rounded voice, reminiscent of a bishop or Shakespearean actor.

"Tweedy?" Roger queries.

"I have a penchant for wearing tweed jackets," his smile is tacked on, "but I'm not overly of my given name, not even the shortened version."

As if to clarify, Tweedy points out his tweed jacket anchored on the back of his chair.

Roger notices it is of venerable vintage with artistic worn, leather patches on the elbows.

"Until he goes out on a sales call," Lucy smiles sweetly, "and then it remains screwed up in his car, doesn't it, T-w-e-e-d-y?"

Tweedy's wrinkled corduroys had long ago lost their crease matching his faded, checked shirt, the collar of which appears slightly frayed and crowned with a carelessly knotted, woollen tie. Strong jawed with a long face and a humorous chin, Tweedy is clean-shaven, topped by an untidy mop of thin, dark brown hair. Habitually, he rearranges his comb-over from out of his eyes, which results in it fluttering about his head like the tattered pennants of some failed crusade.

Tweedy's aristocratic English accent matches his blue blood Victorian manners, which unknown to Roger, are born into a place where old money and new dollars easily commingle.

For Tweedy that money is now long gone. He dreams of leaving the pest control business and breeding exotic birds. Much on a par with Roger's quest for Seal Flipper Pie.

"Delighted to have you on board, Roger. Looking after all of Brisbane has been a big ask for me," Tweedy explains with a pained look. "Now I can breathe as I'm south side."

"Tweedy's always running late," Lucy explains. "He's also an excellent bullshit artist, aren't you, Tweedy?"

"All part of essential sales, dear Lucy." Then with a furtive glance at Jack, "I'll catch up with my calls, sooner rather than later."

Lucy holds out a fistful of messages for Tweedy written on telephone call back slips.

Jack's frown deepens. "Anything in there that's north side, better give to Roger."

"Twenty call backs," Lucy's jaw is set so square she looks thoroughly pissed off as she separates the calls, whittling Tweedy's down to six.

"Lucy, you're an absolute treasure," Tweedy simpers, dancing around like bare feet on sizzling coals.

Jack heads for the adjoining small front room that is his office. As he does so, he barks an instruction at Tweedy, "Please teach Roger everything you know," Jack pauses, "that is that he might find useful." Jack is hovering as if unsure. He is thoughtful for another moment, "And then afterwards we'll meet for coffee in my office, at say," he studies his wristwatch, "10am. Alright?"

Roger looks at his own wristwatch. It is already 9:45am.

"Will do, Jack," Tweedy responds sheepishly.

Lucy is smiling at Tweedy the way people do when they are pretending to like someone.

The Service Supervisor is an instinctive, clever man nick-named 'Scottie'. He is blessed with the style of broad accent that most people from south of the border, including south of the Equator, not merely Hadrian's Wall, have major difficulties understanding. Fair to say most have to concentrate hard to understand whatever Scottie is saying.

Maybe people like him should come with sub-titles, thinks Roger.

"Aye, as an established player of some years in Brisbane, I cannae give a tinker's cuss for the Blue Blood Brigade Mate, nor anyone else for that matter."

Scottie is built like a keg of beer sitting on top of two tiny legs that look like toothpicks tending to limp. He is a cantankerous, hard-working man, his face the colour of beetroot dip is lived in with sad eyes and a wicked sense of humour.

There is a whole lot going on behind those eyes, Roger thinks.

"Good to have you on board, Matey," Scottie beams, and his brusque hearty tone implies that he means it. "Ignore my hirple."

"Hirple?"

"Aye, that's hobble to Sassenachs."

Roger meets the rest of the staff. A few are from the Old Country with a mixture of broad accents while others are True Blue Aussies.

"Jack's principal focus of the moment is on service operators, sales and administration," Tweedy explains. He squints intently at Roger, "Trouble is they're not within a bull's roar of each other."

"Much the same as—Harold Holt," Lucy adds, flashing her immaculately lacquered fingernails.

The days of Roger's first week blur into one, as do the weeks, he soon falls into rhythm.

The only downside Roger can see is working from dilapidated premises so close to the river.

Roger tells Sue, "All their equipment is old but as it keeps getting wet through constant flooding whenever it rains heavily, why buy new?"

Drab green filing cabinets are leaning against walls damp with mould. Timber desks are swelled with moisture. Time and again staff, who live close by, are summoned as the flood waters rise around them to

143

pass typewriters, files, and furniture out through doorways to higher ground."

An afternoon storm called the '3 o'clock special' rolls in. After a scorching merciless hot day, this daily respite becomes an Earth ending storm.

Hail balls the size of oranges; wind that threatens to blow everyone off the map; rain that is blasting skin off exposed body parts; clouds such a dark green and black it looks like something from hell.

Next day Tweedy explains, "When we're not moving stuff above high water level or hunting something to kill and getting paid for it, we have lots of meetings."

Jack joins the conversation, "We co-ordinate sales with service, and service with sales, and then I write glowing reports with Lucy's assistance to the Snake Pit, I mean Head Office, about it all. There, men in suits high above your pay bracket and mine, sit in judgment on us all. Lean as gnawed bones and cold as axe heads, not one iota of humour or happiness, they are the perfect caricature of corporate men who read reports and missives from the outposts then criticise them before returning their appropriate memo comments; a cartoon of vultures in human form waiting for the next body to drop."

"They're so tight even Peter Pan couldn't make the A-grade," Lucy complains.

"Fucktards and Stupid-visors most of them," Tweedy adds, not to be outdone.

Roger's south side sales colleague, is elected to conduct the next meeting in the absence of Jack who is at home, so as not to be disturbed, busy writing reports about reports.

Suits in the Snake Pit and most clients like the way Tweedy conducts himself and his great command of the English language, however it works against him with the rank and file of service operators, and down to earth union orientated clients think he is a pompous prick with a stick shoved fair up his arse. Service operators are busy demonstrating their extreme contempt of Tweedy's efforts and management skills, in a number of ways.

By contrast, Roger is making a supreme effort to lose his English private school accent, emphasising Aussie speech wherever possible.

Scottie on the other hand wanted to believe that Glasgow had become the cultural city of Europe.

After Tweedy has eventually lured the last operator out of the toilet, another off the telephone to his wife, and pacified yet another with an instant coffee they are about to commence their meeting. Issue now is one has a coffee — they all want coffee, just to really piss Tweedy off.

After everyone else has a coffee in their hand, and has lit up another smoke, the room starts feeling like a gas chamber.

Tweedy rolls his eyes and commences. He reiterates directions about how to fill out paperwork correctly.

Reactions are vocal:

"Yeah, right. And why bother?"

"That's right, no-one reads what we write, anyway."

Finally the meeting arrives at the area of servicing questions and difficulties.

Scottie juggles between the over-riding authoritarian requirements of management and getting the foot soldiers, his field operators, to perform their daily tasks capably.

Today in contrast to his sage green uniform and unpolished, black boots, he is wearing bright orange socks. A colourful change from the one red and one bright green worn yesterday.

Scottie refuses to wear any belt to complement his trousers. When criticised for his appearance by Jack, which is a daily event, Scottie says, "Nay, Matey, I'm too busy working, making money for the company, to concern mahself with trifles like that."

It is his way of making a point, the same as his intense dislike of all religions, which he considers total shite. His reasoning; "Going to church doesn't make you a Christian anymore than standing in a garage makes you a car."

Standing at the front of the room, with the Operations Manual and a face mask clasped tightly in hand, Scottie begins the bones of the meeting with Tweedy by his side.

"Purpose of this meeting, mates, is to pave the way for the introduction of gasses in place of Foggin' Machines. Any questions?"

Crickets.

Sitting proudly at their feet Roger observes the grimy, misused, neglected Fogging machine. Roger is not impressed with fogging machines. They are popular with some because when they work they look and sound impressive. While the insecticide carried within the smoke is effective against small flying insects on the wing, the chemical is only deposited when it settles on horizontal surfaces. Roger remains quiet, with his arms crossed over his chest.

Scottie gives a crooked smile as Tweedy pipes up.

"There are two particular gasses of interest to us," adds Tweedy, "and shortly both will be in our armoury for sale by Roger and myself; Pyrethrins and Dichlorvos."

"Aye, righto then back to these 'ere foggin' machines," Scottie continues waving his gas mask in the air, cutting Tweedy a little short, "they're so simple even you blokes can operate them, and they're 'ere until we get the new gas applicators."

Tweedy undeterred by Scottie cuts in, "Yes. Essentially it's a two-stroke motor with an exhaust pipe."

Scottie glares at Tweedy, "That's right provided there's fuel, and a spark..."

Tweedy not to be outdone cuts Scottie off, "And insecticide in the tank, because then there should be fog. Any questions?" Tweedy puffs out his chest confident in his little win.

Crickets.

Scottie turns slightly away from his audience to face Tweedy. The gloves are now off.

"You know all about these 'ere machines, Matey. and you know how to start one up, don't you?"

Stammering slightly at Scottie's aggressive stance Tweedy blurts, "Yes. Of course I do, old chap doesn't everyone here?"

Unable to meet the intensity of Scottie's gaze Tweedy focuses his squint on the back wall.

Scottie moves aside with a theatrical flourish of his hands as if announcing Royalty and allows Tweedy centre stage.

Tweedy narrows his eyes ready for combat at Scottie's audacity. He slowly and deliberately straightens his bird's nest of a tie.

"First we start the motor," Tweedy explains. "The exhaust pipe soon becomes incredibly hot. Insecticide contained in a light oil base, flows in controlled quantities from the reservoir here," Tweedy points at the tank, "onto the hot exhaust pipe here." Into his stride Tweedy's eyelids begin fluttering, "the oil burns and creates much smoke, which carries the encapsulated insecticide wherever the smoke goes. Simple."

Scottie is unimpressed with Tweedy so far, so he butts in. "Well, aye, that's the theory."

Tweedy continues, "Noisy and visually exciting with lots of billowing smoke their use is often referred to, incorrectly, as a *fumigation*, which impresses many uninformed clients."

Scottie has moved further out of centre stage and is leaning on the table. "There are a number of disadvantages foggin' machines 'ave over gas."

Tweedy beams, "Yes, of course. Not the least being that before fogging machines are used, someone has to remember to notify the local Fire Brigade. That's unnecessary when we use gasses. Can anyone tell me why?"

A voice from the back of the room pipes up, "It's not good if someone mistakes the fog smoke for fire."

"Yes," reinforces Tweedy a little too excitedly, "but can anyone here tell me why it's unnecessary to call the fire brigade with the new gasses?"

Crickets.

Roger offers an answer, "There's no fog or smoke, with the gas products."

A murmur of appreciation echoes around the room.

"Exactly," praises Tweedy, "if a neighbour's attracted by the noise and smoke from a building, it might be justification to call the Fire Brigade? Should the Fire Brigade not be notified of the use of a 'fogging' machine at that address on that day, they're likely to attend expecting the worse."

Scottie chuckling chimes in, "Aye, many a surprised looking operator has had the harmony of his day disrupted by firemen gaining access with big fuck-off Boris style axes."

"Exactly," hammers Tweedy. He squints about the room and detects a few nodding heads as encouragement.

"Usually capped by a bill from the Fire Brigade; accompanied by a claim from the client's solicitor for repairing damaged premises, caused by focused firemen wielding large, heavy, sharp, fuck off axes.

"Care to make any comment, Roger?" Scottie asks.

"In my opinion, the old fogging machines were never greatly effective. Expensive to buy and even when used correctly are prone to putting a coating of unburned oil on horizontal surfaces. This creates additional post-drama mess, and often a claim from the client for cleaning.

The low concentration of insecticide also makes a good target kill unlikely because of the smoke being unpressurised. There is no penetration into 'cracks and crevices.' Fogging is nowhere near as efficient as the use of gas, or more specialised treatment."

Tweedy claps his hands asserting an air of authority. "There. Well put, and quite simple. As with most two-stroke motors, it's guaranteed any fool can start it."

Scottie now standing near the table goads Tweedy. "Go ahead show 'em, Matey."

"Well, yes, of course. You just press the starter, like this," says Tweedy absently.

Confidently he reaches out and presses the starter switch firmly.

He looks genuinely surprised.

"Oh—well," says Tweedy slowly, scratching at his head in nervous wonderment, "It should start. Damned thing."

Scottie's dead pan face never alters. The only give away under close scrutiny are his eyes. No longer sad, now they are dancing.

Crickets.

An attentive operator joins in. "Perhaps, you should turn it on first."

"Eureka! So true," exclaims Tweedy, "silly me. Of course," he slaps his forehead with the palm of his hand, "there's an isolator switch behind the handle."

"Let me help, you," offers Scottie without even having to look for it. "There you go," he offers enticing the demonstration to continue.

Tweedy reaches out. He presses the red starter switch even more firmly this time.

Crickets.

"Well," says Scottie, "There's a bother, now. Perhaps there's nae fuel."

"It should still turn over though," another operator chimes in. One operator decides to become involved. He unscrews the main fuel cap and inspects the contents of the fuel tank and, "There appears to be, plenty of fuel."

"Is the fuel turned on?" offers another operator.

The Three Amigos peer to look, and yes the turnkey in the fuel line under the tank, is definitely in the horizontal—off position.

"There you go, Lad," offers Scottie again, as he deftly turns the knob vertical allowing fuel to flow freely from the fuel tank. "Try her again, Matey, now the fuel's on."

Tweedy reaches out, a little more reluctant this time, and firmly presses the starter switch.

Crickets.

"Perhaps this machine is faulty," Tweedy blusters. "It's no good trying to start a faulty machine, if it should have gone in for repairs we'll be here all day, fruitless, absolutely fruitless." His pale Victorian complexion is now turning a rosy shade of red, accentuating his eyes. He is thinking, *I could go a stiff Gin and Tonic about now!*

"Nay, she cannae be faulty," counters Scottie. "Because if she was, then I'd have a docket for her. Those are the company rules. Fred used this machine yesterday on a job. Didn't you Fred?"

Fred is their eldest and possibly most experienced field operator. Wearing heavy horn-rimmed glasses, and a small well kept grey moustache. He is the quietest of men. Not so much going bald, as getting taller than his hair.

Fred is also known for his reluctance to write things down and for being in the wrong place at the wrong time.

"No, it was working alright," Fred says defensively, adjusting his glasses unnecessarily and wiping them with a grubby handkerchief.

Tweedy begins looking less confident. To start this infernal cussed machine is fast becoming his major goal in life.

Some present are unwilling to be there any longer than they need, while others are in the running for time and a half, bordering on double time. There is always that bottom line motivation.

"Don't forget to prime the carburettor," Roger ventures to help, and immediately wishes he had not, as he feels rather than sees the critical stare from Scottie. As he does not get any encouragement from Tweedy either, he begins melting further in to the background and sets about doing what Jack originally asked him to do:

"Observe only—and shut the fuck up!"

After a few quick primes on the carburettor, Tweedy reaches out with renewed enthusiasm and presses the starter switch.

Crickets.

Tweedy now looks embarrassed. He is now colouring slightly pink from the back of his neck upwards, his face, and ears are scarlet. Competing with the colour of Scottie's beetroot dip.

Scottie, openly chuckling is enjoying himself immensely.

"Give it some choke," offers Fred and then almost as an afterthought, "it never starts first up, not without plenty of choke."

Tweedy's eyes narrow almost to slits of hatred as he glares at Fred.

"Keeping that little piece of information to ourselves, were we? At what stage were you intending to offer that bit of advice? Maybe after we've moved onto gas?"

Roger makes movement to reach out. Scottie gives him a withering look that stops him in his tracks.

Scottie, still chuckling at Tweedy's predicament pulls the choke knob out for him.

Tweedy's hand is now unsteady. He reaches forward and presses the starter. He looks as though more than one stiff Gin and Tonic might help him.

Scottie steps back. All necks crane forward.

CLICK.

"There it goes," cries Tweedy. "Oh, thank, Christ."

Granted a tad over enthusiastically, he continues to press the starter switch like a man possessed he is wishing this infernal machine into life.

"What's that red flashing light, then?" Fred asks.

Indeed, a red flashing light is now quite obvious, in the gathering gloom.

"I had a red light," says Fred as he ponders thoughtfully, almost as though he is talking to himself, "but it wasn't flashing then, it was just sort of constant."

Scottie's face is a study. If nothing else, the focus is changing from one to the other, and Tweedy looks almost grateful for the distraction.

"Aye, and what do you think, a red light might mean, then, Fred?" asks Scottie. His voice has an edge to it.

"I don't know, it's just sort of there."

Sucking in his breath Scottie tightens his grip on the manual almost to stop himself from throttling Fred. His knuckles are white. His eyes are like little gimlets. His mouth now resembles a sucked out lemon.

"A red light, Matey, is a warning light. It isn't like a green light, which in case you don't realise it, is a go light. A red light always signifies caution, or stop. When it flashes, it means if you haven't seen me yet, wake up for Christ sake, Matey, I'm 'ere, look at me, I heed caution. Anyone not heeding caution had better watch out. I don't remember seeing any report docket from you, Fred."

"Well, no, Scottie," Fred replies, "but I was going to mention it to you, the next chance I had. I'm not convinced anyway that it is a caution light. When I turn on my electric kettle at home I get a red light and it isn't really a caution light so much as it just sort of means it's on."

"Fred, had you mentioned all of this before we commenced the demonstration, or had you put in a faulty work docket, old chap, I wouldn't have been standing here making a complete arse of myself for the past fifteen minutes," Tweedy's features look troubled.

Everyone starts to snigger, a few laugh outright like drunken sailors, but are cut dead in their tracks by Scottie.

"If arseholes could fly, this would be an airport," Scottie says angrily. "It'd be a bloody miracle if any of you blokes know the first fucken thing about what you're actually trying to do here. Red can also mean aggression, and I'm feeling that right now!"

Scottie swivels his laser gaze around to Tweedy, "And you. You should know better. You're supposed to know all this stuff and set an example to these blokes. Here you are giving a demo' and you haven't got a bloody clue."

Tweedy begins to bluster, "Well ok, then," he says sharply, "I confess, there. I said it. No. I don't know how to start the bloody thing!"

Scottie positively beams. He has achieved his objective and is almost as giddy as a schoolboy wagging school.

"Oh, that's alright, Matey. I suppose you can't be expected to know it all. After all you are sales, and cannae ever be service orientated."

Ouch, thinks Roger. *That was a swipe for sure.*

With a more serious entry to his voice and a look that speaks volumes. "But you should all know how to start a fogging machine, though shouldn't you, Mates?"

Scottie takes centre stage and surveys the room, slowly face by face. "Aye, what you've all overlooked is the safety on the oil reservoir. On this model, it mixes its own two stroke fuel as it goes, and if the oil level in the oil reservoir is below the safety line, it cannae start until you top it up, with two stroke oil," Scottie announces smugly.

"Or, tilt the machine, Scottie," offers Fred, "just to make it think it's got more in it than it has, like I did, yesterday..."

Roger winces. It is the first truly discordant entry for a long time and it seems to strike deep with everyone.

For a full moment—no-one dares to speak. Then a few stifled chuckles, while the main players stand and glare at each other.

"You should take care, Fred. You might be flying dangerously close to the sun," Tweedy scowls.

Scottie speaks with a fixed grin, "Nay, we don't do that, Fred," he says gently, "That's considered poor work practices around 'ere, that is. Aye, what we do, is we do the job properly, that's what we do, Fred."

As he is talking, Scottie's already topping up the almost empty oil tank. With a generous gesture, "There you go, Matey you can try her again now."

Tweedy reaches forward, as a robot unseeing on remote control. He presses the starter switch.

The engine turns over confidently, it chugs, it splutters. It bursts into an abundance of noisy life.

They can see each others' mouth moving but cannot hear any voices. The machine's noise is deafening under the corrugated iron roof as it continues to gather momentum.

Smoke is now pouring from the exhaust pipe.

Scottie vanishes behind a billowing curtain of thick black smoke. He is the only member of staff correctly wearing a face-mask. Everyone else stands as if mesmerised as the thick pall mounts and spreads.

Through the growing haze Scottie reaches out and turns off the chemical tank immediately ceasing the eruption of oily smoke. He then deftly turns the machine off.

The silence is palpable.

"We cannae risk a call out from the local Fire Brigade, no' on my watch, can we? I'm guessing no-one here would have notified them, so we'd better, just end your demo here then, Matey. Aye, also let that be a lesson to you all to turn the bloody chemical tank off before you turn off the machine. If I've told you once I've told you a hundred times, you must turn the chemical off first, then when it stops making smoke, then you turn off the engine," Scottie explains.

"Yes, thanks for coming everyone," says Tweedy. He has recovered with near perfect composure.

"Everyone's been so helpful. At least if the Fire Brigade had turned out we could all have had fun hooking their hoses around. My goodness is that the time? I'll be shot I promised, I'd not be too late home today— time to piss-n-off-sky, with the speed of a thousand startled gazelles," says Tweedy as he pivots to leave.

Scottie is thinking to himself if plan B fails, there are plenty more letters in the alphabet.

Chapter 15

MATES

Art and his missus, Kim, have recommended a north side builder. "They're nothing fancy, although I s'pose they could be, but the word is they're as honest as, so why not give them a call?"

Roger is reluctant, "Our house hasn't been sold yet, might we be getting ahead of ourselves?"

Sue replies, "It won't hurt to meet with them, just to see."

Builder Man is old school. A carpenter by trade, he arrives at their Wooloowin unit in his work clothes. As broad as he is tall, with his face like a dropped pie, he can lift single buildings with one hand and is Aussie to his toenails.

After listening to Sue and Roger's predicament and making a few notes, Builder Man says, "I can do a block of land and the house as a combined package without any payment down and then wait to finalise when your money arrives."

"We shouldn't have to wait too long," Roger promises, "at least we hope not. Fingers crossed."

"Thank you," Sue gushes, "we were warned when we first arrived not to build in a gulley or at the bottom of a hill."

"Well no fear with my land. Good advice," says Builder Man, "who told you that?"

Roger flashes his relaxed smile, "Actually, the taxi cab driver!"

"Clever man," Builder Man says, "rest assured any block I show you, will be high and dry from flooding when it rains. Guaranteed. Otherwise it's very expensive to make water go uphill," he finishes with laughing eyes.

Builder Man drives them far out to the north side, to view the few blocks he has available. Sue has no trouble deciding where she would like to be. She chooses a block of scrubland in the suburb of Kallangur where a few modern homes are already built.

"According to those already living here," Builder Man announces with a knowing smile, "Kallangur in Aboriginal means *Land of the Mosquitoes*," he lets his head loll as if in wonderment, "at times, when the locals disappear in a grey cloud of insects I'm sure they ponder the genius of the indigenous for the obvious. Nevertheless, price wise it fits your budget."

On one of their follow up trips to where Casa Del Kallangur is about to be built, they meet their neighbours to be.

Steve and his wife Sophie, with their two small children Linda and Adam, aged similar to Jayne and James, are neighbours on one side. Other than their different coloured hair, it is difficult to tell them apart.

"Quite the kindergarten area, isn't it," Roger says to Sue.

"Oh, but isn't it wonderful, James and Jayne have so many friends already."

Steve cannot wait to track down Peter, nick named Picasso, due to his house painting business. A tall man with a narrow face and a long nose, his short, cropped, black hair gives him the appearance of a Doberman Pinscher.

"Mate, I've got good news and bad news."

"What's that, Steve?" Peter is elbow deep in his beehives collecting honey. The last thing he needs is to kill any bees thanks to Steve's interruption.

"We've got new neighbours building on the block next door," Steve pauses, "that's the good news."

"Okay, Mate. What's the bad news?" Picasso who has been moving with the slowness of a man handling high explosives is no longer elbow deep in his bees.

"They're fuckin' ten pound Poms!"

"How'd you know?"

"Blind Freddie would know, Mate. All you have to do is listen when they open their mouths. The kids are cute, though."

"Let's hope they're good ones, Mate. I can't stand a whinging, bastard pommy."

"I'm with you, Mate, no-one can." Steve pauses to roll a smoke, "I'll bet a penny to a pound the prick will be wearing fuckin' sandals over his socks."

"That and a fuckin' big hat. Remember the larger the hat the smaller the property," Picasso is holding his hand out for Steve to roll him a durrie.

Both men light up.

"Cute kids you say, how old?" asks Picasso.

"A pidgeon pair same ages as ours.

Picasso nods his approval. "Just what we need around here, more kids."

Back at Wooloowin, Roger rehashes his sums. "Even by Aussie standards we're a long way out of town," he groans. "Christ, Sue, we're further out than most people go on their holidays."

"Well, thankfully you have a company car. Never mind, over time the perception of distances might change. That or you'll make heaps more money and we can move closer to the city."

"Ok, then. So, we're about to commit to a twenty four perch size of scrub just large enough for a small high set house and a back garden for our children to play in.

According to Steve, and based on what he paid for his block the land we bought from Builder Man is overpriced at $2,000 especially as he paid less than $1,000 for it…but that was a few years ago…and he has to make a profit!"

Sue asks, anxiously, "Doesn't matter then does it? Can we afford it?"

"I don't think Builder Man making a profit is unfair, and I think we can afford it. Now that Casa Del Coxwell has finally sold and the funds deposited. It'll be tight, but if I've figured correctly the value of the house and land corresponds to about double my annual salary. If we convert pounds to dollars the Kallangur package price is similar to what we paid in Coxwell. No garage but there's space to park underneath. The Commonwealth Bank is prepared to loan $8,000.00 joint mortgage even without you working, and over twenty years that's $56.00 per month repayments. Only problem is…"

"What?" Sue interjects.

"Well, that's all based on the timber option similar to the houses already there. We can't afford the brick option, which means you'll have to accept the chamfer-board alternative. The brick version is another $2,000.00 on the cost of the house, and the bank won't increase their mortgage. Otherwise we'd have to apply to a Building Society at probably a higher rate of interest than the 8%."

Sue beams. "I don't mind living in a timber shed in this climate. I really don't. That's fantastic, Roger."

"And don't forget."

"What?"

"There are no floor coverings like the nice carpeting that we had at Casa Del Coxwell."

"I'm sure the builder will polish our floor boards, if we ask. We won't need carpets in this climate."

"Alright then. There's no stove included."

"Doesn't matter because we've got our oven arriving soon from England."

"Okay. Just means we'll need to be heavily invested in insect repellant, then."

At their next meeting, Builder Man explains, "Your new three bedroom house will have one bathroom, and a seperate toilet. It's to be built on high concrete stumps like the ones nearby, and the same as I showed you that we're just finishing off at Lawnton. That will facilitate additional homely spaces that can be filled in later underneath if required. To keep out the weather they'll be chamfer-board timber clad walls, which is more modern than the wider weatherboards, and an almost flat asbestos roof.

When it rains you'll hardly hear it because asbestos is strong and absorbs sound. Under a tin roof you wouldn't be able to hear yourself think.

Your timber floor will be polished and we'll apply an Estapol interior as a clear finish. Kitchen, dining, and lounge are open plan in an L shape as you've seen.

The eyes of your new home will be aluminium sliding glass windows."

"Sounds great," says Roger, "to save money I'll construct our own fly-screens."

"If you wish. You'll not need a builder's permit," he smiles thinly, "only a set square, good hacksaw blade, and a steady hand. Good luck both of you."

They shake hands; Builder Man puts his Akubra back on and waves as he drives away.

"Well, that's it, *Woburn Abbey* it's not but as long as you're happy, Sweetheart."

Sue is ecstatic. "I can't wait to move in."

The two carpenters assigned by Builder Man are true blue Aussie characters. Their durries are so thin the paper sticks to their lips and goes out almost as soon as they light them. They are constantly relighting each other's smokes with battered flint lighters. Each wears a blue singlet that looks unchanged since the great depression.

Both ends every sentence with a single word; "But!"

But-One says, "It's going good, but," and But-Two adds, "Your quality Iron Bark flooring will arrive tomorrow, but."

Trucks stream in and out like ants following a trail of honey each carrying bundles of timber, pallets of fibre board, and windows followed by work utes with signage Plumber, Electrician, and Painter.

But-Two has half the intellectual wattage of his mate, but, they are both superb craftsmen.

There is reticulated mains water and electricity. No town gas, no sewerage. Out back sits a septic tank high enough out of the ground to be used as a table. The backyard quickly becomes a barren quagmire. Finally, a home and it is theirs. They move in with what little they have and run up hire purchases for their essentials; beds, and a fridge.

Roger holds his head in his hands, "We need more, Sue. A lounge, a table."

Sue agrees.

Steve leans over their adjoining chain link fence. "There's not a tree to hang Judas from," he laughs, "which at least means a clean start, Mate."

Sue laughs, "When it comes to gardening, Roger would rather open his wrists, than go horticultural."

Steve continues. "Might be a while before it needs mowing, Mate."

"Good job," Roger beams, "we haven't bought a mower yet."

"Wouldn't bother yet, Mate. Getting a mower now would be tantamount to leaving the porch light on for Harold Holt."

When Jack hears their possessions are in a container on a ship bound for Brisbane, which appears to be travelling via outer Mongolia, he enthusiastically rallies the troops.

"Since your unit at Wooloowin was fully furnished, you'll have next to nothing to eat from, or cook with," Jack states the obvious.

Jack and Lucy arrange a collection of loan items to help them through.

"Old sheets at the windows will prevent the sun from fading your children," Lucy says.

Shades of Coxwell, Roger thinks, *hope to Christ Sue gets her curtains soon.*

"You're both young," Jack beams, "you'll survive. Look upon it as character building."

Jayne spends her days spinning, twirling and tapping around the almost empty house like someone who has let the wind in. James struts around the house like a new born pony, getting along with himself quite well.

Believing a clean well-kept house to have the same effect on her family's mental health as the unconditional love of a cocker spaniel, Sue grimaces at any trace of dust.

Jayne asks, "Daddy can I have a rabbit?"

"Yes, absolutely, Sweetheart."

Jayne beams.

"But only in a pie," Sue adds.

Jayne pulls a face that reminds Sue of her own, when she is less than impressed with Roger.

BBQs become weekly events with friends. Sue and Roger meet the rest of their neighbours.

Picasso's wife is May. A fit and vibrant woman, whose lips always look as if she is attempting to suppress a smile.

The children play and make a mess with slices of watermelon. They play a game of seeing who can spit the seeds the furthest. Brett wins hands down.

Sheilas, as predicted, prepare the food and the blokes burn it. Snags, which are sausages, are mostly two shades of black and the smell of cooking onions wafting on the breeze is to die for.

They sing songs, and sometimes a mate strums a guitar, everyone tries to sing along. The men drink copious beers while their wives sip cask wine. They all discuss the fate of the world.

Kallangur lives up to its name, mosquitoes are present during the day, more noticeable on dusk. It is agreed that any socialising be adjourned to indoors before dusk.

"Our fly screens are in the main functional," Sue says.

"In the main?"

"Well, they're not a perfect fit," Sue glares at Roger.

"I won't attempt them again, Sue; next time, we'll get them custom made. I should have measured twice or thrice, and then cut. Not the other way around."

Their ship finally comes in and the rest of their belongings arrive. The stove that has been on the high seas stands like the unspoken Elephant in the room rearing its ugly head and waiting for the electrician to install.

"It can't be connected due to the inconsistencies in the manufacturer's switching being non compliant with Queensland State law," Electrician Man explains.

"Thank you, bloody, Fretsaw," Roger raves.

The old oven is collected as part of the $10 deal. Electrician Man asks for the instruction book!

Shades of the vet, Roger thinks. *Oh well, a new one at $100, why not?*

Next on the spend list, a new mower is $100 from Myer's department store, Fortitude Valley requiring a deposit of $10.00; a preloved, reconditioned mower that would have performed well enough, from the local Esso Garage in Kallangur, is the princely sum of $30.00 cash.

"I find it amusing that we're buying a new mower not because we want or need a new mower, but because we can't afford the second hand one, Sue."

"You've got the best style of BBQ, Mate," admires Art, "just a plate and a few twigs, and a real fire. There's nothing like the sound of pithy fireworks, I don't reckon the new fangled gas crap will catch on."

Shorty and Judy arrive. "Smelled your smoke, and thought we'd drop in," Shorty says.

"Cheers, to that," Art says, "I hear there's moves a foot to ban any form of open fire in the future."

Judy groans, "Next they'll be stopping people from smoking."

"We haven't seen much of you two lately," Roger says to Shorty and Judy.

"Been flat out like a lizard drinking, Mate. What with my job and Judy's, there's no time to scratch ourselves."

"I've been itching to ask," Sue has a twinkle in her eye, "how did you two meet?"

Shorty looks at Judy, Judy looks at Shorty.

"It was at a friend's housewarming party," Judy replies. "Similar to here today, I suppose."

Shorty is thoughtful. "When I first saw, Judy, I noticed that she was taller than average."

"Thanks," Judy says.

"But no wider," Shorty says quickly. "It was the dress, her pearls, the nylons, the shoes."

"You noticed my shoes!" Judy exclaims.

A smile was playing about the corners of Kim's mouth. "He must have noticed more than your shoes."

"Her face, her hair. I was besotted."

"What happened next?" Sue asks.

Judy looks embarrassed. "Well, I've always been attracted to large men. After the party, Shorty drove me home."

There was a long pause.

"And," prompts Art. "This is as painful as pulling teeth."

"Well, if you want the gory details," Judy offers with a smirk.

"We do! We do!" exclaims Sue, who has moved forward onto the edge of her chair.

"Well. The short version is we had sex, and got married," Shorty sums up.

"What about the longer version?" Kim asks.

Again Shorty looks at Judy, Judy looks at Shorty. Judy shrugs "Okay."

"I ran my fingers through her hair," Shorty explains, "swept back her left side and sort of tucked it behind her ear."

"Then what?" Kim wants to know.

"Then I took my hand away," Shorty answers.

"I told him, now do the other side," Judy says, as if in a trance.

Shorty's thoughtful. "Her neck was slender and warm. And then, she put her hand flat on my chest. I thought it was a warning to stop."

There is absolute silence.

Judy breaks the silence. "But I didn't want him to stop. And so then we went to the bedroom."

"That's when we stripped, Judy climbed on top, and we burned up the bed sheets," offers Shorty with a smirk.

"Ok," Kim draws out the word, "that might be a tad too much information!"

"Those pearls of mine certainly swung and bounced about him a lot," continues Judy.

"I stayed the night," Shorty adds, "and afterwards we lay together, looking contentedly at that half painted ceiling, much as if we'd just finished making love in the Sistine Chapel."

Judy leans into Shorty, and kisses him tenderly on the cheek.

After another round of drinks, Steve and Sophie, from next door, join in.

"We'll need to build you a BBQ chimney, Mate," Steve is waving away the smoke.

"Shorty, Judy these are our neighbours from next door, Steve and Sophie. Their children Linda and Adam are already playing with James and Jayne. Steve works for the Fire Brigade."

"You a Firey, Steve?" Shorty asks.

"Sure am, Mate."

"Always been a Firey?"

"Only since Vietnam," Steve replies. "I was one of the lucky ones who returned."

"I was always a sucker for a man in uniform," Sophie adds with a laugh.

"After Vietnam," Steve explains, "I needed a job and wanted out of the army. I'd made Sergeant and thought briefly about joining the police force, but then I reasoned that I'd be locking up people often only guilty of shit I'd done. So, being a Firey rested well with me."

"And the uniform," Sophie prompts. "Don't forget the uniform."

"Been up the coast in *Kermit* yet?" Kim asks.

"Yes," Sue replies. "Last Sunday we drove up to Currimundi Lakes."

"Lovely, safe spot for the kids," Kim adds, "we know it well. How'd it go?"

"Alright," Sue replies. "Roger enjoyed his trudge along the beach from the carpark, didn't you?"

"It's a lovely beach," Roger says, "the soft sand above high tide could bog a camel."

"And do you know what he said about it?" Sue prompts. "Go on tell them."

"No need," says Art. "I can just picture it. The poor bastard was dying. Rog doing the fire walk on hot sand carrying the esky, fold up chairs slung over his shoulders, terry-towelling hat skewiff, sun brolly in t'other hand and in long socks 'n sandals."

"Sue bringing up the rear with the towels and the two kids hanging off her elbows," Kim adds.

Sue continues. "You're spot on. His face was red as, teeth gritted in grimace of pain, sweating in his striped collared T-shirt and shorts just creeping below his knees. And what did you say, Roger? tell them!"

"It's only guts and determination that's keeping me going," Roger repeats smiling.

"Understatement of the year, Mate," Art grins, as he downs another beer.

"And do you know what he said next?" Sue says as she pours another wine.

"No what?"

"He reckoned Scott went to the Antarctic with less gear than he's carting."

"Gravity must have seemed to be sucking you back into the earth, Mate," Art laughs.

"I was gasping for air like a fish flopping out of water. On the way home, the car had its own unique aroma, a heady cocktail of fried fish and chips, and sun spray."

"Never again will they be babies, Roger," Sue admonishes.

"Yes, Roger. You'd better catch those times while you can, how quickly they'll go," Sophie adds. "That's right isn't it, Darl?"

Steve and Art nod.

"No children for you yet, Judy?" Sophie asks.

"Not yet," Judy replies wishfully.

"We're enjoying the preparation for them though," Shorty adds dead pan.

As summer gets into its stride, sand flies and mosquitoes threaten Sue's Christmas shopping outings.

One evening, the children fed and in bed, the adults are about to turn in, when there is a Newsflash on TV.

A frightful whining noise is accompanied by gyrating circles.

CYCLONE WARNING blares from the set!

Roger and Sue are immediately alert and vigilant.

The news flash continues.

"A cyclone is expected to cross the north coast of Queensland between Townsville and Cairns in the early hours tomorrow!

CAUTION is the keyword.

"What do we do?" Sue asks Roger.

"Shush, listen. They're telling us."

They remain glued to their TV and listen as the commentary preaches preparedness. Instructions are clear. Batteries for torches, fill all available containers with drinking water, fill the bath, close all windows!

Roger looks outside. The street appears in total darkness. Not even a sickle moon.

"No-one else is awake," he says peering into the gloom, "not a light on anywhere."

"Should we alert our neighbours?" Sue asks, "what do we do?"

"I don't know, Sue. Maybe they don't know yet?" Roger looks at the clock it's a little after 10pm. "Let's start by preparing and then check the street for lights again. Maybe we're ahead of them all?"

They work feverishly, without waking their children. The bath is filled, batteries, torches and transistor radio are found. Sue checks their pantry for tinned food.

"We'll go buy more tins as soon as the shops open," Roger says, "best make a list."

By 2am they are as prepared as can be. Utterly exhausted, and still the only house with any lights on in the entire street, they fall in to an exhausted dreamless sleep in their armchairs.

First awake is Roger; he hears movement next door, and guesses Steve is preparing for an early start at work.

He bounds down the back steps and calls out softly to Steve, not wanting to sound too alarmist.

"What's up, Mate?" Steve asks.

"The cyclone!" Roger gabbles, "are you prepared?"

"Cyclone? What cyclone?"

"Newsflash last night on the telly, it's expected to cross our coast."

"Where?" Steve asks, a tinge of concern in his voice.

"Up north between Townsville and Cairns, they think."

Steve's face breaks in to a broad grin. "Oh, that, don't concern yourself, Mate. Nothing to it. We never get cyclones this far south." Steve's generous grin disappears, "You might like to prepare for rain though, Mate. We always get a low and buckets of rain following those northerly cyclones, you 'ave a good day.

Steve now has an amusing story to elaborate and share at work about his pommy neighbours.

When Roger reports back to Sue, she is unconvinced.

They remain in a state of preparedness for several days, by necessity they have to empty the bath.

The knock at the door does nothing to settle Sue. She has a feeling of concern. The postie is cheerful with his request for her signature. The registered mail is addressed to Roger. It looks very official. It also has a bank insignia on the envelope.

Sue is afraid to open it. She leaves it conspicuously on the table waiting for Roger to return home from work.

Roger sighs, as he opens the letter. It is brief and to the point, a demand for payment in relation to his personal guarantees.

"How on earth did they find us?" Sue asks.

"We've hardly been in hiding nor had a flexible relationship with the truth. No doubt they have their processes. We have seven days to respond."

Chapter 16

TERMITES

"When your roof caves in, the walls collapse about your ears or you fall through the floor; then your furniture falls to pieces — that's a termite infestation that you don't want."

Roger is receiving a crash course on termites in the bar at a local hotel.

"There are a number of options," Tweedy explains tongue in cheek, "the ancient Greeks worshipped Rhea, the Mother of all Gods."

"Aye, that's alright then, Matey," Scottie smiles broadly, "you could— worship Rhea or the Queen termite."

"Another option is to visit your Mother Church," espouses Jack, "but whatever you decide to do, now is the time to come to terms with your current phase."

"Current phase?" Roger queries.

"Whether you're a pest controller or a client requesting a quote it's likely to become disruptive for one, and expensive the other. Hence current phase," intones Jack, "as the man in charge of a territory you have now progressed from irritating bugs that crawl, scurry, worry, and annoy, such as cockroaches, silverfish, ants, spiders," he is counting off on his fingers, "anyone?"

"Aye, carpet moths and rodents," adds Scottie.

"An occasional friendly snake under a bed is something akin to an art form," enthuses Tweedy.

"Roger," Jack says sympathetically as he puts an arm around his shoulder, "you're moving up the ladder to management, you now have to step up to match."

"I understand," Roger says, smiling, as he sups his second beer. "Clients need professional help, oh, but wait on a minute, I am the professional help."

"Never mind," assures Jack shelling out for another round, "we all might need some additional professional help soon. Latest word from Head Office is that if anything is ever fraught with legality, worthy of courtroom misadventure—Termites are it!"

"The suits in the Snake Pit have got their knickers in a bunch over a mammoth claim pending in Sydney. Thank Christ it's their fuck up, and not ours," laughs Scottie.

"What happened?" Roger asks.

Jack pauses while he takes a sip of his beer. "Some poor bastard's signed off on a termite inspection prior to a house purchase, and when the piano arrived, guess what?"

"What?"

"It fell through the floor, literally."

"Whoops! SNAFU," says Tweedy shaking his head. "Thank fuck no-one was underneath it, manslaughter is a box no-one needs to tick."

"What's SNAFU?" Roger asks.

Tweedy smiles his resigned smile, "Situation Normal All Fucked Up," he replies. "If you ask me it couldn't happen to nicer people than the Sydney crowd. I hope it was a senior suit who fucked up and not some poor bastard lower down in the pecking order."

"Many pest controllers don't quote or service termites now," Jack announces. "They prefer not to have anything to do with them."

"Aye, in some ways they cannae be blamed, Matey," Scottie agrees, "after all if a job goes well they may only make a modest profit."

"Provided they quoted it accurately in the first place," Jack reminds. "and if the job goes badly for any one of countless reasons, all parties are likely to need more silks than a Balinese trader, and the ear of a cashed up insurance company. God help us all."

"Termites are the perfect epitome of an unwanted house guest, I see that," says Roger.

"But unlike fish they don't go off after three days do they? My shout, same again?" Tweedy asserts.

There are nods all round.

"Now here's a group worth talking to," the cultured voice is a stranger to Roger but well known to the others.

"How are you, Chris?" Jack asks, rising as he was taken completely by surprise. "You're not a regular visitor to Brissie."

"Something I hope will change one day," Chris smiles.

Roger is introduced to a slightly overweight man, sporting an expensive, Italian, tieless suit. His English sounds as if he is a news presenter from the BBC, neatly bearded he has the appearance of an academic.

Jack hastens the introductions, which confirms Roger is the only unknown.

"Welcome to the group," Chris smiles, "I'm sure you're in good hands, we've known each other for years, haven't we, Jack?"

"Indeed," gushes Jack, "and how's your pest control business going? Snuffa…"

"Bug," Chris finishes with a broad smile, "Snuff-a-bug. We're only small, not in your league, Jack, at least not yet. Please excuse me, I mustn't keep the lady waiting."

After Chris has departed to rejoin his exclusive guest, Jack hastens to explain. "Christopher Wright aka Legend Man, is a bit of a mystery man with money about town. As you can see," Jack nods towards Chris's table, "he is a bit of a ladies' man."

"Who's the lady?" Tweedy asks, taken aback by her stunning appearance and warm smile, as if someone had just rung the dinner bell. "He didn't choose to introduce her, did he?"

"Who knows? Probably an air hostess he's met on the plane. He runs Snuffabug but appears wealthy by other means. Last we heard he'd bought a controlling interest in a small chain of Sydney fish and chip shops."

At that point Chris reappears carrying a tray of beers and places them on the table in front of Jack, "I think I owe you and your colleagues a few, Jack."

"You shouldn't have, Chris. I was just explaining to the boys about your fish and chip venture, how's it going, by the way."

"It's making money," Chris smiles, "but I'm not sure for how long."

"Oh, why?"

"Well, it's based on a gimmick."

"Gimmick?" Tweedy asks.

"Yes, we sell the original English style fish and chips, the sloppy result wrapped in newspapers. I've secured a supply of Times Newspapers that I get flown over, and that goes down really well with patrons, but…" Chris hesitates.

"What?" Scottie prompts.

"Well, there are moves afoot to ban the supply of cooked food in newspapers in Sydney, even protected by grease proof paper, and we might have to switch to approved polystyrene food containers. Not good for the image we've established."

The group are silent.

"But never mind, if that door closes, another will surely open." Chris smiles his widest concierge smile as if driven by some kind of quiet internal vigour and confidence. Glancing down at his gold wristwatch the size of a sundial that only emphasised his personal awesomeness. "Goodness, is that the time? I must go, I promised to get the lady back in time for her evening flight.

See you, Jack. Good to meet you fellows again. and welcome to the industry down under, Roger."

"Alright," says Jack, after Chris has departed, he certainly makes a big impression wherever he goes. Doubtless the lady will enjoy more positions than an Olympic gymnast." He turns to Roger. "You've just met one of our industry's surprises. A great white shark dressed in Giorgio Armani indeed. Legend Man is, allegedly, all over it like seagulls on a chip. Back to our business in hand. Termites."

Jack pauses, as if collecting his thoughts, the surprise meeting with Chris, a man he knew to be capable of running any National Pest Control company and probably better than most, had thrown him. Was it a coincidence? Why was he in Brisbane? So many questions and not enough answers.

Jack continues. "When you have termites they're rarely difficult to find. Roger, I see you're scheduled to look at your first termite job in Ipswich tomorrow. That's just southwest of Brissie, why are you going and not Tweedy?"

"Lucy changed it because I've got full day scheduled in Toowoomba," Tweedy explains, "Roger said he'd go."

"Very well, good luck then. The biggy termite, at least commercially, is the subterranean fellow often referred to inaccurately as a White Ant. Incorrect, because they're not white and they're not an ant but anyway it's important because there are plenty of them, and generally they devour the cellulose out of timber."

"Remember, even if it's a brick house they comprise a fair amount of sawn timber, especially pine," Tweedy says, "little bastards love hoop pine."

"Aye, you'll find it in wall frames, architraves, door frames, and skirting boards," adds Scottie.

"Another species, not as commonplace, is the dry wood termite and this little critter doesn't need to keep tracking to a nest hidden somewhere, usually underground. To kill them sometimes a large plastic sheet is placed over the building and methyl bromide gas is pumped in," says Jack. "But I see no reason to concern yourself with the Drywood Termite as we rarely encounter them."

"Except the West Indian Drywood Termite," Tweedy reminds.

"Yes, but that's a government contract due to a stuff up by the powers that be," Jack says.

"Quite so," agrees Tweedy, "a relatively drab and boring insect."

Roger is now zoned out, the beers are making his head fuzzy and his thoughts have turned to home; he has had enough of being educated for today. "Righto then fellows, I'm off, enjoy your evening."

At Ipswich, the house is an older style high set weatherboard home. Roger notes that the job involves drilling and trenching around all of the foundation stumps. He quotes the job as heavy work, and hopes the assigned team will not become too carried away in the soft, damp ground. Instead of a shallow trench around each stump, they might unintentionally expose the footings.

The job sold, Roger returns to the office to complete his paperwork for Head Office and instructions for the work.

It is only after the team arrive at the site to commence treatment that Scottie halts all work and races back to the office.

Scottie reports to Jack, "It's nuttin' but a tits up disaster, Matey.

Roger has quoted the entire property for the control of Subterranean Termites," Scottie pauses, and takes a deep breath, "but they're Dry Wood Termites."

This might sound inconsequential however they are different creatures, needing different chemicals, and applications to what Roger has advised.

His faux pas could only be likened to in medicine as the removal of an arm instead of a foot.

"In Roger's defence he has received little or no training," Jack reinforces.

Roger had quoted to dig around and drill each stump and flood with an aqueous solution of Aldrin instead of Dieldrin.

Admittedly, until the shit hit the fan, he was fairly proud of himself as the job had been signed off at $590.00. Now he feels as confident as a chocolate teapot.

"Roger. You'd better step in to my office," Jack says sombrely.

Summoned to the inner sanctum Roger listens intently as Scottie tells the sorry tale of woe.

No matter how nicely Scottie tries to describe what has happened, in pest control parlance, it is still a SNAFU of gigantic proportions.

When Scottie finally draws breath, Roger has visions of handing over the keys to the company vehicle, and getting the train home. Inwardly he sighs. This would let him off the hook of taking Jack into his confidence and discussing the personal letter from the UK bank regarding the guarantee for his father's loans, that upset Sue big time.

Jack sits quietly for a while. He leans well back in his chair. His face remains as placid as a bottomless lake. He splays his fingers behind his head before bouncing forward and placing both hands flat on his desk. He takes his reading glasses off, and he puts them on again. Several times. He bows his head. Unsure whether to shy, shit, or run.

Jack rolls a pencil between his fingers.

"So, what you're telling me, Scottie, is that, Roger here has totally fucked this up."

Scottie shuffles his feet. He looks nervously at Roger. "Aye, that's right, Matey." Scottie has developed a liking for this Pommy bastard, as much as any Scot could, he is now reluctant to see him go.

"He's not only misdiagnosed the species of termite but he's also made out incorrect treatment instructions already copied to Head Office, and instructed the use of Aldrin instead of Dieldrin, is that correct?" Jack hammers home!

"Aye, that's right, Matey." Scottie's shoulders are slumping.

Roger wishes he were somewhere else, hell even at the dentist having a tooth drilled without anaesthetic.

"So let's see it this way, had Roger been right in his original diagnosis, with the style of house construction, the treatment intended and the time the job would have taken, would it have been profitable to this company at $590.00?"

A broad smile creases Scottie's face. "Aye, and a good margin for error, Matey."

"Very good; so if I were to authorise you to change the treatment, discard the Head Office blue copies, the incorrect use of chemical, and prepare changed paperwork to the correct style of work, do you think that would still be the case?"

A wider smile edges across Scottie's face, "Well, aye, that's about right, Matey. In fact I can see a small saving. No' every post needs intensive work."

Scottie is jubilant, his face is a very ruddy red, the sad eyes are sparkling, he has saved his new fledgling.

"Very good," says Jack. "I'm sure you'd agree the mistake is one easily made by someone still learning the ways of termites and not properly trained here in Oz. Make out new work sheets and advise the snake-pit, I mean Head Office accordingly."

"Aye, right you are, Matey." Scottie practically dances a jig out of the dark inner sanctum.

Scottie is behaving like a cave dweller seeing light for the first time in weeks.

Jack looks at Roger over his glasses. "Roger, you have work, yes."

Roger leaps out of his chair. "Yes, Sir. Thank you, Sir."

Roger inadvertently earned a bonus that day.

A few days later over a coffee in their lunchroom Tweedy decides to share his knowledge of the dreaded, crawling, blight. "Termite jobs are not always easy to access and the ones pesties dislike most are those under low set buildings. Any minimal crawl space under the floor is dreaded, but your Ipswich job was easy, wasn't it, Scottie?"

Scottie ignores Tweedy, their tussle about the fogging machine has not been totally put to rest.

"They're never shown like that in the books and diagrams, Matey, the books dinnae prepare anyone properly for crawling on their guts under bearers where they constantly scrape the back of their shoulders and cannae move properly."

"Or of the effort involved with pulling gear along behind and constantly thinking what piece of kit will I need that's been left in the truck?" Tweedy offers with a smirk.

"Aye, laying stretched out on the ground, often avoiding pools of nameless muck from old plumbing or animals, cannae be fun," Scottie emphasises.

"Or bracing your feet against a pillar while trenching, digging or drilling," Tweedy continues.

"Aye, and scrabbling for toe holds when the fucken drill's too heavy or goes silent because your last move pulled the plug from its socket back outside," Scottie speaks as if elsewhere, obviously reliving some unpalatable memory.

"The desire to strip off your overalls and protective gear at times must be almost overwhelming, particularly when the sweat stings your eyes," offers Lucy, as she reboils the kettle.

"Aye, any delusion of desirability just died in the arse, didn't it," Scottie comments. "Instruction books cannae tell of the creeping exhaustion."

"The sudden feeling of panic when claustrophobia sweeps over you and for a moment you get stuck, cannot move your breathing restricted in the crawl space. Made worse with poor light or no light," offers Jack who has just come in for a cuppa.

"The only sobering thought is the posts, which have stayed in situ for many years, suddenly decide to give way and the building crushes down upon you like a folding pack of cards," Tweedy adds dismally.

"Aye, grown men, me included, have been known to have nary a quiet cry under circumstances such as those," Scottie says, "and then trying to wriggle into a better position, just to trench a wee bit deeper or change drill bits to burrow further into a timber stump. Coal miners would be perfect for the job."

"It's usually at about that point in time, no matter how much the operator has tried not to, that the drill bit will become stuck fast. It happens all the time and when least expected. It happens drilling through concrete with a Kanga hammer," Tweedy says.

"Aye, then begins the laborious effort of trying to wind the bit out by hand with a spanner hoping it won't break because that's no' costed into the job," adds Scottie.

"Surely, there must always be a time during any termite job when the thought occurs; will you successfully finish?" Lucy asks.

"The mind filters speeches to the client, 'The ground was a lot harder than we ever imagined, Sir.' Or, 'The concrete was a lot thicker than shown on the plan, Sir.' Or, 'There was reo where the plan said there was none, Sir.'" Tweedy suggests.

"Not really going to enlighten the client to recommend us when we keep putting our hand out for more dosh," Jack injects as he sits down with them.

"As the worst is anticipated, suddenly something goes right?" Roger asks hopefully.

"Aye, like Ipswich?" Scottie says, raising his cup.

"Like Ipswich," nods Tweedy, raising his.

"Like Ipswich," Jack repeats, joining in.

"Aye, thank Christ the drill didn't burn out," Scottie says.

"Agreed. The job looks profitable," says Jack.

Roger smiles and nods his acceptance of his lucky escape.

"Fellows, thank you, I have a meeting to attend, adieu," as he pivots out the door.

His looming appointment is with the solicitor about the bank's letter.

The solicitor reads the letter, twice. "You've known about this debt?" Legal Eagle asks.

Roger nods. Briefly he explains the story of his father's business loans and his involvement as a company director.

Legal Eagle is thoughtful. "We'll do a response. Short and brief or they'll continue to hound you."

Roger feels some relief but remains concerned. "What will you say?"

Legal Eagle smiles for the first time. "We don't acknowledge the validity of the debt, and should they pursue the matter, it will be rigorously defended. That's our starting point."

"Will that get them off my back?" Roger asks.

"I don't know. We'll see, but I do have another question."

"Shoot."

"How did they find you? You're not even in a telephone book yet, and if you had tried to evade them you couldn't have done a much better job."

Roger is thoughtful. "I don't know. What's your thoughts?'

"Well," Legal Eagle leans back in his chair and twiddles his biro, "looks to me like someone has dobbed you in. Maybe your father?"

Roger is stunned. "I'd never considered any such possibility."

"Well, someone's helped the bank, that's for sure, there's no way this just happened, and certainly not within this time frame."

Roger asks. "Is there any way we could find out, who?"

"Everything, and anything is possible," Legal Eagle smirks. "Leave it with me, I'll see what I can find out. Can't make any promises, and it might take a while."

"Thank you," Roger says and he means it, "it's been a heavy burden — the worry."

"I don't doubt it," Legal Eagle says, "but you did the right thing."

"I did...how?"

"You didn't try and handle it yourself, writing letters getting involved, it's a lot easier if solicitors can handle it from the beginning — like this."

"What if it goes badly?" Roger asks.

"Badly: value the house, force you to sell it, you going bankrupt might be the solution."

Roger is looking glum.

"I wouldn't worry too much if I were you, didn't you say your property is in joint names, you and Sue?"

"Yes."

"Unlikely, they'll go down that path, especially as there's no money in it for them."

Roger left Legal Eagle feeling a little less apprehensive, now to break the news to Sue.

At home Roger explains the situation.

"Legal Eagle is not as impressive as my boyhood hero of Boyd QC, and banks are renowned for swooping like birds of prey if you miss a payment by ten cents. Only time will tell," Roger reiterates to Sue, "that's what Legal Eagle said, "we'll just have to sweat it out but it's unlikely to proceed because the house is in joint names and too few dollars are involved."

"Oh, Roger, someone has passed on our address and details? What does that mean?"

"It means someone's a snake in the grass," Roger replies.

Chapter 17

SETTLED IN

"He looks fit and trim," Roger says to Sue, referring to neighbour Steve who is walking on the roof of his house checking his guttering for leaves.

"And handsome in a rugged, weathered way," opines Sue, "his face is the colour of oiled saddle leather, don't you think?"

Roger nods in agreement. "Like a slab of granite that's been eroded by running water for a couple of millennia, you mean."

Steve's lithe six-foot frame is accentuated by his neatly trimmed black moustache sitting under his military style haircut. He is one of the lucky ones who returned home intact from Vietnam.

"He enjoys working with his hands, carrying out improvements around the house and yard, Sue. Clever boy; he has a Bondwood trailer sailing boat that he's built himself."

Roger is not keen on sailing, he prefers powered boats, but Steve is persuasive.

"I'll organise a morning's sail from Scarborough's boat harbour. Just a short sail to give you a taste, Mate. We'll be back early arvo."

Sophie chips in with a laugh. "Australia's been a great place to live since cocky was an egg. Roger, I'm sure you'll love our Moreton Bay."

"I'm sure I shall," Roger says, "everything's wonderful here."

"Here in Queensland," Steve puffs out his chest, "it's even better. I swear if I planted a feather it'd grow into a chook, wouldn't it, Darl?"

"For sure," Sophie pastes on a smile.

Steve is in his element running around preparing the boat. A novice on board is fraught with danger, and as Roger is a non-swimmer, Steve prefers him safely out of the way.

Trussed up like a Christmas turkey in an ocean going life jacket, the light and whistle options fascinate him.

Steve expertly guides his boat out of Scarborough harbour into the bay using his small outboard motor before hoisting his mainsail and picking up a paltry breeze.

Somewhere inside Steve is indeed a mariner; just itching to climb into oilskins and escape.

Out on the water Roger is impressed. "It is very relaxing."

"We might have to cut our sail shorter today. Given the wind is more suitable to power boating and Sophie wants me back early, would you believe we've got bloody visitors?"

Roger sits upright like an obedient German shepherd beside Steve at the tiller. The water of the bay sounds like a drawn out sigh as it breathes past in a long, sad repose.

"The water's quite clear," observes Roger, peering gingerly over the side.

"The depth can be deceptive," Steve's eyes remain deep and alert. For a while neither man speaks as they share the environment.

Steve does a couple of minor adjustments on something called a jib.

"Couldn't do this down south," Steve says after a while, "it'd be windy enough but too cold. Have you ever seen Penguins?"

"Yes, in Regents Park Zoo in London."

"They live wild here, down south that is. Thousands of them. I saw some once near Adelaide in South Australia." Steve laughs, "I'd never seen chooks in dinner suits before."

Steve cuts their conversation short as he unfurls and hoists his main sail.

With both sails up to catch what wind is available they sail southeast across Moreton Bay and cross the Pearl Channel. Steve changes direction and heads back northwest.

"Have you tasted crocodile yet, Roger?"

"Crocodile? No. What's it like?"

"If they're in captivity and been eating chook, then they taste a bit like chook," Steve pauses thoughtfully, "but if they're in the wild and been eating people, I suppose they'd taste like people," then he looks serious, and gives Roger a dead fish-eye gaze, "but when they've been eating each other, they taste just like crocodile."

"That's where I came in, Steve."

"I suppose it's a cross between pork, fish, and chook its texture a bit like overcooked crayfish."

"I'll look forward to trying some."

About ten kilometres out from the Redcliffe peninsula, Steve asks Roger, "Fancy a taste of fresh sand crab, Mate?"

"I'd never say no to that idea. Why? You got any?"

"Sand crabs do live in the bay, and we are on the bay," Steve smiles, "but you really should stop peering over the side for crocodiles. We are too far south!"

"You got me, was I that obvious?"

"Yes, but I've just spotted a professional fisherman's pot on my port bow. As I sail close by, I'll drop the sail, while you grab it. You'll only get the one opportunity. Be sure to get it."

Roger is unsure. Back in the UK this would be stealing. He wonders if it is different here? There are no signs 'Trespassers will be prosecuted' nor 'Keep Out' but in his head he feels sure that what they are about to do is wrong.

Roger does not want to offend his new friend and neighbour but is unwilling to steal another man's crabs. He leans out to grab the float as asked, his awkwardness and lack of experience on boats is showing.

"You think we're gonna steal his crabs don't you?" Steve states accusingly, with a wicked lear.

"It looks that way," Roger says a little grudgingly, as he hands the float to Steve.

Steve laughs. "No. Not at all, Mate. I'd never do that. Look see."

The crab pot they pull up is large, heavy and rectangular in size. It takes both men to haul it aboard.

"How's about that," Steve says, "he's got six fine looking sandies all bucks."

Steve, while displaying the dexterity of an octopus in a bed full of oysters, notices the wire pot is devoid of bait. He swiftly removes two large sized crabs by holding them behind their rear flippers and carapace, and puts them aside in his galley frig. He explains, "Cool them down a bit, that'll slow them down ready for cooking so they don't throw their claws."

Steve re-baits the pot with mullet frames from his small freezer and places two stubbies of XXXX® beer into the pot.

"I think we've done the right thing — a beer for a crab's fair enough. Only one problem remains."

"What's that?" Roger asks, feeling much better now.

"Getting out of here before we get shot, Mate. He might be holed up somewhere with a high powered rifle, the crosshairs trained on our heads."

Roger looks around. They were a long way from land. "He'd need to be a very good shot."

Roger's highlight of their sail was eating the fresh sand crab. Steve cooked them in his galley using clean seawater he'd scooped up in a bucket from over the side.

"You know what people say about sailors don't you?" Steve asks as they finish their meal.

"I'll bite. What's said about sailors?"

"That because we get our power for free, we expect everything else the same way."

They had shared Steve's beers, and Roger makes a mental entry that he will provide the next beers at home.

"How come you're not working?" Roger asks.

"I'm on a sickie, Mate, but it sort of backfired."

"How come?"

"Well, I went down to see the local quack. My plan was simple. Tell him I had the shits. He'd probably ask why, like he always does. I'd say because of work. I've done it before and then he'd shrug his shoulders and give me a certificate for three days off."

"Sounds like a plan, so what happened?" Roger asks.

"He wasn't there. He's on bloody holiday and I got his locum instead. A young quack colleague from Canberra would you believe. That place is about as much fun as having a dingo in your chook pen," smiling Steve adds, "it's a breeding ground for politicians. They're all like mudguards."

"Why mudguards?" Roger asks.

"Shiny on top but shitty underneath, Mate."

"So what happened?"

"Well, not knowing him, the locum I mean, I played it straight. I wasn't prepared to take him into my confidence like I'm used to doing with Arnold. Trouble was he took me really serious."

"How come?"

"Shits?" he said, "that could be indicative of a far more serious and deep rooted problem. We'll need to look in to this. We'll start with a blood test, and a colonoscopy, and an x-ray. You'll need two weeks off work initially."

"Shit happens," Roger grins thinly.

"Touché. Fuck. All I wanted was three days off. I feel as fit as ten men. Admittedly nine are in bed and one is dying."

Roger laughs. The return trip ended all too soon.

Back early so as not to annoy Steve's wife Sophie. She is petite and dark haired with an almost olive complexion. An easy smile and a pair of startling, smiling eyes dominate her facial features. A seamstress by profession.

Sue hears them in the yard and hurries to join in, interested to hear the run down about their outing.

Sophie asks, "Where's my sand crab then you, Wanker?"

"No time, Love. We've been buzzing all over the bay like out of work blow-flies," Steve replies, lighting up cigarettes for himself and Sophie. They both have smokers' raspy voices.

"Right," Sophie scowls, "so you've got me laughing like a shark in a kid's pool, Darl but I would have liked a fresh sand crab, none the less. Would you like a roll for lunch, Darl?"

"No! The grass is too damp!"

Sophie ignores him. She turns to Roger. "I've always wanted to visit England, I can't get over how old your buildings are.

Besides lousy weather what else didn't you like about the old country?" Sophie asks intently.

"You could say that we've left narrow horizons, Sophie. A country so riddled with class distinction, that it colours every aspect of life."

"Where was it you came from in England?" Steve asks.

"No-where in particular," Roger grins.

"You can't come from no-where, you have to be from somewhere," says Sophie.

"A very small place, the village of Coxwell," Sue replies.

"Oh, okay," Steve looks at Sophie.

Sophie looks at Steve, and then they burst out laughing.

"That's just about as no-where gets, we suppose."

Changing the subject to politics, Roger tries, "Put another way everywhere we looked the Right were turning into the Romanovs and we were on the outer," Roger replies.

"Steve and I have never agreed on politics," Sophie says. "Isn't that right, Darl?"

"If you say so," Steve counters.

"Steve votes Labour, while I vote Liberal," Sophie states, "makes for some interesting pillow talk, don't it, Darl?"

Roger laughs and quotes an old English proverb, "*If wishes were horses, beggars would ride.*"

Chapter 18

KNOCKABOUT

Sue greets Roger when he arrives home from work, "Mummy wants to come visit Down Under."

Roger is stunned. "When?"

Sue's frown softens. "They haven't said when."

"They?"

"Minnie and Aunt Audrey."

"Visit us?"

"Yes."

Roger groans. "What's the point of her visit?"

"I don't know but she must have one."

"Just to ruffle our feathers no doubt!"

"I hope not. Her letter says she just wants to visit. To see how we are. How we've settled in."

"Shit! Can't we just tell her?"

"My sentiment *entirely*, and double shit."

"How long until they arrive?"

"It's not planned yet."

"Can't we put her on the back burner? Or tell her we have terminal diseases and will get back to her in about ten years."

"We could try."

"How long will they be staying?"

"About two weeks."

"Fuck a whole fourteen days," Roger groans. "Double fuck!"

"You might as well have the rest of the good news, I thought I'd hit you with that first."

"There's more?" Roger is shell shocked.

"There's more," Sue says, "I'll get you a beer."

"Is it that bad?"

"Could be tricky. Picasso's son Brett is becoming a problem for Jayne."

"Surely not, aren't they still too young?"

Sue laughs. "Not that style of problem. Sometimes she runs home from playing, 'Mummy, mummy, Brett keeps hitting me'," Sue explains, "He's bruising her on the upper arm."

"Little shit probably likes her."

"We have to do something, Roger."

"I could have a quiet talk with Picasso, I'm sure that he and his wife May would be sympathetic toward our little girl. But is that the best solution?"

"What do you mean?" Sue asks.

"Well, no-one can be constantly watching over Jayne. Maybe there's a better way."

"Such as?"

"Well, if Jayne could stand up for herself a little more with Brett, the problem might sort of solve itself. Won't it?"

"Yes. But how?"

"I'll teach Jayne how to defend herself, but on the QT."

"Do you think it might work?"

"It might. His parents are True Blue Aussies I'm sure they'll be alright with it."

Roger starts. "Jayne the best way to stop Brett from hurting you, Sweetheart, is if Daddykins can teach you how to stand up to him. Show him that you're unafraid. How'd you feel about that?"

Jayne's eyes are alight with enthusiasm.

"First you need to learn how to do this with your hand, make a ball," Roger shows her bunching her fist as a weapon.

Bit by bit Roger coaches her, while Sue becomes a supportive audience and second in the ring.

Jayne learns how to throw the bunched fist straight with the weight of her small shoulder behind it. Jayne has a tendency, as many do, to swing her arm, but once she has perfected the technique of a straight, right-handed punch, there is surprising strength behind it.

Sue is impressed. Jayne is punching Roger's open hand with such force that he is reluctant to let her hit him full in the face.

"Now," Roger explains, "You'll need to make Brett see you're not an easy target. Hit him right on the nose. Do you think you can do that?"

Jayne is sure — actually she is over confident. At not yet five years of age she shows a determination to hold her own against the bigger boy.

"I'm proud of you, Sweetheart." Roger hugs his little girl. "You'll only get one crack at this. And it has to be the big one! You understand?"

Jayne nods.

"Is she ready?" Sue asks. She looks concerned.

"She should be, she's just won five in a row. I'm confident, Sue, she'll pack a punch better than any boy her age."

"Don't push or pick on Brett," Roger warns Jayne. "It's only when he hits you."

Jayne is nodding so hard, Sue thought she would give herself a headache. Off she goes to play out in the yard with the other children.

When Jayne returns home, she is excited.

"How'd it go with, Brett?" Sue asks, nervously.

"Good. He hit me on the arm and it hurt, Mummy," she pauses and rubs her sore arm. "And then I hit him, hard, just how Daddy showed me."

"And?" Roger prompts.

"Nothing," then Jayne's face breaks into the barest hint of a smile, "then blood spurt from his nose and went all down his front."

"And?" Sue prompts.

"He ran to his Mum crying."

"And?" Roger prompts, again.

"May said, 'That'll teach you, you little bully. Now leave, Jayne alone.'"

Sue looks at Roger, Roger looks at Sue. "Maybe she's pulled it off?" Sue says.

"Time will tell," Roger replies.

A few days later Brett tries to hit his sister Debbie over the head with a hammer, but after she enlists the assistance of Jayne, all is peace and light.

Their neighbours on the other side are Trevor and Elizabeth. Roger patrols the fence like a whippet while Trev mows the other side.

Eager to make new friends Roger asks through the fence, "Trev, what are you doing?"

"I'm mowing."

"How long will you be mowing? We thought, maybe a BBQ, and a few beers. Meet some mates?"

"I'll stop when I've finished."

"Alright, what's Liz doing?"

In exasperation, Trev pauses and then he says, "She's out front welding the front end of the car."

Roger is unfazed, "So you'll join us then?"

"Okay!"

They are a family of three. Trev is a big man, nearly as broad as he is tall. His round face adorned with a neat black beard.

"Trev is no show pony," Roger comments to Sue.

"That's because he has no backside to his jeans."

"With his crotch ending at his knees, in a suit he'd look like a large parsnip squeezed into a condom."

Wife Liz is of similar size and demeanour and their daughter, Rose, is similar in age to Jayne.

Trev and Roger both look forward to their weekends. They drink beer with the enthusiasm of Triathlon runners, while eating seafood and BBQs as if they are their only meals. The women like barbies, as they call them, because it is light work for them.

"My pet hate," says Kim as she downs her wine and looks for a refill, "is making a pot of soup."

The other women look interested in her comment, and so she continues, "I can't make soup. I prefer sex."

Suddenly she has a greater audience. "I'll buy in," Sue smiles.

"Well," Kim says, now into her third glass, "sex takes five minutes, a good soup takes days so Art never asks for soup, do you, Love?"

"I don't ask for much of fuck all," Art says, "except you keep house, and look after me." He turns to Roger with a smirk, "That's why they gave women smaller feet, so they can get closer to the sink, Mate."

"You must try calamari in breadcrumbs, it's to die for!" Kim exclaims, changing the subject.

"What's calamari?" Roger asks.

"Fancy name for squid," Steve explains.

The men spend their time regaling each other with old fishing stories, embellished and polished to the degree that only distant memories could inspire.

The second year is passing more quickly than the first. Enjoying their semi rural existence, offset by close proximity to the shops and not too far to the city of Brisbane.

Summers feel hot and sticky even as they acclimatise. With their leftover income they invest in ceiling fans in their upstairs rooms.

Without a breeze, there are often so many flies, they sound like radio signals. Insects find the food within seconds and within minutes it takes an endless corroboree to keep them out of their faces and eyes. Eating inside is the preferred way to go without resorting to Aerogard.

Not far away is a cane farm. A few days before each field is to be harvested, it is set alight. A dense black fog rises from the earth; foul smelling smoke full of floating glowing ashes hangs over the area. Often Steve would get prior advice and warn the women not to wash their clothes for a few days. The clinging black soot gets everywhere. When children went out to play, they came home looking like coal miners who had been in a fight with a cat.

Enrolled in the local Kallangur State School, Sue takes Jayne to settle in with all the other newbies. She feels slightly down as she progresses through the morning at home with only James playing at her side.

Sue answers a knock at the front door.

"What's the matter?" Sue panics, "why aren't you at school?"

"I've had enough of that, I wanted to come home."

"Have you indeed young lady. Well, that's not the way it works. You have to stay until they ring the bell at 3pm, and then I'll be there to meet you and walk you home."

Sue promptly walks Jayne back to her classroom.

"My goodness," says her teacher, "I was wondering where she was. She just got up and walked out. I thought, maybe she's gone to the toilet. I'd better keep an eye on her."

"Yes, you had," is Sue's terse reply.

That night as the globe spun on its axis, providing another part of the world with daylight, Roger receives a phone call from his sister June.

Roger's voice quivers as he speaks with her. "It's so terrible that

Gramps has passed away, I'm so sorry, I'm going to miss him a lot. Poor Gran alone in Portsmouth. Is father going to help her out?"

As long distance calls go this is harder with the delays and the emotion of the phone call.

Unable to answer Roger's question about father helping out June continues as though nothing is amiss.

"Dad wants to know if you'd like anything said at the funeral on your behalf?"

Roger is thoughtful. "If I were there, June, I would like to say 'Goodbye, Gramps. A long time ago you meant the world to a little boy, and the man he has become will never, ever, forget you.'"

"That's really nice, I'll tell Dad."

"Thank you, Sweetheart, love you."

"Love you too. I have to go!"

"Any other news about poor Gramps?" enquires Sue.

"No, and I decided not to give her our local stuff."

"Why ever not? She might have been interested."

"What? Like what other highlights of our year? Besides us running up more debts, and the proposal by the parents' committee to name the school swimming pool after Harold Holt, and oh, yes, that *The Sound of Music* could only be fitted into the end of year school program by cutting out all the songs."

"Probably a blessing in disguise as for all of their intellectual gifts — most have ears of stone."

Jayne and James are allowed a dog, which Sue keeps under strict control. An attractive female Weimaraner puppy named Sasha takes the place of Fred, whom neither child can remember.

In addition to Sasha, they add a cat, Tamarind, some kind of caterpillar creature that Jayne promises will turn into a butterfly, and a gold fish. Jayne insists on having a blue budgerigar in a cage. The bird is named Bluey.

A blissful afternoon is shattered by the dulcet tones of Jayne, "That little fucker savaged me!"

"Jayne, please watch your language. That's not ladylike, Sweetheart," Sue admonishes. "Why did the bird bite you?"

Jayne looks sheepishly at her Mum, "Cause I was feeding him this." She holds up a worm from the garden.

"Yes, well no wonder. Now leave the poor bird alone, outside with you," Sue shoos her out the door.

James makes imaginative drawings and enjoys painting on bits of wood without revealing a shred of talent, while he also collects brightly coloured cards of things about which he has absolutely no understanding. His style of organisation is putting his toy soldiers in a row and he shows a talent for building model aeroplanes from balsa wood kits.

"You've done well, James," Sue gushes admiring his effort, "not as much glue on your fingers as last time, a big improvement."

Jayne reads comics with great care, as though she is trying to understand what motivated the characters or the person who had written it. She likes all of her parents' favourite cartoons; *The Road Runner* and a large Texan cockerel, *Foghorn Leghorn*, who keeps saying things like, 'I say boy use your initiative!' This quickly becomes a family saying no matter who it is aimed at.

Sue progresses to stitching up a hem on Jayne's school uniform instead of using Sellotape. "I hate sewing," she confesses. Most times Sophie assists her. What took Sue ages takes Sophie seconds on her industrial sewing machine.

At school, Jayne learns about God in a Religious Instruction class.

"The Bible's all well and good, but should we give her another perspective?" Roger asks Sue.

"What? While she's clutching her bible like a much loved teddy?"

"Well, yes."

"I'm an Atheist, and you're an Agnostic. Might not go down real well with the bible punching Christian teacher, she promotes an afterlife in paradise where they live happily forever."

"If true, that would be like being in an insane asylum until the twelfth of never."

"Maybe just touch on the horror of the First Testament, then."

This results in frightening the stuffing out of James who now cries.

Roger continues. "God, if you believe HE is your creator, gave you canine teeth so that you can rip the flesh from the bones of animals."

"Trust Jayne to like that teeth part, Roger, but James is crying, again."

Sue and Roger exchange glances. "It's a challenging proposition this bringing up children," Sue observes.

"So's hang gliding, that doesn't mean we shouldn't try to do it." Roger opens the fridge as if giving himself somewhere to look. "Not sure if I'm wanting something or just contemplating the creation of the Universe."

Roger has been stricken by feelings of guilt over his Dad and his sister June.

"Family after all is family," Sue says in matter of fact tone. "He's your Dad. Even if he did screw us over."

"If I call him it could rebound on us."

"How?"

"Well, reminding him he has a son doing well in Oz might give him ideas?"

"What ideas?"

"How to better take advantage of us from 16,500 miles away could be a start. We really don't know for sure if it was he who told the bank where to find us, or his Nazi cow of a wife?"

The guilt Roger feels now is like a rusty barnacle sunk deep into his skin. A free radical roaming inside his body, seeking a place to nest, grow and corrupt him. How could he continue to enjoy the fruits of Down Under without at least speaking with his Dad?

The 2nd February 1973 is fast approaching. It will be Roger's Dad's 50th birthday.

"Ignoring time differences," Sue says, "never will you find a better excuse to call him. Why don't you wish him a happy birthday by phone from Down Under?"

"I don't know...." Roger instantly feels as if all his organs are shutting down as his mind races wildly through the possible doomsday reaction. "I'm feeling as fragile as ice on a hot day, Sue."

Sue stares pitifully at him. "Well, he only gets one birthday a year. If you miss this one, you'll have to wait another twelve months. Have another beer and think about it."

Roger drinks two more beers.

"Don't look back, Roger, too many regrets start popping out."

"Even if I do ring, he might not accept my call, you know."

"Well, that's something you'll never know unless you try. Will you? I know I'd call my Daddy if he were alive."

"Sue you were there. You lived through the hell they put us through."

"Yes, I did. And I lived through the hell that followed it. And I know what fiends your daddy and Zelda were to us. But that was then, and this is now. We have a marvellous life here. No reason not to let bygones be. Think of him as a black hole of need. And think of her..." Sue is momentarily lost for the appropriate words to describe her nemesis Zelda..."think of her being the control freak she is, and hope she eats cardboard with a little tasteless tofu for breakfast."

Roger looks up his Dad's number off the letter from June.

He calls the overseas operator and asks for assistance with placing the call. "What time would it be there, please?" he asks.

"Seven in the morning."

Roger is shaking so hard Sue is worried the floor might vibrate.

After about five rings, the call is answered by Zelda. Roger recognises her voice straight away. The unmistakeable German bastardisation of English.

"Zelda, it's Roger. I've called to wish Dad a happy birthday. Is he there?"

"Vait a moment. I'll get June to go call your fader."

Roger covers the mouthpiece and whispers to Sue, "It's Zelda. She's sent June to get Dad."

Sue's flirtatious gaze turns suddenly cool as a cucumber. "No 'How are you? Hello?' Not even 'How are the children?'."

"My thoughts entirely. No. Nothing."

"Maybe she's gone away to slip into something more comfortable? Like a coma," Sue giggles.

When Roger's, Dad eventually comes to the phone he sounds breathless, like he has been running.

"Are you alright, Dad?" Roger asks, "I hope I didn't catch you in the middle of something." There's an edge of sarcasm to Roger's voice.

Edward does not answer right away. When he speaks, his voice quivers slightly.

"Yes, thanks, Son. I'm fine. We've missed you here," he pauses as if collecting his thoughts. "It's been a bit like Christmas, but without a tree."

"Shit happens, Dad."

"True, son. How's Sue and the children?"

"They're very well, Dad. Thanks for asking." There's a catch in Roger's voice.

"You know about your Gramps."

"Yes thanks. Not much we could do or say from here," Roger manages a weak smile and thinks *16,500 miles, we might as well be on the moon, all the good we can do.*

"Your Gran's alright. I spent some time with her. Looks like you've just missed out on Vietnam, Son. Well, done."

"I might have been too old, Dad. As you know they prefer the younger ones. Those without any knowledge of horror. Expendable cannon fodder."

"Armed forces prefer younger, bullet proof, candidates, Son. That's historical fact. You're on the money."

Within seconds Edward's hardened exterior simply crumbles. His relief is palpable. His son Roger has come back to him.

"Look, Son. I can understand that having Zelda as a step mother wouldn't exactly be a walk in the park."

"Nice of you to say that, Dad. But I didn't call up to speak to Zelda. I called to speak with you. To wish you a happy birthday. That said we, that is Sue and I understand, you and her are the package deal. I'm sure Jayne and James miss having you as a granddad."

There is a long pause. So long that for a moment Roger wonders if they have been disconnected. And then, "You're right, Son. On reflection maybe our tribe has been apart too long?"

"So, how are *you*, Dad?"

"I'm well. My weight hasn't changed much over the years. The last time I saw a bone was on an X-ray."

They both laugh.

"Let's keep in touch, Dad. We'll send a few photos when we can."

"Thanks, Son. Pleased you called."

Roger lets out a long sigh of relief. "That went alright, Sue."

"More than alright, it sounded like it went very well."

"Is Grandad coming to visit?" Jayne asks.

Sue and Roger exchange looks. "Maybe," Roger says tentatively.

Chapter 19

FAUNA

Roger is convinced by their new True Blue Aussie friends that all Poms should become swimmers; but impersonating a fish is a big problem for him, as he has no gills. James and Jayne take to the water like ducks. Sue who swam for her school in England has no problems with water except now she prefers not to get her hair wet!

To help alleviate the situation Sue convinces Roger that for the good of their children they should buy a small to medium sized above ground pool. Secretly she is hoping it will also help Roger overcome his fear of water.

Sue finds a special deal at Myer Department Store, Fortitude Valley. It seems not long after payment than the pool kit is delivered.

"Here'll be your perfect spot, Roger," announces Steve, running his measurement tape out across the ground beyond where their car is usually parked.

"Close to a power point for the filter, and the tap for topping her up," Roger agrees.

Willing hands help prepare the ground, removing weeds, stones and raking it clear and level. Steve supervises with his carpenter's belt full of tools while Sue organises refreshments.

Finished in half a day they celebrate with their ubiquitous BBQ, while waiting for the pool to fill. To accelerate the process hoses from four different houses are run across the gardens in between.

"No dramas," Art beams, "that pool'll soon fill up. Time to blow the froth off a few coldies, Rog."

Roger breaks out beers as cold as a slab of refrigerated meat.

"Once you get used to our Fourex, you'll want to try Fourex Draught. It's available in long necks, or stubbies, Roger. It's a better drop." Trev smiles through his neat black beard.

"Less talking more drinking," Art suggests, flipping the cap off a bottle of beer, and smiling at the hiss of the compressed air escaping. "Love that sound."

After an hour Sue chimes in. "If you go on like this — soon you'll be speaking in Braille, how's about getting the job finished first?"

They take the hint and get to it.

With the new pool filled with water Sue notices a few bees hovering about on its surface. Not wanting the children to get stung she eyeballs Picasso, "Do you still have a bee hive in your yard?"

"I've got two bee hives, Love."

Sue continues sweetly eyeing the growing swarm, "Might your bees be checking out our pool?"

Picasso scratches his head. "It's possible. Good question, but are they my bees? Could be from anywhere?"

"How can you tell the difference?" Roger asks.

"Well," muses Picasso, "question is have any of them got a white dot on their head?"

Roger gets up from his seat to check.

Beer in hand he moves closer to investigate. Peering more closely at a single bee, he announces, "No. I don't think this one has a white dot on its head."

"Oh, well, there you have it. Not my bees, Mate."

The bees buzz for a few more minutes then depart; the BBQ ending when Roger and Art are the last two standing.

Daily Roger ventures into the pool. There he submerges his head, but it is not working for him. When he attempts to swim, it is only the breaststroke.

Co-ordination was never his strong suit, his arms are working together but his feet fail to get the message.

"My attempt at swimming," Roger concedes to their friends over many a beer, "has largely been unsuccessful. It is more of what to do? Pat my head or rub my tummy."

"It's tantamount to Mozart and Chopin playing different tunes on the same piano at the same time," giggles Sue.

Picasso is becoming used to his Pommy neighbours and often cracks up at Roger's antics. On one occasion, Roger is standing on the very top step of their rear porch for vantage and bellows, "Jayne! Jayne! Where are you, Jayne?"

When he has her attention, he continues.

"Jayne your dog's shitting in the yard because you're not walking her enough, Sweetheart. What are you going to do about it?"

Using reverse psychology Roger is hoping that given the choice of cleaning up after the dog or actually walking her, as she had promised to do, care problems would be resolved.

Meanwhile the Pug belonging to Picasso's children likes bashing its ball backwards and forwards against Sue and Roger's garage tilt panel door. *Crash! Crash!*

Roger's patience runs thin, he calls out loudly, "I say, Mate, your dog keeps bashing its damned ball up against our garage door. Can't you train him to use yours?"

May's bored voice returns, "Tie the mutt up to the bloody fence post and the kids can bring him home at lunch time."

Chapter 20

BEING A NATURAL

Thanks to Roger's trial by fire in the Motherland, here in the lucky country he is what some would describe as a natural salesman, having no problem meeting and often exceeding the Snake Pit's budgets.

"I don't know how you do it," Tweedy is shaking his head genuinely impressed.

"Do what?"

"Get higher sales figures than me. Our territories are similar, we have about the same number of leads and call outs. It doesn't make sense."

"Well, what's the one thing customers want?"

Seeing Tweedy's blank expression of bewilderment, Roger presses on, "To feel special, customer service. I focus on that. They deal directly with me for all things, any issues, problems, questions, my direct line, and by doing that I've increased my prices as it's an additional service. I'll help you if you want."

"That sounds good, okay then, shoot."

Tweedy can see the merit in Roger's advice. They set out a plan, practice it with role playing in the office. After a week, Tweedy is on his own.

Two weeks in to it, Roger finds Tweedy skulking in the office lunchroom, "How's it going?"

"Ah Roger, I think it's more for you. I've tried, really I have. But I'm finding it very difficult. I might scale it back a bit."

"Sure thing, you do what's comfortable for you."

When Roger arrives home that night Sue shatters his thoughts about Tweedy by waving a letter from Minnie who finally announces the dates of their visit.

Nice way to end a day, thinks Roger.

To take his mind off the horror of the impending arrival of the sarcastic mother-in-law from hell, he changes the subject.

"I feel I need to assist Tweedy further to get him onto the right track. He's timidity is in spades with his approach to raising the figures; perhaps if I go with him to some of his quotes…"

"Oh I wouldn't do that," Sue suggests, a bit taken back with the change of topic. She is shaking her head vehemently, "it smacks of the old days when you worked for your father for nothing. Tweedy will get the commission whilst you get a pat on the back. It's not your job leave it to Jack."

"Perhaps you're right, Love. As that old saying goes time heals all wounds."

Roger is now in regular contact with his Dad back in the land of grey and rain. Their relationship is progressing quickly to being back on track. Edward is undeniably impressed with his son's advancement down under.

"Yes, we are Poms," Roger announces at the weekly BBQ, "but now we have Naturalisation documentation to prove we're Australians."

The gathering cheers and glasses are solemnly raised, and that raising continues well in to the small hours of morning.

Walking into the office on the Monday with a slight hangover Roger is greeted by Jack.

"I see big changes coming if you continue like this; I know of no-one in Australia who's clocking up as much in commissions as you are."

Jack has sent the Snake Pit one too many antagonistic memos and reports. The suits in Sydney have their backs up, and high-rankers are flying to Brisbane to set Jack straight.

The Suits arrive, suitably dressed as suits are, straight into Jack's inner sanctum.

Bets are being placed by staff as the suits are confirmed on their afternoon flight back to the Snake Pit from whence they slithered.

A raised voice echoes around the unnaturally quiet office, "Trouble with you," says a buttoned-down suit, shifting his weight from one arse cheek to the other, "is you've got champagne tastes on a bloody beer income, Mate. Your name isn't Christopher bloody Wright. Just look at your rising costs."

Eyebrows are raised. Suddenly the phones are taken off the hooks. Staff suddenly need to be speaking closely with Lucy on some imaginary urgent issues.

"What's that about Christopher Wright?" Roger whispers.

Lucy moves in closer. Roger can almost feel the heat of her body through her thin chiffon blouse. "Word is he's spending money like water at Snuffabug. Blew $4,000 on a business luncheon for three last week."

"How do you know this?" Roger asks.

"Contacts," Lucy smiles, "not much gossip goes on down south that gets past me. Shut up now I want to listen…"

Jack's head is bowed as if in conciliation. He is aware that he might have pushed the Snake Pit too far this time.

Roger who is hovering now between Lucy and Tweedy rolls his eyes.

"No doubt the poor bloody air hostesses were impressed on their plane ride up," Lucy whispers.

The loud voices continue, increasing in pitch and volume.

"We've spoken with the board and you'll take their instructions and ours, is that understood?" the second suit delivers with a condescending smirk.

"Will the instructions of the board and yours be the same?" Jack asks with a straight face.

The seated suit shifts from one arse cheek to the other again. The standing suit begins to pace, while glaring at Jack. As he does a pass of the door, he notices the staff gathered, glares at them, and slams it shut. That made listening in on the conversation more difficult than winning the Lottery.

"Christ," Roger exclaims, "I'm surprised the door didn't break free and come flying over here."

The others all scurry and scatter away in case the suit got a good look at them. Roger hangs in to hear the voices muffled but decidedly very angry.

"Wow! This could get interesting and more complicated," Tweedy suggests.

"Might it swing the other way?" Roger responds.

"Jack knows his stuff," Lucy says, "but he might be too much of a nuclear red button at the Snake Pit. He's making too many enemies with the new guard, particularly as they believe few out in the provinces can barely sharpen a pencil."

The door opens, suit one and two walk out without a backwards glance or goodbye to anyone. Jack remains in his office for another fifteen minutes, then scuttles away like a whipped dog with its tale between its legs.

Tweedy says, "I'll bet that's a conversation he wishes he never had."

Roger agrees, "That was damned poor form by the Snake Pit."

A couple of quiet, uneasy days pass, Roger walks into the office to find both suits standing with Lucy.

The Chief of all Chiefs accompanies the suits, Ricky the Ringmaster himself. He looks like a prosperous grandfather, probably because he is. Some refer to him as the Godfather, others more cynically the Codfather, but there is no-one senior to Tricky Ricky in Oz.

It is said that in a previous life Tricky Ricky sold real estate and dabbled in land development with his brother.

What is not widely reported, but discussed in hushed whispers, is that much of the land he sold went underwater on less than a King tide!

Carefully groomed, with a gossamer halo of silver hair, lengthening jowls, he wore semi-round gold framed glasses covering the eyes of one who rarely loses at cards. He wears an immaculate pinstriped suit, with a red paisley necktie hanging from his shirt stud. With his shiny brogue shoes Ricky boasts great prosperity.

They exit the building with Jack in the middle of the pack. His expression is one of chilli in his porridge!

This meeting takes place off premises, a few hours later Roger receives a call at the office, inviting him out to join them for dinner. Sue is not included. For the remainder of the afternoon Roger's intestines are twisting into pretzels. The office is abuzz with gossip.

At dinner after some initial chitchat, Roger notices Jack seems quieter than usual. Ricky the Ringmaster looks calm, as if he had eaten a good lunch, taken a Nanna nap, and checked that the balance on his retirement fund was good.

Ricky opens with, "We can't pay you these commissions, Roger."

Roger is taken back.

"Why not, Ricky?" Roger is dumfounded, shocked, and angry. "I haven't been fudging the figures. They're genuine enough."

"We know that. We didn't take your word for it, we always audit commissions before they're paid."

"I don't understand, Ricky, then why can't I be paid my commissions?"

Ricky leans in across the table, as if to impart some great secret. With a watery smile he says with sincerity, "We can't pay you that much commission, Roger, because if we did you'd be paid more for the year than our State Managers. Hell, you'd be getting nearly as much as our General Manager, or me." He grins as if that will take away Roger's pain. "I'm sorry," he sniffs, "but it's not our policy to pay consultants more than Senior Management. Oh, nice main course by the way," Ricky bestows his sales winning smile at the waitress.

Roger is crestfallen. He has completely lost his appetite. The rare eye fillet steak cooked to perfection with fresh seasonal vegetables suddenly seems unappetising.

Ricky leans back in his chair. "Jack, do you think now is the time to tell, Roger?"

Jack smiles a relaxed smile for the first time since devouring his oysters natural. "None better, Ricky."

Ricky becomes placatory. "Look, Roger, we sense your disappointment."

I'd say he's on the money with that, Roger thinks. Forcing himself to think of fluffy white clouds and rainbows.

"We've decided to reward you for all your hard work in another way, a way that better suits our policy for advancement. Are you interested?"

Roger is unsure how to behave. He needs a job but is still coming to terms with being shafted out of his commission. What he could do with that money; how much it meant to him and Sue, now just taken away. To him, it is a disaster, especially as he and Sue had already planned the spending of it.

Ricky looks anxiously at Jack before continuing, "We're about to offer you a promotion, Roger. Regional Manager, with an excellent increase in salary, better car, and your own office and staff as a sub-branch."

"Did I hear you right?" Roger asks, unsure if he really did hear the words, or if they were his imagination trying to reassure him.

"What do you say?" Ricky asks.

Although Roger has lost his commissions, the increase in salary would be a step up. The autonomy of the new office could suit him well. The only negative would be living up to the Snake Pits inflated expectations.

He looks at Jack, and thinks he sees an almost imperceptible nod of his mentor's head.

"I accept your kind offer, and thank you very much," Roger answers with his best salesman's smile.

The relief on Ricky's face is palpable. He holds out his hand. It is spongy and damp.

"Great!" exclaims Jack. "I'll organise celebratory drinks."

"Just one question?" Roger asks.

Jack pauses mid forkful to his mouth, as if a great hand holds onto him, followed by a long pregnant silence.

"Yes, and what would that be?" asks Ricky quietly, blinking a couple of times.

"Will my new salary be capped? Or will I be eligible for commission on sales, or bonus if the job progresses well?"

"There's no holding him down, is there?" Ricky's mouth curves to reveal a generous smile and winks at Jack, "I'm sure we'll be able to work something out, Roger."

Roger forces a smile.

Breaking the news to Sue is easier than expected as she is delighted with his news about being promoted.

They celebrate their successful day with a bottle of New Hope Wine, while he tells her about the gossip surrounding Christopher Wright and the report by Lucy about the expensive business lunch.

"Could he spend $4,000 on a luncheon for three?" Sue asks.

"Dunno. It sounds incredible to me, but I suppose if you throw in a brothel and a few expensive ladies anything's possible."

"Lucky boys. Tell me more about this, Christopher Wright."

"Well, I've only met him the once. He's a man with the gentle forgiving eyes of a priest, who in my opinion is capable of selling just about anything, to anybody."

"He sounds clever."

"Yes, he's quite a legend in his own right, hence his nick name Legend Man.

Word is Chris was expensively educated somewhere overseas in

Europe, hails from maybe Russia, he might be a Croatian Jew, speaks multiple languages, and his English sounds like he's a news presenter from the BBC.

With his concierge smile, and sporting a gold wristwatch the size of a sundial, Chris makes a big impression wherever he goes. His ties and smiles are as wide as the Hume Highway.

Story is that he even managed to convince the Australian Taxation Office that his 92 year old mother really is the proud, registered owner of the brand new red Porsche sports car imported from Germany, and in pride of place in his garage."

On the next scheduled call to his father, he brings up his promotion. Roger's stories filtering back about the way they live, contrary to Edward's own ambitions, have quite simply impressed him.

"It vill not be long before you are ze scheming how you too can be Down Under except for ze few hurdles. Remember mit our ages, and our teenage girls, ve vill not be eligible for ze subsidised government sponsorship program."

"That's on the verge of being scrapped, Zelda. The ads about them have already begun to dry up signifying significant budget changes to come," Edward replies absently.

The more Edward thinks about it problems seem to arise.

"Being an undischarged bankrupt is high on the list, Zelda, and then there are our health issues."

Zelda has been diagnosed with having had a very mild form of tuberculosis when as a younger woman she left Germany, and with his own lifetime of smoking Edward is unsure how he will measure up with being tested.

"Mein Gott, you may be over simplifying," Zelda snaps, "and to you, this is simply a case of dee grass in next field being greener. Ja, it all makes perfect sense to you."

"Our expensive Marine Gate lease is gone with our recent move," Edward reminds Zelda.

"Ya, managing a small private hotel property in South Wales. June and Charlotte hate it 'ere, and so do I."

Chapter 21

UP SELLING WITH ARACHNOPHOBIA

"Sue, this promotion is more demanding than I expected," Roger smiles sheepishly, "however, if this keeps up we can afford to buy another mud crab."

"Don't toy with me, Roger." Sue's eyes are alive and dancing with mischief.

Roger, realising he might have opened a can of worms, tactlessly changes subject.

"With all the impending changes we have a new chief of pest control."

"What happens to Jack?"

"He's being sidelined, heading up a new division. He'll still be based in Brisbane and in our same office, same staff. Frankly, Jack feels totally fucked, not unlike General Custer at Little Big Horn."

"Who's your new boss?"

"George Lancaster. He's an ex-JFL manager from interstate, a big talker and keen as mustard to impress the Snake Pit in Sydney."

"JFL?"

"Job For Life Pest Control.

Word is George measured Jack's office curtains and was ready to move in before Jack could even vacate."

"How old is he?" Sue asks.

"No-one knows. He looks older than his stated years. Those who doubt his age, like Scottie, point to his Certificates of Merit displayed prominently on his new office wall. Anyone who looks closely at them might notice their decorative frames partially obscure the lower part of the year awarded, so we have no clue." Laughing Roger adds, "George is a big man who likes wearing suits and ties, his appearance is complemented by bushy eyebrows of caterpillar size. Scottie reckons he could brush his fucken shoes with them."

Next morning it is the usual meeting.

"Spider control is good business according to the Snake Pit," George announces at their next sales meeting, "and they think we're being slack by not increasing sales."

Roger looks concerned. "Sydney does have the Funnel Web, George. Surely that must reflect in their sales."

"It is supposedly the deadliest spider on our planet, Chief," reinforces Tweedy.

Roger's relationship with spiders has been an uneasy one since he was four years old. His mother's grim unsmiling face while screaming at full volume for assistance when one dropped dead from the ceiling of their Kensington flat harmlessly to the floor, had traumatised the life out of him. His dread had now become paranoia driving him half crazy at times with worry.

Scottie chips in. "Most Brisbanites, me included, would prefer it stay in Sydney, Matey."

"There's a Funnel Web in Toowoomba and according to entomologists it's related, but according to the Queensland Museum, it's not of the same deadly variety," George explains raising his 'Coco the Clown' eyebrows.

Tweedy is upbeat. "I guess the closest we have to a dangerous spider here is the Redback, its bite can be lethal if left untreated."

"And it's quite pretty, which is a problem especially with children," Lucy adds.

"I thought your experience interstate was fumigation," Lucy's voice is scratchy.

"I know these things," George grins tapping his oversized nose.

"Well, if the Snake Pit wants us to go hunt Redbacks," says Roger, "we shouldn't have to look far."

"Aye, back in the day when Brisbanites did nowt else but shit on a can dunny in their backyard, them critters thrived under the toilet seats," Scottie adds sagely.

There is a prolonged silence.

"Come on," prompts George, "name a *bastard* spider."

"The Mouse Spider," Roger volunteers "it's big, it's ugly, and only its mother would love it."

"Name another?" George sounds impatient.

"Huntsman's fifteen centimetres across when fully grown and can jump," Tweedy offers, "big and hairy, but harmless."

"Aye, but there's nowt but two deadly bastards, Matey," Scottie states, "and they're the oil black Redback and Funnel Web."

"We've covered them," George reminds, "come on, imagine you're spider hunting."

"Bird Eating," Roger suggests, "but I've never even seen one."

"Aye, the White Tailed's flesh eating," Scottie offers, "I've heard them bastards reside in tropical rainforests."

"And prevalent in Sydney too! What about the Australian Jumping Spider?" George asks.

Everyone looks blank.

"It's a *jump out at you* bastard spider! FUCK ME!" George waves his arms in exasperation his features rigid.

"Cannae remember seeing it Matey, nae jumping nor anything else," Scottie's shaking his head, "but in the Amazon it's said they have a Tarantula capable of carrying off human babies from their villages."

"Alright," George is rolling his eyes, "moving on because we've a suit coming up from the Snake Pit to explain…he'll be here soon…short and not so sweet."

A groan arises from all present.

"Wait for it, *and* he's going to show us how this can be better done," George explains.

"What's special about him?" Lucy asks demurely.

"His speciality is Spin," George explains.

"Spin what?" Lucy persists.

"Official title is Spin Doctor, no-one heard of them?"

Lucy meets George's soft gaze. "What's a Spin Doctor?"

"It's really a fancy name for being a professional liar," Tweedy eyes them harshly, "becoming more popular these days in government circles."

"He's a spokesman for the company whose speciality is putting out a favourable interpretation of events, particularly popular with political parties," George is in overdrive, lowering his voice unnecessarily. "Roger you get the short straw and he's all yours — this afternoon."

Afterwards Roger explains his day.

"The Spin Doctor turned out to be quite personable, Sue. He's a True Blue Aussie and not a bad bloke. The lady client we visited claimed she was unhappy with our services because she'd seen a Redback on her clothes line."

"On the washing line?"

"Yes. Believe it or not. I inspected the area, with the Spin Doctor in tow, but neither of us could find any signs of infestation."

"Nothing?"

"Not even a trace of a web. Interested to see how he intended to sell this service up, I stood back, and waited. I reasoned he's on a higher salary than me."

"What happened?"

"The advice from our expert to the lady client was, I thought, a tad unusual."

"Why? What on earth did he say?"

"'Next time you see a Redback Spider on your clothes' line best spin your contraption super fast so any spiders get dizzy and fall off.'"

"You're joking."

"I'm not joking. True as I stand here, that's what he actually said. When I tell George tomorrow he'll blow a gasket laughing for sure."

"So, what happened?"

"To say the least the Spin Doctor and his advice, came across less than impressive to the client. No extra services were quoted. On our way to the airport he agreed how it's impossible to sell up under those circumstances without finding a problem."

Shortly after the Spin Doctor's drop in, visits from the Snake Pit tailed off.

Roger wondered about the Hills rotary hoist theory, only as far as wondering whether a Lazy Susan in a Chinese Restaurant was really invented by Susan?

George explains at their next weekly sales meeting. "With spider control on the outside of a building, one train of thought is not to remove any cobwebs prior to treatment. Thoroughly soak the webs with residual chemical. In theory the spider, if it doesn't get drowned during spraying, will come into contact with the spray when it re-enters its web. If it's a female carrying young, they will also die."

"So if it isn't glowing in the dark before we sprayed, it will be soon after," Roger confirms.

Roger receives a withering look from George.

"Aye, the difficult part, Matey," Scottie continues obliviously, "is convincing the client, that for the good of their treatment, spider webs should be lightly brushed down after a few weeks, and cannae be hosed down at all as that washes chemical away."

"Speaking as one who has a phobia about them, not sure I'd like the webs to remain, but okay, I'll try to impart that valuable tit bit to my clients." Roger counters, "I was once met at the door by Sue in a near state of panic. She was convinced her unwelcome visitor, was a huge spider," Roger spread his hands wide as a breakfast plate, "and had taken up lodgings in the bathroom."

"What did you do?" asks George sarcastically, "call another pest control company?"

"Would you like a saucer of milk with that comment, George?" asks Lucy sarcastically.

"No, my self-control was evaporating as I moved tentatively forward..."

"No doubt ready to retreat at a moment's notice should you sight old hairy legs," Lucy offers with glee.

"And when I did, it was the biggest spider I'd seen outside of a museum."

"You should have captured it. Put it in a jar!" George states with some pompous authority.

"Fuck off, Mate, it's a monster bigger than a tennis ball and with long hairy legs." Roger continues with a shudder, "Sue's hiding behind the door with Jayne, James is fast asleep. I got the feeling that if I tried stomping it to death it might even throw me on my back. This was shades of Wacol-Hilton with that damned cockroach."

"Aye, if only the bugger would remain perfectly still while you summon help, Matey, but wait on! You are the help," enthuses Scottie.

"Bloody thing moved," Roger is reliving the moment, "Sue and Jayne are armed to the teeth, I've got nothing, I didn't know whether to shit, shave, or shower? Pass me something!" I said. "Sue handed me a shoe. I said, I'm wearing a pair of them, Sweetheart."

"What happened next?" asks Lucy.

"I got a rolled up newspaper and an egg slice and started taking swipes at it. If only it had stayed still, I'd have got the upper hand."

"Maybe, you should not advertise your arachnophobia," George warns with a frown.

"I'm trying to keep said spider at arm's length in the bath, while I call for backup, George. Give me a break, here!"

"Aye, what sort of backup?" Scottie asks.

"Well, besides the obvious tank, armoured car, and rocket launcher, I was hoping for an aerosol can containing insecticide."

"The spider isn't an insect," George reminds again, pompously, "you'd need something stronger than fly control."

"A man has to work with what cards he's dealt. By the time I'd emptied the can, said spider would at least have slowed down, its eyes watering for long enough, maybe for me to kill it."

"And so you won the day," Lucy laughs.

"Admittedly the bugger never looks as big when he's packaged for disposal in wads of toilet paper, but it's always best to have a ceremonial viewing by family members of the remains—prior to flushing," Roger announces proudly.

"Why do you have to show Sue a dead spider?" George asks.

Roger shrugs, "Convinces all interested parties the victory has been won and not still residing in among the towels I s'pose."

"What better ceremony before the vanquished has an unguided tour of the city," Tweedy adds, a gleam in his squinty eye. "Flush twice!"

"Talking of spider control," George leans back in his chair, "the Snake Pit has decided to mount displays in major shopping centres and I'm told they want us to do one, here."

"What's the stand like?" Tweedy asks.

"It's supposed to be the brain child of our new General Manager, Frank Moore."

"Anyone met him yet?" Roger asks.

"I have," volunteers Jack, "at our interstate meeting. He spoke at length during which he lost my goodwill and any deference I'd harbour for his position. He went on and on impressing us with his own importance."

"His importance?"

"Yes, occasionally he looked me up and down and snagged me with a dead cod like gaze. He's no chin to speak of."

"A chinless wonder?"

"Exactly. And he's short of stature."

"Short?"

"He's short and fat and sullen as a stick. He has absolutely no sense of humour, which goes well with his Hitlerian toothbrush moustache resembling a horizontal slug trail. Coming from bed manufacturing he has no knowledge of our industry. He wouldn't know one end of a cockroach from another. Word is he's an accounting whiz!"

"Great start," Roger groans, "might work better if he knew something about pest control."

"What he knows about pest control would fit in a thimble," Jack emphasises.

Lucy asks, "How short is he?"

"The top of his bald head barely reached my shoulder," Jack says.

"Is he a dwarf?" George asks.

"Close. Built like an egg and bald as a badger," Jack replies with a cautious smile, "with his smudge of a moustache under his nose and a red biro permanently in his left hand. He's a south paw with an enormous ego."

"Most short men are egoistic," Lucy adds.

"A few years ago I suggested featuring a live Blue-Ringed Octopus. Said live animal was scheduled to be caught and sent over to Brissie in a sealed container from Dunwich on Moreton Island. However, that wasn't a popular suggestion with the suits of the day."

"Why not?" George asks.

"Too dangerous having it on display alive."

Lucy adds, "Although of interest in drawing a crowd, it's not a pest to be controlled either, is it?"

"According to the Snake Pits' chief spear thrower white mice or rats are more popular with visiting children and their parents, particularly if the children can handle them as pets," George adds.

"That was suggested back then also," Jack is thoughtful, "we even got the university at St. Lucia interested in loaning us some white laboratory animals."

"And so?" prompts George.

"Trouble is we're not trying to promote the idea of rodents as pets and that concept sort of collided with the idea of us being the best option for killing them," Jack explains. "Another problem with the live rodent idea was caring for them without taking them home at the end of each day."

"Just to make it clear," Roger states, "if I end up manning the stand I have no intention of being foster father to rodents out at Casa Del Kallangur. Not even pretty white ones, Sue would kill me. And I need not mention the eight legged creatures."

"Centre management were not rapt in the idea either," Jack continues, "rodents getting loose among their shops, even if they were tame, and white, and to top it off our staff would have to feed and water them, and keep their cages clean. All in all it's a lot more practical to show photographs of pests and have samples of packaged poisons and equipment on display."

Discussions take place with the Snake Pit and Frank's new chief spear thrower, wants live creatures on the display to attract more curiosity. He feels strongly that if more people visit the display stand and engage in meaningful conversation, any sales staff, even those of limited ability, should be able to follow his simple formula to secure record-breaking sales.

"He's right, and he's wrong," Jack concludes, "but no point in upsetting Centre Management, or offending prospective customers. It's a company display stand not a bloody three-ringed circus. Roger it's your baby."

Stated wishes of Frank, to display live creatures, never eventuate. Frank blames Jack. Jack blames spear thrower Wayne, then George. George blames Roger. Unsure whether he should be proud or ashamed, Roger mans the stand personally for the duration at Toombul Shopping Centre. At least it is a break from office politics and the Snake Pit for a while.

"Seven days straight you just did!" Sue reminds him, as she pours his second beer.

"Long days," Roger comments as he holds the glass of frosty amber liquid aloft. "Often with periods that ranged from extreme boredom to utter bedlam when, for some inexplicable reason, everyone wanted my attention at the same time."

"You performed quite well," Sue asserted proudly giving him a tender kiss on the cheek.

"Yes, I collected many names and addresses but never enough to satisfy Frank. I told him, 'I'd done jolly well with twenty leads and do you know what he said?"

"What?"

He shook his head from side to side fixing me with those cod like eyes. "Don't say 'jolly' you sound like a damned pom!"

"What did you say?"

"Nothing. He made me feel like something dying on a hook."

Chapter 22

KIN

Roger has enjoyed talking with June by phone and now she is writing regularly. Communication between the two families has escalated rapidly.

Roger is now getting the drum on the gossip.

Zelda going cold on the idea of a life Down Under is clear but how much will her political manoeuvrings behind the scenes with Edward affect Charlotte's decision?

Roger and Sue have offered sponsorship to their family no strings attached. That comprises written guarantees that accommodations will be provided, as neither Edward nor Zelda are eligible for any government assistance.

"What's the difference?" Roger comments, "besides the subsidised air fares and a few days at their Wacol-Hilton we've never received any government assistance, anyway."

Edward applies successfully to be discharged as a bankrupt, even he is astonished at his good fortune.

"You suffered long enough, Edvard," Zelda says comforting him.

"Subject to them having successful health checks life Down Under is becoming a distinct possibility. Do you think your Dad will get work here?" Sue is understandably concerned about the family guarantees she and Roger have undertaken.

"I hope so, we don't want to have to support them here forever. I'm flat out supporting us four."

In between building his region to please his new boss, and their social life at weekends, Roger has become excited about the impending arrival of his family Down Under.

Sue has already sorted out beds and bedding. Jayne and James are to share temporarily. That frees up a room for Edward and Zelda. The two girls, June and Charlotte, are to be on camp beds in the living room.

"It's tight as but workable for a short period," Sue explains.

Jayne's understanding of tidying her room was making a pathway from the door to her bed, shoving unwanted toys under said bed.

Sue standing at the door, her arms folded, judges, "Not good enough, young lady."

After some childish petulance and a Mexican standoff, begrudgingly Jayne tidies her room.

Four weeks after the 1974 Brisbane floods have subsided, Roger's contingent are excited, finally awaiting the arrival of their kin from the old country. As the sliding doors from Customs and Migration part at the Brisbane International Airport Sue's tissues appear from nowhere. Dabbing her eyes from all the built up emotions. Like startled, stunned, and bewildered deer, the passengers begin to file out through those doors.

Twenty people are through when Roger catches sight of his father. Roger hears before he sees his sister June, her squeals of delight echoing about. She runs and almost knocks Roger over. June cannot decide if she wants to hug, Roger, Sue, Jayne, or James, or all at once, while Sue is handing out tissues.

Jayne and James are both excited. "Granddad!" In unison they run to hug grandpa's legs and body. In return, Edward leans down, smiling, to embrace both children at once.

Roger hugs his father and notices that Edward looks as if he has aged ten years. His posture is not as straight, his hair seems less thick and more grey: the man's energy level is not as robust as he remembers.

Zelda's eyes, the colour of dark chocolate and as round as billiard balls, continually sweep the space around them reminding Roger she is tougher than a goat's knee.

A smile spreads across Edward's face from ear to ear, which is only a reflection of Roger's own. Edward's statue melting smile blows away many old recriminations like leaves in a storm.

"How was your flight, Dad?" Roger asks.

"Excellent, Son."

Brief cordial hugs are exchanged with the Iron Maiden Zelda, her face an easy read of disapproval at being touched by commoners. Now Jayne wants to kiss granny hello.

"Vat is dis?" Zelda is horrified. "I am not ze granny! Nein dis is forboten! I vill only be called ze nanny. Ya, dat is better, is dat understood?"

Jayne is horrified at the rebuff.

James clutching grandad's leg looks about to cry.

Her answer is vacant stares of disbelief.

The sound of silence is earth shattering.

"Anyway, you are not my real grandchildren," Zelda responds with an embarrassed huff.

"Thanks for reminding us," mutters Sue, who nothing less than gracious forces a tired smile as they help guide Edward and Zelda with their luggage. It is then that Roger notices no Charlotte. Instead, a teenage boy is hovering about.

Much to Zelda's annoyance, her daughter had not turned up at Heathrow Airport. Numerous phone calls went unanswered until it was too late for Charlotte to join them. She finally advised, "I've decided to stay in the UK."

Allegedly, a boyfriend of some significance was involved with her decision, is all Edward will disclose.

Barry shakes hands with Roger and family, introducing himself as June's boyfriend.

He at the last minute was able to take advantage of Charlotte's unused air ticket. Sue and Roger share a glance that spoke, "Somehow this was in the works well beforehand."

When Barry smiles at June, his pale brown eyes disappear behind his pallid cheeks. He is medium height, broad shouldered, and sullen. The muscles of his triceps look surgically carved.

Sue and Roger look at each other in amazement. "Doesn't help us much with the bedding arrangements," he whispers to Sue.

"Maybe we shouldn't concern ourselves with their sleeping arrangements," she whispers back, "from the way the two are eyeing each other off, and the bemused expression on his face, I'm sure love will find a way."

Zelda shows visible signs of distress about Charlotte not making the plane, and who could blame her.

Initially Sue and Roger feel sympathy for her, but she soon puts their minds to rest with her Teutonic attitude, "Mein Gott, I vill vrite to Charlotte, and she vill be here soon."

A big Welsh lad, Barry is a forester by trade. Quite what that means no-one seems to know but it appears the lad has been cutting down trees for firewood.

Barry is quiet, very quiet. At times, Sue and Roger are unsure if their woodsman-come- forester is on their same page.

"He met June while carrying out gardening work at the estate where we lived," Edward continues, with his best winning and inscrutable smile.

Zelda is conspicuous as vengeance dressed up as enthusiasm, she huffs and puffs, while chain smoking her un-tipped French cigarettes.

Their journey from airport to Casa Del Kallangur is full of excited chatter from June and Edward, while Zelda and Barry remain silent.

Roger and Edward unload the car under the guidance of Sue. Zelda stands out front smoking like a chimney.

Sue is not at all happy with Zelda making up for valuable lost time puffing away at her French cigarettes in their car.

Roger is of similar mind: Oh, that distinctive harsh tang and that smell that would prompt the memory — a bit like cat's piss.

"I see your taste in smokes is unaltered," Roger says to Zelda hastily trying to clear the air around him by waving his hands.

"I've positioned ashtrays for our visitors," Sue explains testily, "and can only hope they give up smoking or leave before our freshly painted white ceilings turn yellow from their smoke."

Zelda's response, besides a grunt of acknowledgement, is a serious facial expression that probably has been permanently stamped on her features since about one week before arrival.

Barry continues to annoy Sue. The big lump of a lad sits on the sofa with June at every opportunity. June flashes proudly her multi-coloured fingernails at every opportunity.

Barry picks his nose.

Sue sees him wipe his errant finger on the fabric of their adopted love seat. When she eyeballs him, knowing he has been spotted, he sucks his fingers.

"He's about as classy as a meat pie at a dinner party, Sue."

"I really don't understand what your sister sees in the man," Sue whispers later in the privacy of their bedroom, "he eats his own bogies."

"He has the sex appeal of a lump of coal," Sue giggles, "but your sister likes him."

"She's not thinking of becoming a lesbian, then."

Late that night Roger awakes with a start.

Instead of searching for his elusive Seal Flipper Pie he has been dreaming of catching multitudes of crabs. Pleasant enough until the relatively docile captured sand crabs turn unpleasantly into enormous, snapping mud crabs — each with three claws!

Calming himself down, he pulls his emergency torch from beside the bed to avoid disturbing the household by turning on lights. Cloudy the night is so black there is zero visibility; even dawn might not break it. He decides to venture to the kitchen for a glass of water. On his way he tiptoes past where June and Barry are laying, only to be rewarded with the sight of a bare, male arse, pulsing up and down in the beam of his torch. A female hand, one with familiar multi-coloured fingernails, is clutching Barry's back as if she is holding on for dear life.

Nothing is ever said, although Barry is hanging around June like a bad smell in a lift.

Zelda continues to distinguish herself by perching on the edge of a chair like a dowager countess, forced to accept the hospitality of a peasant.

Sue makes multiple efforts; offering coffee, with or without cream, brown or refined sugar in cubes and loose, assorted biscuits between meals; even homemade muffins and fruit to appease her.

"Nothing seems to work," Sue is downcast.

Tears start to brim, threatening to roll uncontrollably.

"Barry's visibly distressed," Sue's maternal emotions are in overload.

"All of the bounties offered by Down Under appear singularly unattractive to Barry even with the support and love of June," Roger tells Edward.

"He hates it here, Roger."

"What's to hate? It's paradise on earth."

Edward is counting off on his fingers, "The Australian heat, the sun, the shops, the beach, the beer, the food, and even the trees."

"The trees?"

"Even the trees."

Knowing Barry had worked as a woodcutter in England, Roger researches work for him in the forestry industry nearby.

No. Barry is not interested.

"Nothing's working, Roger," Sue is downcast.

"Maybe if we could give them their own room?"

"He's missing his Mum," Sue explains, "their own room won't cut it."

Barry's mood deteriorates to such a point where there is only one option.

Barry, with June in tow, returns to England.

Meanwhile Zelda has been consistent. Her constant letters, telegrams and telephone calls to Charlotte eventually prompts a reaction.

"I've decided to stay put in England. Better the devil you know," are her parting words to her mum.

This puts Zelda and Edward in dark moods.

"I'm unsure what's more complicated, Sue?"

"What?"

"Being a father or having one."

"Stop stressing over stuff you can't control," Sue rolls her eyes, "like I have. Roger, when will they all leave? I just want my life back."

At work Roger's office phone rings loudly. He answers it. "May I speak with, Roger, please?"

"Speaking."

"Roger, it's George Hamlin, your bank manager."

"Hello, George. What's up?"

"I've been talking with your Dad, Edward. He says he'll understand if you tell me to go to hell."

There is a long pause, "You have my full attention, George."

"Your Dad has a big favour to ask."

"Favour?"

"Yes. Because he's a newbie he has no financial history here in Oz. We see he's been bankrupt in England, and so to borrow money and get started here, well, he needs a guarantor."

Roger cannot help but feel that the forces are conspiring against him.

"What does that entail, George?"

"Your dad hates having to ask you. Basically a rubber stamp from you and Sue. Provided your father meets his obligations, that's it. But

I have to point out that if Edward, that is your Dad, falls down owing the bank money, then we would come to you for restitution."

"Okay, George. I don't see as we have too much choice with the matter. I can hardly say no as we are sponsoring him. How much will it be the guarantee?"

"Ten thousand dollars."

Chapter 23

TIDAL WAVES!

Sue takes the news well, "You really didn't have much choice, let's just hope your Dad behaves like a proper boy scout. We have no assurances back yet from the solicitor over that letter. Only his bill with his hand in our cookie jar."

"Maybe we won't hear further. But no news must surely be good news, in this instance at least."

Eager to have their own digs Edward and Zelda rent a timber high-set home, not unlike Sue and Roger's, but a little further out north side at Narangba. Zelda dislikes it the moment she moves in, even with all her own furniture, she is constantly whinging at Edward, and anyone else within earshot.

"I did not come 'ere to live in a chamfer board monstrosity, Edvard."

An unpleasant lady with a nasty response! She might be missing the girls doing her housework and ironing, but she does not miss a beat at putting her foot in it.

"Yes, dear," is Edward's only response.

"Nice back handed compliment, Roger. Having it rammed home that we live in a chamfer board monstrosity."

"It's not that Zelda dislikes the house. It's more a thinly disguised passionate, loathing," Sue explains.

Edward and Zelda both land jobs. Edward as a used car salesman at Kedron, and Zelda in a Medicare office in Chermside.

"Dad's new sleazy occupation's only one rung below real estate sales and lawyers. Come to think of it funeral directors are yet to be put into a similar category."

While the family are no longer estranged Roger sees visits to Edward and Zelda as duty calls, and neither grandparent shows any more than a passing interest in Jayne or James.

Roger sets about cutting his Dad's grass. He uses his own mower and performs much the same task as at home.

After the second cut his Dad timidly confesses, "Zelda's not happy with the way you're cutting the edges, Son. She wants a straighter line, and also she'd prefer you place the grass cuttings around the base of the bushes rather than taking them away to the tip."

"Might, let it go then in future, Dad. Best let Zelda make arrangements more suitable."

Sue is ropable, "That SHE-leopard hasn't changed her spots," she raves.

Upset and confused that his kindness has gone against him, Roger confides in Trev and Steve at their weekly BBQ.

"Can't buy respect," Steve says, shaking his head nonchalantly.

"Can't make them like you," Trev says. "Your conscience should be clear, Mate, you've done all you could."

"Talking of family," Sue tells Roger, "Mummy wants to come visit Down Under."

Roger is stunned. "I know, you told me that already."

"That was before when I told you that she and Auntie Audrey wanted to visit us, but they hadn't said when."

"Yes, Minnie and your Aunt Audrey. I understand."

"Yes. But her latest letter's beside your chair. She says now we've settled in they're on their way."

"Shit!"

"My sentiment entirely. Double shit."

"How long until they arrive?"

"They leave Heathrow on Monday week."

"Shit. How long will they be staying?"

"As I said before, about two weeks according to her letter."

"Shit! A whole fourteen days," Roger groans.

All he can think of is fourteen days of continuous mayhem.

His voice is quivering. "Oh, my God, why me, why us?" is all he can say.

"Well, Roger, we did bring yours home for keeps…one rule — and all that crap! Family," Sue sighs, "it just doesn't get any more complicated than that, does it?"

Kim says, "I can vouch for that, can't we Art?"

"Most of us can," offers Trev.

"We've only just got rid of one lot, and here we go again," Roger's voice is hollow.

"Back to the subject in hand," Trev reminds.

"What's that?" asks Roger irritably.

"Our favourite pastimes, Mate; fishin' and crabbin'."

Roger brightens.

"All fishermen are liars, except you and me. And sometimes I'm unsure about you!" Art says, downing his beer. "Time we went and left these people to their misery; come on, Love."

"You all do love your fishing," Sue says, "will you take Minnie and Aunt Audrey out fishing while they're here?"

Roger looks horrified. "Is there no end to the potential of this nightmare? I need to wake up," Roger pinches his own arm.

Sue ignores him. "Did you know that Trev tried commercial fishing? Pro fishing, I mean; but Liz said life on the trawlers wasn't easy as a deck hand."

"Trev is easily the best fisherman of us all," Roger says, "Steve's a close second, with Art and myself squaring off for most improved."

Next day Roger makes a phone call. "I'd like to speak with Art."

"No way! He's not here, Bro," answers Art's big Maori mate.

"Where is he?"

"Dunno, Bro! But if he's not here, he's gotta be somewhere else."

Trev's encounter with a nosey neighbour a few doors down on the opposite side of the road was the catalyst for Nosey becoming their new BBQ mate. A small, slight man in his fifties with unnaturally-blond hair.

"I-I-I've not l-l-looked after my c-c-cat vewy well," Nosey explained, "he was a stway I-I-I befwiended."

Trev nodding sagely in agreement.

"If he had ink for brains, he wouldn't have enough to make a full stop, let alone take care of any animal." Trev explains to the group.

"How nosey?" Roger asks, politely overlooking Nosey's speech impediment pronouncing.

"I was digging a hole in my front yard. Nothing to do with bloody Nosey here, but I'd picked a nice soft area in the shade of your Jacaranda tree."

"Nice an' easy to dig. This Nosey bastard leans on my front fence and asked, "What you doing?"

"Not that it's any business of yours," I said, "but I'm digging a hole.

'W-W-Why?' Nosey joins in, in recollection.

"I'm burying my budgie." Trev continues with the story, "Nosey scratches his head.

'B-b-big hole for a budgie, Twev,' Nosey continues his part of the story.

"That's because it's inside your fucking cat!"

"What did he say?" Roger asks, as Nosey skulls a beer.

"Actually, he took it quite well, after I explained the special circumstances."

"What on earth were the special circumstances?" Roger asks, feeling put out for Trev who would not normally hurt a fly.

"His bloody cat had been eyeing off my budgie for weeks. Can't blame the cat for doing what comes natural I s'pose. Although Nosey 'ere should be caring better for his animal."

"Agreed, so what happened?" Roger asks.

"Well, finally, the cat won out didn't it. Found a way into budgie's cage. I came outdoors and the cat's already swallowed the poor bloody bird like a Pizza. Last few telltale feathers are stuck around its mouth. I s'pose I startled the cat, it knew it shouldn't be there doing that, so off it goes like a streak of light, heading home."

"And?"

"It never made it; right under the wheels of a passing car — one dead cat. So, I cleaned up the mess."

"So, what did you say, Nosey?" Roger asks.

"I-I-I ended up t-t-thanking Twev for buwying my cat; offered to help clean up, or b-b-buy him a beer."

"You're not a bad bloke," Trev acknowledges.

"A-a-and here I am," Nosey beams.

Instead of Roger testing out their new chimney at their BBQ, the wives insist on cooking the fish indoors.

Indoors resembles Santa's workshop. Charged glasses in hands.

Roger protests, looking over Kim's shoulder, "I don't like eating mullet, after all it is sold as bait, isn't it?"

"Not all mullet is bait, Roger. You should try this fresh ocean mullet."

"What's the difference?"

"Ocean mullet's too good for bait," Trev explains. "Debate rages about how best to catch them but I say square hooks are best."

"Square hooks?" Roger queries.

"He means nets, Rog'," Art explains.

"Best way to catch Ocean Mullet," Trev continues, "and these here are their melts."

"Melts? Whats's melts?" Art asks.

"Don't ask," volunteers Kim.

"No, really," Art persists.

"Semen from the male mullet," Trev explains.

"I'm not eating funky spunk, Mate," states Art, "not even from a mullet."

"It's a fish delicacy," Roger reinforces, "You don't know what you're missing, I've always liked melts, not so much the roes though, that's the eggs from the female."

"It's a bit salty in taste, Art," Sue offers, a twinkle in her eye, "would you prefer it taste of chocolate?"

"That's ridiculous. Spoof doesn't taste of chocolate!" Art says.

"How'd you know it doesn't?" asks Trev with an impish smile.

Glasses are recharged.

"I like boats and being on the water but we can't really afford a boat yet, can we Sue?"

His only practical experience of boats was what he remembered after his parents visited the annual *Earls Court Motor Show* in the 1950s to buy a new car, returning with a boat.

"Why don't you go somewhere to watch boats, then?" Sophie suggests.

"Somewhere where the children won't get bored straight away," Steve cautions.

"Why don't we go sit by a boat ramp?" Sue suggests enthusiastically.

Roger is thoughtful. "Could be a good idea. Scarborough has an excellent wide ramp, plenty of parking, and places to sit, even a shop that sells lollies."

Jayne's face brightens.

"Why don't we check it out, and if it's interesting enough your Mum and Auntie Audrey might be interested?"

"Good idea."

Sunday morning they troop off to Scarborough Boat Harbour to watch mariners doing their thing. The harbour twinkles green and calm under the morning sun. Roger is able to join with some of the more taciturn, weathered old sea dogs waiting to retrieve their own boats and show Sue where he and Steve had launched his trailer boat.

An expensive lump of fibreglass boat on a triple axle trailer arrives at the boat ramp. Its little crew of misfits comprise three adult women, tanned, lean, and strong of limb; dressed in bikinis, and a spritely little jerk around Roger's age. He is dressed in white shoes, long white socks, a splendid white silk shirt, crimson cravat, and a blue sports jacket. He stands observing where his backing has landed him down the ramp beyond the water's edge. He appears impressed.

"I have to admit Pretty Boy has made an excellent job of backing, Sue."

"You think so?"

"Yes, the boat is positioned perfectly to glide backwards off the trailer and into the water without being beached on the ramp."

They watch the three women take care of launching the boat expertly.

After the boat is clear of its trailer, Pretty Boy goes to park the late model Toyota Land-cruiser and boat trailer. He returns and Roger is surprised to see he remains fully dressed.

"This'll be interesting," Roger says to Sue. "I wonder how he intends to board his boat without getting his feet wet?"

Two women make a chair with their arms and support him into the boat.

The boat is well away from the ramp into deeper water when Pretty Boy starts his twin 200 hp motors. He begins reversing further away from the ramp.

Roger leans in close to Sue, "He'll want to stop soon or he'll cross those slack mooring ropes to the port side."

Pretty Boy crosses into the mooring lines, his propellers become entangled and the motors cough to a halt.

Pretty Boy looks confused. The boat is sitting against the tide. The motors are silent. Someone is going to have to free the propellers, probably with a knife.

Sue and Roger exchange looks.

"This is becoming most interesting, Sue."

Without any discussion, the women leap overboard.

On occasion one surfaces for a breath taking turns at freeing the motors.

Finally, with the women back on board, Pretty Boy restarts the motors and departs the harbour, his female crew by his side.

"Wait until I tell the boys about that. I'll bet they'll never believe me."

Over many a beer Trev reinforces to Roger the importance of tides, fishing early morning, baits, and being quiet on the water; also about Fisheries Regulations, which of course vary in every State.

"Next best thing to actually fishing," Trev explains, "is the preparation."

They are spending many enjoyable evenings drinking beer while making ready their fishing and crabbing gear for the weekend.

"It's never good fishing at weekends," Trev says, "but as we all work at regular jobs except Steve who does shift work, we have no choice. There'll be boats all over the river and bay by mid morning so we'll try and beat the system by starting before first light and being home about when everyone else is getting started. Serious fishermen are not hell bent on killing everything that swims only what we're targeting."

Roger cannot hide his disappointment.

Trev sighs his deepest sigh. "It's about more than being a purist. If we're serious about putting time, effort, and money in, we need to target what's best for our larder. Now, Roger, our enemy is the wind," Trev explains. "Since Mary had the measles it's best to fish when there's little or no wind. *Smooth to slight* means the surface of the water should be like glass."

Lowering his voice Trev continues, "To ignore it, Mate, would be like taking no notice of blood in your urine."

Trev being a big man. His mates at work refer to him as the big bastard.

Trev grins, "If I jump into the water you'll be able to collect the fish out of the trees."

Steve has a formula as to where to fish when conditions are perfect.

"It's simple, if Sophie is laying on her side with her legs to the left when I get up, I go north to Caboolture. If she's laying on her side with her legs to the right, I go south to the Pine River."

Trev is thoughtful. "What if she's not laying either way? What if she's laying on her back, with her legs spread left and right?"

"Then I have a bloody good reason to stay home, Mate."

Roger's ocean reel from the old country holds 500 yards of 80 lb. breaking strain line. Ready rigged with four barbed hooks the size of cup hooks, a brass paternoster, and a lead sinker the size of an egg cup.

"What the fuck have you got there?" Trev asks.

"My British fishing rig," Roger says with some disdain. "Last time I used it was off the pier at Brighton."

"Did you catch anything?"

"No!"

"I'm not surprised. We're not going after the fucking Kraken," Trev explains, "we'll be in the estuary of the North Pine River!"

Sometimes Roger feels as vacant as he looks.

Trev rolls his eyes. "You're fishing too heavy, Mate. You need a side caster reel, or an eggbeater, and 4 lb. line. Better to use a pea sinker or even no weight at all if we're fishing a slow incoming tide."

"Your blood's worth bottling, you know that Mate?" Roger grins.

"Remember to always fish light," Trev reinforces, and then with a sheepish grin, "you'll stack up fish quicker than empty plates at a pie-eating competition."

From the boat every cast of their hand lines, baited with a small piece of squid or worm, produces a wriggling Winter Whiting.

When they take their children along for a treat the little ones shriek with pent up excitement.

Trev preaches caution. "It's all right to let the kids take the Winter Whiting off their hooks, Mate. It's good fun for them, but watch out in case they snag a problem fish. They're called Smudge Spot, Spine-foot's, or commonly known as Happy Moments."

"Why?" asks Roger.

"Because if they spike you, you'll get a short burst of happiness followed by many hours of severe pain."

"What's the happy part about, then?" Roger queries.

"That's when you start dancing around like a dick-wit trying anything you can possibly think of, anything that is besides trying to teach Roger how to fish, just to take your mind away from the pain," Trev explains.

Trev enjoys his winter fishing, but Roger does not like the colder weather. After he becomes acclimatised he prefers the warmer months.

"Trouble is," Trev says, "the bigger fish are about in the winter months. There's also less mozzies or sand flies in winter.

Let's go crabbing," Trev suggests.

"With crabbing it's easy," Roger espouses, "basically anything female gets put back unharmed and to be a keeper it's got to be fifteen centimetres or more across the carapace. Easy."

"Translating that from English to Australian, Mate, is return Jennies to the water, and keep the bigger bucks."

That Sunday before the arrival of Minnie and Aunt Audrey the sun is warm on Roger's back. He is content with a gentle breeze to his face while they labour in the back garden mending and replacing the suicide dilly nets.

"I've been telling Roger about crabs and crabbing," Trev tells Sue.

"Oh, dear. Now I suppose he'll want to become a full-time crabber."

"Strewth, I hope not. With him in the mix it'd be like trying to herd a bunch of cats! Come to think about it, more like cats with an attention deficit disorder!"

Roger is dreading the day of Minnie and Audrey's arrival, but when it arrives, they are truly charming and easygoing.

James and Jayne have a ball showing the two old biddies off to all their friends.

Neighbours and friends rally to include Minnie and Audrey in social get-togethers and imbibe them with the best of local foods, and their favourite tipples.

Edward and Zelda are conspicuous by their avoidance to mix in, which Roger and Sue think most rude.

Minnie and Audrey like everything they see, which includes a weekend bush rodeo out at Dayboro where they clap and cheer the riders.

Highlights besides the rodeo, are visiting the Gold Coast, the Sunshine Coast, eating squid in breadcrumbs, and visiting Scarborough boat ramp where Granny shouts James and Jayne ice blocks. Another fun thing was playing cards. The old girls liked to play a hand or two of poker before bed, and to spice up their evening with a fine rum, port, or a malt whisky.

At the airport Minnie kisses Roger farewell, "Thank you for loving my daughter, and caring for her the way you have. You are a dear, young man."

Christ, Roger thinks, *this is a big bloody change in attitude.*

After their departure, Roger and Sue feel a little flat.

Roger admits, "I was almost sad to see them go, Sue."

"Hold that thought, Roger. There's something I haven't yet told you."

"What's that?"

"It was Minnie who dobbed us into the bank."

"What?"

"You heard. She meant no harm, but when they came knocking, investigating next of kin, she told them."

In the winter months, Trev goes fishing with Art. Steve prefers sailing all year round or working about the house. In the summer months, they go crabbing with Roger.

Roger explains, "We travelled 16,500 miles to escape the cold. Not to rug up like Michelin Man to go to the beach! For me it's cooler than a polar bear's toenail."

Roger's first boat is a twelve foot tinny.

"Light weight, easy to maintain, and they don't need a big donk, that's slang for motor, to push them across the water, Sue."

A new *Savage Snipe* with a 9hp *Evinrude* outboard motor. On a new *Tinka* trailer he is as proud as punch. Sue admires the new rig standing on their driveway.

"It's like your new baby," she grins. "Boys and their toys."

Trev shows Roger how to keep the wheel bearings greased up on the trailer so they can submerge it at boat ramps for easier launch and retrieve. Another concern is the 2-stroke motor as Steve does not trust premixes. He shows Roger how to prepare his own mix with the same care as when he had been a warrior in Vietnam checking his pre-battle supplies.

"I've seen too many motors run hot and blow on account of incorrect mixtures," Steve warns.

Sometimes when they missed being on the water, they would sit in their boats in their backyards, pretending they are out on the water.

Sue laughs at them from an upstairs window.

"Caught any fish yet, boys?" she asks mockingly.

"Only a few small ones," Roger replies coyly. "They'll be alright for crab bait — but."

Sometimes out on the water they would just sit at anchor in silence.

Both loved the early morning, if the light is right they would be anchored or drifting in the murky, grey light of dawn, enough to see by, but dark enough to need navigation lights.

"Notice how the only sounds are distant traffic," Trev murmurs.

"And the water as it laps past the hull."

"Ah, the tranquility."

They are broken rudely from their thoughts by screeching tyres, crunching metal, and what appears to be haywire headlights coming towards them.

"The commotion's a ways from us," Trev observes, "but over water sound travels great distances."

"It would appear, Captain Ahab," Roger says collecting his thoughts, "that a car has driven full belt from the road, over the boat ramp, and out into the water."

"Partially submerged with headlights still full on, might he be hunting Moby Dick?" Trev asks sarcastically.

Roger looks at Trev. Trev looks at Roger.

"Fuck," Trev says, "that's bound to upset the fishing!"

"We might have witnessed an accident, Trev."

"He'd have to be as dumb as dog's shit to do that."

"No good fishing now."

Moments later flashing lights and sirens herald the arrival of Queensland's finest.

Again, they exchange glances. "Fuck," Roger says. "Should we do something?"

"There're plenty of people at the site to sort it out. We're displaying our riding light. If they want to talk to us, they can see we're here. Let's fish on!"

"We might get lucky and see a stray fish scale on our line before it's time to go home."

"Stop jumping around like a fart in a bottle."

"Okay."

"Pass the coffee."

A man is struggling ashore from the car and appears to be taken into custody but clear vision of his features is obscured by distance.

"Looks like he's dodged an unwanted trip to the mortuary."

"Should we pull up the anchor and motor closer?"

Trev shakes his head. "Not much point. By the time we get there it'll all be over."

It takes them a while to connect the dots but by the middle of the following week after Nosey's been missing for a while, it turns out that it was him, Nosey, in that car. Apparently he had ventured down to check on his new mates and misjudged but being full of alcohol can do that to a man.

Chapter 24

SAME SHIT DIFFERENT DAY

A wise man once said: *It's never good to start a day out in the boat hungover from the night before.*

That cocky in the mouth furry feeling, the seedy stomach that is so close to doing flips and disorientating, eyes feeling as though there is grit beneath the lids, head pounding each time the body is slightly less than vertical, is Roger and Trev on the day after they had promised to take the tinny out crabbing.

Going through the motions, much as a condemned man supposedly enjoys eating his last hearty meal, Trev steers expertly against the gentle nudge of the tide onto their first dilly float. Now it is Roger's job to lean over the port side and catch the float as they slowly pass by.

First one, empty!

Roger rebaits and drops the dilly back down again.

They are progressing towards the second float when Roger, dressed like Scott of the Antarctic and starting to roast like meat in an oven bag, has an overpowering urge to remove his heavy sea coat. Sweating because of the alcohol in his system, his sleeve becomes caught on his heavy divers wrist watch.

The float looms closer.

Trev bellows, "You ready, Roger?"

"Yes, I think so," Roger replies weakly.

Trev starts to chuckle as he circles the boat around the float, waiting patiently for Roger to extract himself from his clothing. Roger joins him. They become convulsed in helpless, hysterical laughter.

Gasping for breath, Trev asks, again, "Are you ready this time, Roger?"

That sets them off laughing again.

"You're flopping around like in a dick in a bucket, Mate," Trev says.

Hysteria overcome, heavy coat finally stowed away up front among the anchor rope, they soldier on.

Second dilly; one buck, third dilly; empty, fourth dilly; empty, fifth dilly; three good sized bucks and one Jenny.

As the sun begins to beat down on them, the only breeze appears while their boat is underway. They decide to pull the pin.

"We learned a valuable lesson today," Roger tells Sue back at home. "If we're going out on the water it's wise to cease drinking early the night before."

"What did Trev say?"

"Well done, captain Obvious. Fuck we're stars."

As Jayne becomes older, Sue allows her out in the boat more often but with firm rules laid down. Unlike her brother James, Jayne loves boats, and enjoys being on the water fishing or crabbing, whichever.

Slowly Roger begins to trust Jayne holding the boat beside the ramp while he parks the car and returns. That and Jayne's keenness to join him on the water at every opportunity means he has a new loyal fishing mate. Slowly, he teaches her the practicalities of boatmanship, hooks, and bait.

Together on any beach at low tide, Jayne and Roger have great fun gathering live bait; pippies, yabbies, occasionally Roger throws a bait net.

Jayne becomes excited at pulling up the dillies as she finds crabbing contagious. A net approaches the surface through water so clear, her keen eyes aboard search the water for any colour hinting the presence of a crab.

Often they have a couple of sand crabs enmeshed in the net with another barely hanging on by a foot or a claw. Jayne speedily hauls the net aboard.

With mud crabs in the boat, Jayne is quarantined to the bow of the boat up over the anchor and ropes, to stay there until the wily crustacean is safely ensconced in a wet hessian sack.

Back home they fill the concrete laundry tubs under the house with live mud crabs. Monstrous brown nightmares, waving their arms and snapping their claws, arching up high on their rear swimming legs, just daring a hand closer!

"To cook them you can just drop them into boiling water," Trev explains. "They'll die instantly but throw their claws. It's better to chill them down first. Puts them to sleep. Also makes cleaning the pot easier as there's less mess.

First boil the water, and then put the crabs into the boiling water. Time the actual cooking from the second boil; allow seven minutes for sandies, twelve minutes for spanners, and twelve to fifteen minutes for muddies depending on size and weight. Remove crabs from boiling water and cool in an iced slurry."

"Why?"

"Well, otherwise they'll continue cooking in their shells even after you've removed them from the water!"

Another late afternoon they put their boat in at the boat ramp in Dohles Rocks Road adjacent to the Pine River. They crab a pretty part of the river upstream, where it winds through a soft green paddock.

For a change they decide to cook their fresh caught muddies on the bank of the river using salty river water over a bush fire.

"We'll only eat just one crab," they agree. "The smallest one!"

Roger is sitting on the bank under a great gum tree admiring the early evening. That last few minutes of sparkle before the water loses any translucence and fades into darkness.

Trev remarks, "When you're quite rested, maybe you won't mind helping with the cleaning up?"

Recalled from his pleasant thoughts to the mundane present, Roger pitches in.

"What to do with our sucked out shells?" Roger asks.

"Unless you want to take them home, show them to Sue, and keep them for posterity," Trev says pointedly, "I suggest they go back into the fucking river from whence they came."

"Might look a bit unsightly."

"When I said put them in the river I meant out deep," Trev barks, a general look of disapproval on his face. "Not a neat little pile on the fucking bank, Roger."

Without clean running water, they remove grime from their hands on the grass, and use a stick of wood and tuffs of grass to clean the worst scum from their pot.

Roger finally polishes it with Trev's old, wet T shirt.

They sit back again in their moored boat. Trev has a quiet smoke.
"Great life."
"Yes, it is." Roger agrees.
"It's a lot easier cleaning up after cooking at home."
"Yes, it is."
"And at home we get some assistance from our women."
"Yes, we do."
After a while they motor back to the ramp.
Trev reflects, "Although the majority of our crabs would pass muster, mightn't one or two be marginal size wise?"
"You could be right. Measuring by rule of thumb the way the Romans used to is not as accurate as using a ruler, Trev."
"Tell you what, just to be on the safe side, and to avoid a right kick in the balls, how's about we be a bit clandestine at the boat ramp?"
"Clandestine?"
"Yes, just in case the Green Shirts are out on patrol."
Roger's blank look leads Trev to explain. He means Department of Fisheries inspectors.
"Good idea," Roger acknowledges, "how's about as we approach the ramp I'll kill the motor and we can drift quietly ashore to avoid noise."
"And we'll kill the lights, as it's now quite dark."
"Roger that," laughs Roger.
As the outline of the Dohles Rocks boat ramp comes into murky view, Roger disconnects the fuel line. The motor continues to run at idling speed.
"What the fuck are you doing?" Trev asks. "I thought you said you'd kill the motor."
"Well, I have. I'm just running out the carburettor."
At that point the noise of the motor escalates before it coughs silent, finally out of fuel.
"Fuck me," mutters Trev.
"Slowly and quietly does it," Roger reiterates.
Roger has misjudged the speed of the boat and the final distance to the ramp. The bottom of the aluminium hull now hits the concrete ramp quite hard. There is a very loud clanging noise followed by the sound of metal grating on concrete.

Trev murmurs in a stage whisper, "Well — that was quiet. What part of drifting quietly ashore did you not fucking understand?"

There are no lights, no welcoming committee, and no apparent Green Shirts in attendance.

Trev starts to laugh, and then Roger. Their uncontrollable laughter rises to a crescendo, mouths open so wide they can see each other's tonsils and beyond. Their merriment abates, and wiping tears from their eyes, they continue with their tasks in hand.

"Fucking poms," mutters Trev.

Chapter 25

APOLOGIES

The following weekend Sue and Roger invest in a heavy-duty tent with a sewn in ground sheet.

"Maybe we should have a dummy run with it in the backyard?" Sue suggests.

"Absolute waste of time, Sue. I see no point in putting it up for no purpose."

Quite the campers, their gear stowed in their new, larger Clark Abalone boat and trailer, they set off for their first weekend away at Elanda Point.

"Why pitch the tent here?" Roger asks innocently.

"That's a very good question," Sue replies with a smirk, "in case you haven't noticed the kids are already off playing, and 'here' as you put it, is convenient to their shop and not too far from the toilets."

"Alright," Roger acknowledges, "better get the canvas up first, then we can relax."

"It looks simple enough. We take the poles and fit them together, a bit like gigantic croquet hoops. Then hang the tent inside them."

"Easy peasy, ten minutes tops," Roger says confidently.

They take up the hoops, and begin dropping them into their sockets.

Roger complains, as one hoop exits its socket and swipes him across the chest.

"That might not be the best way to put up this tent," Sue observes.

"Oh, deep joy," Roger exclaims, "what a bastard contraption. When the right hoop goes into the right socket, the left one pops out again."

The hinges in the middle, while Roger is concentrating elsewhere, nip closed on whatever delicate part of his body is exposed. Sue wrestles with one side of a hoop that swings back behind her when she is not looking.

"If we don't get a move on," Roger warns, "night will be upon us."

Their children appear.

"We're hungry," Jayne announces, "when's dinner?"

"Just as soon as your father and I have got the tent up, everything sorted, and then he can start the BBQ," Sue announces.

Both children groan.

"We're hungry," pouts James.

"Well, how's about you chip in and help?" Roger suggests.

"Do we have to?" James argues.

Roger becomes irritable, "No you don't have to, but some assistance would go a long way towards making it fun for your Mum and me as well. You're not the only one to be considered you know."

James storms off, while Jayne stands by quietly to assist.

"I think you've bungled it, Dad," Jayne says.

Endeavouring to get the hoops to do their duty, Sue finds herself stretched between two hoops while trying to snag the loop of the canvas roof.

"I need three hands," she says, mournfully. "Jayne, hold this, please."

"That's it," Roger announces, "I think we've finally cracked it, Love."

"Is the groundsheet supposed to be up off the ground?" Jayne asks.

Sue and Roger are dumfounded.

"I thought it was going so well," Roger says.

"If you think that," Sue says "I fear you're delusional."

"What's this?" asks Jayne, holding up what was obviously an instruction sheet from the tent bag.

"The instructions," Roger says lamely. "Appear to have been written by Taiwanese school children."

Sue speaks intensely, her hands painting pictures alongside the words.

"I'm amazed, that a man so brilliant in many ways, can be so lacking in commonsense."

"You sound like my Dad," Roger replies.

Roger has quickly learnt that to guarantee a feed of mud crabs, their pots have to be sunk without markers.

"The bastards who rob them, don't even have the courtesy to rebait or close the trap door afterwards," he raves. "It's a club, and they're known as the 'No Pot Club' where members set about deliberately stealing other fishermen's crabs. This is not an honourable pursuit, Sue, someone should call the police or break out the cavalry!"

Jayne asks a really good question, "How do you know where the pots are, Daddy?" Roger explains. "I take approximate land bearings and triangulate to put myself in the ball park, and then I guarantee success by tethering each pot to its neighbour about 5 metres apart. That way when I dredge I only have to be successful once, and I have a connection to each pot."

Their trip away comes to an end on Sunday, when packing up is quicker and easier than pitching.

Soon they settle in to weekends away that becomes better organised each trip. Collecting cooked chook from a takeaway at Nambour on their way through negates a BBQ on arrival. Crab pots sunk without markers while bordering on illegal produce mud crabs.

"Life's sweet," Sue confirms.

In an effort to share the pleasures of Elanda Point they became quite vocal about it.

Occasionally Jayne and James bring their young friends along for an overnight.

Roger fishes and crabs the lakes, while Jayne and James venture out on Sail Boards watched over by Sue, or on occasions with Roger on a small catamaran. They wear lifejackets that are compulsory.

On the other side of *Lake Cootharaba* it is possible to trek through to an ocean beach. There Roger stands on a large stretch of arcing white sand. His feet or more specifically his toes, slowly disappear into the soft wet sand. Just Roger, his ankles, and the sound of breaking waves.

"It's a bit far for you to trek, I think, Sue, but what a place it is."

Friends Art and Kim come for an overnight tester. They like it so much they became regular visitors.

"Fish are a bit light on," Roger tells them, "but I've found a great spot for muddies."

"The Everglades alone are worth a visit, and the stories about Mrs Fraser and the Island that bears her name are unbelievable."

Their weekends are filled with fresh crabs, BBQ's, greasy spoon breakfasts, more grog, sun, sunburn, and sand everywhere.

The following weekend Trev has a brilliant idea.

"Roger, if you're prepared to tow the Abalone to Mooloolaba, word is we could clean up on crabs."

"I didn't know we could catch sandies or muddies at Mooloolaba," Roger replies.

"I mean Spanner crabs, Mate."

They leave early. 2am! Slip the boat in before dawn and head cautiously outside the harbour. There is a gentle swell and they bob along until anchoring in about eight metres of water, a mile out from the main beach.

Eight dillies down, each with extra weights fixed to their hoops, they enjoy their early morning coffees and Trev has his heart starter smoke while they watch the dawn.

Trev declares, "I think it could get lumpy by mid morning. We'll give the baited dillies a full twenty minutes, then check 'em."

They finish their second cup of coffee.

Approaching their first dilly there is more than a little anticipation in the air. This is their first attempt at catching Spanner crabs, and the furthest they have travelled on a whim.

"It's a bit bloody heavy," strains Trev. "I think it might be stuck on the bottom."

Roger drags out his local chart and peruses their exact location. "Only sand is shown on the chart, Trev. Not even a gravel bottom."

"Well, there's something. It's not wanting to budge, maybe it's caught on an old anchor or part of a wreck?"

"Well it's got to come up, that or I cut the rope. We'll both pull."

"Fuck me it's heavy, but it's moving," Trev says, as both men strain with effort, "what's the chance we've got part of an old car or something?"

"Not bloody likely about a mile out from the beach. Not even Nosey could achieve that with or without a boat ramp. He'd have to have wings."

The two continue to struggle pulling up the dilly, as it comes into view through the clearer surface water they can see what the net holds.

"Christ, Almighty," utters Trev, "it's crabs, it's so full of crabs I can't see any netting, they're triple stacked."

Not only is the dilly full of Spanner crabs but they are hanging on and off from each other. As the two men manhandle their catch into the boat, the full significance of their success hits them.

"Too many to count," Roger says sincerely, let's get them off into buckets and sacks. Time to rebait."

"Hold your horses," Trev cautions, "if this net's anything to go by, we've got another seven to go. We won't have time to rebait."

"We won't have room for any more crabs either."

"We're gonna need a bigger boat."

Each dilly retrieved is the same. Ladened with good sized Spanner crabs.

"I've never caught Spanner crabs before," Roger says, "never realised that they're a reddish colour when alive."

"They look like they've been cooked already."

Five sack loads fill the front anchor well. More amidships.

The boat is so full of crabs it is riding lower in the water.

Two hours after their arrival, the prevailing South-easterly winds are building.

"White caps are decorating the tops of each swell," Trev announces.

"Time to get out of here."

At home, they count 240 Spanner crabs.

Roger's big pot holds four, Trev's about the same. Steve is enlisted to help and they prepare three pots on three gas rings. Children's toy blackboards are used to record cooking times.

"Even in shifts we're going to be busy at this all day," Roger observes.

"And half the damned night as well," joins Trev.

At about quarter way mark Roger asks Steve and Picasso.

"Please offer free Spanner crabs to anyone you know."

"On one condition," Trev stipulates.

"What condition?" Picasso asks.

"They take them live," Roger says, "we're not cooking them to give away."

The following weekend Trev and Roger take stock.

"If we do that Mooloolaba run again," Trev says, "we'll need to rethink."

"Rethink?"

"We don't need so many crabs, Roger. What with changing their water after every second boil because of the iodine from the crabs. Time wise about 40 crabs would be plenty."

Jayne pleads to be allowed to go.

Trev looks at Roger. "I've no objection. It'll be safe enough. It's your call."

Roger looks at Jayne's pleading eyes and then looks to Sue for maternal guidance.

"Go on, take her," Sue smiles, "she'll never forgive you if you don't."

Jayne is not just excited, she is clearly over the moon. Up and dressed at 1am without prompting, and making coffee, tea and sandwiches for their outing, one hour before Roger's alarm clock.

They leave on time for Mooloolaba.

"Have you checked the weather forecast?" Trev asks.

"Just before we left. Latest recorded advice was 7pm last night. Seas smooth to slight, no warnings current."

"That's good, pretty much agrees with what I heard, too," Trev agrees.

All the way they chat and sing songs. Enthusiasm fills the air.

When they arrive Jayne has been so patient, she has never even asked once, 'Are we there yet?'

Roger parks near the boat ramp.

"Trev, I don't like the look of those trees."

"I'm thinking the same thing, Mate."

First to get out is Jayne.

The wind nearly blows her over.

"It's not calm," Roger announces.

"It's certainly not smooth to slight," replies Trev. He holds his hand up to the wind, a handkerchief dangling from it, "I'd say we're looking at an unfriendly 15 to 20 knots."

"Thing is, Trev…is it abating or building?"

Trev tries to shield his lighter to light his cigarette behind his coat. "Bloody wind's so strong, I can't even light my smoke."

"There isn't any light reflecting off the water," Roger says.

"It's chopped up too rough."

Roger looks at Jayne, who is busy preparing the boat for the water.

"Jayne!" Roger calls, "better hold off on that, Sweetheart. We might not be going anywhere but home."

Jayne's face is a study of disappointment.

Roger is thinking of his next chess move. "Look, there's a slim chance it might abate. I'd hate to call it off and then learn if we'd waited we'd been alright."

Jayne's face lights up with anticipation. "We can still go?"

"I'm not sure yet, Sweetheart. How's about we drive up onto a hill where we can view the area of sea better? If we go it means a later start."

From on top of the hill the scenario appears no better.

Roger looks at Trev. Trev looks at Roger.

"If anything the wind is increasing, could be gusting 25 knots," Trev declares, "but it's your boat, your call, Roger."

"I'm sorry, Jayne, but I'm calling the trip off, Sweetheart."

Jayne says nothing. She curls back up in the rear seat all the way back.

When she gets out of the car at home, she mutters something that sounds like, "Gutless bastards," before storming off back to bed where she rolls up like a pickled herring.

"I'm sure you did the right thing," Sue reassures Roger.

Later that morning Trev calls out over the fence.

"Roger!"

"Yes, Trev."

"Authorities have just issued a strong wind warning, Mate. They've been slack arse on account of it being a weekend. You were right to call it off."

Roger looks up at his daughter's bedroom window where the curtains remain tightly closed.

Chapter 26

SMOLFALA

The Snake Pit again broaches the subject of Roger's escalating commissions, which with accrued bonuses are amounting to the equivalent of a suit's annual salary. This is not sitting well in Ricky's corporate world.

"Changes are to be based on their audited net profits instead of my branch sales turnover," Roger explains to Sue.

Sue kisses Roger lightly on the mouth. She tastes of flour and butter and sugar and eggs.

"Just another little misunderstanding over their goal posts," she chides.

"Galileo and the Pope, now that was a little misunderstanding. I was hoping they'd leave well alone. I'm performing for Christ's sake, isn't that what they want?"

Sue hands him a beer.

"They'd like me in Sydney, a promotion to the Snake Pit, more salary, but I'm dubious at best."

"I'm pleased you're *dubious*, we're settled and like it *here!*"

"Maybe it's time to look for another job, or do we just accept their fluid rules?"

"The devil you know, is better than the devil you don't, there's no guarantee that if you change jobs your new employer will be any fairer, or more ethical."

"Quite right. George doesn't speak highly of Pests For Ever nor Job For Life Pest Services. That's why he left and came here."

"You have your answer," Sue gives Roger a big hug.

"Word is State Pest Control Licensing will commence next year," Roger announces, "it's going to mean a lot more administrative work for managers."

"Might help with you getting more salary."

"I doubt that."

At a meeting, Ringmaster Ricky explains.

"Our sister company in the US is NEV."

"NEV?"

"Never Ending Vocation Pest Control is run by close business associates of mine. With our proximity to the Pacific, we have an arrangement where we manage it from here. We were lucky to have Wayne Thomas available."

"Wayne Thomas?" The name rings a bell in Roger's mind; Frank's new spear thrower is starting to make sense. Blood is thicker than water, or so they say.

"Yes, he's Frank Moore's brother-in-law. He's done an excellent job standing in for the retiring CEO. At short notice the authorities waived a lot of their bureaucratic bumpf, but insisted on the usual."

"The usual?" Roger queries.

"Birth and marriage certificates, proof of citizenship, company references stating no citizen with those skills is available, no criminal record, and so on but now they expect Wayne's successor to be their last ex-pat recruit."

Roger remains silent.

"So, Roger," Ricky continues, "I've been under great pressure to reinstate Wayne, but we're now offering you the Smolfala Archipelago. What do you think?"

"Sounds challenging, Ricky."

"As head Poobah over there you'll have the whole gambit; anything pest related is yours, with a large staff. You'll be based at Head Office, which is on a main island with branch offices spread throughout Apia in Western Samoa, Pago Pago in American Samoa, and Nuku'alofa in Tonga.

You'll report directly to myself of course, and to the New York board in writing. Copies of all US reports to me, is that understood?"

Roger nods. "I've had some reporting functions with Frank Moore."

"Frank is very well connected, you would do well to remember that, but he will have his work cut out here in Australia," Ricky smiles but firmly to make his point, "remember you only call me. Our turf in this is to be protected at all costs."

"What about accommodation?"

"All sorted, Roger, a rented house, all found, but remember you'll be up against it."

"Up against it?"

"Yes, Smolfala — the area attracts all sorts. The good, the not so good, the mad, the bad, the plonkers, and the totally fucked up, needing that special white coat with an all expenses paid padded room."

Roger understands Sue does not want to leave Brissie, but she does want new shoes, matching handbag, and to pay off their debts. He realises that he is probably being played but so what? Welcome to another world of plonkers.

He drinks in Ricky's bad toupee and mustard coloured shirt, which is setting off his barstool gut a fair treat.

Seeing the concerned look on Roger's face, Ricky is quick to continue, "But you're very fortunate, Roger. You're following a succession of excellent men. What we, and the US board, expect from you is a steady continuation."

Ricky takes a pause. He is running the backs of his fingers under his jowls before speaking. "I've decided I'm bumping you up by ten percent this year."

"I understand, Ricky. Sounds a wonderful opportunity, thank you."

"Good. Irrespective of the relaxed island attitudes, we expect you to maintain our high standards and continue to improve the bottom line. You'll achieve this whilst nurturing the style of harmony we enjoy in Sydney and the US demands in New York. Any questions?"

Roger has none. Although he is already wondering how these places might be compared with Sydney and New York. His mind is now a whirl of nothing, all he wants to do is get home to Sue, his sounding board of reality.

Ricky breaks through Roger's thoughts. "Employees fall into categories of ethnic groups. By law all companies operating have to employ a percentage of locals, who are without any doubt, the most charming but difficult to train, motivate, and control."

"Moti Mukherjee will be your assistant, and I'm sure you'll get on well. On the bright side I'm told there are no termites," Ricky pauses, and with a conciliatory smile, "so there's no need to concern yourself there or refer it up the food chain, but I suggest that you do something after you arrive."

"Something?"

"Yes, nothing too expensive," Ricky hastens to add, "but something to reflect your new management."

"Such as?"

"Maybe have the roof painted a different colour — don't go too extravagant. Has to be something visible to impress locals, maybe a new front door, or a small rock garden out front."

Later at home, Roger shares the day's news with Sue.

Sue makes a face. She is not exactly thrilled at the prospect of leaving Brissie. She sighs deeply.

"On the bright side," Sue brightens, "we'll get to try out our new Aussie passports."

1st August 1977, a few days before Jayne's tenth birthday, excitement in their household runs high. Sue is consoled by Roger's assurances they will return to Oz afterwards and their house is rented out following their departure.

Main farewells occur before departure at their regular get-togethers but they are officially seen off at the airport by Edward, Zelda, and a few friends as a celebratory occasion.

"Zelda looks stern today," Roger comments quietly to Sue.

"She's so tough, she'd burn her bra while wearing it," Sue replies in a tragic whisper.

"She gave me her hand in a way that made me wonder if I was meant to kiss it," Roger whispers back.

Zelda's terse smile unsuccessfully hides the timbre of her voice, which barely masks the quality of her hostility while she adjusts a pinkie nail with her emery board.

Edward being old school is dressed in a three-piece charcoal grey business suit, with a tight fitting waistcoat and tie.

Roger is amazed at how little his dad has learned to fit in. Roger whispers to Sue, "He's dressed like a pale, pox doctor's clerk. Mad as a cut snake in this weather!"

"Don't you feel terribly uncomfortable dressed like that?" Sue asks, "It's a real stinker today."

By way of response, humourless, Edward loosens his tie, which appears to bring him some relief, while Zelda takes a couple more swipes with her emery board.

Roger is comfortably dressed in a loose fitting Safari suit as they wave their farewells.

Their Air Pacific flight is pleasurable. Thankfully it is uneventful.

Sue is on tender hooks clutching the armrests with her eyes firmly shut for almost the duration of the flight.

As their plane circles on the approach, Roger falls in love with the Archipelago at first sight. The rugged green hills spilling out into the sea are sights of great beauty.

Passing through Customs and Immigration, each family member exits adorned with an overpowering frangipani lei before boarding a smaller plane. There is a small band playing to welcome visitors with a small market outside the airport, and locals are wearing sulus and colourful 'Hawaiian' shirts. It is hotter and more humid than in Brissie.

They are met by Wayne Thomas who has arranged a day's changeover to settle them in.

Wayne is small, thin, and handsome with the face of an altar boy, and gives the impression that he is on his way up. His neatly trimmed hair is greying at the temples. His tranquil brown eyes are relaxed but when he shakes Roger's hand, it is as if he is searching for a pulse. His voice is as dry as dead leaves.

Wayne is wearing khaki trousers and a yellow cotton shirt. He explains with a disarming smile, "Your home is not far from Head Office, commuting's a breeze."

Wayne hands Roger the keys. They pile into his car, luggage and all, and head for their new home.

Wayne does not look like a personality powerhouse. Roger observes that the poor bastard looks in need of a sandwich or a good feed. He does not appear to be happy leaving.

The house is upmarket and large enough inside to lose the 8th Army.

Their landlord, a retired Member of Parliament, lives elsewhere. Locally the residence stands out from the crowd, like a zit on a nose, fronting the bay with a verandah the length of the house. The garden, a terraced affair, is surrounded by low stone walls.

"Your landlord is intelligent, well educated, well respected, and Indian." Wayne explains, "He has the look of a man for whom life has held no hardships. His wife is Indian, his driver come bodyguard, chef, and housekeeper are Indians.

All of the MP's important jobs are carried out by Indians. Your landlord is used to supping from a well that never runs dry, which includes cocktails served in half a coconut by barefoot natives most days."

The interior is expensively decorated with heavy solid furnishings and an Indo Pacific theme. Timber floors, highly polished, the colour of honey gives way to tiles in the bathroom and kitchen areas. French doors open out onto the front verandah, which is wide enough to discourage direct sunlight into rooms. The dining room sports the noble lines of a sideboard with a matching table, long enough to land a B52 on it.

James and Jayne have their own rooms. Outside the main house is the servants' quarters, occupied by a married couple, Lilly and her husband, Brutus. Both have served previous Poobahs as long term employees, as has Shandy, the ever present guard dog.

Lilly is house girl and cleans. Husband, Brutus, tends the gardens. He has the heavy shoulders of a circus strong man and is bald as a badger. More tattoos than teeth, sleeveless checked shirts and Popeye forearms, he resembles some crazed 'Odd Job' type character with a big fuck-off axe in one hand.

Roger doubts he will need the axe. Nor any other weapon as he is one!

"Heaven only knows what sort of music those two are capable of making together? Him being without a dollop of doubt the strongest man I've ever met and her the strongest woman. It'd be like watching the ritual mating of two grizzly bears," says Wayne shaking his head in disbelief.

"Hopefully as gentle as lambs with us and our children," Roger adds.

Wayne is silent.

"If you tried wrestling him," Sue says quietly to Roger, "it would be like a gnat taking on an elephant."

"I'd get away, I'd have to. He could bend me into a figure of eight without even trying. I'd be seemingly jet-propelled — swish! Like a heron over water."

A quick walk around the humungous unfenced garden finds it ends after sloping down towards a creek. The tide is running out and the air has the sharp tang of the muddy smell of mudflats and mangroves. Rotting silt and vegetation fills the air.

The few brown cows walk down the beach in the late afternoon in search of garbage as food, while the child vendors offer banana, coconut and rice treats to carry them over to dinner time.

As the technicolor sunset light show begins, mosquitoes the size of dragon flies continually buzz around them, followed by virus infected bats flying in random patterns, staining everything with betel nut juice. Ah the call of nature.

Once Sue and Roger have sorted the family and baggage, Wayne drives Roger to work.

The NEV offices and warehouse are on a corner block in an enormous three storey brick building. The stucco over brick and orange terra-cotta tiled roof needs urgent TLC. Set on half an acre Roger notes that there is plenty of room for expansion.

Roger's very capable Assistant General Manager, Moti Mukherjee, has a string of Agricultural qualifications after his name. Taller than most Indians and devoid of facial hair, Moti has an athletic, long limbed body and a commanding presence. Married with three small sons he is devoid of any main interests outside of his family and work.

Moti has a surprising trait in that he possesses a wicked sense of humour. He regards golf as an expensive way of playing marbles and enjoys good food and wine.

Their Financial Controller is Vijay Prakash a qualified accountant. Vijay is trim and of medium height; his calming brown eyes shield an incomprehensible intelligence that lurks behind his gold wire frame glasses. In his early thirties, Vijay is married with two small girls.

Vijay has two passions outside of his job and family. A keen golfer and his car — a Toyota Celica sports car.

Roger and Wayne retire to Roger's new office where they complete the handover.

After Wayne departs, Roger has a question for Moti, "Is it true there are no termites in the islands? If so it removes a significant problem from servicing but hurts us turnover wise."

"We have Subterranean Termites and Drywood Termites throughout Viti Levu," Moti responds. "We've never treated any in Tonga or Western Samoa, Western Samoa, or American Samoa, but we've just treated one incident of Subterranean Termites in Sigatoka."

"Okay," Roger says slowly, "how was that treated."

"We tent fumigated it," Moti says proudly.

"Oh shit," Roger says, "we might have white anted ourselves! Remind me we must talk about that sooner than later."

Chapter 27

LIFE IN THE ARCHIPELAGO

Vijay presents the end of month figures to Roger for incorporation into the US.

"What report would that be?" Roger asks.

Vijay explains, "A monthly trading report has to be sent to the US."

Roger peruses said report.

"I'm impressed, Vijay," Roger says with a friendly smile. "Unlike me you can add up without using your fingers."

Vijay beams.

Roger asks, "Tell me, are you our financial controller, or are you just ornamental?"

Vijay appears confused.

Roger continues, "Why isn't the US report being prepared and sent by you?"

"It used to be," Vijay replies, "but Wayne insisted on preparing it and sending it himself."

Roger appears flummoxed.

"Vijay, I think as financial controller, that should be your duty, not mine. I'll be pleased to check it, rubber stamp it, or discuss it with you, if needed."

Vijay's mouth stretches into a wide smile, so broad, you could have easily mistaken he was about to take a long lunch.

"Although you're Hindi, Vijay, it's as if all your Christmases have come at once," Roger jokes to lighten the mood.

"If it was Christmas," Moti beams, "we should ask him how the turkey's going?"

"Dead and decapitated, but that's Christmas for a turkey," joins in Wasume. She is Roger's secretary, senior lady and at times mother hen at the gate. She completes the trio of senior management. In her early twenties, she is pretty with soft dark hair coiled around a long, slender neck and curvy under her sari.

The most sensual piece of clothing a woman can wear. It requires some practice to drape but hugs in all the right places. Wasume is mesmerising not because of what she reveals but what she does not. It is like watching a peach doing the rhumba in ivory silk.

Her slight build borders almost on anorexic in appearance. She is newly married and has a mind like a steel trap. A saucy authority she is sharp, intuitive, and has a voice that can drive birds from the sky.

Quickly Vijay disappears.

Later he approaches Roger.

"We may have a problem," Vijay announces.

"What sort of problem?"

"Well, when I tried to reconcile this report with the figures that were last sent to the US; I couldn't."

"Couldn't what?"

"Reconcile."

"Vijay, you might have to elaborate."

"The last report sent to the US bears little similarity to my own."

Roger is shell shocked, "Exactly, what do you mean, Vijay?"

Vijay looks embarrassed.

"Wayne prepared the summaries himself and kept them locked in his, I mean your office. This is the first time I've been privy to what he's been sending."

"You're not serious?" Roger is dumfounded. "We'd better call in Moti and Wasume."

"What's going on?" asks Moti.

"Tell him, Vijay!"

Vijay takes a couple of attempts to start, and then blurts out, "The summaries submitted to the US over the past quarter, bear no correlation to my own."

"Your figures must be wrong," Moti accuses.

"No, no!" Vijay hastens, "my figures," he stretches his arms, "our figures are correct. It's the summaries to the US that are inconsistent."

"How inconsistent are they?" Roger asks.

"Very!"

Roger sighs, "Vijay, getting a verbal report from you, is about as painful as pulling teeth!"

"Come on, Vijay," Moti urges, "spill the beans."

"The figure is so large that it carries over into the next column and makes a mess of the page!"

Moti, Roger, and Wasume exchange looks.

"We're out by hundreds of thousands of dollars," Vijay shrugs. "The US summaries show profits whereas our figures, the true figures, show significant losses."

"So how come we've got contradictory sets of figures?" Roger presses Vijay.

Vijay looks deeply troubled, "As I said, Wayne never involved me with the figures that went overseas to the US," he looks sheepish, "they were always formulated without my input."

"Without your *fucking* input," Roger explodes, "you're our financial controller for *Christ's* sake!"

Vijay and Moti both look mortified.

Roger laughs, "What? Never heard the word *fuck* before, you'd better hang around."

"It is an extremely good word," Moti says in an exaggerated Indo accent, "and it is a word we can truly grow to love and enjoy."

"Oh, fuck," Roger says.

"Oh, double fuck," Moti agrees, nodding vigorously.

"What do I do?" Vijay pleads.

Roger stiffens, he pulls his shoulders back.

"First, Vijay, you, that is we, must be absolutely certain that your figures are correct, and the US summaries are incorrect. Is that quite clear?"

Vijay nods. Moti sits down. Wasume fusses.

"This is serious," Roger continues, "and I'm not sure of the correct process, yet. I'm assuming all figures are intended to be accurate, are they?"

Vijay looks blank. "I've only checked the last quarter, I'll need to check further back, maybe to the last audit."

"Yes, you will. Question is, Vijay, do I notify Ricky first, before we do that?"

"I have a contact at the auditors who comes out here six monthly. I can call him as a matter of routine before you do anything drastic. He can at least run a routine check."

"If they come here six monthly, then why didn't they pick this up, six months ago?" Roger asks.

Silence.

"Good point," adds Moti.

"A very good point," joins Wasume.

All eyes are on Vijay.

"Wayne had lunch with the auditors, and their previous official visit was deferred," Vijay says.

"Deferred?" shouts Roger. He calms. "Alright," he murmurs.

"Sounds like a plan," Moti says to the room.

"But don't let the auditor find anything, Vijay, you must show him your findings, okay?"

"Alright," Vijay replies, "if you're sure."

"He's the auditor, Vijay. You're the financial controller. Let them see it as it is. You have found this problem not them. No need for white lies, nor padding. Just tell it as it is."

Vijay looks relieved.

"Vijay, what did you expect me to say?"

"I hoped you wouldn't ask me to cover it up."

Roger reacts badly, "Are you used to covering shit up, Vijay?"

Vijay reddens and shuffles from side to side looking like he wants to throw up. "The capital depreciation register has become…"

Roger looks up sharply but says nothing.

"Become what?" Moti asks.

"It's not as accurate as it should be."

"Fuck me," Roger throws out angrily. "Any more good news?"

Vijay still looks uncomfortable.

Roger has telephone calls to make. He starts with Ricky in Sydney. He chooses his words carefully and speaks slowly.

Ricky the Ringmaster listens intently but reacts quickly.

"You'd better call the auditors, Roger. Tell them I've authorised it."

"Alright, Ricky," Roger replies, "it's going to be an interesting week."

Ricky takes pause. "I'll throw in a $5,000 bonus if you perform, Roger."

Roger is taken back. Quite the unexpected. Does Ricky know something that he, Roger, does not?

"Thank you, Ricky."

After a lot of hemming and hawing, a young Indian with almost identical gold-rimmed glasses to Vijay's arrives and sits beside him scrutinising the figures.

They work together for about an hour working their calculator keypads like virtuoso pianists while grumbling something inaudible.

Roger is waiting anxiously in his upstairs office for any tidbit of information without him needing a crow bar.

When nothing happens, his patience runs thin. He phones downstairs to Vijay. "Anything happening yet?" he asks.

"The auditor is on another line to his Head Office. I think he's speaking with his boss, the Chief Auditor. He might be talking with the US. It's serious."

Not long afterwards, Roger gets a formal visit from their Chief Auditor. He is tall, fit looking, and plays squash. To Roger, he looks as if he could jog forever without being winded. Certainly, fat would not dare attach itself to his body. His brown hair is cut short, his brow naturally furrowed. His spine is as assuredly straight as the ironed crease in his trouser leg. Roger sees nothing inviting or welcoming about Straight Man who looks permanently serious.

"We've found Vijay's figures are correct and something's definitely wrong with the summaries presented to the US."

"Not right?"

"Well, totally inaccurate actually."

Roger pauses, "Who pays for all of this auditing?"

"The US are picking up the tab, but…" Straight Man lets the last word hang in the air, "ultimately it will be charged back to here."

"This just keeps getting better and better." Roger holds his head in both hands.

Straight Man has a binder of reports with a myriad of entries and a list of required actions.

According to the reports, any profits evaporated entirely between the arrival of Roger and Wayne's departure. Under scrutiny, it is doubtful the Archipelago Office has made any profit for its last year.

Roger watches dismally as all the black plusses on the balance sheet now fall away like dominoes tumbling into the red columns.

"And with your personal belongings from Oz still in a container, tossing about somewhere on the high seas, it's debatable whether you'll see them again outside of Oz," Straight Man clarifies. "It's not an auditor's decision, nor yours, Roger. This has to be referred to the board. We are here to advise only."

"And your advice is?" Roger asks.

Straight man responds unequivocally, "It's a choice between trying to trade out of the problems or closing down."

Roger absorbs this for a moment and then allows it to rattle around the room. He tries not to look too shattered. Straight Man gathers his files to depart.

"Good luck," bestows Straight Man as he walks out through the door.

Wasume with a severe expression suggesting she has lost her pet hamster to a feral cat, walks straight in. It was a good thing that the door was already wide open because if it had been closed, she would have crashed right through it like Popeye.

"So," Wasume pauses, "in the words of Lenin, what is to be done?"

For a long moment Roger says nothing, then slowly as if he has been shot with a tranquilliser, "Things usually go well until they stop going well."

Roger's thoughts are in turmoil. How quickly things can turn to shit. He looks and feels as if leeches have exsanguinated him. Suddenly all the fun has been sucked out of life.

Chapter 28

CHOICES

Thursday — FIVE A.M.

Roger blinks awake. Sue is beside him fast asleep. For a few seconds he is unsure where he is.

He gets up quietly and pads to the bathroom. Jayne's room is across the hall and her door is wide open. Like Sue, she is fast asleep. He closes the bathroom door quietly behind him so as not to wake the house. He peers out the closed window. It is still dark.

For a while, Roger becomes a classic case of glass half empty.

The stress of maybe having to close a business down so soon after he has arrived unsettles him.

Finished in the bathroom, he pads to the kitchen, *a cup of coffee will help me think.*

He sits on the front verandah, sipping coffee, watching the bay fade into light as the early sun catches particles of dust, and stirs newborn flies that buzz around his head like a halo. With a gunner's view of the bay he philosophises with Rudyard Kipling, *The first condition of understanding a foreign country is to smell it.*

Right, he thinks. *So much for a relaxing morning. Admittedly, the place is a bit on the nose.*

Later on the way to work, he invests in a packet of cigarettes. He is taking for granted he will need them. After sucking his first life-saver down to the filter, he wishes he had not. He reassesses, surprised that he has started smoking again.

"There's nothing wrong with the cart," Roger tells himself, "it's who's been pulling the damned cart's the problem."

"You're an idiot," he tells himself. "Correct. It's not easy to educate an idiot. Better to argue against a hundred idiots than have one agree with me."

"Lung cancer slow or closure of business fast? What's the real difference? Time? Who gives a shit? Just do, whatever you've got to do. Remain detached as a surgeon would removing an infected limb."

You are lucky you have a good, young management team. They're enthusiastic about what they are attempting to do. Run with it!

Roger's office looks like the command bunker of an army in fighting retreat. He is trying to quell the rising panic in the eyes of his staff. He smiles his most assuring.

"I'm sure we'll all get along, really, really, well," Roger confesses, "at times I have trouble remembering my own phone number. I'll need all of you to help me and give your best support in this very difficult situation."

The day passes uneventfully. No panic phone calls from Ricky, none from the US, even the auditors are quiet.

"I don't like it here," Sue states later at home in the gloom of their bedroom, "on the rare occasion when the sun actually does shine the place smells and it's filthy."

"You might be over stating."

Sue raises herself up on one elbow. "What's to over state?" she replies indignantly. "In town stinking rivulets of water run in what are called gutters, but are actually open drains. On occasions, everything from night soil to small dead animals flow through those and at times it's like a council project to liquefy the contents of our bowels. But the trick," Sue says reinforcing her comments, "is never to examine anything too closely, keep moving, and sometimes hold your breath."

"What else?" Roger asks, "besides hygiene."

"No television, limited entertainment, poor standards of delicatessen, a few fresh foods are imported from New Zealand. Little or no window shopping," Sue slumps back down, "whoopee do!"

"At certain levels your logic is awfully compelling," Roger shakes his head. "I'm so far out of my comfort zone here, Sue. It's like this is my first rodeo. I've always had to make sales and profitably, but I've never had to turn a business from a bloody great loss and fast, not since Dad's hotel."

"Back then you never even had a chequebook, and your father and Zelda were working against you. This is different."

"Maybe we should just admit defeat and let them close it down?"

"Yes, but what about the others who have lives here, families and homes? True, we can just return to Oz, to our house and friends, but what about them? Don't you owe it to these people here, to give it your best shot?"

Roger is thoughtful. An old saying fills his mind. Good, better, best. Never let it rest until your good is better and your better best.

"Yes, of course. But what if it becomes a case of how fast support from the turkeys at the Snake Pit will fade away?"

Sue's voice rising to a horrified squeak holds no conviction, "Surely that can't happen quickly, so what could possibly go wrong?"

"Quickly? It would happen faster than the financial support of a candidate with plummeting poll numbers."

"If I nominate closure of the business the losses are contained. If we trade on and the situation deteriorates then I've failed and my career, such as it is, is in the toilet."

"But if you do pull it off, Roger, surely that will guarantee your future back in Brisbane?"

"You'd think, wouldn't you?"

The clock seems to stop as the walls close in on Roger.

Then he laughs.

"What are you laughing at?"

"I love the irony, what I was told by Ricky, 'But you're very fortunate, Roger. You're following a succession of excellent men. What we expect from you is a steady continuation.'"

Roger works late in to the nights with his management team while they perform an autopsy of the business. It becomes very intense.

"How'd it go?" Sue asks when Roger eventually trudges home.

"Besides vehicles being depreciated long after they're sold, or transferred, the capital register now looks in reasonable shape, or at least it will after a succession of write downs."

Sue is sympathetic.

"Want a beer?"

Roger shakes his head. "I think I'm past it but a sweet tea would be nice, thank you. It's the trading register that holds the worst news. That said, in order that our bottom line doesn't vanish like a fart in a fan factory, we'll have to stick to some pretty strict ground rules. We've problems at Apia Branch. There is a bunch of unaccounted stock. Moti advises we close Apia as it's too difficult to administer from here. I think he's right."

Roger asks Wasume to make photocopies of something for him he calls his reminder sheet, but asks her not to show it around until he tells her to do so.

"The problem," Vijay explains, "stems from sales being inadequate to support the overheads. Even with the closure of Apia Branch."

The culprits quickly become apparent.

"A succession of your predecessors has been reluctant to increase prices for fear of upsetting clients and looking uncompetitive. Whenever I've suggested price increases I've been shouted down faster than an Indonesian abattoir," Vijay blurts out.

Moti is thoughtful. "Whenever I submitted a quote Wayne always wanted me to reduce the price for a quick sale."

"This problem would have been a lot easier to cope with if minimal increases had been instigated in line with inflation over time," Roger states.

"People in high places could get very ticked off after they find out," Vijay shakes his head.

"When we tell them," Roger announces calmly, "it'll be reminiscent of Russia and the United States doing war dances."

Vijay looks worried.

Roger tries to put his mind at ease. "There's no future in selling our services based on price. If that's what the competition is doing, then we should let them fail, and without our help."

Roger looks about him. All faces look troubled.

"Wasume would you please release those photocopies. Now appears to be the perfect time."

Wasume bends decorously at the knees and prepares to pass around the reminder sheets.

"Keep one for yourself, Wasume."

Roger holds his copy up after the group have theirs. As if inviting questions but none arise.

"Something I like to remember from time to time, team," Roger begins, "and I hope that as we read this together it might make sense to you all. Put simply it's a quote by Ruskin a famous philosopher who lived many years ago from 1819 – 1900. Roger coughs to clear his throat and begins.

"When you buy on price alone you can never be sure.

It's unwise to pay too much, but it's worse to pay too little.

When you pay too much you lose a little money—that's all

But, when you pay too little you sometimes lose everything

Because the thing you bought is incapable of doing the thing it was bought to do.

The common law of business balance prohibits paying a little and getting a lot.

It cannot be done.

But, if you deal with the lowest bidder it is well to add something for the risk you run, and if you do that, you will have enough to buy quality."

Roger pauses for effect. "Not bad advice from the 1800s, team. I'm sure we could rewrite it in more modern language, simplify it even, but that's not really the point, is it?"

Roger is unsure whether he has got his message across. Hoping his team has taken the bait.

"I think Mr Ruskin was a clever and deep sighted individual," Vijay declares, "from his mouth to God's ear."

Wasume remains quiet; safer not to speak, unless spoken to, until she knows him better. However, she is impressed.

In the final analysis Vijay craves information. Finally he has been given the green light by his new boss to do his job the way he always intended. No more being excluded from management talks, no more being side stepped by the auditors.

"Agreed, I'd like to get started straight away."

In a moment Vijay is barking orders at his team of girls downstairs, "I want a full audit on cash payments over the past two years, and I want copies of every report that went to the US without me seeing it first."

Vijay has a wide smile plastered across his face. He knows he is going to have a far more interesting job from now on, providing of course he has a job.

Chapter 29

TAKE THAT!

The auditors send their best people; two clever ones and thirteen nongs, who make copies of everything and then disappear back to their Snake Pit.

"This event is most embarrassing to all concerned." Straight Man is less than confident.

"Could always be worse," Roger replies.

"Worse?"

"Wayne Thomas could have been caught in the middle of the night by a journalist, wearing fish net stockings, and with an apple in his mouth...."

"Then we could have disowned him," Straight Man's smirk looks sly.

Back at his office, he ignites a firestorm in New York with a single memo. A firestorm Tricky Ricky might have trouble putting out.

Those at the meeting do not look overly surprised, but confirmation of what has been muted for a while, receives broad smiles all round. Prices are about to be increased big time.

"What do you want us to say to clients on the telephone?" Wasume asks tongue in cheek.

Good question.

"We'll cover that shortly in detail, Wasume," Roger promises calmly.

In response, Wasume looks down at the floor.

"If after spending time with me you feel confident, and would like to tackle some on your own, please feel free to do so," Roger tells Moti.

Moti is ecstatic. To him this is manna from heaven, a feather in his cap, and a step forward. He is the chosen one — the one Roger is now training to take over. For over twelve months it had been a plan but without any start date. Now Moti sees his future ahead and the awakening within effuses his whole being.

"Our ploy is simple," Roger tells his team, "we tell our clients the truth, except that there were two sets of figures. I see no advantage in discrediting my predecessors, although a few clued up clients may give us knowing smiles. Price increases are to be graduated over a six month period culminating in target sales predicted by end of year."

"Is that it?" Wasume ventures.

"We need to concentrate more on our PR, make our clients feel extra special; our customer service must be second to none. We need to focus on that. They deal directly with a nominated staff member for all things, any issues, problems, questions, a direct line to someone who cares, and by doing that we'll increase prices in line with additional services."

Everyone is fidgeting; no-one is looking overly confident.

Roger is thoughtful before continuing. "In particular we are going to announce that if our servicing fails to live up to our Clients' expectations — it's free."

"Free?" is their resounding chorus.

"Yes, free! We're charging top dollar now, and so we need to provide top warranties!"

Crickets!

"What's up? What's the problem?"

Vijay was first to answer. "I see where you're coming from, but…"

"But what?"

"Well, might clients take advantage?"

"We'll have to wait and see won't we?" Roger replies. He stands up and rubs his red, swollen eyes.

Wasume is hesitant. "You seem very sure of yourself."

"Well, if I can't be, who can?" He felt his scalp tingle. His first rodeo.

As the meeting disburses. "I have another duty I should perform," Roger says.

"Can I help you, with it?" Vijay offers.

"Yes, thank you. I need to track down Wayne Thomas. He left here for Europe and I want to speak with him by telephone. I think I owe it to him, to tell him about the problem found with the two sets of figures."

"Surely, he already knows that," Vijay muses aloud, "after all it was his doing."

"Yes, but I would feel better in myself by talking to him. And before the US catches up with him and spoils his holiday."

"I'll track him down," Vijay promises.

Vijay found Wayne in a London hotel.

Roger finds the long distance echo disconcerting.

Wayne sounds indignant, "What's the matter, Roger? Why are you calling me here and at this hour?"

"It's urgent, Wayne, or I wouldn't be calling you at all," Roger pauses, "we have a glaring discrepancy with the figures. Vijay's monthly actual doesn't match up with what you've been sending to the US."

There's a long silence, and then, "Oh, I see," another delay as if Wayne is collecting his thoughts, "but surely there's not much of a difference?"

"It's the difference between profitability and substantial losses. The auditors are working the figures now."

"Why have you called the auditors?" Wayne's voice sounds panicky.

"Ricky authorised it."

"You've spoken to Ricky about this?"

"Yes, of course I report to him and the US board, why wouldn't I?"

"Well, it might have been better if you'd contacted Frank first; after all, he is in charge."

"In charge! Of what? I report to Ricky."

"Have you got that in writing, Roger?"

Roger is taken back.

"Wayne, I have nothing in writing, except a copy of a work visa."

"Exactly, had you spoken to Frank, you may have taken a different direction."

Roger's head spins.

"You have me at a disadvantage, Wayne, if you're privy to information that I'm not."

Roger ponders Wayne's reaction, which has certainly taken an unexpected direction.

Frank? Why Frank?

"The auditors are doing a complete audit, Wayne. As a courtesy, I thought you should know."

A silence descends between them. It is far from companionable.

"Are you still there?" Roger asks.

When Wayne replies, Roger senses from his staggered almost incoherent speech that something is surely wrong.

"Roger, it's not what it seems, really....but I'm so sorry."

"Sorry, for what, Wayne? Sorry you left me in a mess? Or sorry I'm here with my wife, two kids and part of our home on the high seas living on a knife's edge trying to sort out your problems?"

Wayne's voice is close and then distant, as if he is moving about.

Roger covers the mouthpiece and speaks to Vijay.

"It's as if he's pacing a trench through the hotel room's carpet."

"You still don't understand do you?" Wayne says accusingly.

"Maybe I'd be ashamed if I did."

"Frank promised me a bonus, this holiday all expenses paid, all I had to do was show a small profit to the board and hide the loss. That's all."

"Pity you didn't tell me what was going on, Wayne. I'm out of the loop here."

"Maybe you should have spoken with Frank first, Roger. Word is Ricky's about to take early retirement and Frank's the new man in charge. He's the man I answer to. Probably you too."

Wayne ended the call.

Is Wayne being entirely honest with me? muses Roger.

"What did he say?" Vijay asks.

"He was like Fonzie trying to say he's 'sorry'," Roger replies with a smirk.

"How many times, this sorry?"

"Only once. But he's not half as sorry as I am."

"His reputation is now shipwrecked. Surely no suits will want to acknowledge his existence. Perhaps Ricky will sack him?"

Roger is thoughtful.

"Agreed up to a point, but the suits who appointed him must surely share some responsibility. Wayne insists that Frank Moore is really in charge, even gave me a heads up that Ricky is about to retire."

"Who's this Frank Moore?" Vijay asks.

"Very well connected at Head Office. Not the most popular of fellows."

"Why?" Moti asks.

"He has no knowledge of our industry for starters, he has an accounting background from a bed manufacturing industry second, and third, he's a motivator of personnel by fear."

"Just the sort I wouldn't want marrying my sister, if I had one," Vijay exclaims.

"Good one!" Moti adds, slapping the palm of his hand on his thigh, "just what's needed in business, a damned theorist."

"Something's not quite right," Roger ponders, "I can't quite put my finger on it but there's no evidence of theft. Why cook the books? Wayne's brought it on himself with his terminal inaccuracies."

"Terminal inaccuracies?"

"Lies."

"A sin half concealed is always easily half forgotten," Moti quotes sagely.

"There are always consequences to choices made," Wasume says haughtily, "he'll have to quit or go under a bus."

On the way home, the rain has passed and Roger thinks he can actually see some sunlight trying to break through the cloud cover.

Over dinner, Roger tries to play down his problems at work. An animated James talks about his school cricket match that afternoon and is full of his misadventures at the crease.

It revolves around him standing on the green field, as stiff as a board, while the ball bears down on him like a guided missile.

Jayne recites her lines from an upcoming play, although it does not appear that trees have much to say.

Sue has spent the morning trying to discourage Lilly from punishing the furniture with her sa sa broom as the bunch of twigs is pulling threads.

"Inside and outside it's the same damned sa sa broom," Sue complains bitterly to Roger.

Lilly is an Amazon of a woman; Roger guesses she is about fifty, mainly as that is the age she looks.

Lilly is forty years old. She is no femme fatale, but had once been pretty. The years had caught up with her early and her frame is better upholstered than it needs to be, but her heart is in the right place. She looks capable of lifting tall buildings with one arm.

They are interrupted by an impromptu visit by Moti.

"Just thought I'd check that all is well here," he smiles nervously.

"Come on in," Roger announces, "you never need an invite, Moti. We were just talking about Lilly and Brutus."

Moti visibly relaxes. "It's a bit frizzy around the edges," he says sadly, "but word is Lilly can't have any children of her own. Meanwhile Brutus is a bit of a mystery man."

Moti in awe reveals, "I watched her lift a stove with one arm once, and just to beat a mouse to death with her free hand."

"With her sa sa broom no doubt," Sue smiles grimly.

Lilly's smile is of mostly missing teeth; those that remain are blackened or broken. She enjoys scooping up both James and Jayne, one in each powerful arm, and kissing them.

Then Lilly roars with laughter saying, "Oh Marama, these are Lilly's babies."

"When we're going out without Jayne and James, Lilly and Brutus become babysitters for us, although our two are hardly babies."

"More a case of child minding," Moti agrees.

"The last thing I say," reinforces Sue, "as we're getting into our car, 'And under no circumstances are the children allowed up on to the roof of the house to play. Is that quite clear, Lilly?'"

Moti is thoughtful. "The roof here is flat with a parapet surround quite safe I think, but climbing up on to the roof via a ladder could be hazardous."

Sue ignores Moti's helpful advice and continues, "'Yes Marama,' is Lilly's confident reply."

"Sometimes when going out we need to drive past due to errands, and yes, there they'd be up on the roof. Waving at us as we drive past!" Roger explains.

Sue continues, "Lilly and Brutus are in attendance, all four of them up on the roof playing and dancing around like fools, having a wonderful time together."

After Moti leaves, they listen to the world news on Radio Archipelago, the bastion of broadcasting worthiness.

Sue finally turns it off after bad world news turns into dreadful then passes on to terrible.

"What a world we're leaving for future generations," Sue opines, "we've seen genocide in Africa, Asia, and Eastern Europe that would bugger the imagination. All since the conclusion of the Second World War."

"And the Korean War, and the Vietnam War," Roger reminds, "I doubt it will get better. Where there's conflict, there's profit. The bigger the war the bigger the lie and the bigger the bottom line ever since Plato was a lad."

Chapter 30

SHANDY

Their neighbours on the other side are a family of three from the Gilbert Islands. Zayn Kiribati is an engineer; his wife Selina, a stay at home Mum, and their young son Jason, is about the same age as James.

"Never go swimming in the creek," Zayn warns the children, "as you just don't know what lurks under dirty water."

Selina's skin is the colour of milky coffee; she has enormous, long-lashed, liquid brown eyes radiating intelligence. Topped with a mass of long, shiny, black, hair, she could easily be an International model travelling the world, but because she is in love with Zayn, she wants to stay put.

As with most Gilbert Islanders, in addition to being highly skilled, Zayn plays the guitar and is easy on the ear. Zayn is a gentleman in the truest form.

Sue and Roger are visibly impressed to have such wonderful, friendly neighbours.

"In addition to his Polynesian good looks, he's always relaxed and smiling," Sue reflects.

"He gives the impression of utter peace and inner calm at all times."

If there are insufficient chairs, they all sit around on picnic rugs, sarongs, and tapa cloths.

A pit in the Kiribati's back garden produces great Lovos, something similar to the Maori hangi. Popular and always included is wonderful Palusami (Taro leaves and coconut cream) and Dalo (the edible root of the Taro leaves).

Palusami is very labour intensive. Brutus collects ripe coconuts and splits them with a mighty blow from his cane knife.

"He could probably tear them apart with his bare hands," says Roger.

Where possible they save the coconut juice, for which Roger and Sue have developed a taste.

"Be careful," warns Zayn, "too much coconut juice is like too much drivel, it will make you *sleepy*."

Lilly sets to scraping out the ripe flesh of the coconut that she then squeezes in a muslin bag, to produce the rich cream.

Roger watches on in amazement as the rich cream from the coconut flesh builds up in the bowl, leaving desiccated coconut to be discarded from the bag.

"If the cream is too thick they add some juice from the coconut in place of water," Zayn explains.

The food that comes out of the Lovo is tender and falls apart as it touches the tongue. It is almost like cooking in a massive crock pot. Plenty of drink, music, open pit fire, yummy food, it is a time of great celebration with a few sore heads the next day.

"The gourmet result is to die for," Sue coos. "As anyone with children knows feeding them can be tricky but even Jayne can't get enough Palusami."

"If God made anything better than Palusami," Zayn says, "HE keeps it for himself."

Zayn prepares his first bites of Palusami carefully, equal amounts of leaves, fish, and meat drenched in the rich coconut cream. His eyes are half closed as he slips a forkful reverently into his mouth. "Dreams are made of this."

"Another favourite is a fish dish called Kokoda." Roger licks his lips.

"Agreed. A raw fish dish marinated in lime and coconut cream."

The Kiribati family have three dogs; a mongrel Pinky and two Great Danes — one black and the other beige. They all roam the properties as a free K9 patrol.

James and Jayne have two brown dogs of the Heinz variety that mix in with the other three, and then there's Shandy, another brown bitzer.

They patrol the grounds with the fervour of holy warriors and dribble dangling from their chops.

"Things are going well," Sue says brightly. "It's early morning, already hot, and after a few minutes shirts are already sticking to everyone's backs."

"Have you noticed how few dogs are barking here?" Roger fires back.

"Not until you mentioned it, no," Sue replies.

"Maybe it's because they're always asleep. They do sleep a lot."

"I've noticed that there aren't many of them about, except where expats live," Roger adds, "locals generally are not popular among the expat dog population, but to be fair, neither are dogs overly popular among locals."

"Unless from the inside of a pot, and about to be eaten."

"I've deduced that dogs here are either super intelligent or rely heavily on their acute sense of smell."

"Why?"

"Because guaranteed if a white person approaches for any reason the dogs will not even stir a recumbent ear, but if it's a dark skinned person, then all hell breaks loose." Sue is thoughtful, "the exception is for Moti and Zayn. Dogs take no notice of them at all."

"Agreed, but Moti and Zayn are exceptional."

"There are few pedigree dogs on this island, the emphasis is on bitzers; adopted mainly by expats for their children to dote on."

"Moti has warned me how he ensures Vijay has an abundance of dog licences always to be held here or at the office. Dog licences are very important. To own a dog without one is a very serious offence. Police arrive, often in pairs, comfortably ensconced in their 4x4 vehicle to count dogs and check the validity of licences at homes of expats."

It being an indictable offence, Roger would not want to experience the sights and sounds close up and personal of the local gaol.

Speaking of which they have an impromptu visit on Wednesday, by men dressed a lot like policemen, the local constabulary no less. Most view the local constabulary as incompetent, lazy, corrupt, or lacking resources.

Two police officers commence a conversation with Sue through an open laundry window, adjacent to the drive-way.

Sergeant Rock Star put his head half way out through the laundry window and enquires, "Do you have any dogs and dog licences, Missus?"

A fair enough question, thinks Sue, even if she is up to her armpits in suds.

In the process of drying her hands, Sue is about to explain they have a number of dogs and will gather their licences from the main house area, she moves and in so doing nudges Shandy, who is asleep at her feet.

Shandy suddenly realises there are visitors and, more importantly, they are not white nor Moti or Zayn.

Shandy does not like anything indigenous.

She leaps up with her front paws on the window sill to get a better look at Mr Plod. Her ears are back and down.

Shandy sees him and produces her most menacing growls, low in her throat. Retracting lips display two rows of razor sharp teeth the size of rifle ammunition.

James and Jayne nicknamed this the 'Shandy grin' — the style of which any carnivore would be justly proud.

Sergeant Rock Star, is standing adjacent to the laundry window, falls back immediately to a more defensive position. Heavily supported on his colleague's arm he mumbles, "Yes, oh yes, nice big doggy."

With that, both officers fall over each other, waving their arms as if directing traffic, in their rush to get back into their vehicle through the one door nearest the window.

They drive away.

Shandy resumes her original pose, shuffling back to Sue's feet and for the mild inconvenience to her day, without so much as a murmur.

"Interesting," Sue giggles, "they never did see the dog licences. I wonder if we'll get another visit from them."

The policeman obviously thought Shandy is the style of guard dog capable of tearing his face off.

Unlike Fred, Shandy has no papers and there are many opinions as to her parentage. Her dominant genes are large, playful, and intelligent. She plays with children.

Shandy watches other dogs closely, particularly those living next door, and it is with almost a look of disdain when they drink from a puddle.

As the neighbours' dogs hump furniture, lick their own balls and drink from any toilet bowl, Shandy remains unimpressed but they all have one thing in common. They avoid walking on the road because most locals would risk life and limb to run them down. That or being eaten in the local village would be their likely fate if they wander too far.

One of Jayne and James' dogs, called Tiger, is hit by a car and promptly replaced by Tanya. There is no plan or process. Appearing from nowhere one morning, Tanya was adopted after Shandy allowed her to drink from her bowl.

Roger treats himself to a smile after Tiger is buried, and remembers the tale told in Oz by Trev about Nosey's cat.

"What's so funny?" Sue asks Roger.

"Just thinking about Trev burying Nosey's cat; and the fact that Brutus dug this hole for Tiger."

Chapter 31

MORE PLEASE

At a Friday evening BBQ Roger learns about cultural difficulties first hand.

He is criticised by his Indian guests for serving meat on a holy day as well as cooking pork on the same grille as the beef. On a visit to the toilet he sees someone downing a beer, someone who had constantly bleated how they never touch the dragon hell fire of alcohol. Roger shakes his head at wonder of the hypocrisy of it all.

At another BBQ, this time on a holy Tuesday, Roger, on Moti's advice, serves an abundance of fish.

"Can't go wrong with fish," Moti smiles coyly, as he genuflects towards the kitchen and another beer.

On yet another occasion, carefully orchestrated not to be a holy day, Roger is quizzed by both Muslims and Hindus as to the origin of the content of the sausages. Having explained they had been purchased from a reputable butcher's shop in town, he opts to leave Abdul the Muslim arguing with Prasad the Hindi, and for good measure someone's wife of Sikh Punjabi ancestry, whether the shop bought chicken hamburgers might contain any traces of beef or pork?

"Yousef the Muslim is the equivalent of a lapsed Catholic," Sue whispers to Roger.

"You're right. He has no quarrels with his religion, as its rituals and ceremonies provide him with comfort but he ignores anything in the Quran that gets in the way of his enjoyment of worldly things."

"He also works most Fridays."

"The only thing that he finishes by Friday, is Thursday."

The next up worry for Roger will be what juices on the hot plate may contaminate the damned fish.

"I'm over it," says Roger to Sue.

"Grill it and they will come," Sue replies, then adds after a significant pause, "mostly we seem to alternate somewhere between laughable and non-existent. I'm missing home. BBQ's in Oz were a lot easier to cater for."

Roger raises his glass to Sue. "A toast — here's to not buggering it up."

"Life here's about as basic as you'd ever want it to be," Sue agrees, "but where there's a will there's usually a way."

Moti often calls out before or after work, sometimes with his wife or children, ostensibly to keep a watchful eye out for the family from Oz and in part to keep a watchful eye, on his mentor, Roger. It is subtle, but Roger and Sue notice and appreciate it.

"Brutus isn't as happy about being here as Lilly is," Moti observes.

"Is there a reason for that?" Roger asks. mildly.

Moti looks uncomfortable and squirms in his chair. Sue pours him a fresh coffee, and puts milk and sugar in front of him. "Thank you, Sue."

"Come on Moti, spit it out. What do you know about Brutus that we don't?"

"This house has a history," Moti explains, "and that history is why it's available at such a great rental price."

"I had wondered," Sue opines. "It's a terrific location and so grand compared with other expat homes."

Moti considers his words, carefully. "Some say the house is haunted."

"Wonderful, tell us more," Sue grins encouragement.

"Well," Moti continues, "a young house girl was murdered here a few years back and the culprit was never arrested."

Jayne becomes interested. "Wow! A ghost. Can I see the ghost?"

"Shush," Sue says, "let Moti finish his story."

"Not much more to tell," Moti laughs, "truth be known it might have been her lover, or boyfriend. He hit her that hard with a cane knife he decapitated her."

"Is she carrying her head under her arm?" Jayne wants to know.

"Okay," says Sue. "We might leave it there for now. Off you two."

"Might we have to kick this ghost out of the house?" Roger asks, a twinkle in his eye.

"Just leave that to Jayne," Sue suggests, "as long as she doesn't drop a few brain cells along the way."

It does not unduly worry their family that some poor girl has been killed, apparently outside the house in their carport. Lilly remains unmoved but Brutus often becomes distracted, by what, Roger is unsure. Without proof it is just a ghost story.

"Talking of ghosts," Moti continues, "it's said while they're intimate with the place they haunt, they're never of it."

"Maybe this ghost, if it's friendly enough, could do the housework while we're not looking," suggests Sue tongue in cheek.

"Does any of this make sense to you," Roger asks Moti.

"More so, when I've been drinking," Moti replies with an impish smile, "but about Lilly and Brutus, it's good that Brutus is as gentle as a lamb, best you try and keep him away from the grog or heaven help us all."

"Is he a drinker?" Sue asks innocently.

"Who isn't?" Moti replies. "But he's strong. After a bad storm last summer, a few trees were down. The gardeners eventually cut off their branches and built a fire. Brutus, without any effort, bent down, picked up a solid tree trunk and balanced it up high on his shoulder. Then he walked to the far edge of the grounds and threw it on the bonfire heap. I doubt I could have lifted one end even with help."

Lilly and Brutus go through a rough patch as some marriages do. She accuses him of having sex with another woman, her sister actually, and throws him out.

He has tried flowers, even plastic ones, but Lilly is not having any of the get-out-of-gaol card they represent.

Moti preaches caution. "Your household has a mentally disturbed Brutus who normally wouldn't swot a fly, sitting in a tormented heap on the floor in your lounge while he plays with Jayne and James with nowhere else to go. I'll have him watched. Do you know anything about marriage counselling?"

"Nothing at all," Sue replies, "I'm sure it's like climbing a mountain of treacle."

"We need a good result. Maybe Brutus lifting up their local church so Lilly can sweep under it, while not disturbing the congregation too much," Moti cheekily suggests.

It is time Sue and Roger practise their non-existent skill at marriage counselling on their living room floor. Both Lilly and Brutus sit obediently while Sue and Roger feel like Roman Emperors seated on dining room chairs.

Sue looks at Roger. Roger looks at Sue.

Both prepare to cock sympathetic ears to the delinquents.

Sue is pretending she is riveted by every word coming out of the guilty mouth of Brutus, while Roger is balancing integrity between Malcolm Fraser and Ronald Reagan. Suddenly the room seems smaller and hotter!

Sue begins a new tack with Lilly. "Now Lilly, we've heard that you've thrown Brutus out because you think he's slept with your sister. Is this correct?"

Lilly replies, her head bowed both out of respect and embarrassment, her voice barely audible, "Yes Marama."

Sue looks at Roger.

Roger gives him a discerning look to ensure he has not been drinking. "Ah hem, uh hm," then more sternly, "Brutus is this true?"

"No Turaga!" Brutus raises his head with his eyes wide open, pleading his innocence.

"DON'T YOU DARE SAY THAT!"

Both Sue and Roger have grabbed the arms of their chairs in shock at this sudden high-pitched not-so-subtle reply from Lilly.

Sue tries to placate Lilly, "Why Lilly? What proof do you have?"

Before she can answer, Brutus brushes the mat in front of him with the back of his hand as if brushing away crumbs.

"She's always dreaming."

A menacing growl comes from Lilly, "You good for nothing laze-a-about! My own Sister told me!"

Brutus snaps around to look at her in total shock.

Sue and Roger snap around to look at Brutus in total shock.

At the same time, Lilly gets up and runs outside.

"Is this true Brutus?" Roger is trying to look wise and grey like an elder.

Before Brutus can answer, a whirlwind of frizzy hair, bright and colourful and the ever present sa sa broom come flying through the door and suddenly pounces furiously all over Brutus's head. Being big and cumbersome, he cannot get up quick enough to flee or deflect the torrent of blows about his head, back, and flailing arms.

It reminds Roger of the cartoon of the Tasmanian Devil and the true call of the Tasmanian Devil fills the room.

Roger and Sue at first lean back in their chairs, almost toppling backwards to evade the thrashing sa sa broom. Once they are up, Roger attempts grabbing Lilly about the arms from behind. She is a big lady and he can hardly get a grip. Sue watches on as the rodeo unfolds in front of her, not knowing what to do.

Thankfully just Roger's touch stops Lilly in her tracks. She had never had a white man touch her before. She becomes embarrassed and stands quietly, the feeling of the touch lingering like moss on the side of a tree whilst Sue takes the sa sa broom gently from her.

Brutus, still sitting on the floor, has hundreds of little scratches all over him that trickle with blood. He just sits there with a hangdog look about him.

Roger decides this is his cue, "Well now Brutus, I think you know now, how Lilly feels."

Sue is thinking, Surely they all should know how Lilly feels by now.

"And I have a feeling you won't do this again will you?"

"No boss."

"And Lilly, I think your punishment is enough to embarrass Brutus for a week whilst those cuts heal. He looks as if he's remorseful, are you Brutus?"

"Yes Turaga."

"What do you think, Lilly? Will you forgive him like a good Christian woman and take him back?"

Silence.

Sue puts in her best, "Lilly, you can walk with your head held high now that he walks with scratches all over him. What do you think? I think your punishment was a good one. Besides you need him."

Lilly encouraged by this suddenly stands proudly and smiling at Brutus with satisfaction exclaims, "I will take him back! He can walk to church with me on Sunday with his sa sa scratchings."

More hangdog than ever Brutus gets up and slowly lopes out the front door with Lilly following and her sa sa broom held up high.

Roger looks at Sue, "Well if that's marriage counselling, I think I'll stick to pests and vermin. Let's have a sundowner early today."

"I'm with you there," Sue agrees, still looking a little shell shocked.

Next day at the office, Roger reports the satisfactory outcome to his team.

"In the villages there's a hierarchy," Moti explains, "at the top the Ratu (Chief). He receives all monies and offerings and it's up to him to disburse goodies to the villagers."

"Some huts or cabins have thatched roofs over timber or earthen floors. No hot or cold reticulated water, no phone, and no electricity," Wasume offers. "The Kava drinking ceremony is the ultimate sign of respect for one another."

"An acquired taste," Roger says.

"Exactly; Kava or (Piper methysticum) is an age old herbal drink that is the beverage of choice for the well to do families of the Southern Archipelagos. A drink consumed for centuries by islanders it was only during the voyage of Captain Cook to the Pacific in 1768 – 1771 when white men first encountered the plant. Interestingly; It does not show up on a breathalyser."

Vijay confirms, "Yaqona is a soothing drink with proven medicinal effects, which include relief of stress and anxiety."

"Allegedly," says Roger, "I still think it's unlikely to catch on in Oz."

When Sue tries a sip of Kava for the first time, her face is a picture; puckering up like a Sharpei dog.

"Yuk, Roger you can keep that. It's gritty in the mouth and as unappetising as drinking mud. You're telling me locals actually like this?"

"Absolutely. So much so, we have a tanao in the office, just to offer visitors."

James and Jayne want to try it.

They both agree with Sue. "Yuck!"

Chapter 32

MORE PROBLEMS IN PARADISE

"At what stage did you decide to trade on, and not close," Moti asks cagily.

Roger pauses, replying with what he hopes is an ingratiating smile. "Not that I'm a lover of cake and balloons, but when I realised that closure would ruin my going away party,"

Moti's frown deepens. "We might have a problem with a client."

"Only one?"

Moti simpers and crosses his legs. He is unwilling to make eye contact with Roger. "One client in particular."

"Okay. Shoot."

"It's Uncle Jim's Chinese Restaurant. Not easy to find. Its access is up via an unimposing stairway between two shops on lower Main Street."

"Besides watching your feet climb the stairs, is there another reason for that?"

"Well, besides unnecessary melodrama," Moti continues with a grin, "probably not. Then again it's a first class restaurant although food might not be their only source of income."

"More melodrama? Or are you going to tell me?"

"Rumour has it the owner deals in drugs, the restaurant being where they launder their money."

"Okaaay. Clutch the pearls, Moti! This is getting interesting, money laundering, drugs."

"Agreed," Moti smiles.

"We carry out monthly servicing there for rodent and cockroach control but as our prices have risen upwards by about 500 per cent, the owner's complained."

"Are we surprised?"

"Well, no, but not for the reason you'd think." Moti drinks some of his beer. "On further inspection and discussion it turns out not to be about the price increase at all but our substandard service."

"Our what?"

"Thought that might get your attention," Moti grimaces, "they're unhappy with our standard of cockroach control."

"How long has this been the case?"

Moti looks embarrassed. He shuffles his hands and feet. "Service staff have all been there taking it in turns, even the service supervisor, but no-one could find the source of the German cockroach problem. I've been there myself, but it's, how do you say a 'toughie' that's been placed in the too hard basket. As all the usual culprit places have come up clear of infestation our staff is pretty well left scratching their heads."

"I'll give it some thought, Moti."

Sue frowns when Roger tells her about Uncle Jim's.

"Informing you at the eleventh hour, and only then just as the client is threatening to go to a competitor is maybe Moti's way of ensuring you continue to earn your high salary."

Roger agrees but needs to buy time while he tries to sort out the servicing problems and time to put user friendly processes in place to avoid future calamities.

Next day he involves Wasume.

"I want you to make me appear important to Uncle Jim's Chinese Restaurant, Wasume. If you could please make a big deal about booking a family table for me personally with the restaurant owner."

Their meal at the Chinese Restaurant is superb. So many dishes on their menu are unique. Their spring rolls are to die for with a cooked spring onion threaded through the middle and the tastes are unbelievable, even before they sample the fresh made duck sauce.

Roger is convinced that their man in the kitchen is an absolute artist.

"Pity he is a half cut, on half cut opium," he tells Sue, "whose speciality is a collection of skinned frogs floating about in a washing up bowl.

"Time to enjoy fried frog cutlets and lucky duck as the main course," Sue enthuses.

"The saying fish you eat today slept last night at sea does not leap to mind here, Sue."

None the less, Sue and Roger have a great night. After James and Jayne have finished eating, they take advantage of the restaurant being quiet, by laying out on the bench seating.

A large table to one side of the room no-one notices or cares about two children processing to the next stage when they curl up on the floor for some much needed shut-eye while owner Lee and Roger party on.

Lee has a question for Roger, "Have you ever tried marijuana?"

"No," Roger answers truthfully.

"How about you, Sue?"

"No, absolutely not," she replies a little put out by being asked.

"Well," Lee responds, "would it surprise you to know that it's grown here," he gestures with conviction throwing his arms wide.

"I wonder what it's like to smoke?" those words slip from Roger.

"Oh, I'll get you one to try," Lee is most eager to please.

"No! No! I don't mean it like that, I wasn't hinting, Lee." Roger immediately regrets what he has said.

"There are many things people do try, maybe once, and then never again," Sue says, "but I'm sure Roger never intended to take a wrong turn here, we're just not into...." she lowers her voice to a mix of dread and morbid curiosity, "DRUGS!"

"Don't worry, you two, I'll get you one to try for yourself, but remember that to get the best result, you must persevere!"

"One what? Persevere?" Roger panics.

"Not at work, not on the way to work, be relaxed."

Sue and Roger look at Lee in blank panic.

"Try dimming the lights, maybe play some soothing music, and remember it's very important."

"What's important?" Sue asks, her patience running thin.

"To be in the mood, and not just a single puff. Enjoy with many puffs, for best affect."

Sometime later Roger pays the bill and leaves, in his customary good mood having drunk a little over his quota. It is then that Lee hands Roger what looks like a crude hand rolled cigarette, dark brown in colour, folded closed at both ends.

"Lee, I don't even smoke anymore. I regret speaking."

"Doesn't matter," Lee is unstoppable, his face a picture of evangelistic passion. "But remember, not just a single drag, continue smoking, best if you finish the entire smoke."

They are almost home when Sue remarks how quiet their children are.

"Oh, Roger, we've forgotten them. They're still asleep on the floor at the restaurant."

They return, Roger hastening upstairs, Sue in tow, and there they are, just as they had left them, asleep under the table.

Getting down low to pick them up one at a time, much to the amusement of Lee, Roger has to crawl under the table and seating and it is then that he notices a slight flurry of cockroach activity.

Sue helps with the children, while Roger very much alert now investigates further.

The German cockroaches are coming from inside the tubular legs of the chairs and tables.

Roger is aghast. *Pure arse pest control man*, he thinks! Excited he is already planning to send a supervisor not an ordinary visor!

Without explaining why he is so confident, Roger gives Lee his personal assurance that his cockroach problem will be resolved, and the very next day, or he will be refunded in full.

The next day two service operators, service supervisor, and Moti are down at the restaurant early, before they open for business.

The hollow legs are gassed with Pyrethrum then sprayed inside with residual chemical and cockroaches begin dying in their thousands. The restaurant has no early diners for lunch, which is a stroke of luck because they have difficulty vacuuming up so many dead and dying cockroaches throughout the remainder of the day.

Roger uses the truth about how he has solved the problem as a training tool with Moti but they agree to keep the details quiet, "Because," as Moti confides, "that's the stuff of legend in the islands, Roger."

"I am an imperfect human being, Moti."

A few nights later Roger is standing in their bedroom thinking about how he has successfully given up smoking.

"I don't feel very clever," Roger says staring at the gift Lee had given him. "What should we do with it?"

"You could throw it out, flush it down the loo, or maybe you could try it?" Sue prompts.

"What about you?"

"Not me, I'm not trying it, but at least if you do try it you can tell Lee what you thought of it."

"Okay. He said that I need to be in the right mood, as in relaxed, right?"

"I'll lower the lights, but you're not getting music. The children are asleep."

"Alright."

Roger lights the smoke with some apprehension. "I feel like a naughty teenager," he giggles.

He takes a light puff, and feels nothing.

"Lee said not just a single drag, continue smoking, best if you finish the smoke, remember?"

Roger takes a deep draw and holds it in his lungs for a few seconds. Sue is looking on.

Roger begins to cough. With his eyes watering slightly, he tentatively takes another drag.

"How is it?" Sue asks, looking worried.

Roger falls back hacking so hard he thinks he might crack a rib. When his coughing subsides, he cautiously takes another drag.

Roger forces himself to keep smoking, but in between he cannot stop coughing. Through now watery eyes, Sue is beginning to look like a mirage. "Fuck me!" is all he can say.

"Are you alright?" Sue is concerned. "You are looking unwell." feeling his forehead with the palm of her hand, she adds, "you are quite flushed and maybe running a temperature!"

"My face does feel hot, Sue, this isn't fun."

"Well, you should stop then!"

Roger feels nauseas.

Operating on the instinct of blind, suffocating panic, he scrambles along on his hands and knees into their bathroom. There he clasps the porcelain toilet bowl to his bosom, as if it were an estranged English relative. Sue is looking down at him. Her face is a taught mask of high agitation and concern.

Sue then runs around the house closing doors as quietly as possible without her happy face on, while Roger first grade rocket scientist of the year, continues vomiting, but not quietly.

Short sharp breaths between retching and coughing, it takes some doing, but remarkably Roger has an occasional puff. For some insane reason is he trying to finish the joint?

If I had a brain I'd throw this down the loo.

"Nearly there, Sue!" he splutters, slipping further into the abyss of nowhere memorable.

Forcing what little bile is left in his stomach to make an appearance, Roger feels incapable of winning an egg and spoon race, let alone rejoin the human race.

Roger remains lying on the bathroom floor, motionless, until Sue tempts him back to the comfort of their bed.

"How are you, really?" Sue asks.

Roger hears himself say, "Don't cry and hug my teddy comes to mind."

The next day Roger comes awake with a loud snort and looks around.

Sue asks, "Do you feel slightly better?"

"Sue, I don't know why I didn't get Lee's promised high, but I certainly won't be doing that again."

"What will you tell, Lee?"

"The truth of course, that it made me very sick. I might make a joke of it, like next time just cancel the pest control contract, Lee, you don't have to kill me as well."

Roger is greeted at the office door by an obviously worried and agitated looking Vijay.

"What's up?" Roger asks, looking at his watch — it is barely 8am.

"We have a major problem with cash flow liquidity."

"And..."

"We can't pay our major accounts together by the stated 30 days." Vijay is thoughtful, he straightens his spectacles, "Which do I pay first? The US of A, or Oz?"

"Does it matter? They're both in-house accounts?"

"Normally I'd pay the US, and let Oz run to 60 days, but..."

"Sounds like a plan, Vijay. But what?"

"You report to Oz and letting them wait over 30 days could become a political issue."

"You're right, Vijay. It could. I appreciate your concern, but I suggest you carry on as usual and I'll deal with any fallout."

Chapter 33

FISH ON FRIDAYS

Sue and Roger are living as royalty, so why is she unhappy?

Well to be fair, she is happy with the financial side of things. Pleased to be getting ahead of the game; their mortgages, bank loans, and hire purchase with something left-over for shoes and handbags.

Sue's face droops like a rain-slacked flower. She is terribly homesick for Brissie. "What's not to like in Oz?" she opines, "living there's like heaven on Earth."

Does Sue keep her promise? Of course she does. She never, ever—cries. Well, not more than once a day.

"Do I complain too much?" Sue asks.

Roger's thoughtful. "Yes."

"But I like complaining. I complain well. I do it all the time, and I'm good at it."

"Alright. But remember James and Jayne are having a ball."

Sue has the last word. "Yes, but living in Oz is truly like having won the lottery of life! Here," Sue waves her arm around, "I'm not much fond of here, it's not my type of paradise!"

"James and Jayne stick out like the proverbial; two white marshmallows in a sea of black treacle thanks to attending the district Primary School," Roger adds, "but thankfully, they've been accepted by the locals."

"Most times walking about daytime is about as dangerous as taking on a Nun in a ruler smackdown," Roger says defensively.

Wandering barefoot about the local villages at any given opportunity, James and Jayne would probably stay the night with anyone who invites them.

Strangers hug them and kiss them, and talk only the kind of rubbish that younger children admire over the world.

When dining out, they usually go to restaurants that have passed the various hygiene tests set by them, and as always they are clients of Roger's.

"Makes it easy, as," Roger declares, "I can ensure there's no salmonella hanging around in their kitchens, the toilets are clean and they have hand washing facilities and toilet paper."

The permanent kit carried by Sue in their car, for occasions such as these, is an inexhaustible supply of tissues, changes of children's underwear, soap, and towels.

"Some of our most recent clients have more fingerprints on plates than you'd find at a police station," laughs Roger, "but even that's better than eating where rats are hoofing it under tables, or stepping around someone sat cross legged on the floor beside an open drain preparing vegetables, just to get to a toilet."

"It's unfair on rats," Sue says.

"Why's that?"

"Well, when you think about it they're only a bushy tail away from being hand fed in a park."

"Agreed. Do you think if they realised that, they'd be resentful?"

"Absolutely."

"Why do some toilets only comprise a hole in the floor? Surely, that's inconvenient for all? I feel like a contortionist each time I go, and the children, well it's an adventure keeping their feet dry."

Early one morning on his way from the bathroom Roger spots through the open door an obese looking rat sitting beside the skirting board in Jayne's bedroom. He quickly summons Sue, who gasps, "Jayne? Jayne! Are you awake, Sweetheart."

"What d'ya want?"

Jayne needs her beauty sleep.

"Mummy and Daddy don't want to alarm you, Sweetheart, we'd just like you to get out of bed slowly and come to us."

Her movements are Flash Gordon fast! Probably because Jayne hates spiders! However the rat, the size of a medium dog, sits undisturbed.

"It's a rat, Sweetheart," Roger explains.

"It's a big, brown one," whispers Sue her eyes as big as saucers.

Roger is unsure what to do. "I think I'll call Moti," he says finally.

Moti is understanding. "We don't want the local papers latching on to this. I'm on my way."

By the time Moti arrives, Roger has summoned Lilly and Brutus.

Moti explains, "If we let the dogs in they'll handle it but damage the house. Best we drive it outside where the dogs can take care of it."

Jayne summons the dogs from the rear garden to outside the front door. There is controlled canine chaos.

James collects up a sa sa broom for each defendant.

The rodent is slow moving thanks to its claws scratching against the highly polished timber floor. It's a bit comical, looking like a cartoon character, trying to ice skate. As it exits Jayne's room, it has difficulty gaining traction, and spends many precious seconds running on the spot in the doorway.

Lilly is in full cockatoo flight, screeching hysterically, which is better than fainting.

Jayne is displaying a fair attempt at an Irish step dance, by stomping her feet, which would surely have killed the rat — had it been there.

Sue has progressed to standing up on a chair getting ready to scream or faint like it was Christmas and New Year rolled into one.

Roger is trying to look brave. He is positioned behind Moti. The beating and waving of the sa sa brooms on the floor, as if they are pounding kava seed, have the desired effect.

When Rattus norvegicus, sees the open front door, it high tails it out of there for freedom.

Lilly clobbers it a sideways blow. Tumbling it rolls outside, where with yellow eyes glowing, the excited dogs trip over themselves to get at it. Two manage half a rat in their mouths and struggle in a tug of war.

"And that," states Moti, "is farewell to the rat."

He looks at his wristwatch, pivots and leaves.

Chapter 34

FRIENDSHIPS

One of Roger's clients is a wholesaler selling a wide variety of local and imported goods and food ingredients. The manager is an expat who hails from New Zealand.

"Not really surprising," explains Moti, "as there are more Kiwis in the Archipelago than Australians and Poms put together."

Kiwi Man is on a three-year contract with twelve months to go and he, his wife, and three children have settled well. Since his wife enjoys the life so much and Sue does not, they agree to mix in and spend some social time together. "My wife, Mandy, might influence Sue in a good way," Kiwi Man explains, and the kids should all get on.

Kiwi Man and his family are interesting people.

According to Kiwi Man's wife Mandy, most nights he drinks himself into oblivion only to fall asleep outside on their lawn.

"He takes to crashing up on their BBQ table, which should feel incredibly unnatural, but at least the dogs don't pee on him," explains Mandy.

"Maybe he thinks that if he pulls his belly button in, it might take some weight off his legs?" Roger jokes.

Needless to say, Roger and Sue soon determine that Mandy's opinion of her husband is at times, below par.

Sue explains to Roger, "The local villagers leave him alone because he's a big man who tends to become aggressive when he's had a few too many. He boasts to them that he's some sort of karate champion."

"My god Sue, "He may be capable of killing a man with his small toe."

Roger for one is not putting him to the test.

Kiwi Man arrives at Roger and Sue's, his family in tow, and Mandy driving because he is so damned exhausted from working.

"He does work dreadfully long hours," Mandy explains.

Roger is unsure. "Sue, might he be one of the few ex-pats who works that hard?"

"He doesn't smell at all of alcohol," Sue whispers to Roger.

Roger takes Sue into his confidence, "I think Kiwi Man has that rheumy eyed look because he is stoned out of his mind."

After drinks have been served, Kiwi Man holds court, "Alcohol's never been a problem for me," he says with a smirk, "only for the fuckwits around me at times."

Roger and Sue are concerned. Might Kiwi man be less than a class act?

"Oh, he's so tired, poor darling but he's been so good and promised me he hasn't taken a drink all week," Mandy explains.

Later Roger ventures to Sue, "Is Mandy swallowing this crapola hook, line and sinker? I don't think he's dragging his tailpipe because of tiredness."

Kiwi Man sidles up to Roger and asks in his suitably slurred, oops, sorry, that is tired tone, for his soft drink bottle to be topped up with neat Vodka, "So Mandy won't know."

Sue and Roger are caught up in this like hares in the headlights.

Roger explains to Kiwi Man that he is not prepared to be complicit in a quarrel between him and his wife. "If I do what you want, then we're actively betraying Mandy," he explains, "and if I tell her, then I'm betraying you. I don't think you should be putting us in this position. Why don't you sort your shit out!"

They continue having groups around for BBQs. A good mix of people they know, with a few people they do not, senior staff, company clients, a few prospective clients. Families are welcome!

Some are typical desperadoes like Kiwi Man. Most are solvent and house-trained. Rarely do they expect to find randoms sleeping on their couch.

Sue and Roger become accustomed to a style of entertaining, getting into the rhythm, even hiring a film projector and showing movies on the outside whitewashed end wall of the house.

On one occasion, Roger has a Hindi senior partner from a legal firm, insist in front of his wife that Roger be extra careful not to serve him a pork sausage, then behind her back, he asks Roger quietly for just a small pork chop.

On Fridays, it is popular to BBQ fish, which satisfies Kiwi Man's family as they comprise the Roman Catholic contingent. Chicken and goat for the Hindi and Muslim persuasions, beef and pork for locals, Kiwis, and Gilbert Islanders.

If any quacks are present, after a few glasses of bubbly, they revert to showing how they behaved as medical students, while the children enjoy friends of every persuasion. Their new Kiwi playmates stay over as hubby is too tired to drive.

At another BBQ, staunch Roman Catholic guest Mandy decides to represent her one billion or so fellow catholics by stepping in to assist with her opinions on religion and food.

What she delivers to an Indian guest is, "What a silly, small, minded twit of a man you are for not wanting your food contaminated by other animal juices."

Mandy, unlike her husband, is sober. Her eyes are flashing, shoulders forward, mouth ready to savage all comers.

To his credit in maintaining peace at a social event, the Indian backed off grinning like a drunken jackass, and apologising profusely.

Sue hastens to pile his plate high as consolation, with enough agreeably uncontaminated chicken, to satisfy any starving village.

"Go for it!" instructs Mandy's slurred husband, "don't back down. Be a fucking man. The cow's had it coming a while," he turns to his astonished looking wife, and adds, "you should try rubbing alcohol in the wound, which tastes delicious by the way."

Dark looks, head shaking, shoulders rising and falling as Mandy pushes her sunglasses up onto her forehead and stares rigidly at her husband with glacial warmth.

Kiwi Man sways slightly, with obvious tiredness, "You shouldn't wear hats. They don't suit you."

"What's wrong with my hat?" Mandy asks, reaching up as if to adjust it.

"Too small it looks like you've got a pikelet stuck on your stupid head," Kiwi Man steadies himself, "and it's too big. Looks like you're living in it."

"Wanker might be an apt description?" Sue whispers.

"Agreed. Mandy should put him on a skewer and fire up their grill but back at their place, please."

"It's the perfect hat for here," retaliates Mandy, fingering the yellow crown within a lovely white brim. She is tearing up with rage.

"Looks like it needs some crispy bacon on the side," slurs tired Kiwi Man, "you might carry it off, but you're not exactly the warmest person."

"I'm not affectionate?" Mandy retaliates.

"About as affectionate as that burnt chicken."

Roger ignores Kiwi Man by concentrating on his wife, Mandy.

"I don't see the difference between the Indian gentleman for religious reasons preferring not to eat pork or beef related products and your insistence of eating fish on Fridays?" Roger pursues.

"Are you out of your fucking mind?" Mandy objects, "of course there's a difference." Her smile is bright and cold, like winter sun on a frozen lake.

Mandy's children, who have been snacking between projector shows now take active sides against their Mum. Their death stares are pay back such is their hatred for fish.

Roger insists attitudes about food preferences should cut both ways.

To Mandy, her reasons are legitimate enough, while for the Indian his are foolish in the extreme.

After their guests have left, they let the evening draw around them.

"Aren't people strange?" Sue says.

"None so strange as folk," Roger replies.

Mandy does not speak to Roger for weeks after that and refuses to allow her children to sleep over, which means Roger cops the brunt of his own family's displeasure for being too outspoken.

Since Mandy enjoys the life in the Archipelago so much more than Sue, their agreement to mix in spending social time together was for Mandy to influence Sue in a good way, but it went in an entirely different direction; Mandy running Sue and Roger into the weeds whilst being safe in her own bedroom are givens.

Chapter 35

The complexity of Witch Doctors, it is said, is that they have a reputation for being unfathomable, primitive, and superstitious. They imbue the moment with mysterious stories, such as refusing milk in coffee for fear of the cow being cursed.

"Is Lilly having an encounter with the ghost that walks?" Sue asks.

"Moaning and creaking noises," Lilly explains, her eyes are open wide.

The moaning and creaking noises continue.

"No wonder Lilly's frightened if this is what she's hearing," Roger whispers to Sue.

"Should you arm yourself?" asks a worried Sue.

"With what against a ghost?"

"The noises are coming from the rear of the house."

"I think I hear creaking and scraping noises."

The noises become louder. Roger reaches for his trusty torch before he realises that it's faulty. He hits the torch hard and the bulb flickers and gains in intensity.

In a dreadful moment of suffocating panic, Roger worries that they are not alone.

"Don't fumble around in the dark," Sue attempts in a stage whisper. "Put on a light."

"I don't want to flood the house with daylight and wake the children."

Roger aims the fragile beam ahead of him. In the blackness he senses rather than sees something animal and substantial approaching. Its laboured, distressed breathing, alerts him to being attacked by some beast.

With the light from the torch now working, the sound of movement ceases abruptly. In two great strides Roger reaches the back door and tears it open, bringing his arms up as if to protect himself, and sees in a split second in that artificial light the eye of something possessed bearing down on him.

"Brutus!"

Brutus looks surprised, "I live here, Sa."

"Yes, of course you do, but why are you creeping about and frightening Lilly and us, at this hour?"

Brutus looks embarrassed. He raises his two hands in mock surrender, either one the size of a telephone book. "Brutus's been drinking, Sa. Lilly doesn't approve, I'm sneaking in."

Roger feels an overwhelming relief, and sorrow for Brutus.

"Okay, that's fine, Brutus. As long as you're alright."

Back in their bedroom, Roger brings Sue, up to date with developments. "I wasn't mauled to death by a monstrous ghost."

Sue lets him know how funny she finds that.

Lilly engages the frail, large nosed Witch Doctor whenever she is sick. This sinister looking individual wears opaque shades, a set of pure gold teeth and strings of amulets adorning her neck and arms. Unfortunately, the lady with admirable powers becomes a regular visitor.

"Admittedly, the chanting is a bit off key," Roger complains to Sue.

"And it goes on well into the night. It unsettles me," Sue gives an involuntary shiver, "but the children think it's great fun. When they're tired of listening, they just go to bed. Frankly, at times they could sleep standing up."

After one visit, Lilly announces. "The special doctor from the village can do many things."

"I bet she can," Sue says. Roger gives her a stern look.

"I will ask special doctor what else you would like?" offers Lilly.

Roger looks outside. Further discussion might be somewhat difficult; competing as it is with the sound of heavy rain on their metal roof.

"For the sun to come out will do, Lilly," suggests Roger.

"You tax their powers, Sweetheart," Sue chides.

Lilly gets the message and withdraws; obviously these white folk are not enlightened.

To commemorate their twelfth wedding anniversary next day Sue and Roger decide on a slap up meal at a fine dining restaurant.

They order fresh crayfish complemented with a bottle of wine.

"Will you require dry or off dry, Sa."

"Do you stock Mateus Rose wine?" Roger asks, scanning the wine list.

The waiter is thoughtful, "Is that a red wine, or white, Sa?"

Roger and Sue settle down to enjoy their alternative white wine, unfortunately served un-chilled.

Thinking he might be able to latch onto a home supply, Roger asks with a trusting smile, "Do you know where this wine comes from?"

"This bottle, Sa," is the toothless reply, "how would you like your crayfish cooked, Sa?"

Roger and Sue are thoughtful. There are no choices listed on the menu, which only states fresh and cooked.

"Not overcooked, please," Roger asks.

The waiter does not look confident. Maybe the term 'overcooked' is new to him?

Sue tries to explain, "We like our seafood al dente," she smiles reassuringly.

Roger senses a communication problem exists, "How would your chef normally cook fresh crayfish?"

"Under the grill, Sa," is the waiter's confident retort.

Sue and Roger exchange looks, and in a wordless display of communication, everything that needed to be said was said. Their preference is to avoid the grill altogether. Too much danger of their prized delicacy becoming too dry.

Searching for other words to describe 'under or over cooked' Roger tries, "We prefer our crayfish more 'au natural' than that, at which the waiter's face lights up with understanding.

Presented within a few minutes is a beautiful, crayfish. Not long dead, it is green, raw, and served cold on a platter.

"We can't eat this," Roger says to Sue.

The waiter looks disappointed.

Sue has a brainwave. "What we want," she explains to their troubled looking waiter, "is the crayfish cooked in a pot of boiling water, just like you would in your village."

The waiter's face explodes in to a wide grin of understanding and the crayfish is soon returned to their table cooked to perfection, with a theatrical flourish.

"Well done, Sue, we have our translation. In future it's as cooked in their village."

"At this price the crayfish should sing, dance the Macarena, and introduce us to a mermaid."

Next day more good news.

"The office is fielding myriads of complaints from island resorts. It's serious," Vijay explains.

"It doesn't make sense. We've ensured the operator's doing all the right things, I'm baffled," Moti looks sideways at Roger for an answer.

"You've got nothing?" Roger asks.

"I've got less than that. We're getting a great result with good control around all but the majority of the islands don't mirror the same story. Why?"

Convinced his team is missing something simple Roger puts all of their best brains to work. Admittedly they are floundering.

Moti returns a week later from a brief management tour of the problem islands, "I'm convinced if we don't do something soon we're likely to lose contracts. It's almost as if we're spraying water and forgotten to add the damned chemical, so poor is the result."

Roger consults various technical experts by phone but they all provide noncommittal noises assuring him no-one else, anywhere in the world, has reported a similar problem.

Moti suggests, "Roger why don't you do a quick tour yourself of the problem islands. If nothing else, by you showing your face as the big boss, it might help buy us some time."

Moti is better qualified than Roger in agricultural chemicals. Roger's the expat white man. Putting in an appearance would carry more weight, even with his lack of technical knowledge.

"When can you get me to the nearest problem island, please, Wasume?" Roger asks.

"Early morning to Thai Island it is," Wasume announces.

Roger calls Sue to pack him a small overnight bag and departs for Thai Island.

To save company money Roger hops an ocean cruising yacht from the Marina at first light. Had it been crewed by Nordic beauties and sailing further away from his problems rather than directly into them maybe he could have fantasised. However, not knowing any Nordic beauties the closest to that daydream would be the Nils Master fishing lures displayed on board.

The time warp journey takes over four hours but it is cheap compared with jumping a chopper or a sea plane. He sits astride a deck hatch seat where immediately he feels over conspicuous.

All around him are holiday makers in board shorts and bikinis, singing ditties along with the local guitar player.

To say the least Roger feels out of place.

Not nearly as out of place as he feels when he removes his shoes and socks, before rolling up his strides to wade ashore the lovely island.

The expat American manager puts on a brilliant water skiing display.

The cabins are small and in need of renovation but there are so many cockroaches Roger's embarrassed to admit he has anything to do with pest control.

German cockroaches are everywhere and not a tubular hollow leg of furniture in sight, everything being in heavy, solid timber.

After a good look around Roger sits at the bar and begins drowning his sorrows.

"You get a few American guests staying here," he mentions.

The Barman replies, " Heaps. Mainly women. A lot want to get laid by a black man."

"Plenty of black men in America, aren't there, why here?"

"S'pose so, but maybe they want something different? Have you tried American beer? We stock some here."

"No. Is it any good?"

The Barman's eyebrows wrinkle in amusement, "American beer is a bit like making love in a canoe."

"Love in a canoe?" Roger smiles cautiously, "I'll buy."

The Barman lowers his voice to almost a whisper, "It's fucking close to water."

"That's clever. No, I'll have a local beer, thanks."

Barman pours Roger's beer from a stubby.

"I've got a problem," announces Roger.

"Yes, I know. You're the pest control guru and we've got too many cockroaches."

"You've got it one, but what I can't understand is why our treatments work well elsewhere but not here."

"Sorry – I can't help you, Sir."

Roger has a couple more beers, a chat with the resident manager about improving services forthwith, and then anxious not to be too exposed whilst vulnerable, he is about to retire when he hears a voice like water. "Looks as if more than flotsam has turned up here!"

Roger turns to look into the familiar face of Christopher Wright with probably one of the most beautiful women he has ever set eyes upon, hanging off his arm.

"Bula, Roger, are you here alone?" asks Chris.

Roger is quite taken back. "I'm sorry," he says, "I never expected to run into anyone I knew here," and then as an afterthought, "least of all you, Chris. What a surprise."

"It's a small world, Roger. You should realise that, but we're only passing through, aren't we, Sweetheart?"

The lady without a name gives Roger the style of smile usually reserved for very special people or slaying Adonis, and cuddles innocuously closer to her date Chris, as if confirming her unavailability.

"Putting two and two together," Chris smiles, "I'm thinking you're here because there's a problem with cockroaches." He pats his date's arm reassuringly, and adds, "I'd be absolutely devastated if Snuffabug was performing like this, here."

Roger colours. "You're quite correct, Chris, mine is not a social visit. To be honest, I'm worried as are we all, and here trying to sort it out."

"Good on you, Roger. I hope you get it fixed. Too late for our visit but no doubt those who follow here will be most grateful. You'll have to excuse us, Roger, we're on a tight schedule."

"Yes, of course," Roger extends his hand. "Will you be swimming here? The waters are welcoming, and without cockroaches."

"I doubt we have time and anyway I'm a non-swimmer, Roger. It's an eastern European thing."

When Chris's date extended her hand, Roger was unsure whether to shake it or kiss it. Chris roars with laughter. "Don't let us keep you, Roger. You keep looking into it."

"I'd rather be looking into a loaded gun," Roger attempts a half-hearted laugh. Never one to place too much importance on his looks, but suddenly he wished that he could have run a comb through his hair, put on a pressed shirt, and splash on a little cologne.

Next morning Roger is up early and the day looks miserable. Monsoon rain is streaking down through a mounting smog. It quickly turns the small island paradise into a different style of adventure. He feels like a castaway on a sandy shore, trying to come up with a plan, in front of him an endless ocean.

Great, thinks Roger, *not the best time to be returning to the mainland on that bloody yacht. I'll be huddled below decks and probably get sea sick.*

Roger takes a quick shower, which proves difficult. When he tries to lather up it won't work. To get around it he rubs the soap bar over his body and hopes it will wash off.

When dry he feels slightly sticky for all the wrong reasons. Wiping himself down with a dry towel he is uttering several words most have heard before.

He heads to reception to see whom he can bribe to get him get to the mainland not on that blasted yacht hoping like hell not to run into Legend Man.

In between bouts of the palm trees touching their toes and the sheets of horizontal rain there is one hope of salvation. The resort manager explains, "A seaplane is scheduled to collect one elderly American lady and if she has no objection you could ride along for the appropriate fee."

The New York lady is delighted at sharing the cost of her ride and they're told to present themselves at the beach forthwith. After Roger's farewell to the manager with promises he's unsure how to keep, he finds a four seater seaplane taxiing into knee deep water. The lady's baggage is already at the water's edge.

The usual friendly group of locals are steadying the plane and assisting anyone who looks as if they might want to be included in the day's revelry while they wait patiently for the pilot who has taken a toilet break.

He appears wearing a distinctive flying cap, white shirt with epaulettes and neatly knotted tie. Below the waist, he is wearing swimming trunks and has bare feet.

"Are you the pilot?" asks the New Yorker by way of greeting.

"If I'm not lady I must be late for a fancy dress party, and I'm not, so I must be," he beams, with a broad Kiwi accent.

Kiwis are everywhere. Should be a law.

The New York lady is large and has been travelling first class. This accounts for the four locals it takes to put her luggage on the plane.

El Capitan removes his hat and starts scratching his head in disbelief.

"I don't know if we won't be overweight," he muses. Then looking at his two passengers he starts calculating his overall weight. "Never mind, we'll give it a go, if I can't get her up in the air, I may have to taxi you home."

Squashed into their seats the single prop plane makes its way out from the beach and then at full throttle hurtles bumpily across the waves. All the time El Capitan is muttering to himself while Roger flinches.

They seem to travel very close to a few moored boats.

"Hypothetically, if we were about to make a parachute jump from the seaplane," Roger asks El Capitan, "at least how high should we be?"

"Three days of steady drinking should do it, Mate."

In the distance, Roger can see his original ride making heavy weather of it and muses at the absence of the guitar group on the deck where only a few now huddle in wet weather gear.

A few times El Capitan throttles down and drives around moored boats, then as the open sea beckons, he lets her rip.

Roger's surprised how long it takes to lift off the water and when they do they seem to hover only a few feet in the air. Slowly they climb but not very high.

They clear the mast of a small yacht, then the boat that brought Roger by only about fifty feet, and looking down Roger feels no remorse.

The lady from New York has a question for El Capitan, "If you can't see where you're going, do you fly by instrumentation?"

"Lady if I can't see, I don't fly."

El Capitan has permission to land and taxi into the beach.

Another group of friendly locals help with baggage and in order to remain dry, money swiftly changes hands.

Roger farewells his fellow lady passenger who is staying overnight before boarding her international flight back to the US.

As Roger is about to leave he mentions to the pilot how he has a problem to solve trying to fathom the differences between Thai Island that they had just left and other places.

El Capitan looks thoughtful for a moment, "What apart from Malafafa being owned by the Chinese and the other by Yanks?"

"Yes, apart from that."

"Well," El Capitan scratches his head thoughtfully, "much as I like Thai Island's toilets," he smirks, "I don't like washing in sea water and that's what most of the islands serve up around here. Malafafa's the only island I know with fresh water showers on account of their ship, the South Seas Malafafa, carting the bloody stuff out there every day – rain or shine."

Of course! Why had he not thought of that?

Roger hurries past groups of excited Japanese travellers to be met by Sue. She has brought the car and children for a drive to meet him and he has the best ever escort home.

"How'd you go?" Sue asks after they had all exchanged greetings.

"Well, besides bumping into Christopher Wright on the island with a lady who looked like a very hot date, I feel like Sherlock Holmes. I think I've solved the mystery. It's mixing sea water from a tap with chemical concentrate instead of using freshwater. Renders wettable powder emulsions unstable. Do you mind if we stop by the office on our way home?"

Chapter 36

SADNESS

The Australian authorities are unsympathetic about James and Jayne wanting to bring pet anythings back from overseas. Shandy is their chosen one above all others but migration wise she is an unwelcome illegal.

"What's the point of breeding animals if each generation doesn't improve on what went before?" is the catch cry of a friendly customs officer, hardly wrapping himself around them like a friendly cat.

The day they leave, Shandy senses something is wrong. She becomes agitated and Roger feels guilty as shit as if he has betrayed her. Let her down.

"No-one wants to take her," Roger says sadly, "and as I'm the last expat to pass through, Shandy is now redundant."

Shades of Fred.

Moti asks around a final time, "Shandy has befriended a succession of expats and their children over her ten or so years' tenure," he explains to anyone who'll listen, "but now her future is uncertain."

Roger feels wretched. Jayne and James are crying, and Sue's crying because her children are hurting.

Moti has news, "Shandy is to join a Kiwi family," he explains with relief, "a ute will collect her soon."

The ute arrives but the driver is an islander, not a Kiwi. When questioned he is all smiles, and all yeses, but seems extra vague over his destination.

Shandy does as she is told and jumps up on to the back of the ute. For a moment her eyes meet Roger's and in that split second he reads the animal's distress.

"I did all I could," he says stroking Shandy's head for the last time, "sorry, Girl."

It was as if Shandy is saying, "I know it's not your fault, but I'm blaming you anyway."

"I'd rather have an inch of a good dog than miles of pedigree," Jayne argues sagely.

After the ute carrying Shandy has departed the official farewells and parties come celebrations carry on for about two weeks.

"Are you sad to be leaving?" Sue asks Roger.

"Yes, I am."

"If you want to stay on I'll agree."

"No, a promise is a promise, and we're going home."

The Isa Lei is the traditional farewell song. It is sung throughout the Pacific and at each and every one of their farewell staff gatherings. It is also performed by the local village at their rented house, performed by Lilly's church choir, again at selected hotel foyers after dinners and speeches. The final performances are held at the airport departure lounges and again on the airport tarmacs, accompanied by multiple flash cameras, which litter them and their children with blindness.

Sue is sure other travellers are wondering whom are these people getting all this attention?

Roger has a special goodbye with his team.

"We never did paint the roof a different colour, did we, Moti? Maybe you should do that after I've left."

"What you've achieved is more lasting than a colour change of roof or a rock garden," Moti adds with conviction.

"We, Moti. What we achieved. Not me, alone."

There are more presentations, more photographs, and many gifts.

Wasume gives Roger hugs and Vijay keeps blowing his nose and cleaning his glasses.

"You saved us," Moti has tears forming in his eyes, "how can we ever repay you for what you have done?"

"Do well here, Moti. I can then bask in your success."

Roger held out his hand.

After their departure they receive word from Moti that Shandy eventually made her way back to the rental home. There she befriended children who adopted her as a friendly stray.

They hope that she might end her days peacefully roaming the spacious grounds of the very house where she had lived for so much of her life.

Chapter 37

RE-ENTRY

On re-entry to Oz, Sue, Jayne, and James are literally vibrating with excitement at being back home and reuniting with their friends. Roger is apprehensive with a lost expression on his face.

"I'm pleased you and the children are happy."

"Yes we are, but so should you be. You've made good money, so, it was worthwhile being there."

"Most definitely. I've calculated it's enough to pay off the mortgage."

"So, what's wrong?"

"I feel I'm being treated as little more than a used bus ticket."

"Who by? Not me."

Roger sighs his deepest sigh, "Like a myriad of middle managers who've performed in corporate positions before me, I indeed have performed, Sue. And now this."

"What?"

"Problem number one is major changes in their Snake Pit hierarchy. None of the new guard wants me back in Brissie. I'm twisting in the wind."

"Oh, Roger, that's so unfair. They knew we were keeping the house and wanted to return."

"I know, but Ricky has put his cue in the rack. Frank is now Ringmaster and his preference for me to work elsewhere, anywhere, preferably in another company, another hemisphere, another planet, is obvious. We have cultivated a mutual dislike for each other."

"What will you do?" Sue is clearly concerned.

"I dunno! Maybe it's me? Am I out of touch and delusional? According to Frank I'm about as useful as a cat at a dog's show."

"No! You're not!" Sue is adamant, "think positive, you kept all your promises. You turned the US company around and we've returned to Brisbane just as you said we would."

"Alright. Maybe it's time to dust off my resumes?"

"Maybe it is?"

"But getting another high level job in pest control now would be like playing Russian roulette."

"You know the very best part?" Sue finds herself laughing and crying at the same time.

"Tell me."

"Jayne and James are easily entertained. They remain glued to the television even the ads, and their reunions with all their mates. It's like they've never been away."

At work the next day Roger meets up with a few familiar faces.

"Aye, you have to take Frank seriously, Matey," Scottie warns, "he's a bit of a ratbag, sacking blokes an' sheilas left, right an' centre. Jack's gone. He sent one memo too many about Head Office crapola! Lucy's gone too. Word is she was too supportive of Jack."

"That's a shame, they're good people, Scottie."

"Aye, Wayne Thomas of all people ha' been promoted to run the pest control division under the watchful eye of Frank, he's a right toss bag. A case of like minded people, promoting like minded people."

Roger replies sadly, "You're right, they are sycophants."

Scottie rolls his eyes. "Sycophants?"

"Aye, that's a good description, but blood's thicker than water, Matey. Did you nae have some problems with this Wayne Fuckface?"

"The auditors did, Wayne covering up the true figures nearly closed the operation down."

Scottie beams, "Aye, you've made enemies of the cockheads at the Snake Pit, Matey, I'm so fucken proud of ya. You're as popular as a turd in a swimming pool."

Some at the Snake Pit make a perfunctory effort to smile but to keep their jobs they follow their leader and care factor shown towards Roger is zero who continues to wallow in self-pity. "They're simply following the culture from the top," he summarises.

"Welcome back to Brisbane," is the official Snake Pit line, but they have to create a job for him, make a company car available, and they do not want to do any of that.

Frank the Ringmaster sports a few more wrinkles around his

cunning mouth since Roger last set eyes on him. The rotund dwarfish man stares Roger down; it is obvious that he has also adopted a more arrogant demeanour since being promoted to the top job.

"You could have applied to go to Jakarta." Frank makes no attempt to suppress his anger. His Hitlerian moustache is ticking with barely contained fury revealing that he is indeed a dangerous man to cross, "Wayne declined that appointment after your debacle."

Roger is angry. He lets fly. "Sue's a neat freak who likes inhaling Windex and ginger potpourri. Jakarta, even as a port of call, has to be one of the least likeable cities on earth. A hell hole of poverty in any language. Hot, sticky, dirty, polluted, annoying and generally mind-numbing. Also nothing much apart from a couple of poky museums to see and an occasional condom festival. Now was that not tactful of me to decline as I did?

Anyway. My debacle? It was Wayne who falsified the figures to the board. Not me!"

Frank exhales heavily. His eyes flicker about his victim like search lights, scanning for a kill zone. "Sorry to hear that your testicles have slipped into your socks, but had those figures been acted upon, the board would almost certainly have closed the operation down. Your damned interference," Frank's voice becomes a malevolent sneer, "prevented that closure. Have you thought about that?"

Roger is aghast. "You mean, you set it up, you set me up. You wanted their operation closed down?"

Frank lowers his eyes, "You should know businesses get bought and sold all the time, sometimes for their share values, others for their assets, or are you so fucking naive as to still believe in the tooth fairy."

Roger's anger is starting to rise, again overtaking his nervousness. He knows he is in danger of completely losing his cool.

"If you, and your relative Wayne, conspired and were foiled by me, simply by doing the right thing, then you have only yourselves to blame. If this was a company plan then why wasn't I told?"

"Because," Frank's cod like eyes are narrowing with hatred, "you're the fucking boy scout, the noble prick, incapable of seeing the wood for the trees. Ricky's boy, well now Ricky's gone."

"It wasn't a company plan though, was it? You and Wayne are up to no good."

"I don't like Pommy bastards and in particular I don't like you! This company would perform better without you. Ricky should have sacked you over your termite fiasco, and you're disloyal, Roger."

"Disloyal, how?" Roger is more than a little piqued by Frank's superior rebuke seeping from every pore.

"You should have paid your Oz accounts on time, and let the others wait for theirs. Remember what side your bread's buttered, Roger. You tend to forget that."

"Irrespective of any account delay of 30 days, if you and Wayne got caught out doing the wrong thing, don't blame me for your fuck ups and look for petty excuses!" Roger shouts.

Their voices are rough around the edges. They both try to compose themselves.

Frank sits motionless as though he has been suddenly bronzed. Then he fingers his Hitlerian moustache ruminatively, "The only option for you here is a factory job, so you'd better get used to it. It's time to get over your highly paid Pacific holiday and get your hands dirty," Frank sneers humourlessly, "you'll never make any more big money like that, not in this company, I'll see to that. Ricky should have kept Wayne there, extended his term like I asked him to do, but no, he wanted you."

Frank crosses his legs and picks a piece of lint from his immaculate trousers it is a gesture that shows his anxiety level has increased a notch. While Roger's throat feels as if it needs oiling.

Without qualified staff Roger is expected to run and expand a new business Frank has in the developmental stages; all very hush, hush.

In the event of failure, which is likely, Frank will need someone to blame.

"Frank wants to diversify and compete into wider products," Roger tells Sue, "trouble is the opposition are light years ahead and have got their act together. This has disaster written all over it."

Later Roger stands in an old deserted, ramshackle, building situated near the river and next door to a food processing factory. He stares at an antiquated rusted hopper, some decrepit mixing equipment, and a stack of broken timber pallets. He shakes his head in wonder and disappointment.

"To make matters worse," he tells Sue later, "it floods when it rains, which is another biggish problem."

Sue looks concerned, "Is it that bad?"

"Bad? I'm supposed to be mixing dangerous poisons together in an area adjacent to restaurants and food processing factories; our only separation being single fibre walls, with full sacks of poisons sitting exposed on drums and now a few broken pallets trying to keep them above flood water height."

Roger is unsure how to handle his situation. On the one hand, he needs his job; on the other, he has major concerns with his employer and safety issues. Unlike Goldilocks he does not have three options.

Next day Wayne approaches Roger. He flashes his television smile and for a moment looks as if he is the good model in a dentistry commercial. He makes a show of careful deliberation, "I'm truly sorry for the way you've been treated, old chap. I'm embarrassed at being placed above you in the chain of command. I'll try to keep a low profile."

"Them's the breaks. Not your fault," Roger replies testily, "but why couldn't you tell me the truth before you left or when I tracked you down in London?"

"Truth?" Wayne is looking shifty.

"Yes, Frank's so filled with hate and revenge, I found out about his grand plan to close it down."

Wayne's face turns as white as his shirt. "Oh, my God, I know nothing!"

"The Sergeant Schultz defence, 'I see nothing, I hear nothing, I know nothing!' You are a lying, bastard, Wayne!"

"But even if I over played Frank's hand I meant no harm."

"Harm! Your actions nearly closed a business down and for self profit — greed. You deserve to be charged, maybe fraud."

Wayne looks as though he has been punched in the stomach. "Fraud? Oh, shit, no, I don't want to go to prison."

"Gaol? What about all the poor bastards you and Frank were prepared to sacrifice for profit?"

"I only did what I was told to do, honest, Roger," Wayne is whimpering. He slides both hands up his face and presses the palms to his forehead in horror.

"That's what the Nazis said after the end of the *Second World War*," Roger takes a deep breath, "you and Frank are the pits."

Wayne's face betrays his concerns.

"I, am the one loose end that could bring you two jokers down, have you thought about that?"

"Well, I'm embarrassed at the way you're being treated, of course."

"Embarrassed? You'd want to be. I should be sitting in an ivory office, with hot and cold running secretaries; instead, Frank has put me in charge of a joke of a factory, loaded with poisons incorrectly packaged, on the verge of contaminating the nearest three suburbs adjacent to the damned river!"

Wayne freezes up before scurrying off in a funk to report to Frank.

"We might have another problem with Roger," Wayne tells Frank.

"You've only just come to that conclusion."

"I've just left him. He's not happy, and he's becoming threatening and demanding."

"Threatening? What can he do to us? Nothing!"

Frank's confident demeanour is betrayed as Wayne watches him nervously smoothing his moustache. When he had given Roger the worst job he could create, he had been confident the man would quit.

"I just wanted to keep you informed," Wayne says quietly as a church mouse. His face scrunches up in something that might have been a smile, but could just as easily be a heart attack.

Roger catches up with Scotty in the staff lunchroom.

"They've treated you badly, Matey, but you aren't Robinson bloody Crusoe. Most of the good blokes are gone, present company excepted," Scottie smiles coyly.

"What's happened to George now Wayne's taken over?"

"He's gone across to the enemy, Matey. It was a toss up between companies but he's shifted camp. Not sure how long he'll last."

"Big changes appear to be afoot everywhere."

"I'm chucking it in, Matey."

"Can't say I'm surprised," Roger replies, "what will you do?"

"Starting out on my own. Not right away. Planned it while you were overseas. Couldn't tell you until I was certain. First a short trip down memory lane back to Scotland to see the folks."

"Good luck," says Roger, "I hope you get to leave before they sack you, Frank detests your coloured socks routine and your practised surly demeanour. You do know that."

"Aye, Matey, I do."

Scottie and Roger shake hands. "End of an era," Roger blinks.

"Tweedy's got some news, too, haven't you, Matey?"

"Yes, I'm off soon also," Tweedy sighs. "I've always enjoyed breeding exotic birds as a hobby, and there's money in it if you do it right. I'm very sorry to hear how they've treated you, Roger. You deserved better. I'll keep in touch."

At home Roger unloads on Sue, his mood is dark.

"You get any darker," Sue quips, "and you'll be putting in for land rights."

At school the children learn more about Britain than Australia, which Roger thinks is also strange. *Is there a pattern?* he wonders. *Perhaps it's not just my world that's gone to shit?*

Then the children try to forget all of that British stuff because outside their window is a strange land, different to the one they are being lectured about. *Surely, the priorities are wrong*, Roger contemplates.

"Sue, nothing appears in their school books about this land that is as old as time, burned brown by the sun, and according to legend, filled with the magic of *Dreamtime*."

"You're right. They look forward to 'Boney' with James Lawrence on Tuesday nights, which teaches them about the outback. Maybe changes are needed."

Roger shakes his head. "If you ask me, raising teenagers is a bit like trying to nail jelly to a tree. Get it wrong and it'll get away from us like a blow torch on grass."

On the social side of their calendar, it is as if they have never been away.

Roger easily slips back in to weekends of fishing, crabbing, BBQs, and drinking to the point where they become the major highlights of his week.

Roger confesses. "It is a milestone in most peoples' day, their week, their lives."

"We'll drink to my downfall," Roger announces, "and what are you doing now?"

"I've done a mixture of jobs from labouring for Shorty's mob, driving for a courier mob, to now filling in the late shift on taxis."

Sue looks troubled, "That graveyard shift can be dangerous, can't it, Art?"

"As a city boy I'm down to the last knotty, twisted helix of my DNA," Art jokes, "she'll be right, but Kim's not impressed."

There is a silence, awkward as a stepladder.

"Our marriage is in freefall at present," Kim confides tearfully.

Roger exchanges looks with Sue, memories of Lilly and Brutus are flooding back, but they doubt anything they say here will be helpful. Instead, they commiserate with their friends with offer to help.

"Sorry, things are not going well," Roger says, and he means it.

"Embarrassed at our situation we should binge on chemical stimulants," jeers Art.

"Good idea," Sue looks embarrassed but pours more drinks.

"That's what I do," Roger announces changing the subject, "I drink and I know things," he taps the side of his nose just like George used to do, "so much has changed in such a short space of time."

"In other words, we'll get double pissed, that'll fix it!" Art exclaims, downing his beer with less enthusiasm than usual.

Chapter 38

GLASS HALF FULL

Roger takes a surprise phone call from Christopher Wright in Sydney.

"I hear through the grapevine that you solved lots of problems for Pest Dispatched here and overseas," Legend Man pauses, "and that they're maybe showing their ungrateful side."

"I think you might be on the money, Chris," Roger replies quietly, almost offhandedly, as if it were a given, similar to darkness falling every night.

"I might have something of interest for you, Roger. It's early days but we have a scenario. Details are yet to unfold," explains Chris, "but I wouldn't have called you unless I'm sure that the plans to expand Snuffapest will proceed. You are wasting your time where you are. That much is clear. Sleep on it and I'll get back to you, soon."

"The offer, should it eventuate," Roger tells Sue trying hard to stifle his excitement, "is to take up the new role of Queensland State Manager. It looks as if I'm being head-hunted."

Sue is all smiles. "Your reputation for being an over achiever might have caught up with you after all?"

"Maybe? Certainly my time there has impressed Christopher Wright who owns Snuffabug. He told me his grand plan's to go National and then International; he's interested in employing me."

Roger's final interview is in Sydney.

Christopher Wright aka Legend Man meets him at the airport in his sporty red Porsche upholstered in quilted black leather, dressed in another Giorgio Armani. He is the same overweight, if not rotund, bearded academic, who Roger remembered from Oz and the island. Clearly not worried about cholesterol. Roger watches fascinated as Chris levers himself back into his driver's seat, a surprisingly cramped space, by swinging off the frame of the car's door.

The interior is a shit tip; papers and debris strewn about. This is not a tidy man, Roger is thinking, but he is wealthy.

"Sorry, about the mess," Legend Man explains, "I didn't want to keep you waiting."

"Thanks," Roger replies, "my first time in a Porsche, the hire purchase company and I in another life, once owned a red MGB."

"This car makes a noise like a fallen angel on amphetamine," Legend Man jokes as the engine bleeds noise.

Back home, after his interview Roger concludes, "Yes, I'm probably being played, Sue, but at a salary significantly higher than now, bigger car, an unlimited expense account with the title of Queensland State Manager. Why argue?"

"So, why not give it a go?"

"Digging too deep might uncover something best left unfound," Roger summarises, "we know little about Snuffabug or their backers, I may add. His version of events sounds well rehearsed, even sanitised, but thorough enough not to lose anything important in translation."

Sue smiles broadly. "It's good to see you happy, again, Roger. You have that kick back in your step."

"If things transpire according to plan, we could do well," Roger says hopefully.

Roger's letter of appointment has barely fallen into his hands before he pens his resignation to Frank. Nothing flowery, no lasting thanks, just his resignation. He never mentions his new appointment.

"None of their bloody business," Roger tells Sue through gritted teeth.

Roger receives back by return mail his termination cheque and a demand signed by a secretary that his car be surrendered immediately. Roger is not required to work his notice.

Roger is well pleased.

His first duties are to take delivery of his new car, which when he turns the key her four cylinders purr commiseration, and seek suitable premises to rent somewhere in Brisbane.

Sue goes with him to whittle down the short list. He chooses a two-story property with an adjoining warehouse in the suburb of Northgate.

The following week Legend Man flies to Brisbane where Roger collects him from the airport in his new Ford station wagon.

"Bit bigger than yours," Roger comments.

"Not quite as fast," is Legend Man's considered response.

Legend Man approves Roger's property selection and insists on having dinner with him and Sue that evening at a charming restaurant near his city hotel.

Roger introduces him, "Sue has the great misfortune of being married to me."

"Agreed," beams Chris, as he takes Sue's hand and presses it to his lips for a moment longer than necessary.

Sue's impressed, Roger's surprised, even more so when Legend Man orders a $400 bottle of wine to celebrate.

"Too expensive for my tastes," Roger shakes his head, "I'm reluctant to even taste it."

"Why?" asks Chris.

"Well, for starters, I might like it, and that's a problem since we can't afford it."

Roger resists the temptation to request a take home pack.

Legend Man is an exceptional salesman alright. He may well be able to talk ten hungry dogs down from a Butcher's truck, but he needs Roger, who is tempted to maybe take four bottles home, no make that a carton, he thinks.

"You're not a bad salesman yourself, Roger," Chris beams, "you could sell wine to Jesus, I'm sure of it."

After the main courses they get down to business.

"You'll need staff, Roger. I have budgets I'll leave with you," he reaches down and takes a manila folder from his briefcase, and with a sly grin adds, "I think the salaries quoted will be sufficient for you to attract the people we want. We're not so much interested in profitability at this stage, as growth. Your job is to secure turnover, big turnover and fast, a portfolio of contracts from the competition is what we want, and in order to make that a reality, we're prepared to be ultra competitive, if you get my drift."

Roger nods.

"Only for the first two years or so," Chris cautions, "there will be a day of reckoning."

"Of course, Chris," Roger replies. "There's always a day of reckoning."

"But not in the early years, on that you can rely," Chris continues, "if capitalism were a religion, I could see myself as leader of an extremist sect. Drink up."

Sue is impressed with Chris's academic appearance and his Oxford style accentuated English.

Chris enjoys the reciprocal attention of good looking women as his two former wives would attest.

"How are you? Correction, we, justifying these initial losses, Chris? I need to know if I'm to convince the right people to join us."

"My backers have allocated very large sums of money to purchase pest control companies to accelerate growth. My plan is simple, by incurring a significant trading loss by employing you to do what I know you can do, we're saving about three million dollars in capital expenditure."

Roger now understands Chris's strategy.

"Man should possess the divine right to make money unfettered by government regulations and conceal it wherever he pleases," Chris concludes, "avoidance of taxation should not be a choice but a moral duty. My backers are experts in these fields."

Roger is relieved that he said avoidance and not evasion. On the face of it there is no talk of illegality.

"I do have one question, Chris?"

"Shoot, Roger."

"Well, the final interview; meeting yourself and those accountant pointy heads at the bank premises, seemed very low key. I didn't have to answer any difficult questions to get this job."

"And nor should you, Roger," Chris beams his most benevolent smile, "you were on a short list of one, dear chap. But we had to go through the motions."

The following day, Roger makes a call to Tweedy.

"How's the exotic bird business going."

"Slowly, Roger. I hear you've fallen on your feet."

Roger gives a thin smile, "News travels fast."

"Word is Frank is ropable," Tweedy laughs, "they could hear him shouting interstate!"

"That's good to hear, Tweedy.

Would you like to get back into harness for a while? A year or two, maybe help supplement your other business interest? And if I'm honest, I'd like you to help me upset Wayne and Frank."

"About the same dumbstruck fury but one step short of the way Moses looked when he smashed the tablets," counters Tweedy. "I'm all ears, Roger. What's the gig?"

"I need a salesman, Tweedy. I need you."

There is a long silence, as if the information is being considered.

"I fear I'm not really your man, not for that job."

"Why'd you say that?" Roger asks.

"I've never been good at quoting up, Roger, you know that. I have trouble quoting and selling at top dollar."

"Well, believe it or not, this job is right up your street."

"How come?"

"My function is to achieve growth, irrespective of profitability it seems, at least for the first few years. No guarantees after that."

"But there's always a day of reckoning," Tweedy responds.

"I know, but that's not our concern right now, we need a portfolio, and we need it in a hurry. Frankly, I'll need you to poach every contract you can, and you have licence to quote on price alone. Look upon it as a useful way to utilise an enormous advertising budget."

Tweedy brightens, "Salary?"

"Of course and commission; more than you were getting."

"I'm in, when do I start?" His voice increasing in enthusiasm.

"Why not now? See you soon at our new offices. You do know where they are? Oh, and Lucy and Scottie will be there."

Chapter 39

TRIPPING OVER THE FAMILY

Roger has been chasing his Dad about finalising the initial bank loan guarantees for the original ten thousand dollars.

"Damn I'd forgotten about those."

It was Edward's eyes that gave him away; *you are a lying scumbag,* Roger thinks.

"Oh, yes, of course. I'll remove those.

I have some important news, Son." Edward's voice trails off. The smoke from his pipe still trailing around him like a steam engine.

Concerned, Roger waits with baited breath.

"Actually, I've had a stroke of good luck," Edward gushes.

Roger relaxes, "Good news we can handle, Dad."

"A casket win of $100,000."

Roger is somewhat taken back. Pleased for his Dad, this good news as it sinks in also means Roger, need not concern himself with his father's finances in the future.

"I'm delighted for you, Dad. I really am. I'll talk to Sue, we must have a get together, our shout, to celebrate your good fortune."

There is a pause.

"Just so you know, Son. It's not enough to give you any."

Roger laughs. Has he come full circle? All those years of being cheated by his Dad, and now only relief that Edward has come in to a substantial sum of money. Yet his Dad is too tight and selfish to share any of his good fortune with immediate family.

"You'll never change, Dad. I don't even need you to shout the dinner. Let Zelda know that if you want to mix in and celebrate with us, it's our shout. Get back to us, okay?"

"Yes, Son. Thanks."

Sue is absolutely gobsmacked, "Your Dad said what?"

"His exact words 'Just so you know, Son. It's not enough to give you any.'"

"The old bastard," Sue is amazed. "Well, a $100,000 casket win certainly means that we should never have to concern ourselves with their financial future."

"My thoughts exactly," Roger grins broadly.

"Your Dad's news let's us well and truly off the hook. What's he going to do with the money?"

"Retire, I hope, a win of $100,000 should set them up comfortably, as they only paid about $12,000 for their low set brick home with pool on mortgage."

"What else did he say?"

"Nothing, I hope to find out more over dinner."

Sue bought a new dress for the dinner with Zelda and Edward.

"It's a wonderful occasion, don't you think?"

"Certainly, should be," Roger replies with fermenting annoyance.

At the table, after they have ordered, Roger is impatient. He is excited to learn of his Dad's plans.

"Will you resign from your job and retire now?" Roger asks excitedly.

Zelda and Edward exchange looks. Her artificially arched eyebrows are at attention.

"What?" Roger presses.

"I've decided to go back in to business again," Edward announces.

"What?" Roger tries to hide his true feelings but is incapable of concealing his surprise.

Edward looks pleased with himself.

Roger bit the corner of his lip. "Not surely in to hotels!"

"No, not hotels. Zelda has agreed we go in to the Real Estate business."

"I 'ave studied and got my licence in de real estate, so zhat ve can make more money."

"There's big money to be made in property development in this state, Son," Edward's smile falters a little as he explains, "we're going to invest big in buying houses, property, and then resell after the boom. There's a boom coming, you do know that."

"Right," Roger is looking sideways at Sue, "well, if you've decided then that's that. You do realise that with $100,000 in the bank, you could kick back and relax without any risk. Why not take a trip?"

"We do intend to take a short holiday first, Zelda wants to visit Hamilton Island, don't you, Sweetheart?"

"Ja, dis how dey say, 'Hammo' I vant to go dare."

Back home after their meal Sue and Roger discuss his Dad's plans.

"He's a braver man than I am, Gunga Din," laughs Roger, "good luck to the old bastard."

"How will he do it, Roger?"

"What take the bitch Zelda to Hammo, 'cause she vants to go dare." He mimics.

"No his business venture, silly."

"My understanding is that he's going to open a Real Estate office somewhere on north side where he and Zelda will function together in sales. Good luck with that one!

Meanwhile, with a shrewd eye on the market he intends to borrow heavily against his winnings and buy houses on mortgages at rock bottom prices."

"In effect using his casket win as multiple deposits."

"Yes. Maybe tart them up a bit, maybe not. Then after the boom, resell them all at an enormous profit; notwithstanding the horrendous interest bills, and hopefully being the big plate of hope they're wishing for."

"Admittedly, retirement doesn't suit everyone," Sue intones.

"Then again while it might suit Edward for a while, Zelda prefers her own agenda; fluff on the carpet and all that."

"And having Edward following her around all day like a six year old in the school holidays will only drive her up the wall."

"Good one then, the old bastard should go for it!"

"Shush. That's not nice."

"I know, but real estate salesman are considered by many to be good liars as are used car salesmen, even lawyers."

"Will it work?"

"I have no idea, but at least we're off the hook."

"But if he fails won't he expect us, you to bail him out?"

"Me? Us? He might, but no way. Remember he said, 'not enough to give you any,' which is good really."

"Why?"

"Well, if they did give us any money, and then hit hard times, with his track record he'd expect it all back, probably with high interest."

At work, Roger realises that he has not felt this good in weeks. It is as if a massive yoke has been lifted from his shoulders instead of feeling as if ice cold water has been poured over his genitals.

In their first year, they made a big hole in the opposition's portfolio.

Tweedy is in his element, "Every time I take a contract," he explains, "I feel like celebrating their rotten house tumbling down upon itself. A pox on their house and all that."

"Keep it up, Tweedy" Roger encourages, "Chris's backers want it all, and we want it now."

While Legend Man is doing cartwheels down his office corridor in Sydney as staggered payments roll in from his backers, Roger is attempting to do the same. He speaks with his Dad regularly by telephone, and by doing so is avoiding calling in face to face.

"Whenever we make a social house call it's never long before Zelda misbehaves," Sue sighs.

On one occasion while her Yorkshire terrier named 'Cuddles' happily leaps all over the settee and armchairs, Jayne and James are pointedly instructed to sit on the floor.

On another occasion they sit outside in the backyard, and while the children play in the pool, Zelda admonishes them for splashing.

While Zelda's back is turned, as payback James and Jayne lure 'Cuddles' to the poolside, where miraculously he falls in!

As Edward's sixtieth birthday approaches, Roger discusses with Sue what they should do.

"If we could take him out without her, it would be alright," Roger atones.

"Bit difficult."

"Impossible."

Jayne has a suggestion, "Granddad likes seafood, why not take him a mud crab on his birthday?"

"Bloody brilliant," Roger agrees.

"If you caught it yourself, and took it to him, it would mean more to him than buying one at the market and just dropping it in," Sue suggests.

Roger is thoughtful. "If I take a cooked mud crab he won't know I cooked it myself, but if I take a live one and cook it there in front of him, it would be perfect."

"Only problem is I can't see you cooking it in Zelda's kitchen, Roger. She'd never shut up, the mess, the smell. My God can you imagine."

On the 2nd February, 1983, and by appointment Roger is at his Dad's door with an excellent, 'A' grade, live mud crab. He beams, "Caught it myself, especially for you, Dad."

From the back of his station wagon Roger takes a portable gas ring, small gas cylinder, and cooking pot, which he sets up on the kerb-side next to the gutter outside his Dad's house.

With Edward looking on Roger boils the water, cooks the crab, cleans it, cracks the claws, dresses it, and delivers it into his Dad's waiting arms back on the doorstep.

"Happy 60th birthday, Dad. Sue and the children send their love."

Edward is overcome, Zelda is looking mildly embarrassed, and Roger, exhausted from his efforts, hails a fond farewell.

"How'd it go?" Sue asks, as she assists Roger with the cleaning up, back home.

"Absolutely, fabulous," Roger beams, "worked a treat. Dad didn't know whether to go shit, shave, or shampoo, while his bitch of a wife had absolutely nothing to complain about."

"She will of course."

"Yes, of course she will. I can imagine her as we speak."

"Go, on then," Sue urges.

"Well, I'll bet she's hit her straps, bitching and winging about the smell of the freshly cooked crab wafting into the house even before Edward put it into their frig, and then she's probably attacked me viciously for rudely remaining outside, and, wait for it, not bringing her flowers or chocolates."

"It wasn't her birthday, it was Edward's."

"No good deed ever goes unpunished, I can tell you. It's likely I'll be asked not to do it again, so as not to offend. Remember the conditions about mowing his damned grass?"

"Do I ever."

Next day their predictions are reinforced with more good news delivered by Sue, who has been busy all morning on the telephone running between Zelda and Roger's Dad, in a low hum of instant panic.

"After comments about the smells and neighbour's strange looks; your sister June and her new boyfriend Dennis are about to visit Down Under on holidays and will be staying with Zelda and your dad," Sue explains, a little breathlessly as she feels as if she has been co-ordinating it all.

Roger is delighted. He had heard little from his sister since her return to the UK with Barry the Woodsman in tow as if resigned to her fate.

"What's happened to Barry the introvert Forester?" Roger asks.

"A tragedy," Sue explains, "apparently the poor fellow's dead."

"Dead? He was only young."

"Yes, well big heavy trees don't differentiate between the old and the young. According to Zelda, and I quote, 'he came off zhe vorst when zede big tree he vas cutting down fell on top of him. Kaputt.'"

"My God. When do they arrive?"

"This weekend."

"Plenty of notice, then."

"About the usual."

There is excitement in the air at Zelda and Edward's house.

With so much to talk about, it is a bit of a shemozzle as to who will speak first.

End result, everyone chats at once and no-one is listening to anything.

June wants to show off her new beau Dennis, who is a fine young man from an agricultural background in south Wales. Between farming sheep, and putting up fences, Dennis is a busy boy back home, and unlike Barry the Woodsman, Dennis is personable, talkative, and interested in Oz.

"Nor does he pick, nor eat his own bogies. A positive indeed," Sue says to Roger.

Zelda is repeatedly telling everyone how hard she has worked, how sick she is and might be, how impossible Edward is to live with, and the awful smell of decaying crab shells in the bins although triple wrapped. Every sentence begins with, "Oh, mein Gott."

Jayne and James amuse themselves playing with 'Cuddles' who appears to bear no malice from his impromptu swimming lesson in the pool.

Roger goes to help Sue cleaning away in Zelda's kitchen.

"I don't want to leave a thing for her to do," Sue says casting her eyes back to the living room, "did you pick up on how long it takes her to tidy after we leave? And the smelly crab shells?"

"I'm beginning to think we're the only normal ones, Sue."

"You could be right, I might be getting too old for all this crap."

Roger gives his wife a hug, but they are soon joined by June.

"And how is 'what's her face' really?" June asks, an unconcerned look behind her thick black rimmed glasses. She looks the epitome of the intellectual she is.

For a moment Sue and Roger are taken aback, until they realise June is speaking in a derogatory way about her step mum Zelda.

"She's progressed then from 'Thingy' to 'What's her face'," Roger grins.

"The cow reorganised the table after I'd laid it. Each knife, fork, and spoon into some microscopically different configuration that was somehow better than the original. Queried how many eggs we ate for breakfast this morning? Argued with me over a fucking boiled egg! Can you believe her? Weird, they're the ones who offered us to be here, they're the ones who didn't want a cent from us."

Sue is sympathetic, "If it's not going well there, you know you can always come and stay with us, can't they, Roger?"

"Yes, of course."

"I doubt we'll go the distance here," June puffs. "The cow whinges she feels sick, then swallows a fully cooked, fried breakfast, I'd forgotten how fucking evil she can be."

"Looks like being an interesting stay," Roger counters.

June lasts a whole three days.

Roger receives a personal phone call at work. He snatches the receiver from its cradle.

"Is Sue's offer still available that we come and stay with you?" June asks, "I've had it here."

"Yes, of course."

"Good, come and get us!"

The line goes dead.

When Roger arrives at his Dad's house, he is unsure what to expect.

First, he lowers his window and listens for sounds, any sounds. There are none. Nor any bad smells. Encouraging. No raised voices.

As he is about to exit the car, the front door bursts open, and June comes rushing out lugging a suitcase and calling out to Dennis, "Come on! Keep up!"

Roger is opening the rear tailgate to facilitate the luggage at about the same time as Zelda appears with Edward in the doorway. Roger is about to raise his hand in salutation, when June, turns on her heel to face Zelda. June's tall and leggy frame is dressed in jeans and knee-high boots.

"And you, you German cow, you can stick your boiled eggs up your arse!"

Roger notices that his Dad has positioned himself strategically between his wife and daughter.

Beside the front door is a medium sized pot plant with something pink growing in it. With one swing of her booted right foot, June sends the pot flying into orbit, before it crashes against the front wall of the house. Bits of pot, pink petals, and potting mix cascade all about.

Leaving the luggage for Roger and Dennis to stow, June jumps into the car, and exclaims, "Roger take us to your place, *please*."

Unsure of the etiquette in a situation such as this, Roger decides discretion being the better part of valour, he puts his head down and picks up the luggage to vamoose.

On the way back home June declares, "I need a drink."

Roger replies, "We've plenty at the house, but I'm sorry, I never thought to bring en route supplies."

They are greeted at home by an anxious Sue.

"Well done give the girl a clap — not the clap," beams Dennis.

"June has one hell of a kick on her," Roger adds.

"Try that a bit closer to Zelda, right between the…" chuckles Dennis.

A week into their stay with Roger and clan, a registered parcel is delivered.

Addressed to June, she opens it with a frown. "Who'd be sending something to me here? No return address."

Once opened two UK passports fell out; her's and Dennis'. No other note.

"Fuck him and fuck her," June says. "We must have forgotten them in our haste; I'd not noticed."

In between bouts of sightseeing Roger spends some glorious times with his sister doing what they call 'Zelda bashing' and everyone else including the children join in.

Even their neighbours and friends thought that unique as it is said how there are many sorts of Zebras in the herd.

When Roger calls his Dad, he is greeted frostily. He takes that as an indication that as an ally of his sister, he is now under grave suspicion.

"Should I do something?" Roger asks Sue later.

"Like what?"

"You could write him a letter," Jayne suggests.

"Or do nothing, if you're unsure," Sue opines, "you know the saying 'when in doubt.'"

Roger opts to do nothing, which results in no speakies with his Dad for about a month.

The remainder of June and Dennis's trip is pleasurable.

With Sue's agreement, Roger suggests that if Dennis has enjoyed his visit as much as they think he has, they might consider a return trip or even a permanent move Down Under?

"We'll think about it," June says later in a drawn out long distance telephone call, "Would you and Sue be prepared to sponsor us, Roger?"

"Yes, of course."

Contact with Zelda and Edward continues but in a somewhat diminished, patchy way.

"Do you think your sister will return to Oz?" Edward asks Roger.

"I hope so," Roger replies irritably, "we've offered to sponsor them. Why do you ask, Dad? Her last visit to your home did not end well."

There is a long silence.

"Dad?"

"Yes, Son. I'm just thinking that if June does come back, I'd like her assistance."

"Assistance?"

"To assist Zelda, as you know, she's not well."

Roger is thinking that his Dad has got about as much chance with that as a mouse leaving a cat convention. Zelda has been exaggerating how she is at death's door for the past five years but up there nor down there or even Evolution wants that aggravation.

"Good luck with that, Dad. But I'll let June speak for herself."

"Would you talk to her, Son?"

"Dad, if you and Zelda want June to help you, I suggest you talk to her. How's your real estate business going?"

"I've bought three houses so far, Son, waiting back a bit for the boom."

Chapter 40

A DISH BEST SERVED COLD

In their second year, Snuffapest continues performing remarkably well. Roger asks Chris if he should apply the brakes to their wild ride of acquiring contracts from their competition.

"Word is we're hurting them badly," Roger explains.

"Keep going, they're not squealing loud enough yet, although word is they're putting off staff."

"Yes, I know," Roger replies, "I feel partly responsible for that."

"You should, and you are," Chris says, "enjoy it. You've heard the good news about your nemeses Frank Moore and Wayne Thomas?"

Roger is surprised, "Chris, I've heard nothing about them, what's that about?"

"Well," says Chris, warming to his task, "allegedly, the dishonourable Mr Frank Moore has been caught out with his hand in the till."

Roger is aghast.

"What?"

"Apparently, Frank did a deal. He bought a pest control company, probably trying to shore up their failing turnover, thanks to your efforts I may add, but the prick got greedy."

"Greedy? How?"

"Frank did a back door deal, like, 'I'll pay an inflated price for your company if you look after me,' nod, nod, wink, wink. The sort of thing politicians are renowned for doing, but Frank got caught a beauty! Last I heard the board have dismissed him without notice and are filing charges against him for fraud and embezzlement."

"Wow!"

Roger is speechless.

"You want to hear about smart arse Wayne, baby?"

"Yes, please. Was he involved in the deal?"

"Wayne? No! He'd taken a holiday authorised by Frank, but without his wife, to guess where?"

"Tonga?"

"No! Not Tonga. Up my arse and to the left. He was without his wife. Have another guess?"

"Bali?"

"The Philippines! But he got caught out having sex with a fourteen year old girl in his hotel bedroom. Apparently, the authorities might have let the case drop, him being a stupid foreigner and the girl, well in fairness to Wayne, she looked a lot older than her years."

"What happened, Chris?"

"The girl turned out to be a runaway from a respectable, wealthy family, and they wanted revenge against the man, who had defiled their innocent daughter."

"Defiled? Innocent?"

"Yes, well, parents tend to be a bit one eyed about their kids, and so your friend Wayne's been instantly dismissed and is waiting to hear his sentence in a Philippine gaol."

All Roger could think of to say is, "Wow! So who's running the show now?"

"They've appointed a new Chinese board member with interests in Casino property development."

Roger is aghast. "Still no knowledge of our industry?"

"None whatsoever," Chris beams.

Chapter 41

MORE SURPRISES

Roger celebrates his fortieth rotation around the sun on planet Earth. After attending as a member of Rotary International at Strathpine Branch, he returns home to find his neighbours and friends have organised a surprise birthday party for him.

Sue and the wives have been busy all morning preparing the food, while neighbour Steve has organised drinks, and Nosey put in charge of the BBQ.

Morning of the day after, Roger is leaning against the kitchen wall, phone propped between his ear and shoulder. He is nursing a little man who insists on banging up against the inside of his skull.

"It's complicated," Chris explains, "the backers' accountants are convinced that they bought into a business that's measured up less than expectations. Some say they've been duped. But all that's bullshit to hide their real motives. They smell a fine profit and want to sell us."

Afterwards Roger repeats to Sue, "Sell us. I knew it might happen one day but wasn't expecting it just yet. I'll try to find out more."

Roger calls a senior accountant he had had dealings with in Sydney to get another perspective of Legend Man.

"Roger, he's so crooked, that if he swallows a nail, he'd shit out a corkscrew," Accountant Man continues, "by the time Chris, aka Legend Man had finished with the backer's accountants they were not entirely sure whether they're right handed or left?"

Roger tells his team.

"Bit unfair," Lucy rattles off, "after all we have run the business successfully for three and a bit years."

"And with good profits on paper, if you allow for a ten percent advertising component, to build a multi-million dollar business from a zero base."

Roger has a private meeting with Legend Man in Sydney.

"Sorry, about the wait," Chris says blandly, as he comes out of his private toilet, "takes longer than my third marriage these days."

Roger remains calm. Legend Man has called the meeting and is paying over the clock.

Do not say anything until the pitch is over.

"End result," opens Legend Man, "is who will buy us in. Who'll pay the big bucks? I was hoping that it might be a big Chinese company. But no!"

"What's the bad news?" Roger asks, getting a little impatient. So far this could all have been handled by phone.

"Well, to answer your question," Chris takes a deep breath, "after about six months of waiting around the cashed up buyer turns out to be Pests Erased."

"You're joking!" Roger is appalled.

"I'm not, no! Frankly, I realise that this outcome could not be worse for you and your small team. But you can take some solace."

"Solace?"

"It was your determined efforts stripping them of their entire portfolio that spurred their interest."

"So, the only way to win back their contracts is to buy us out."

"Exactly."

"So, why am I here, Chris? You could have discussed this by telephone."

"Yes, very astute of you, Roger, but then you always were clever, very clever."

"Why are you blowing smoke up my arse, Chris?"

Legend Man pauses.

"I'm putting a deal together, Roger, a very big deal, bigger than Snuffapest, if you know what I mean?"

"I have no idea what you mean, Chris."

Roger looks at his watch, if he hurries he can make the 3pm flight home.

Chris notices Roger's ebbing interest.

"Have you ever heard of a drug called Ecstasy, Roger?"

"I can't say I have, Chris. I have heard of marijuana, I even tried it once."

"How'd it go?"

"Made me as sick as a dog."

"Well, if you ignore all the bullshit, and government red tape, ecstasy is actually safe, harmless, and I may add very profitable to those in the know. No-one can deny that it does a lot of good, although equally, none can deny around the edges there has been harm. Overall no-one should ever underestimate the appeal of getting high. It's a beautiful thing that makes many people feel the best ever.

I'm setting up an enormous cartel in Sydney, Roger, I'll need someone with discretion whom I can trust to run Queensland for me. Absolutely, no risk. You'll employ others to do all that, and I have contacts who can help. You'll enjoy the lifestyle, customers are so grateful and enthusiastic they hum with desire. It's not like other jobs you've worked. What do you say?"

Roger is thoughtful. Unless his hearing has deceived him, the reason he is in Sydney, is to discuss a major drug deal to do with ecstasy, with a budding drug baron none other than Legend Man himself and he, Roger, is to be the chosen one.

Roger coughs. He feels uneasy. He and Chris lock eyes. Roger feels uncomfortable. Might he be like the disciple Peter? Except he has not heard a rooster crow. He takes a deep breath.

"Chris, I'm sorry if I've given you the wrong impression, I really am, but there's absolutely no way I'm prepared to become involved in anything, illegal or criminal, no matter how well you sell it to me."

"Roger, you do realise that it's only a matter of time that clock is already ticking, not long before laws change and the sale of recreational drugs becomes legal. We're not talking the shady side of life here. Addicts using a needle in a public toilet. It's a clean, easy to take, pharmaceutical pill. They're made in a laboratory by pretty girls in masks."

"That maybe the case, Chris. I'm sure the girls are pretty, heavily scrutinised even, and hold the test tubes up to the light at the right angle, but in the meantime, and strictly from a selfish point of view I'm not prepared to subject my family to the fears associated with criminal activity."

"Sydney, in particular the city and eastern suburbs is Australia's drug capital with double the national consumption. I'm offering you a great opportunity in Queensland."

Roger is shaking his head, emphasising his point. "The constant worry radiating off me. Possible Police visits. Something going wrong. We're not talking here about pest control problems, which I feel confident handling, we're talking illegal activities, Chris. Imagine the possible upsets."

"What upsets?"

"I don't know. Suppose. Deranged druggies hammering on my door at 2 am for one! Coming home to find drug dealers interrogating my family in the living room with hammers and pliers, or that they've broken in, searching for the damned drugs and torn the place apart."

"Is Sue the nervous type? What's she like to live with?"

Bit cheeky of him, thinks Roger, but he says, "Bit cheeky of you, Chris. But as for your question; what Sue's like to live with? Getting her permission for the three of us might be a challenge."

Chris ignores the attempt at humour.

"But is there another point of view?" Chris asks pointedly, "other than the selfish aspect?"

"Yes, I'm not convinced that helping people to face the gates of death, to risk being hooked on demons, is a correct way to behave irrespective of the legal consequences."

"You're quoting ethics."

"Maybe I am."

"But you weren't so ethical as not to want to bring the opposition down, and for your own profit."

"Chris. You're right *that* I wasn't that ethical, although I viewed *that* as a legally binding business decision."

"How come?"

"Dunno? Maybe I'm an imperfect human being, Chris. But I don't want to be associated with the new gold standard for your affluence. Not my area of expertise. The answer to your offer is still no."

For a moment Chris looks like a shot duck.

Back home with Sue, Roger calls Legend Man and his cohorts all a lot of useless bastards, which does not help his case much. An attempt to numb his pain with alcohol like a man who has been lost in the desert, only makes it worse.

"A meal without wine is called breakfast," Sue says with a faintly flirtatious smile.

At their next BBQ, Art says sagely, "There's fuckors and fuckees, you've had a good run, Rog."

They are interrupted by Nosey.

"Woger?"

"Yes, Nosey."

"When s-s-shall we twy to l-l-light the BBQ?"

Roger is disinterested. "I'd suggest about half hour *before* we start feeling hungry."

Kim has not attended with Art as regrettably they are splitting up.

Art explains he has applied for a job as Entertainment Director with a cruise line, and Kim, broken hearted has taken their child home to her mother.

Roger shakes Art's hand, "I wish you well, Mate. You were my first friend in Brissie, the true blue who showed me the ropes, remember?"

"Blood oath, the bloody pom with a heart of gold who sounded too fuckin' English," and with that Art was gone leaving Roger feeling emotionally drained.

A few days later Roger feels as if he has swallowed a brick when the contract of sale, finally signed, specifically excludes him and other key players of his team, from being employed.

With the weight of the world on his shoulders he meets with his team.

"It's been a good run, Roger," Lucy coos making a mock bow, "who would have thought when Jack first took you on that you'd give those bastards such a good run for their money. I'm going to be a stay at home mum for a while, and I'm looking forward to it. Thank you for the opportunity, I've always enjoyed working with you," and she gives Roger a big friendly wink.

"What about you, Scottie?"

"Aye, well now I'm better cashed up, I'll get back to working for meself, that I will, but I do have one question?"

"What's that, Scottie?"

"Poaching contracts! Aye, we've done it, cannae I nae do it again?"

Roger is thoughtful.

"You are not subject to any signed restrictions, that I'm aware of, Scottie. None of us are. You've been dismissed, and it's in writing that they have refused you even an opportunity of an interview. I know of no law that can stop any man from earning a living. I'm not a qualified lawyer but I'd say go for it. What about you, Tweedy?"

"Well, my exotic birds are closer to maturity now, but Scottie and I are thinking of staying together. I have an intimate knowledge of the contracts as you know, we won't be able to poach them all of course," Tweedy's predatory grin is shark-like, "maybe only 90%!"

"Aye, why nae join us, Roger?"

Roger is deeply touched that his team think that much of him, but shakes his head, "I don't think so, Scottie, but thanks."

Admittedly their farewells have none of the extended celebratory fulfilment of the Smolfala Archipelago but Roger was content in a mild and steadily growing alcoholic haze. A little voice in his head was saying, *Just finish this one and go home.*

"You know it's funny in a way," Tweedy said next day as they are clearing their desks.

"Funny how? Funny hilarious? Or funny peculiar?" Roger queries.

"Well, both. If they'd ever looked after their staff well, you do realise that none of this would ever have happened."

Roger is thoughtful. "You're right, Tweedy."

"As a matter of interest, Roger, how much were we worth, what did they pay to get us out of the way?"

"Five million dollars and change, Tweedy."

Tweedy whistles, "Wow! We did cost them big time didn't we?"

"We certainly did, Tweedy."

Roger is officially retrenched.

As the money from his termination fund begins to dwindle he tires of his fishing, crabbing, and tripping about.

Sue has an idea but wants to carefully choose her moment.

Chapter 42

Roger is smiling sheepishly, the way he would as if caught with his hand in the cookie jar, and then picks Sue up abruptly in a big hug and spins her around.

"Are you feeling frisky?"

"A little."

"Oh, so sexy," Sue says in a tone that suggests the exact opposite. She senses this might be good timing for her suggestion.

"You do realise that you're going through a midlife crisis, don't you?"

"Am I?"

"You're about as shat off with the world in general as anyone could be about now."

Roger inclines his head. "Maybe I should run for politics. Plenty of losers there."

Sue presses. "You don't argue, then?"

"You might be on the money. I am forty. Am I really having a mid life crisis?"

"Yes. You are!"

Roger is thoughtful.

"We can do this, Roger. And it'll be fun." Euphoria is wrapping its arm around Sue as a cloak.

"Do what? What's fun?"

Sue takes a deep breath. "Adopting a sustainable, simple and self-sufficient lifestyle with monetary requirements cut to the minimum."

"Are you serious?"

"Yes. Why not, Roger, and before we're too old? We'll grow our own soft fruit and veggies, and run chooks."

"That seems pretty crazy. But such an idea might work; a sea change but rural."

"You've always threatened that if you had to take a demotion, or go back on the tools, you'd rather do it for yourself. Even though you're terrified of pests!"

Sue looks and feels as smug as a stray cat in a dairy. Knowing that she is on the wrong side of forty and has not changed her hairstyle since Jayne went to pre-school, this is a big deal all round.

"Time to put up, or shut up," says Sue enthusiastically, with a twinkle in her eye, "we'll be like that British sitcom; *The Good Life*. Character Tom Good went through a midlife crisis at forty in the show."

"But where, Sue? In the show they ploughed up their suburban block but there's no room here. Surely, we'd need acreage."

"Yes. Why not acreage? And maybe a cockerel called Lenin in honour of *The Good Life*, perhaps even a cow, or two?"

"Gotta have two pigs then, Pinky and Perky."

"And a goat, Geraldine."

Roger is again, thoughtful. "But where, Sue?"

"Dunno. But it needs to be affordable. Acreage as in twenty, thirty, or fifty acres in or around Brisbane, just isn't, is it?"

"No, I don't think if we sold up here we'd have enough for even one acre in Brisbane. Land is far too expensive here to play at being pioneer farmers."

Out comes their only map, again. The original one with Brisbane circled as an alternative to Perth.

"So, where?" Sue asks, smoothing the enormous map out flat on their table.

"Well, we can't go anywhere east or we'll be in the drink; Moreton Bay. If we travel north it'll be expensive because it's coastal, same as south and I don't see any advantage in crossing the border into New South Wales. That only leaves west, as in rural and the outback beyond."

"How far do you think we'd have to go from Brisbane?"

"Dunno? Certainly far enough to escape city values, I'd say at least three hours driving maybe even further. Remember what Fretsaw told us."

"What in particular? He misled us about what to take on the plane."

"Ignoring that. He reckoned that in the outback many children have never seen the sea. That they've grown up without television in towns little more than T-junctions or a wide spot in the road. Vast stretches of major highways are little more than dirt tracks. Also that if you break down you could be stuck for days — has a ring to it."

"And jobs could be few and far between."

"Alright. We don't need to go that far west."

They draw a beeline south westwards on their only map and see Toowoomba.

"Too expensive. It's a growing city, Sue. What we need is more the back-blocks."

"What about somewhere here," Sue suggests, her finger identifying an area known as the South Burnett Region. "Might acreage be affordable there?"

"Blackbutt, Yarraman, Nanango, Kingaroy!" They read off their map in unison.

"Blackbutt's a pretty little place with just one main street. We stopped there once for lunch, do you remember?"

"Yes, I remember, and Yarraman was even smaller, again."

"Nanango had a couple of pubs."

"Three actually."

"I remember you telling Fretsaw that we preferred our milk delivered from a bottle rather than a teat. So what's changed?"

Sue shrugs. "Lifestyle."

"Alright. But surely we must have electricity; remember Fretsaw was unsure if they had 240 volt electricity in Perth, for Christ's sake."

"Actually, he was not certain. But we now know that much of what he said was wishful thinking."

"Agreed like nappies and baby food for James on the flight. Call me silly but I do like electricity, microwave ovens, refrigerators, freezers, TV, and telephones."

Sue practically radiates relief. "Oh, agreed. We don't want to live like the poorer villagers in the Smolfala Archipelago."

"But we'll need money, Sue. We can't barter with the government for electricity, rates, and registrations."

"That's where you going back on the tools part comes in, Pest Boy. Why not start your own pest control business?"

Roger is thoughtful.

Sue hastens to add. "But the shingle can read," she spreads her hands about a metre apart; *Pest Control — available foggy days only.*"

Roger smiles. "We had nothing, we owed much, and we had nothing to leave to the poor. That's what we said when we arrived in Oz in 1971."

"And now," reinforces Sue, enthusiastically, "in 1985 we are poor people with money; but we owe nothing, and when we retire we'll...."

"Eat and drink it all?" Suggests Roger.

"It would be more economical if we made our own beer and wine, and if we need an income why not sell it — like Peapod Burgundy in the the *Good Life*?"

"Or better still the Aussie version. But I don't know about starting a pest control business in the South Burnett, I know no-one there, I have no contacts, Sue."

"You have multi-million dollar contacts elsewhere but you don't want to use them. Do you?"

"No I don't. And neither do I want to compete with Tweedy and Scottie. Maybe I'm handling things very badly, and a complete change is called for! What about James and Jayne?"

"Well, unless they run away with the circus or try sleeping on the street, I expect they'll come with us."

"Alright, there might be additional opportunities for them if they take advantage of our life style change, I suppose."

"Such as?"

"Well, Jayne likes animals — who knows where that might take her in the country?"

"Jayne's in year twelve, doesn't like school, doesn't want to go to university, and is unsure what she wants to do with her life but I think she'd move with us. James hasn't finished Junior school yet and is in year ten. They do have schools in the South Burnett."

"Could work, especially as neither of them have any daddy or granddaddy issues yet."

They are interrupted by the phone ringing.

It is the senior accountant; the very one that Roger had dealt with in Sydney, who had provided the epiphany of Legend Man.

"How's it going?" Roger asks curiously.

"Do you care?" came the smug but honest response.

"No! Not really, I was being polite, showing the caring side of the unemployed."

"I've spent twenty years of my life working on spin, but I thought you'd like to hear the latest news about your old boss Christopher Wright aka Legend Man."

"Okay, I'll buy. Shoot. What's he done now? Sold the Eiffel Tower to the Chinese? Bought a bank with its own money?"

There is a pause. "No actually, none of the above. Worse than if he got hit by a car and slept it off for a couple of days in the Rocks."

"What then?"

"He's wound up dead."

Roger is aghast, "What?"

"You heard right, Christopher Wright aka Legend Man is with us no more. Dead, as in not breathing, as in dead as a dodo, and dead as the spark of his life has gone to shite! And that's not spin, that's fair dinkum!"

"How? He wasn't old by any stretch. Heart attack? Stroke?"

"Sort of, at least his heart did stop beating. They do that when they drown."

"Drown! How did he drown?"

"It happens when your head goes under water for an extended period of time."

"Ha ha!"

"Well, it's been ruled an accident by the police, they apparently found him in a swimming pool floating face down. Word is he was doing something with pest control at midnight, or something, somewhere. Maybe with another man's wife. Who knows? Anyway, allegedly, that's the police word, allegedly, he fell or slipped, hit his head and drowned in the pool."

"Wow!" is all Roger can think of to say.

"So what's your plans?"

"Need to report back do you?"

"You know how it works, Roger, the wheels keep turning. Pointy heads and their best laid plans. So, what are you planning to do with the rest of your life?"

"Not sure, maybe develop a drinking problem."

Roger smiles sideways at Sue.

"Word is your team's going to hit the company again, good luck to them, we don't care any more. We've moved on — bigger fish to fry."

"Well, since you're showing an interest, Sue and I are thinking of doing a sea change to the country."

"What the outback?"

"Maybe not quite that far out; we'd surely be useless there for any stretch of time."

"Most would be. They say fishing for Yellow Belly is fun when they're on the chew."

"I'm sure they might be, but…"

"But what?"

"I prefer eating fish that come from salt water."

"Oh, well. Good luck with it, Roger — just don't go falling into any swimming pools."

After Roger puts the phone down, he tries to absorb the shock of his conversation with the senior accountant.

He cannot help but tie in his ecstasy discussions with the budding drug baron and that he, Roger, had been destined to become the chosen one. Now joining the dots, Roger is convinced Christopher Wright's death was no accident.

He feels an overwhelming sorrow for a man who had head hunted him in business, paid him well, and done him no harm.

"True he was a non-swimmer, Sue, but from what we see on television drug barons are renowned for fighting dirty, and that means not by Marquess of Queensbury Rules."

"Oh, Roger. Thank heavens you're not involved."

"Agreed. No contest: I'd rather be a live pest boy, than a dead drug baron any day of the week."

Sue swallows. "So, what now?"

"Well, we have the makings of a plan, and unlike when we left the UK for here, we don't have to rely on Brainy at the library."

"Oh, please don't mention that awful flight."

"Agreed. But now we don't have to go that far to check out what's almost on our doorstep, do we?"

"Blackbutt, Yarraman, Nanango and Kingaroy, you mean?"

"Could be a start. Why not?"

"Devoid of the surf and salty sea breezes."

"Maybe we don't need a town so much as a place?"

Jayne appears with a look on her face as if she is the only one who has not received an invitation to an ABBA Concert. "What's going on? Are we moving?"

Roger and Sue exchange the style of conspiratorial look that only their closest friends would understand.

"Maybe?"

Jayne sits down. She crosses one leg over the other, uncrosses them, and then crosses them back again. Something she always does when stressed. She gives a little eyebrow waggle.

Sue expresses concern. "You shouldn't worry, Sweetheart. I'm sure Daddy will do what's best for us."

Roger continues. "You are right that we shouldn't worry, but, in this family; that's a bit like telling water not to be wet. I suppose."

Sue and Jayne are both looking at him, expectantly.

"Is Pops talking in riddles, again?" This from James.

"Alright then, family," Roger beams, "let's go look."

EPILOGUE

Moti Mukherjee and his team continued Roger's good work for many years.

Kiwi Man and wife Mandy divorced back in the land of the long white cloud.

Zayn Kiribati died in a tragic aeroplane accident survived by his family Selina and Jason.

Kim and Arthur (Art) did split up. Roger tried to find them but drew a blank.

Dogs; Fred and Shandy, and budgerigar Bluey played themselves.

LIVING UPSIDE DOWN, is John's debut novel to feature the adventures of Sue and Roger, after writing three true stories.

This novel was inspired, in part by the author's thirty-five years of experience in the global pest control industry, life in the Archipelago, and migrating as ten pound poms.

You can find John at: **www.authorjohnhickman.com**
OR send John an email at: **authorjohnhickman@gmail.com**
OR follow John on FACEBOOK at:
AuthorJohnHickman@facebook.com
OR Books By John Hickman on FACEBOOK:
https://www.facebook.com/JohnHickmanAuthor/
OR on TWITTER at: **WriterJohnH**
John Hickman

ACKNOWLEDGEMENTS

Special thanks are due to several people this time around.

Carole, my wife of fifty-two years, is appreciated as always for her patience in tolerating what has become my obsession. You are my closest friend and confidant. My guiding light through our dark times, when we went backwards financially but in sunshine.

To our daughter Sara Hickman — who bears some remarkable similarities to Jayne in the story; is always the first person to read my pages and she reads them in chunks of chapters. Thanks again for your extraordinary patience, and generous support, Sara. Your unsurpassed loyalty and razor sharp comments about the text have proved invaluable.

To our son Mark Hickman — who is loved, and one day may read one of my books even before it becomes a DVD.

To Andrew Farrell my guru at Dennis Jones & Associates (Melbourne) who has tirelessly over the years mentored and advised on the ways of the world of books. Andrew has probably forgotten more than I shall ever know about the world of publishing. My thanks, Andrew.

To Linda Daniel, my editor, whose patient research has spared me much embarrassment. She really has put her heart and soul into editing draft after draft — ad nauseam.

I like to pay a special tribute to my Gran, Lily, who never lived to see any of my published work, but who if she had would have been 120 this year. You were always the spark, Gran.

You lit the flame that burns in these books with that *Remington* typewriter on my tenth birthday.

Also by John Hickman:
I hope you will check out these earlier books while I am working on my next one.

Reluctant Hero
Tripping Over
Sex, Lies & Crazy People

ALSO BY THE SAME AUTHOR

Reluctant Hero

John tells the true story about his dad Bill's involvement
in the Second World War as a Lancaster bomber pilot.

Pilots and aircrew proved to be a rare breed of heroes.
Bill's own squadron was wiped out numerically—twice.
These were the odds Bill faced for king and country.

Reluctant, he might have been.

Hero—he certainly was.

ISBN: 978-0-9870945-1-3 Paperback
ISBN: 978-0-9870945-2-0 Hardback
ISBN: 978-0-9870945-3-7 eBook

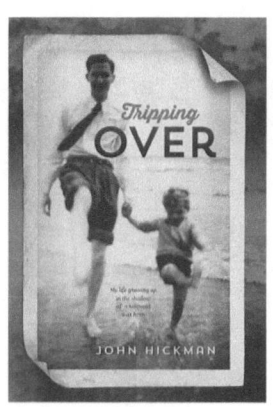

Tripping Over is the sequel to *Reluctant Hero.*

Another true story it depicts life in post war England in the 1950s and 1960s. It tells the story of John, who grows up in the shadow of his dad, a returned war hero. John senses he is different but not in a good way and knows he has big shoes to fill. He is not coping well. Beleaguered and confused, poor judgement and clumsiness dog his every move. When his parents visit the annual Earl's Court Motor Show to buy a new car but return with a boat instead – turmoil follows. Later he is almost killed on a disastrous wild horse ride on Rotten Row but is he really guilty of the police accusation of fraud? As a teenager John explores his sexuality, only to fall in love for all the wrong reasons. John's self-deprecating reminisces are often illuminating as the reader accompanies him on his bittersweet journey of both triumph and disaster.

ISBN: 978-0-9870945-5-1 Hardback
ISBN: 978-0-9870945-4-4 Paperback
ISBN: 978-0-9870945-6-8 eBook
ISBN: 978-1-3103968-3-0 Smashwords edition

Sex, Lies & Crazy People
is the sequel to *Tripping Over.*

John tells the bittersweet true story about his family's involvement in the Harewood Hotel, Royal Tunbridge Wells, Kent in England during the 1960s, interspersed with self-deprecating reminisces. Best described as a true life Fawlty Towers – but without Basil. When John is assigned to the kitchens will he be able to cook any better than his dysfunctional family? He is in good company with chefs who can't cook and waiters who don't speak English. A multitude of international guests include a millionaire addicted to pornography, a con man and his beautiful ex-prostitute wife, a cash strapped film company, a strange little man who reads tea leaves and scientologists seeking spiritual fulfilment. After falling in love for all the wrong reasons John meets Carole – but will their love last?

ISBN: 978-0-9870945-8-2 Hardback
ISBN: 978-0-9870945-7-5 Paperback
ISBN: 978-0-9870945-9-9 eBook
ISBN: 978-1-3107543-9-5 Smashwords edition

www.ingramcontent.com/pod-product-compliance
Lightning Source LLC
Chambersburg PA
CBHW020530020726
47494CB00006B/1701